I0668606

The Wild Part

The Wild Part

Jerry Craven

ANGELINA
RIVER
PRESS

ISBN: 978-0-9883844-1-5
Library of Congress Control Number: 2013906009
Manufactured in the United States

Angelina River Press
Fort Worth, Texas

I dedicate this book to thirteen
of the world's most talented and best people:

Adam
Anna-Marie
Austin
Avery
Brett
Caroline
Jack
Jake
Mary Grace
Miles
Olivia
Will
Zoe

Other Books by Jerry Craven include

Tickling Catfish
Snake Mountain
Becoming Others
The Big Thicket
Searching for Rama's Spear
Saving a Songbird and Other Stories
Tiger, Tiger

Acknowledgments

I am grateful to many people I knew in Venezuela back in the middle of the century past, folk who served as models for characters in this book. These include Sylvia (Rosita in this novel), Ramón, Mr. Noraye (the candy man), an outrageous Texan I remember only as Tex, a clever gold miner known as El Loco, my older siblings Sue and Carl, and my parents, Gorman and Rosebell Craven. Those who read my collection of nonfiction stories, *Saving a Songbird*, will recognize many people in this novel, some of whose names are changed in this story.

For their encouragement, insightful reading of the manuscript, and helpful suggestions, I am thankful to many fine writers and editors: Jerry Bradley, Kevin Casey, Sherry Craven, Gail Fail, Andrew Geyer, A. William Hinson, Susan King, and Dave Kuhne. Thanks to Terry Dalrymple for publishing a piece of this novel as a short story in *Concho River Review*.

Preface

While this is a work of fiction, it is based on my own adventures in the wild part of Venezuela. In writing this story, I drew inspiration from Jerzy Kosiński's wonderful book, *The Painted Bird*, especially from the way Kosiński turned his experiences in wandering around Europe into a novel. As Kosiński did, I write from memory filtered through imagination.

Many of the people who appear in *The Wild Part* are ones I knew, talked with, watched, feared or loved. In another book, *Saving a Songbird*, a memoir and hence a work of nonfiction with its more stringent demands to stick with historical fact, I chronicled some of the same people, and in that book I always used real names.

In the book you are holding now, I sometimes changed names and sometimes did not. My good friend Sylvia from my memoir became in this story Rosita, but the names of the candy man Noraye and his daughter Fatima are unchanged. They lived two houses down from my home in the village named El Tigrito. The bizarre gold miner El Loco in my story was a real man who roamed the gold country of my childhood. He hid his mining activity from bandits just as I report in this novel, and everyone called him El Loco. A man people knew as Tex, an outrageous Texan described by my father as having "gone native without learning Spanish," became Sam Dean from Abilene. Ramón from my memoir remains Ramón in this book, though I changed the names of my siblings—and so on with the telling about real people through imaginative writing.

CONTENTS

1
In the Darkness of Stars

"Maybe," I said, speaking Spanish and talking right into Rosita's ear so she could hear over the roar of the broken muffler, "we could jump out of the truck?"

We stood in the doorway at the back of the candy man's truck and watched the wheels stir up dust. It rolled across the savannah like dust devils. "We might break bones if we jumped," Rosita said. "We must wait until the candy man stops. Then we get out, tell him about how we sneaked into the truck, and hope he can take us home soon."

All we had wanted was to catch a ride to a neighboring village so we could go to a shop we heard about that sold bones of Indios and a shrunken head. The head supposedly hung from the ceiling by its lips. Neither of us had ever seen human bones, and I had never before heard of shrunken heads. But after we hid in the truck, Mr. Noraye, the one we called the candy man, had headed west, out into the wild savannah instead of going east to the next village. He pushed hard and fast over the dirt road, no doubt heading for the interior of Venezuela, toward isolated villages where the natives would buy his candy because no one else brought such treats to isolated places.

Rosita closed the door to the casita, the little house bolted on the back of the candy man's flat-bed truck, and we settled down as best we could in the crowded place between the Gott can of water and the stacks of cans containing the candy. I had shoved my machete among the cans to get it out of our way.

Rosita shifted the nubby pillow the candy man kept on the floor of the casita. "Soon it will be night."

I sighed. "We won't get home today." Mom and Dad would worry about me, would send my brother to search for me, and Dad would walk around the village calling my name. My sister would cry when they didn't find me, and I felt a knot in my stomach.

1

For a moment Rosita grew still, and I thought maybe she was crying. Then she said, "We've done something dangerous, Don, and we'll pay for it when we return. But there's something exciting about the danger, don't you think? You and I will go with the candy maker into regions of the interior where few people have seen someone as white as the candy maker, and none have seen a person with white hair like yours. We'll go into the gold country, into the country of diamonds and bandits and Indios who wear blue skirts, even the men, and we'll see giant iguanas and rivers too big to swim across."

The energy in her voice gave me a surge of excitement. I wanted to see all of the things she mentioned. "Maybe. The candy maker might soon need to stop to get a drink, and he'll find us here and drive us home, maybe tonight, maybe in the morning."

"If he does, I'll be glad. If he does not, I'll not be disappointed. It'll be better than going to the shop in El Tigre, better than seeing the bones of the dead. Better even than seeing the tiny head of the negrito. We'll help the candy man sell his candy, and we'll get to see wonderful things in the wild part of my country." She sighed. "My only real regret is that this is supposed to be a holy day, my grandmother said, because Eva Perón died today, and holy days are not good ones for starting fun adventures."

"Who is Eva Perón?"

"A saint, grandmother said."

As day faded into night and the light leaking into the casita around the edges of the door dimmed into darkness, we drifted off to sleep.

The stopping of the truck awakened us. The candy man killed the engine, stopping the roar beneath us, but my head was still full of the sound of the truck. "Noche," I said. Nighttime. Perhaps we had slept for hours. As we stood, stiff from the cramped space, we heard the slam of the truck door and some voices too muffled by the walls for us to make out what was said. One voice was that of a woman.

Rosita got to the door first, opened it, and turned to me. "I need to find a bathroom fast, but there are lights out there and strange men. Come with me, Don."

I took the machete from between the cans of candy and joined her outside, feeling wobbly and almost dizzy as if still bracing against the movement and noise of the truck. Cool night air felt good on my face. Kerosene lanterns hung from stubby trees beside a single building from which we heard guitar music and singing. The walls of the building looked too low and thatching on the roof stood thick and black in the thin light from the lanterns. "I think the candy man went in there," I pointed, realizing as I did so that the gesture was lost in the shadows of the truck.

"Hurry." Rosita danced around beside me. "I need a bathroom." She grabbed my hand and we ran toward some dark shapes beyond the house.

"I need to find the candy man," I protested.

"Yes. But first I need to go. And you will stand guard to make sure no one sees me." In the shadows of a small tree, she stopped and began pulling up her skirt. "You turn that way and make sure no one comes."

I turned, looking toward the building. Three lamps hung on the side of the house closest to us, and they looked to have damaged mantles or else were in need of being pumped up, for their light was feeble. Two men had emerged from the house to look at the candy man's truck. Perhaps one of them was the candy man, but it was too shadowy to tell. I heard footsteps behind us.

"Someone comes," Rosita said.

I turned in time to see a man take Rosita's arm and pull her to her feet. "What is this?" he said.

"Let go of me."

"Oho. A girl. A pretty girl. Do you work here? Come, give me a kiss." He tried to pull her to him, but she twisted away. He grabbed her hair. "A wild girl. Good. Good. I'm a wild man. Do you like wild men?"

The candy maker's truck roared. I glanced at it and saw it lurch into motion, then I stepped toward the man who had Rosita by her hair, and I held the machete out to give him a whack. But it wasn't necessary. Rosita did something and the man released her and bent over with a sharp cry.

"The truck," Rosita said. "We must stop the truck."

3

As we ran, the truck rumbled into the night, picking up speed and throwing a cloud of dust behind it. We ran into the dust, both calling out for the candy maker to stop. But he couldn't hear us over the roar of the engine and the damaged muffler, nor could he see us in his mirror because of the dark.

Dust from the truck bit into my eyes and throat, and I coughed. Rosita caught my arm. "Running is no use," she said. We stopped and watched the taillight of the truck bob on the uneven road, winking as the landscape dipped and rose. The dust settled, my cough slowed to a few hawks and throat rumbles, and the night noises arose around us.

Crickets and other insects of the savannah whirred and cheeped. Guitar music and singing from the building behind us floated faint and low through the dark, and somewhere to our right we heard the sharp notes of whistle frogs. They were the loudest frogs I ever heard, louder even than bullfrogs because there always seemed to be thousands of whistle frogs so that together they made quite a racket. I stood in the night beside Rosita in the settling dust from the candy man's truck and wondered if there were other frogs out there. Green tree frogs with long skinny legs. Frogs with red stripes on them, more colorful than the giant grasshoppers. Jesus frogs that, according to Uncle Ray, could hop across the surface of water. I wanted to see a Jesus frog and had hunted them in the edge of the El Tigre river but never saw one.

"The sky," Rosita said.

Only at that moment did I realize what we saw around us was illuminated entirely by stars. The sky seemed close enough to touch, and in the cumulative light of the heavens I turned to look at Rosita's face. Her eyes glittered with starlight and one cheek dimpled.

"You're not worried?" I asked.

"Worried? Yes. A little. But Don, the night is so beautiful— perhaps because it is almost ended. Within an hour or so the sun will chase away the stars, and we'll see this new world that the candy maker has brought us to."

"We slept almost all night in the truck?" The notion astounded me.

4

"Yes. We're hundreds of kilometers into the wild and unknown parts of Venezuela. We're so far inland that I doubt people here even know of the death of Evita. There's a marsh over there where the frogs whistle, which means it rained here yesterday afternoon. Dry season is coming to an end, and soon the rains will come each day."

We stood in silence, straining to see in the direction of the whistle frogs. "Perhaps," I said, "we should find a chaparro tree to climb and see where we are?"

Rosita laughed, low and excited. "Yes. But not to see anything, not now in the darkness of stars, but to wait out the coming of dawn. There's water close by, and in the water are frogs. Where there are frogs, there will be snakes. We should climb a tree to keep above the snakes."

I looked down. The ground seemed sinister, shadowy, and things appeared to slither about in the periphery of my vision. I imagined a zillion snakes squirming around, chasing Jesus frogs as they hopped across the surface of water from yesterday's rain, chasing the whistle frogs out of the water and up close to where we stood. "Maybe we should go back to the house where the candy man stopped."

"That's not a house. It's a place where men go to become drunk and to find the wrong kind of women. Putas. There will be men like the one who grabbed my hair. I prefer to worry about snakes in the dark than go to that cantina."

When I looked in the direction of the music, I saw nothing but more savannah. The land seemed flat, but it rose and fell much more than in the region of El Tigrito. In the direction of the whistle frogs, far off and low on the horizon, stood the dark shape of a river jungle. A shallow gully beside us looked as if it might lead to the river. "That way," I pointed. "I think there are trees along a river."

"The jungle at night is a dangerous place to be unless we had several hours of light to get ready for darkness. Then the jungle is the most exciting place in the world. Your idea about finding a chaparro tree is better." She began walking along the edge of the gully; I followed. The gully widened and became so deep that its walls cast shadows too dark to penetrate. Sand glittered in a tiny

5

strip of starlight along the bottom. Before long, we found our tree.

It stood, stumpy and bent by savannah winds, only a meter from the gully. After some fumbling to tie the machete to my belt, I began to climb. "I'll find a nest for crows." The phrase sounded odd to me as I said it, for I was translating the term my brother Todd used to name the place in our backyard chaparro tree where branches forked several directions, making a safe place to sit.

"Are we crows? Do you say so because we look black in the darkness? Be careful not to fall into the arroyo."

The chaparro tree had a proper crow's nest higher than a man's head and hidden well enough among the big leaves. "Give me your hand. We can sit here without being afraid of falling, even if we go to sleep."

She climbed fast and settled in place with her back against my chest. "This is good, Don. You found us a safe place to await the sun. I wonder how far from home we are."

Home. The word conjured up an image of my family sitting around the dinner table, talking about where I was. Todd would say I was off in the savannah hunting tigers and Mom would ask if maybe a tiger got me, and Dad would say that I was too stringy for a tiger to want to eat, and my sister June would say I was in bad trouble for missing dinner. I closed my eyes and watched them finish eating, get up from the table, and go outside to sit in the cool beneath the water tower, and I imagined hearing Dad saying that it was time to go to Ramón's house to find me, and Todd tried but I wasn't there and Ramón said he last saw me with his cousin, who was missing from her house. Todd ran home fast and told Dad that I had vanished with some native girl, and Mom's eyes looked all watery and red and June said maybe some kidnappers got us.

"Rosita, we must get home today." I heard urgency in my voice that startled me.

"Impossible. We rode all night in a truck. How can we walk home in one day? It'll take us a week, maybe more because we don't know which road to take."

"A week? My family will worry. Your family will worry. We must let them know where we are."

"Impossible. And since we cannot do it, I say we enjoy the

adventure we're on."

"I'll write them a letter. We can mail it to them at the nearest town."

"Letter? Nobody sends letters in Venezuela."

"My mom and dad send letters back to the States. They get my grandmother's letters from the States."

"Not in El Tigrito, they don't. Perhaps there is mail in Caracas or one of the big cities. But not in our village. Never have I seen anyone get a letter. Never have I heard of anyone sending a letter."

"What about the letters from the States? I've read some from my grandmother."

"Did someone bring the letter to your house?"

"Yes. No. I don't know—but I saw the letters. So I can write to my family and tell them not to worry, that I'm in the wild part of Venezuela with you, and that we'll be home in a week or so."

"There's no place to mail a letter here. And even if there were, where will you get paper and a pencil for writing the letter?"

"I'll get them. Then I'll find someone who knows how to send a letter."

"Good. You do that. I'll try to help." Rosita sounded sincere. She patted my arm and moved around, settling herself against me and on the branches of the crow's nest. The warmth of her felt good. "Do you think you can sleep?"she asked.

"No." It seemed to me that I could sleep, but the tone of her voice said that she was done with sleeping, that only a simple-minded person could go to sleep there in a tree far out in the wild part of Venezuela.

We listened to the whistles of frogs and the chirring of insects, and perhaps I did fall asleep, for I jerked when Rosita gripped my arm and hissed in an excited whisper: "Don. Someone comes. Make no noise."

The man made a strange scraping sound with a dark mass that he pushed along in front of him. He walked beneath the chaparro, just under our dangling feet, and it was then that I saw he was pushing a wheelbarrow. The sound of the wheel bumping over dirt and rocks continued for only a few seconds, then changed to a softer crunching sound, and the man vanished from our sight. He reappeared in the gully, coming toward us again. We could see only the top part of him because of the shadows, so he looked like a ghost floating in darkness. Beneath our chaparro, he stopped, made some gritty metallic sounds with the wheelbarrow, and began bobbing in and out of the shadows. We heard the sound of digging and of dirt being flung into the wheelbarrow. He muttered as he worked, at first in a low rumble, then more audibly, and I recognized the words as English:

" and I'll hex them sumbitches all the way to Topeka, and if they give me any lip, I'll tell them I'll turn them into snails." He laughed in a humorless way and said the Spanish word for snails: "Into stupid caracoles for chrissake. Caracoles, what a dumb sounding word, heh, heh, heh." Then he broke into song, his voice cracking and off-key. "Maresey doats and doesey doats and little laaaaambsy divy, for chrissake." The song ended with grunts and the crunching of the wheel along the bottom of the gully. He sputtered and groaned up an incline, and when he walked beneath our feet again, his breathing heavy, he smelled like a goat.

Rosita exhaled with a loud hiss when the man vanished into the savannah. "Such a bad smell." She kept her voice low. "That was your language, Don. What did he say?"

"I'm not sure. Strange things."

"Why did he talk about snails?"

"He said he would turn some people into snails because of their lips. But I didn't understand why he said that or how he planned to turn them into snails. The song is one I have heard my mother and sister sing. It's supposed to be funny because the words are all crammed together so they don't make sense."

"Lips?" Rosita sounded puzzled. "I think maybe he's a crazy man. No one digs for gold in the night."

"Gold?"

"But of course. This is gold country where men come to find wealth. Almost no one finds any, my father said. He went into the gold country once and almost starved." She gripped my arm and dropped her voice to a whisper. "He comes again, the one who sings and stinks."

The man seemed to materialize out of a wall of savannah grass some distance from where he had vanished into it. "Maresey doats and doesey doats, maresey doats and doesey doats," he mumbled, making no effort to sing. "Maresey doats, for chrissake, and doesey doats." He pushed his wheelbarrow into the gully again and again filled it with dirt, this time doing so in silence except for an occasional grunt. He did mutter one phrase: "Daylight cometh, crap." And he was right, for the horizon had begun to glow with faint pink, and stars were going out in the area above the pink. When the man pushed again into the savannah, he chose a different spot to do so.

"He's crazy," Rosita said. "He would find it easier to use the same path each time instead of having to push aside grass every time he comes this way. What are these doats he talks about?"

"Those are words from the song that's supposed to be funny. It's something about horses and deer eating oats."

"I would eat oats right now. Come. Let's go catch something for breakfast." She stood in the crow's nest, then became rock still. "He returns."

The man stumbled along, sweeping the ground with a crude broom. "Maresey doats, for chrissake," he mumbled. "and doesey frigging doesey, doesey, doesey doats, not to mention the frigging little lambseys." His sweeping stirred up so much dust that I thought I might sneeze, so I pinched my nose and breathed through my mouth. This time when he went into the gully, there was enough light to watch him. He swept all the way to the place where he had dug, made some noise with twigs and leaves, then retreated, kicking dust with his feet and jabbing at the ground with the broom.

"This is very strange," Rosita said when the man was gone. "He covered the tracks from his feet and from the wheelbarrow. Why would he do that? I think we should go see."

I followed her down the chaparro, then untied the machete from my belt. Most boys in my village carried machetes, a habit my brother and I picked up soon after our family arrived in Venezuela. I loved hauling the big knife around, loved using it for hacking tree branches to make tops, whacking papayas from the shorter papaya trees down in the river jungle close to our house, and I loved pretending the blade was something thinner, more like a proper

9

sword used by men wearing armor and riding horses with plumes.

"What kind of animals can we catch for breakfast?" I waved the machete around, pretending to be in a sword fight.

"A rabbit, maybe. Or an iguana. I don't know. Come on, Don."

When I caught up with her, she was walking down a caved-in place on the side of the gully. The sky glowed and almost all the stars had gone. We stopped beneath the chaparro tree. I expected to see a large hole in the bottom of the gully, but there was none. Rosita pointed at some bushes growing on the wall. "He dug there, which is a relief to me."

"A relief?"

"Yes. I thought maybe he had murdered someone and was down here burying the body. But he was after gold. He's crazy to dig here. My father told me all the gold is in the streams and rivers, washed down among the stones and almost impossible to find. Come."

I stabbed the cliff a couple of times, pretending I had just dispatched the man who had pulled Rosita's hair outside the cantina. "I don't want to eat an iguana."

"Yes, you do. Or you will when you get hungry."

"How about a lizard? Iguanas are too pretty to kill, and too big. We could kill some lizards and cook their tails."

"Lizards are all bone. It would take a hundred lizards to make a meal, and we would have to spend the whole day sucking the meat from the bones. But if you don't want to kill an iguana, then we will set some traps for a rabbit. Maybe for quail."

"Or we could find some people and buy ginger cookies like those sold in the market of El Tigrito."

From the top of the gully Rosita turned to stare at me. "Cookies?"

"Yes. I have the money I brought to buy the finger bone of an Indio."

"But, Don, we're far from villages that have—" She waved her hand. "It doesn't matter. We'll look for cookies, as you wish. If we find none, then we will make some traps for animals. Perhaps we go that way?"

The direction she indicated followed the gully, and it seemed as good as any to me, so I followed her lead. We walked in silence, feeling the sun burn off the chill of the night. The problem of getting a letter to my family kept me from feeling much like talking, for the logistics of the matter became more complicated the more I thought about it.

Didn't letters have addresses on them? Didn't addresses have house numbers and street names in them? None of the houses in our village had numbers, and none of the streets had names, at least not that I knew. Still, there were those letters from my grandmother —how did she address them? I tried to visualize the envelope. It had little blocks of red and blue all along the edge, and there was writing in the center and up in one corner. What did the writing say? With my eyes closed, I could see the writing, several lines of it, but I couldn't make out what it said. I bumped into Rosita, who had stopped walking. "Sorry." It took some quick steps to keep from falling. "I was trying to read the address on my grandmother's letter."

"Someone is ahead," she whispered. "We must be quiet."

"Why?"

"I don't know. She sings."

The voice came to me, low at first, then louder as we walked toward her. It was a clear, alto voice that dropped to butterscotch-smooth low notes, then rushed to notes so high and clear that I wanted to hear more. She sang about a dove who lost its mate and cried over the loss. I had heard the song before, but never sung with such power and feeling. "The woman who sings must be very beautiful," I whispered.

"Yes. And she sings like an angel. Look." Rosita pointed.

The woman stood in the center of a shallow wet-weather stream. Water had washed away enough sand to expose fist-sized rocks in the bed of the stream. Someone had dug a hole beside a large rock to catch enough water for washing clothes. The singer had her back to us and was bent over the task of dunking some clothing into the hole, though how she hoped to get anything clean in that muddy water was beyond me. "Ku-ku-rrru-ku-ku paloma," she sang, clear and beautiful, then became still as if listening, her head tilted at an odd angle. She wore a dirty dress woven in the fashion of Indios with streaks of red and black in patterns that might have once been pretty, when the garment was new. She was poor, then, I concluded—but she sang with such a clear and wonderful voice that I knew her to be a beautiful Indio. It seemed certain that at any moment she would turn toward us and I would no doubt see the prettiest woman in the entire wild part of Venezuela.

"Who's there?" She moved her head in small jerks, scanning the trails that opened from the savannah to the rocky bed of the stream where she stood. Then she turned to face us. "Two children? Why are you sneaking up on me like that?"

One eyelid drooped over an empty socket, and beneath the eye a scar ran a crooked course to her chin. The other eye, which seemed to be opened far too wide, glared at us. Brown stains ran from both corners of a mouth clamped into an angry frown.

The sight astonished me. She was the ugliest woman I had ever seen. "Were you the one singing?" I asked.

"Where did you brats come from?"

"The candy man brought us. We are looking for. . ."

"Shut up, boy. Girl. You answer. The witch-child with white hair speaks foolishness. Candy man, indeed."

Rosita took a step closer to me. "This is Don. I am Rosita, and what he said is true, if you'll let me explain."

"The little rose takes up for her master. The Don, you say? I thought the brat was dead, killed when bandits burned the house of the old Don. Don't talk nonsense to me about a candy man. Why are you watching me?"

"You sing with such beauty. We heard you and came to listen."

"Yes. I sing better than anyone, ever." Her face seemed to soften.

"I need a pencil and some paper," I said. "It's important to write a letter to my father."

"Keep quiet," Rosita whispered.

"Your father is dead. Little Rose, why does the Don talk such rubbish about a candy man and about his dead father?"

"Please excuse us. We have been long on the road and need to find something to eat. Perhaps there is a village nearby?"

12

"Not near here. Over there," she gestured with a nod of her head and a pucker of lips, "is the camp of El Loco Merzi." I glanced at the trail she had pointed toward with her lips. "And there," she thrust her lips in another direction, "some lazy men from Maracaibo dig for gold. Beyond them are the bandits who killed the old Don. All are bad men. Stay away from them. And stay away from me, too. I need no trouble with the young Don who wants to write letters to the dead."

"Who is El Loco Merzi?" I asked.

"Keep quiet, Don." Rosita gave me a nudge.

"The Norte Americano? He is a warlock, worse than any brujo in the world because he has powerful magic, the kind that comes sometimes to crazy people. Dig here, dig there, never staying with one place. How he finds gold is a mystery. Stay away from El Loco Merzi." The woman turned her back to us and resumed dipping clothes in the muddy water.

"That way," I pointed. "We go that way."

"But it's the wrong direction."

"No. That is the right one." I started walking in the direction the one-eyed singer had indicated was the camp of the crazy American. Americans, I reasoned, knew something about letters, so maybe this Merzi fellow could help me send one to my family. I glanced back at Rosita, who stood chewing her lip. She sighed and started after me.

"I don't like dealing with crazy people," she told me.

"Have you ever known a crazy person?"

"No."

"Then you might like dealing with crazy people." I swung my machete about like a fencing sword. "I don't think he'll try to hurt us."

"You keep that machete down. Hang it onto your belt again. Please?"

I tied the machete to my belt and led the way through the savannah into the camp of El Loco Merzi.

It wasn't hard to find, for the American had chosen the top of a rise to pitch his tent. Dad once said that the best place to camp in the rainy season was on the top of a hill because there was usually a breeze, and a breeze would help keep mosquitoes off of you. There were two chaparro trees for shade, a puptent, and a pot suspended with wire from a branch of one chaparro tree. Below the pot was a dead campfire. Hanging by its neck from a branch in the other chaparro tree was some sort of doll about half a meter long. It had arms and legs of grass and a hideous black head protruding from sackcloth made into crude doll clothes. The face of the doll had one eye that was a slit and another that was open too wide. Long teeth hung like tusks from its black lips.

A man sat in the shade of the tree close to the doll. His legs were drawn up so his knees protruded like sticks on either side of his face. Pants muddy enough to have been washed by the one-eyed singer rode up his legs, exposing ankles covered with black hair so thick that I thought it looked like fur. His shirt might have been blue, once, and his face looked like cracked leather. He wore the gray beginnings of a beard, like he had forgotten to shave for a few days. With hands between his jutting knees, the man worked at cutting up a sheet of paper with a pocket knife. Judging from his smell, he was the same man who had pushed the wheelbarrow into the gully that morning. I looked around and located the wheelbarrow down the rise beside a small stream. The man didn't look up when we came into his camp.

"Mr. Merzi, I would appreciate it if you would loan me some of that paper," I said.

"Wipe with a leaf or a handful of grass." His eyes flickered up in a flash of blue, lingered on us only a second, then went back to the pocket knife and paper in his hands. "You ain't getting my paper."

"I would pay for it. It's important for me to write a letter."

"Yeah? I don't give a rat's ass about letters. I need this here paper for rolling smokes. Not that this paper is worth a shit for smokes. It burns hotter than old hoppy's hell fires and can scorch a hole in your lips if you ain't watching." He cut the last of the paper into small rectangles. "How come you talk English? What a stupid question, considering your hair is blond as the sun. Course you might be a German or a Swede, but you ain't cause of the English. So where you from?"

"My family moved here from Texas so my Dad could work for an oil company. That is, they moved to El Tigrito. I don't know exactly where here is because the candy maker drove far into the wild part of Venezuela while we slept." I took a few steps closer to the man, mainly so I could get a better look at the hanging doll. Rosita tugged at my shirt, trying to hold me back.

Mr. Merzi pulled a pouch from the shirt that might have once been blue, picked up a rectangle of paper, and poured some tobacco on it from the pouch. "That's close enough. And how about you, girl? Do you ever talk?" He looked at Rosita. She gripped my arm and met his gaze. "Native girl, huh? That's what I thought. She your servant, kid?"

"No."

"You got a name?"

"Don. This is Rosita."

The man grunted and got back to rolling his smoke. "Call me El Loco. Everbody around here does, and it's a name that suits me just fine. Did you stumble across me by accident, or did you come looking for me? Not that it makes a big crappy difference because you always have to do what you end up doing, no matter what."

"A lady who was dunking clothes in some muddy water told us how to find you."

"She have only one eye? Was she singing about some stupid dead bird?"

"About a paloma. Yes."

"Lady. She ain't been a lady in years. Lady. Heh, heh, heh."

Rosita leaned toward me and hissed, "Let's go, Don."

El Loco pulled a match from his shirt pocket, struck it on the bottom of his boot, and lit the cigarette. "Better do as she said. Hanging around a nut like me ain't going to do you no good."

"But I need to write a letter."

"Tough tiddy, kid." He picked up the bits of paper and crammed them and the tobacco pouch into his shirt pocket. One piece fluttered to the ground, but he was so busy trying to stand that he didn't notice. He put his hands on his knees and grunted while forcing himself to his feet. "I'm too old for this shit." Much to my astonishment, he stood not much taller than I. His first few

15

steps were more like stumbles, and he muttered what must have been curses, directing them at his legs. Then he turned to me. "You hungry? I was about to whop me up some panbread and coffee. If you hang around here long, I'll feed you and then put you to work. Both of you. How come she ain't scared of my voodoo doll?" Without waiting for an answer, he pulled a match from his pocket and handed it to me. "Get a fire going under that there pot. And don't waste that match. I got too damn few of them left." He stumbled toward the pup tent, singing without much of a tune: "Maresey doats and doesey doats and dumb little lambsey, two little lambsey divy, for chrissake, divy, divy, little laaaaambsey all the stupid divy."

2
A Pig in the Cantina

"Beats the shit out of cassava, don't it?" El Loco talked with one cheek puffed out. Every time he took a bite of panbread, he pumped his jaws a couple of times then shoved the bread into his cheek long enough to say a few words before swallowing. Rosita, leaning against one of the chaparro trees, turned so she wouldn't have to watch him, and she grimaced something fierce when he chewed because he did so with his mouth open, making a terrible smacking sound. "You two came just in time. A couple more days and I would be chowing down on cassava. The only critters that can digest them thin little slices of roots are the effing natives and termites. Cassava goes right through me like so much sawdust soaked in castor oil."

Rosita nudged me with her elbow. "Why is he talking about cassava?" she whispered. "We're eating his terrible bread, not cassava."

"Pan terrible, is it?" El Loco laughed and went on in English: "If she thinks my bread is terrible, wait until she tries my beans. Can't cook them sumbitches worth a shit."

"You have the ears of a donkey," Rosita told him.

El Loco nodded and switched to speaking Spanish. "I do have donkey ears. Was born with them, but without fur, and I take what life gives me, not that I have a choice in the matter. From two kilometers away I can hear a goat fart."

Rosita raised one side of her upper lip. "You speak like a puta."

El Loco grinned and winked at me. "That there is a feisty little bitch," he said in English. "Dumb natives like naming their girls 'little red one,' Rosita. But none of them ever say what the little red thing is. But I know. It's a wussy. This gal is a feisty little red wussy." He jerked in silent laughter.

Rosita stood and flung the crust of her panbread on the ground. "Don, this pig is saying nasty things about me. Tell me what he said. Tell me exactly." The tone of her voice said I'd better not gloss over anything.

I swallowed hard, remembering some words from the water

17

vendors in El Tigrito. "He said you are a coña de rosa." These were words Todd had told me never to say to a girl, so it made my stomach jump when I said them.

She stared as in disbelief for a few frozen seconds, picked up my machete, and stomped over to where El Loco sat leaning against the other chaparro. He regarded her with some alarm as she stood over him, machete in hand. "If you talk about my coña again," she said through clinched teeth, "I'll make you sorry. And if you try to touch it, I'll come to you in the night and cut off your banana and both of your eggs." She swung the machete in a sudden arc, burying the blade in the chaparro tree just above El Loco's head. The chop of the blade biting into the wood made my stomach jump again.

"Wow," El Loco whispered in amazement. "Wow."

Rosita tugged on the handle of the machete a couple of times, then released it, leaving it stuck in the tree. "My father warned me about men such as you." She put her hands on her hips. "And he taught me what to do with them. Ask Don what happened to the man at the cantina who pulled my hair." She whirled around and strode down the slope to the stream.

"Wow," El Loco repeated. "I like that little girl. When she becomes a woman, Don, you damn well better marry her. She's got the kind of fire a man needs in his life. Until you're both grown, though, my advice is not to talk about her coña unless you have no regard for your banana and eggs."

"I think Rosita and I should be going now." I stood.

"Not yet, unless you think that one little piece of paper you picked up will be enough for the letter you need to write." He ducked away from the machete and struggled to his feet. "You don't need to look so surprised. I might be an old sumbitch, but I ain't dead. I saw you sidle around and grab up that slip of paper but figured what the hell, you would earn it by making a bean run for me."

"Bean run?" No wonder they call him El Loco, I thought. He doesn't make much sense sometimes, not that calling Rosita names was particularly sensible. I tried to pull the machete from the tree, but it wouldn't budge.

"That chaparro has a good pinch on the blade. I'll have to pull

18

her out for you. Yes, I need beans. Some flour, a bag of salt, and a bottle of Lava Gallo."

I put my foot on the tree for leverage and tugged on the handle of the machete. "You need to wash a chicken?"

"Rooster, boy. Rooster. Gallo is a cock that crows, fights, and mounts chickens. I don't aim to wash one, though. You leave that machete to me."

I stepped back and El Loco took hold of the machete. He grunted and jerked and fumed, but the blade remained stuck. After a string of mumbly-sounding curses, he kicked the tree and turned toward me again. "You need to get a letter into the mail, and I need someone to tote groceries into camp from the cantina over by the digs where the boys from Maracaibo think they'll strike it rich. They won't, the dumb shits, on account of how they go about gouging the ground when they find a little color, but that's no concern of yours. How about it, boy?"

"How about what, Mr. Merzi? I'm afraid I didn't understand much of what you said."

"What you got for brains, cassava? Listen kid. You and that fiery little cun—uh, you and Rosita go to the cantina to get some groceries for me, and I'll help you with your letter. Deal?"

"Deal." I pulled a few more times on the machete and gave up. "The one little piddling piece of paper you dropped won't be enough for much of a letter. Do you have more paper?"

"None that ain't cut up for smokes, and almost none that I ain't got plans for. Here." He pulled another rectangle of paper from his shirt pocket and handed it to me. "I know, I know," he raised his hands to stop me from speaking. "you need a pencil. I happen to have one in my tent. And you need an envelope, which will be more of a problem. But with a little countryboy ingenuity, I can make you an envelope. You go find me a handful of dried savannah grass. Make sure it ain't rotten, cause I need it for string. Go on, now. And tell Rosita that while I have a foul mouth, I ain't never messed with a girl that wasn't growed up and more than willing. Tell her if anyone at the cantina messes with her, I'll jerk that machete out of the tree and go after his banana with it. Not that anyone will mess with her in the daytime, and especially not with Mamacita Moreno anywhere closeby. She would wrestle any man to the ground who tried to molest a little girl. Go get that grass, like I told you." With that, he was finished with me. He turned away and started singing as he headed toward his tent. It was as if I had vanished from the face of the earth. "Maresey doats and doesey doats, Maresey doats and doesey doats, and the frigging little laaaaambsey divy."

There was plenty of dried grass down by the stream close to where Rosita walked about, her brows set in anger. I pulled some grass, tested it and decided it was too old to serve as proper string. "El Loco said to tell you that he was sorry."

"He did not."

"Maybe not exactly in those words. But he did say to tell you he has never bothered a little girl, and he said that if anyone in the cantina tried to hurt you, he and Mamacita Moreno would punish him. With a machete, maybe."

"Don, don't defend that crazy man. We don't owe him anything just because he gave us some greasy bread. Don't make up stories when you talk to me. Ever." Her voice had a dangerous edge to it.

"I didn't make anything up. Saying in Spanish what he told me isn't easy, and I'm trying hard to tell you exactly what he said. Wasn't I honest with the bad word?"

"Yes." Her face softened and she came to where I was grubbing around with the dead grass. "Yes, you were honest. Most boys and men would have lied to me about such a word because I'm a girl, but you didn't. Why are you pulling grass?"

"For a letter. El Loco told me to bring him some grass for my letter to our parents. Look." I stood and dug into my pocket. "Two little pieces of paper. One he dropped and another that he gave me. He's looking for a pencil in his tent, and he said he would make a country envelope with grass string."

"Don, whatever are you talking about?"

I shrugged. "I don't always understand him. But he promised that if we would go to the cantina for him to get something for washing roosters, he would help me with my letter."

"Cantina? The place with the putas? We won't go. That's a bad place with bad men."

"He said it was safe enough there during the day because Mamacita Moreno will be there. She's some sort of wrestler, and the men are afraid of her. El Loco will help us with a letter if we buy some groceries for him. He wants some beans and flour, along with the soap for washing roosters, though he probably will use it for his own baths because he said he had no intention of using it on a rooster." I tugged on some more grass and discarded it when it snapped.

"He needs a bath." Rosita wandered along the edge of the stream, bent down and picked among some plants. "Here. Take him these, if he wants fiber to use for tying something. But, Don, I would rather that we left right now."

"Without my machete?"

"You don't need it. Come on. Let's start walking home."

"I want to get that letter written. El Loco said he has a pencil." I started back up the incline clutching the long blades of grass Rosita had given me. She sighed like she was bothered by something and came with me.

El Loco had a nub of a pencil for me, along with what looked like the top of a shoe box. "Use the cardboard for backing while you write your letter," he told me.

"I would do better writing the letter on the cardboard. There's more room on it."

"Don't argue with me, boy. The cardboard has to serve as the envelope. You just get that letter written."

I sat by the tree with the machete stuck in it, and Rosita sat beside me, casting distrustful glances at El Loco. "Those pieces of paper are too tiny," she said. "You cannot say much."

"I know. And I write large. Give me a few minutes."

I struggled with what to write. Grandma always started her letters with Dear. But that was four letters, and they would take up almost a whole line on one side of a sheet. Dear was out, I decided. "Hi," I wrote. "I'm fine Rosita is fine." That filled the entire first sheet. I turned it over and wrote, "Don't blame the candy man." Then I went to the second sheet: "We will walk home." I turned the paper over. "El Loco will mail this. Don." I read over the letter.

21

"What did you say? Did you mention me?"

"Yes. I told my parents about trying to get to El Tigre by hitching a ride in the back of the truck that belongs to the candy man, but he didn't know about it so they shouldn't blame him for taking us way out to the wild part of Venezuela. I told them you and I are doing fine out here seeing as we slept in a tree so the snakes wouldn't get us, and that we're working out a way to walk home, even if it takes more than a week, and that a friend is mailing this letter for us so they won't worry the whole time we're gone."

"You said all that on that small paper?" Rosita sounded impressed. She picked up the sheets and examined them.

"Yes. Sometimes English uses fewer words than Spanish."

El Loco whittled down the cardboard and folded it over so it looked about the size of a small envelope. He put my letter between the folds, then punched some holes along the edge of the envelope with a pocket knife. "Now," he said, "you stitch this sumbitch together with that grass you fetched up from the creek." He made sewing motions with one hand.

Rosita understood immediately. She took the envelope that once might have been a shoe box lid, picked up one of the grass sprigs, and began threading it into the holes. When she finished, she tied off the last piece with a quick flicker of her fingers. The results were stunning.

"That looks like the letters we get from my grandmother," I told her. "The stitching looks exactly like the red-and-blue spots on the edge of her envelopes, except for not being red and blue."

Rosita looked pleased. El Loco took the envelope, turned it over a couple of times, and nodded. "This will do. Write an address on it or it might end up in Outer Mongolia." He handed me the letter.

With Rosita and El Loco watching, I didn't want to seem so stupid as not to know how to address the envelope, so I wrote,

The Seal Family
Mom, Dad, June, and Todd.
House with a Water Tower in Back
El Tigrito.

I paused, remembering what El Loco said about how somebody

might send it to Mongolia. It might end up in the hands of some Mongolian family just because they had a water tower, and they would be puzzled over who sent them the letter, and my own family would never get it. That would be bad, I decided, so I added:

Estado Anzuatage, Venezuela

South America

Western Hemisphere.

Estado Anzuatage was something I had heard my parents say was the place on the map where you found El Tigrito. My spelling was likely wrong, but I figured it was close enough. "I doubt that the letter will go to Mongolia." I offered the letter to El Loco.

"You give it to Mamacita Moreno at the cantina," El Loco said in Spanish. "If you buy some supplies for me, I'm sure she'll figure out how to get the letter into the mail. Now listen you two. I want five kilograms of flour, one kilogram of sugar, a half kilo of salt, a toe-sack full of red beans, and a bottle of Lava Gallo. You got that?" We nodded. "Good. Say it back to me."

Rosita repeated it exactly, and El Loco raised his brows as in surprise. "You'll have to take my wheelbarrow to haul that much weight back. You ever pushed a wheel barrow?"

"No." I looked at Rosita. She shook her head.

"Then get down there and practice some. It ain't as easy as it looks. When you get to the cantina, cram the bottle of Lava Gallo down inside the beans in case you dump the load. I don't want that bottle breaking. You go practice pushing that wheelbarrow, and I'll get the hard cash to pay for the supplies."

We headed for the wheelbarrow and El Loco vanished into the savannah. We could hear his voice chanting, "Maresey doats and doesey doats, maresey doats and doesey doats."

Just as we got the hang of how to push the wheelbarrow without letting it fall over, El Loco reappeared. "You got a pocket?" He demanded of me.

"Yes."

"Put this in it," he said in Spanish, handing me a chunk of heavy quartz. When I turned it over, I saw it was mostly gold. "Don't you lose that. It's enough to buy everything I told you to get plus mailing your letter. You tell Mamacita Moreno that. Enough for everything plus the letter with some left over. She'll come out way ahead on the deal, so don't you let her cheat you on the amount. You might even try to bargain a second bottle of Lava Gallo from her, just to show that you know how much that gold is worth. She won't go for it, but give it a try just for show."

"Why don't you get your own supplies?" Rosita asked. "Why send us with all that gold and your wheelbarrow? We could take the gold and run away."

"You could but you won't. Don made a deal with me."

"That's right." I felt proud.

"You didn't answer my question."

"There's a chance the men from Maracaibo won't pay any attention to a couple of kids. But if I went to the cantina with enough gold to buy that much food, they'd notice, and they would come here to see if they could find out where I dug up the gold. They would watch me for weeks. Weeks. But what the hell, they're probably watching me off and on right now."

He gave us directions to the cantina, which wasn't necessary because we both remembered how to get there. I pushed the wheelbarrow for the first leg of the trip. It took only about fifteen minutes to get to the muddy hole where the singing lady was dunking clothes. She still hunkered over the hole, singing and poking clothes into the mud, and I thought maybe she had been there, laboring away over the mud hole for the entire time Rosita and I had been with El Loco. How long was that? I wondered and glanced toward the sun.

"Just after noon," Rosita said. "We'll need to eat again. I plan to bargain for some food, along with all the other things for El Loco, using that rock you have in your pocket."

"Ku-ku-rrrru-ku-ku paloma," the one-eyed woman sang. She looked at us and fell silent for a few seconds. "So you met El Loco Merzi?" She laughed without being amused. The flesh hanging over her missing eye quivered and she bulged her good eye at us. "Wait. Stop, please."

I stopped pushing the wheelbarrow when Rosita tapped my arm. "He gave us bread," I said.

"Yes. He can be generous. But beware of him. Did you see his bad-luck doll? It can afflict you with the evil eye."

"We saw the doll. It's only a doll."

"Please," Rosita whispered, "be quiet for now." She raised her voice: "He said he knew you. He said you sing beautifully."

"He didn't say that," I whispered.

"Hush." Rosita pinched my arm.

"El Loco said that?" She looked astounded.

"He helped us with a letter that Mamacita Moreno will mail," I said.

"Hush, Don," Rosita said.

"Letter? Letter? Mailed from the cantina?" The one-eyed lady dropped her jaw, making her mouth into a comical little O, but I managed not to laugh.

"It will be a beautiful day I think," Rosita nudged me aside and took the handles of the wheelbarrow. "Goodbye for now." She started off, leaning into the job of pushing the barrow.

"It'll rain. Perhaps before dark. Perhaps after." The one-eyed woman scanned the sky. "But that'll help, I think, for I have a plan. You will be back in the camp of El Loco Merzi?"

"Yes," I said.

"Please, Don, hush," Rosita said. We walked on.

"Tell him to put away that bad-luck doll, and I'll come tell you about my plan," the one-eyed lady called to us.

"Why did you keep telling me to be quiet?" I asked.

"You talk too much about what we're doing. It might not hurt to do that, but I have a feeling that some strange things are going on. She thinks you are someone else, someone important."

"Do you think I'm not important?"

Rosita dropped the handles of the wheelbarrow and turned to me. "To me, you are the most important boy in the world." Her eyes flashed with such intensity that I took a step back in surprise. What had El Loco said about her? Fiery. That she was fiery, and he said it was good that she was fiery. "We must help each other find our way home," she said in more subdued tones. "And that means we must find ways to eat and to stay warm at night and to keep away from danger. I think we can have fun while we work to get home." She resumed pushing the wheelbarrow.

We walked past the Chaparro tree where we spent the night,

and farther on we found the tracks of the candy man's truck. Rosita again dropped the handles of the wheelbarrow. "You push the rest of the way. People would ask too many questions if they saw a girl doing the work, and I don't want to call attention to us."

Handling the wheelbarrow was more like play than work, I thought. I made little runs at grasshoppers, but they always got out of the way in time. Before I knew it, we reached the cantina. It didn't look like much.

Chickens pecked in the dust all around it, and some wandered into the front door. A couple of skinny pigs stood in the shade of some castorbean bushes, regarding us with piggy eyes and twitching noses. The walls of the cantina had once been white-washed, but most of the color had faded into pink adobe. The walls seemed too low, and palm thatching covered the roof. I parked the wheelbarrow beside the door. A pudgy woman dressed in the reds and browns of Indios appeared in the door. She seemed to have no legs and maybe to be standing there on the stumps of her knees.

"Two children, for the sake of God," she said and smiled in a broad grin of snaggley-looking teeth stained brown and black. "Come in, come in. You both look too skinny to be proper children." She vanished into the darkness of the cantina and called out, "Pepito, two children. One with the golden hair of angels, the other beautiful enough to be Indio. But so skinny. Bring beans and bread."

We stood in the doorway, leaning against each other in our uncertainty, straining to see in the dim light. "Step down," Rosita whispered.

I would have fallen if she had not warned me. The floor was about half a meter lower than the threshold, and I realized that the pudgy woman had been peering out at us from a lower level instead of standing on lopped-off legs. Sun stabbed like spotlights into the room through two windows, and dust motes swam in the rays. When my eyes adjusted, I found myself before a crude table surrounded by chairs made from tree branches and twine. The bottoms of the chairs were woven fibers. At the far end of the room, shelves held greasy-looking bottles, and cooking smells drifted in from a door beside the bottles. A pile of dirty laundry sat beneath the shelves with bottles, and I wondered if the one-eyed lady had already washed the laundry in her mud hole or if Mamacita and Pepito had flung it on the floor until someone could wash it.

"Sit, sit," the pudgy woman said. "First you eat, then you tell me why such skinny angels have come to my cantina. You may call me Mamacita Moreno."

"Yes, Mamacita," Rosita said. She urged me to sit at the table. "I am Rosita. This is my friend, Don."

"El Don. Madre de dios. Have you returned to reclaim your land? I should have known from the hair and fair skin. But you have starved for ten years, and look at you. Pepito, you lazy dog, bring the frijoles y pan de mano before El Don and his beautiful servant fall over and die from lack of food. I should kill a chicken, but that would take too long."

"We aren't starving," I said. "Hungry, maybe. But not starving. And my name is Don, not El Don."

"I'm not his servant," Rosita said, but Mamacita didn't hear her, for at that moment Pepito came in carrying two steaming bowls and hugging round loaves of bread between his arms and body. He looked to be at least a hundred years old. From the smell of him, I figured he hadn't had a bath in at least ninety years, and I doubted his flour-sack shirt had ever been washed. After he leaned over to set the bowls of beans on the table and extricated the bread from close to his armpits, I was in no mood for bread.

"Eat, eat," Mamacita Moreno told us. I scooted my chair closer to the table, aware that doing so had gouged out a bit of dirt from the floor. My toes touched something under the table—a gunny sack filled with flour, from the feel of it, used no doubt by patrons of the cantina as a foot rest. But when I plopped my feet on top of the sack, it came to life, squealed, and headed straight for the door, a route that took it beneath my chair. The bracing on the chair legs was a little too low-slung for the pig to clear. It squealed again and kept going. As the chair spun around and I fell, I caught a glimpse of the pig scrambling out the door. Mamacita leaped over the chair with an agility that amazed me. She snatched me up and hugged me to her breast. "Porbrecito, porbrecito el Don," she muttered, clutching me with one arm and pressing my face into her breast with the other.

It felt as if she were trying to smother me with a pillow. I

27

struggled for breath, pushing to get free of the woman. Finally she set me in a chair and knelt beside me. I snatched in some quick breaths of air and looked over Mamacita's shoulder at Rosita. She winked at me with a slow-moving wink, her face showing no emotion at all.

Mamacita Moreno smoothed out my hair with her fingers. They felt like sticks against my scalp. "Pepito," Mamacita said. "Pepito, you and I will cut that pig's throat today and make a soup of its head for El Don. Never again will such a pig sleep under our table."

"Please," I said, "don't kill the pig. I frightened it by putting my feet on it. Maybe I kicked it in the nose. Todd told me that pigs have sensitive noses, so it serves me right that it knocked my chair over. You must not kill the pig for something I did."

"Mamacita," Pepito said with some excitement. "Look. Gold." He held El Loco's chunk of quartz and gold. It must have come out of my pocket when I fell.

The word gold aroused the laundry piled beneath the shelves of bottles. I watched in astonishment as a man materialized from the pile, stretching and yawning. He stood, hitched up his pants, straightened his belt, and belched. "Did I hear the word gold?" he asked. He turned a chair around across from me and Rosita and straddled it like it was a horse. "Beans. It's too early for beans. Ah, but the bread. I'll eat that."

"No you won't, you raper of goats," Mamacita said.

Before she could say more, I shoved both of Pepito's armpit loaves across the table to the man who had once been a pile of dirty laundry. "I want you to eat these," I said. "Rosita and I want to eat only beans. Isn't that right, Rosita?"

She had also seen how Pepito carried in the bread, so she nodded with vigor.

"El Don," Mamacita said, "This rude man is Carlos Moreno, my good-for-nothing son. Carlos, this is El Don, who has been living on nothing but bread and water for ten years. And this is Rosita, his beautiful little servant girl."

I glanced at Rosita, who had just put a spoon of beans into her mouth. She looked flustered, and she struggled to get them chewed enough to push them into her cheek so she could speak. I winked at her, trying for a stony face in the process. The gesture seemed to make her furious. "No, no, no," she said. "Don is my friend. I serve no one."

"Good morning, El Don." Carlos ignored Rosita.

"It's always this way." Rosita slumped in her chair.

3
Lava Gallo and Bandits

While he ate, Carlos eyed the chunk of gold and quartz Pepito had set on the table in front of me. Rosita spooned beans into her mouth, looking beaten, though I figured such a mood wouldn't last long. I thought Pepito's beans tasted better than any food ever did or ever could. Mamacita hovered over the table, watching me eat, and the pig wandered into the cantina to settle under the table against my feet. Maybe it was another pig, for this one started snoring, and the other one had been so silent that I had mistaken it for a sack of flour. Mamacita and Carlos took no notice of the snoring pig.

After swallowing the last bite of beans, I said: "Mamacita Moreno, we have come here to buy some groceries." I couldn't remember the entire list, and particularly I couldn't remember the name of the rooster soap, so I added, "Rosita remembers the list. She never forgets anything."

Rosita perked up some at my compliment. "Flour," she said. "Ten kilos." She went through the rest of the list, concluding with "One bar of perfumed soap and three bottles of Lava Gallo."

Carlos laughed. Pepito, who was busy sweeping the dirt floor, stopped to stare. Mamacita fixed me with a disapproving look. "You are too young to be drinking such garbage. Are you at such a tender age already a boracho?"

The accusation startled me. Was I a drunkard? "No, no," I stammered. "The Lava Gallo is for a friend who plans to use it to wash chickens." So, I thought, the stuff El Loco wanted wasn't soap at all.

"Not chickens," Carlos said. "Roosters."

Mamacita looked mollified. "For a cockfight, one bottle is enough. Enough for ten cockfights. Tell your friend to spit the whiskey into both eyes of the roosters. It will make them angry enough to kill each other."

"Such a cockfight Lava Gallo causes," Carlos said. He sat back and closed his eyes. "I can see them going at it, feathers flying, flinging cheap whiskey and blood on all the spectators. How

31

beautiful."

"Carlos, don't be so crude. This is El Don you are talking to."

"The old Don used to go to cock fights. When I was a child, I remember seeing him place bets like any ordinary peasant."

"Carlos, stop talking rubbish and get the groceries El Don's servant has ordered." Mamacita picked up the gold, and her entire demeanor changed. "Mostly this is stone with little gold." She hefted it to measure its weight and sniffed in derision. "There's barely enough to cover the price of the beans, much less the other items. Carlos, get only one bottle of Lava Gallo."

"There is more than enough gold there for twice what we are buying from you," Rosita said.

"Also, I have this letter you must mail." I pulled the stitched-up cardboard from my pocket and handed it to Mamacita.

"A letter?" The idea of a letter seemed so novel that Mamacita's voice dropped to a stunned whisper. "A letter? Where do you send a letter?" She turned it over several times.

"It's a letter from El Don to the president of Venezuela," Rosita said.

"A letter to el Presidente," Mamacita said in awe. "I will give the letter to one of the men who brings sacks of flour in a truck, for this letter must be important. El Don, you have indeed come back to claim your land. The people will rejoice. Not the bandits who live in the old house, of course. They will try to kill you. Two bottles of Lava Gallo, Carlos. No one needs three."

Carlos began gathering our order, eyeing the gold the whole time. "For that lump of gold," he said, "I would hand-deliver the letter to el Presidente. For a hint about where to dig for more such gold, I would deliver ten such letters. Twenty."

I managed to get away from the table without disturbing the snoring pig and stood close enough to Rosita to whisper, "Should we ask about the bandits who want to kill me?"

"No."

"Why did you order a bar of perfumed soap? El Loco would never use such soap."

"He would never use soap of any kind. The soap is for us, Don. We must bathe daily, when we can find water."

"The fact is that I don't like to spend a lot of time bathing. You sound like my mother."

She scowled. "Don't you say that. Don't you ever say that."

"I'm still worried about the bandits." I thought it wise to change the subject, given Rosita's scowl and the tone of her voice.

"Los banditos," Mamacita Moreno said. "They are bad men, almost as bad as those scoundrels Carlos calls his friends. I say you should never trust a man from Maracaibo. Those men came here for gold, but they find only tiny bits of gold dust—nothing like the stone you brought in. Not that it has much gold in it, you understand, because it is mostly stone. Still, they bring their tiny bit of gold to my cantina to trade for pleasure."

"Don't talk so much, Don," Rosita whispered to me.

She and I went outside to watch Carlos load the groceries into the wheelbarrow. He set the flour in the front, close to the wheel, then walked around the wheelbarrow, inspecting it. "Did you buy this from El Loco Merzi?" he asked.

"Yes," I said.

"No," Rosita said at the same time.

"I knew it." Carlos laughed. "El Loco Merzi knows how to find gold because he is a wizard. A crazy wizard, to be sure." He loaded the rest of the goods. Rosita took the two bottles of Lava Gallo and put them inside the sack of beans. I lifted the handles of the wheelbarrow and had started to turn it around when Carlos said, "Now you will tell me where you got the gold."

"We will not," Rosita said.

With a suddenness that shocked me, Carlos lashed out, striking Rosita in the mouth. She stumbled back and fell, and at that moment I wished my machete wasn't stuck in the chaparro tree. In a split second I considered pulling out my Barlow, snapping it open, and going after Carlos. But extracting it from my pocket would take too long. I dropped the handles and launched myself at Carlos, leaping on his back. He stumbled forward but didn't fall. I buried my hands in his hair and pulled. He spun around, throwing me to the ground. Then Mamacita Moreno came out.

"Carlos, leave those children alone," she snapped. The command stopped Carlos, but he was plenty mad, probably because I still had a substantial amount of his hair in my hands. I flicked it away, hating its oily feel and doggy smell. "Get back in here, Carlos

33

Moreno," Mamacita said.

Rosita took my arm as I stood up. Her lower lip looked puffy. "Does it hurt?" I asked.

"No. Let's go now."

Carlos turned in the doorway to give us one last murderous look as I again picked up the handles of the wheelbarrow.

Pushing our load back wasn't easy. For one thing, my hands kept slipping because of the oil on them from Carlos' hair. By the time we got to the mudhole where the one-eyed lady washed clothes, I had blisters on my hands. The one-eyed lady wasn't there, which was fine with me, though Rosita seemed disturbed. "I wanted to ask her some questions about why everyone thinks you are El Don and what it means to be El Don. Perhaps we can get the information from El Loco, though I doubt it."

"I want to wash my hands," I said. I picked my way among the stones to the stream. Rosita walked behind me. When I dipped my hands into the water, she handed me her bar of perfumed soap. "Thanks." I thought the soap smelled better than Carlos' hair, but not by much.

When we wheeled into El Loco's camp, Rosita also had blisters on her hands, and two of the ones on mine had popped. The puffiness of her lip had vanished. El Loco was down by the stream, shoveling dirt into a wooden box and shaking it with a handle. When he saw us, he hurried up the slope. "Did anyone follow you?" he asked in Spanish.

"No," Rosita said. "But your stupid wheelbarrow put bubbles of water on my hands."

"Blisters, eh?" He switched to English. "Big effing deal. Men get blisters all the time, right Don? Blisters mean you're earning your living by the sweat of your brow. Blisters are Adam's curse, the bane of mankind, the fault of the serpent and the woman, and all that good shit."

"What did he say?" Rosita asked me.

"He said that women and snakes cause blisters. I didn't understand him so well."

El Loco found the Lava Gallo and whistled. "Two bottles. You're better at bargaining than I ever was." He shoved one bottle back into the bean sack, uncorked the other, and took a long drink, then fell to coughing. "Damn but that's good shit. Strong but good." After wiping his mouth on the back of his hand, he sat in the shade of the chaparro tree where Rosita had stuck the machete, and he took another drink. "Goddam," he said, his eyes moist with pleasure. "Goddam."

"I think we should go now," I said. "We mailed the letter and kept the bargain. Now we start home."

"Not yet," Rosita whispered. "Let El Loco get more of that Lava Gallo into him, and we'll ask some questions. Maybe we can discover why everyone calls you El Don and why Mamacita talked about bandits."

"Bandits," El Loco said. "Banditos. Bad hombres, shit." He took another drink.

"I forgot about his donkey ears," Rosita said.

"Can I ask some questions without you telling me to hush?"

"Yes. Of course."

"Why are you all the time telling me not to talk?"

"I'm sorry, Don. I worried that we might tell too much about ourselves and put us in some danger."

"What kind of danger?"

"I don't know. It's just a feeling I got from the woman who sang and then from Mamacita and Carlos. I don't know. It all seems to have to do with your name, Don."

"Don, Don, the piper's son," El Loco said. "Stole a pig and away he run. Or was it Tom? Who the crap cares? Maresey doats and doesey doats, maresey doats and doesey doats for chrissake. Listen." He sat up straight, almost hitting his head on the machete. "Horses. That means only one thing—the effing bandits are coming to collect taxes. News seems to travel fast around here, when it comes to gold."

"What did he say?" Rosita asked.

"He said he hears horses."

El Loco stood and glanced around. "The savannah," he said in Spanish. "You two get over there where the grass is highest and thickest. Hide in the savannah and don't make a sound. Those men are bad." He began shoving us toward the thick wall of savannah grass at the edge of his camp. "They would probably kill you, Don, and they might do terrible things to Rosita."

35

"Kill?" Rosita said in disbelief.

"Yes. Get in there now. Fast. Lie down and make no noise at all, no matter what you hear the bandits do."

We parted the grasses and stepped into them. El Loco pushed the grass back into shape as we mashed enough of it around us to lie down. He retreated, kicking the sand to cover our footprints.

The savannah grass had a dusty smell to it, making me want to sneeze. I pinched my nose and breathed through my mouth until the impulse went away. "I hear the horses now," Rosita said. We elbowed our way closer to the edge of the grass so we could see out. "That's far enough," she warned. "Get still now. And don't you dare sneeze."

El Loco turned the bottle up. I could see bubbles rise in the bottle and imagined that I heard it gurgle. Then the horses thundered into the camp, kicking up dust. "Five horses," I whispered. "And look, there's Carlos."

"Hush." Rosita nudged me with her elbow.

"Good day to you, El Loco Merzi," the lead rider said. He rode, as all the men did, barebacked, holding reins, and he looked like an ordinary man with a moustache. I was a little disappointed that he didn't carry a rifle and have cartridges of bullets slung across his shoulders. There was a pistol sticking out from his belt, and the sight of it gave me a thrill. The men dismounted and handed their reins to a pock-marked fellow who was small enough to pass for a boy, but he wasn't. Like the others he had a pistol handle protruding from his belt. The pock-marked man seemed nervous, and as soon as he had the reins of the horses, he began edging out of the camp.

Mr. Moustache turned to him and demanded in a querulous voice, "Where are you going?"

"The bad luck doll." The man made the sign against the evil eye.

"Ha," Mr. Moustache said. "Sometimes El Loco isn't so loco." He took the pistol from his belt, made some clicking sounds with it, and fired at the doll hanging from the chaparro tree. The doll jumped and bounced around. "It's evil eye is now dead."

A look of relief spread across the face of the pock-marked man, and he stopped making the sign against the evil eye. He moved forward again, pulling the horses with him.

Mr. Moustache turned to El Loco. "I heard you struck it rich," he said.

"Did I do that?" El Loco looked amazed. "I didn't know. It's good news, though, for now I can retire, move to a ranch in California, and have many women to serve all my needs. Perhaps I should start packing up the gold that I didn't know I had. Can you tell me where to find it?"

The men laughed. "He has gold," Carlos said. "I saw a chunk of it the size of my fist."

"So you claim," Mr. Moustache said. "The nugget grows every time you tell the story. Now shut up. Juan, get the small bit of gold from his tent."

The one called Juan crawled into the pup tent. El Loco took another swig from his bottle, and Mr. Moustache paced around, looking at the ground as if he expected to find chunks of gold everywhere. El Loco began a slow shuffle toward his campfire. Juan emerged from the tent holding a piece of cloth tied with a string. "It feels like very little," he said.

"That's all I have this time, and I'm telling the truth." El Loco edged closer to the campfire and glanced at it.

"If that's all you have, then I'm a bunch of radish," Mr. Moustache said. He watched El Loco with care. "Juan, look inside that pot hanging over the burnt sticks."

El Loco seemed to brighten. "Maybe Juan could wash the pot for me when he checks it for gold? Here, I'll get it for him." El Loco took the pot from the wire hook tied to a branch in the chaparro tree.

"Look," Juan said. "A machete stuck in the tree. What is the meaning of that?" He took the handle of the machete and jerked on it. "It seems to be grown into the tree, carumba." He jerked on the handle a few more times.

"Leave the machete alone, pendejo. Look in the pot like I told you," Mr. Moustache said.

El Loco handed off the pot, then retreated to the burned-out campfire. Mr. Moustache slit his eyes and looked at the remains of the campfire. "Juan. Get a shovel."

"There's nothing in the pot but dried pieces of bread," Juan said.

"I know. Get a shovel and dig where the fire was."

Juan looked around, spied a shovel leaning against the box down by the stream, and headed for it.

"No." El Loco became alarmed. "It is bad luck to dig there. The person who digs there will get warts on his face. The dead fire has been cursed. Anyone who digs it up and looks into the hole won't be able to pee for a month."

"Carajo." The pock-marked man moved back and made the sign against the evil eye.

"This was easier than usual," Mr. Moustache said. He turned to Carlos. "I hope there's enough gold to make our trip here worth my time."

"I do wish you wouldn't dig up my campfire," El Loco said.

Juan returned with the shovel and started excavating the campfire. The third shovel of dirt unearthed something, and Juan dropped to his knees. "This is large and heavy," he said, his voice high with excitement.

Mr. Moustache pushed Juan aside and plucked a piece of tied-up cloth from the hole. He shook dirt from the bundle. "It is larger than usual, but not so heavy." He ripped the cloth and dumped some stones onto the ground. "Bah." He nudged the stones with the toe of his boot. "Pick them up, Juan. There's some gold in them, but they're mostly just rocks. Carlos."

"It took me months to dig that little bit of gold out of the hard ground," El Loco said. "Months. Leave the gold stones for me. Leave half of them for me. Isn't my labor worth something?"

"You bought whiskey with my gold," Mr. Moustache said in tight voice. "I'll leave you the Lava Gallo as payment. Only a man with a stomach made of rock can drink such a brew."

"He also bought flour, salt, and beans," Carlos said. "You could take that."

"And have my servant starve? Don't be a fool. He doesn't find much gold, but he at least finds some, which is more than I can say for your stupid friends from Maracaibo."

"Leave me just one of the gold stones," El Loco said.

"Maybe he gave some of his gold to the children," Carlos said. "Maybe he's supplying El Don with gold for weapons to arm the peasants."

"El Don." Mr. Moustache spat on the ground. "Where do you get such stupid ideas? I killed El Don when he cheated me in a card game, remember? But of course you don't remember. You were a child then."

"His son, the new El Don. That's who I mean."

"Shut up. There is no son." Mr. Moustache turned to El Loco. "You stupid old man, you worked for how long since I last visited you? Three months? Four? And you barely dug enough gold for me to have a meal and a night with a whore. You must stop pushing that wheelbarrow all over the place and dig only where you find gold. Juan, get the rocks. My horse, where is my horse? I've had enough of crazy people. Carlos, if you play such a trick on me again, I will feed your platano to the cannibal fish."

The men mounted and rode away. El Loco took another drink of Lava Gallo and laughed. "A kiddledy divvy too, wouldn't you?" he sang as he stumbled toward the chaparro tree. "What, ho?" He tried to kick the machete, but he couldn't kick that high. "A bare bodkin. Shit." He sat down and leaned against the tree. "They're all gone, all the bad horses and all the bad men who can't put all the gold together again. El Don and La Doña Rosita can now come out of the grass."

"Are we safe?" I asked.

"I think so," Rosita said. "Let's go ask Mr. Jackass Ears about El Don."

"Jackass Ears?" El Loco laughed. "I like that name. You are to call me that from now on."

We stood and brushed the dust and grass from us. "Why is he so jolly?" I asked. "The bandits just took all his gold."

"Hush, Don." Rosita and I approached El Loco.

"You said you wouldn't tell me that again."

"All my gold, alas. Todo. Every bit. Each flake. Every nugget and all the rocks that glittered, goddam, leaving me destitute, poorer than a church mouse, broke as last year's toothpicks, flat as fungus, and without funds, shit."

"What did he say?"

"He said something about a mouse and some toothpicks. It sounded like nonsense to me."

39

"Right on, young man, heir to the throne, the Don of the Orinoco, Prince of Dust Devils, and King of the black caimanes. All of my words are nonsense. That's why the people wisely call me El Loco. To you, however, I am now Jackass Ears. You may call me Mister Jackass or Mister Ears, as you like."

"Don't ask," I told Rosita. "I didn't understand that speech at all."

Color rose in Rosita's cheeks. "You will please talk only Spanish. Please tell us why everyone thinks Don is El Don."

"I am stricken," El Loco said in Spanish. "The bandits take all my gold, and all you can do is to lecture me about how to talk."

"You have plenty of gold hidden elsewhere." Rosita put her hands on her hips and stepped closer to El Loco. "And if you cannot remember where you hid it, then you can find more in the gully beneath the chaparro tree, where you push your wheelbarrow at night."

El Loco stared at her, open-mouthed.

"So are you going to answer my question?"

"Don't talk about that gully," El Loco said in a harsh whisper. He cleared his throat and smiled. "Please sit down and I'll tell you some stories. I'll even answer your question, but you must be patient, for my head is spinning with Lava Gallo. Sit. Sit."

As we sat, I asked Rosita, "What did you mean about more gold? The bandits took all he had, we saw that."

"Hush, Don."

"You told me you wouldn't say that."

"I'm sorry." She turned to me and put her hand on mine. "I truly am sorry."

She looked so contrite that I shrugged and said, "Forget it."

"Thank you, Don, my good friend." Rosita patted my hand and turned her attention to El Loco. When she did, her face hardened. "Stop drinking so you can make sense when you talk. Who is El Don?"

El Loco looked limp and shapeless as a piece of chewed sugarcane. He took a defiant swig from the bottle. "Dead, that's who he is. Deader than a doornail. Deader than last week's belch or the dreams of youth. Deader than a mackerel. I wish I had a mackerel right now. I'd eat that sumbitch without salt. Goddam." He took another drink.

"What did he say?" Rosita nudged me.

"He said El Don is dead and that he wants to eat some fish without salt."

"That's no help. Stop drinking now, El Loco. And please remember that I don't understand English." She offered to take the bottle from him.

He clutched it to his breast. "No you don't, sweetheart." He glanced at the machete. "And you please keep in mind that I ain't flirting. Saying sweetheart is just a manner of talking. And little laaaambsey divy."

"Talk to me in Spanish, you drunk goat," Rosita snapped.

"Bueno. Spanish it is," El Loco said.

I was relieved that he switched languages. "What will the bandits do," I asked, "if I try to get my land back?" Rosita shot me a sharp look, and I expected her to tell me to be quiet, but she didn't.

"Does it matter what you try to do? Not at all. You are not in control of anything—nobody is." El Loco shook the bottle at Rosita. "Not even you, sweet princess of swinging machetes and queen of the curled lip. Nothing you try to do makes any difference, even if you must try to force your life to be the way you want. The bandits are also puppets. We are all poor players in a game with dim rules we don't know about. We work and sweat and kill and die, and nothing we do changes what we will do." As he spoke, his voice became lower, and he looked to be on the edge of tears. "That goddam Chinaman was right. By doing nothing, everything gets accomplished. But I can't just sit and do nothing. I can't—even if what I do doesn't matter."

"I think he is crazy," Rosita said.

"Children and drunkards tell the truth," El Loco said.

"What about my land?" I asked.

"You have no land. You're just a boy. A good one, though, suckering Mamacita Moreno with that chunk of gold rock and getting her for two bottles. Two." He took a drink and continued in a slurred voice: "They'll be here, those boys from Maracaibo, soon as they get a sniff of my gold. They'll follow me around for days, the stupid goats. I won't be able to go near my gold mine for weeks,

41

maybe. You know what those goats do? They watch me dig, then they go dig like crazy men, straight down, finding nothing because there's nothing where I dig." He laughed. "I let them work like Chinamen, then I go dig somewhere else, and they follow and dig there. Wears them out, and they call me crazy for digging all over the place. Soon as they give up, I get back to digging where the gold is, but only in the dead of the night when those lazy goats are at the cantina with Mamacita's women. Won't none of them come into my camp on account of my bad luck doll with the evil eye, heh, heh, heh." He glanced at the doll and frowned. "The stinking son of a goat licker shot my hex doll, goddam."

"The men from Maracaibo and the bandits keep you busy," Rosita said.

"The bandits, yes. Those guys don't care about my doll, mostly. They march right into camp to collect taxes. I pay them, too, but not as much as they might get if they weren't so stupid. And why the hell is Carmencita la Gatita hanging around my camp?" He pointed with the neck of the bottle.

The one-eyed lady stood on the trail, making little jerky motions with one hand, holding the other out in front of her. "Why did you call her Carmen the cat?" I asked.

"She's making the sign that guards against the evil eye," Rosita said, then glanced at the doll hanging from the other chaparro.

"She has only one eye, and I have the evil eye hanging in the tree," El Loco said in English. "It keeps the goddam superstitious natives out of my camp. Except for the frigging bandit tax collectors, of course." He then switched to Spanish and raised his voice as Rosita headed for the other chaparro tree: "You leave that doll alone."

"I will not." Rosita climbed the chaparro fast as a monkey and got the doll. She shinnied down the tree and threw the doll into El Loco's tent. Only then would the one-eyed lady come into the camp.

4

A Stolen Canoe

"Carmen, beautiful and once beloved Carmen," El Loco said. "Though you paint an inch thick, you must come to this."

The one-eyed lady kept casting sidelong glances at the pup tent as she entered the camp. "Why is there a machete in the chaparro?" She grabbed the handle and pulled the machete away from the tree.

"Madre de Dios," Rosita said.

"Goddam," El Loco said.

"Juan must have loosened it," I said.

El Loco closed one eye and looked over the neck of the bottle at me as if he were aiming a pistol. "Don't say such a thing, Don. Don't even think it. Life is too hard without magic, and what Carmen did just now is magic as sure as butterflies ain't made of butter." He turned his attention to Carmen. "You are of royal blood, that's clear. You are the princess of the Savannah and heir to the kingdom of El Don."

"How much has he drunk?" Carmen asked me.

"Nearly half a bottle of Lava Gallo. But he didn't make much sense before he started drinking."

"Out of the mouths of babes," El Loco said in English.

"Speak so I can understand, please," Carmen said.

"He might for a while, but he likes to talk to Don in their language," Rosita said.

"Yeah," I said, "and the words he says might as well be in German."

"Don't listen to him," Carmen said. "It is El Don who is important here. You must reclaim your land."

"El Loco says I have no land, and he's right. I'm just a boy from El Tigrito who was brought here by the candy man. Ask Rosita."

"That might be true. But it is also true that you are now El Don. I believe it. The people who worked for the old Don believe it because I told them about you and your golden hair. Even the ruined men from Maracaibo believe it. Like it or not, you are now

43

El Don."

"Believing it doesn't make it true."

"No, El Don, you're wrong. Believing is the only thing that makes something true. And now that you are a man of much importance, you must help the people who know you and love you and believe in you."

"Goddam," El Loco said in surprise. "That's pretty damn profound for a one-eyed whore."

"I asked you not to speak in English," Carmen said. "What did he say, El Don?"

"I think he said you're right."

"I am right. Now you must hear my plan."

"We need to go home," Rosita said.

"Hush, child. You are the servant of El Don. It is your duty to help him do what he must do."

"My servant, is she?" I chuckled. Rosita slit her eyes at me.

"Yes. I saw her pushing the wheelbarrow for you, as is only proper. Now she will stand behind you when you tell the people to rise against the bandits."

"And do what to the bandits?" I asked.

"Kill them, of course. Look at me. I was once young and beautiful and could see from two eyes so brown that I broke men's hearts just looking at them. I broke his heart," she pointed at El Loco. "Then the bandits slashed me with a knife, cut my face into ugliness, and killed the fire in my eye."

"You seem to have rediscovered some of the fire in your head," El Loco said.

"Yes. And if you had any sense, you would look with your heart beyond my empty socket and scars. But, El Don, ignore him, the stupid goat. The bandits killed your father and butchered your cattle and even now live in the home that your father built."

"My father lives in El Tigrito in a house that has a water tower in the back yard."

"Perhaps. But your father is also dead and I am wounded and ugly, and for what? So the bandits can have the land that gave a good life to many good people. The people are afraid of the bad men, afraid of dying or being mutilated the way the bandits mutilated me. So they do nothing. But if you talk to them, it will give

44

them hope."

"Why me?"

"Because of your golden hair. Because of your age. Because you are now El Don. The old Don had a boy with golden hair. He would be about your age now, but the bandits say they shot him and buried him with his father."

"Then I am not El Don."

"Don't argue with her, boy," El Loco said. "You'll lose. Never argue with a woman with fire in her head."

"Listen to this man," Carmen said. "He speaks the truth."

"But you told me not to listen to him."

"You're arguing with her again." El Loco said. "Now you know why I called her a cat. Have you ever been able to argue with a cat and win?"

"The people are gathering down by the small river. You will come with me and speak to them."

"No I won't. You want me to tell some people to kill some other people. Miss Carmen, I couldn't even kill an iguana if I were starving."

"It's true," Rosita said, "about the iguana."

"Do you value your servant girl?" Carmen asked.

"Rosita is my best friend. She is not my servant." It surprised me to hear myself calling her my best friend, but I knew it was true as I spoke. Rosita looked at me, her eyes rounded in wonder, then she gave me a solemn nod.

"Good enough." Carmen sighed. "I do wish you would come without my having to do this." She turned and called out, "Simón, come get these unruly children." A man wearing khakis and boots emerged from the savannah grass not far from where Rosita and I had hidden from the bandits. He held a pistol, and he smiled in a mean-looking way. Dark, sinister-looking brows slanted into a frown and almost met over his nose, and his cheeks were thin and leathery. A white gash of a scar ran through his moustache, giving him the appearance of snarling. "Simón, if El Don doesn't obey me, shoot the girl."

"No." I leaped to my feet and snatched the machete from her.

"Get back." Simón pointed the pistol at me. "Get back."

"Goddam," El Loco said. "So much for romance. So much for

45

this whore being of royal blood."

"Speak Spanish, you goat kisser," Carmen said. "El Don, you will take the machete by the blade and hand it to me. Your friend is beautiful, even as I once was. It would be a shame if she came to harm."

I handed her the machete. Rosita took my arm and stood close to me.

"And you, you crazy old man. Stand up." As El Loco struggled to his feet, Carmen snatched the bottle from him and threw it down. The whiskey gurgled out and vanished into the dry sand.

"Goddam," El Loco said.

"I loved you once. Did you know that?"

El Loco looked as if someone had struck him in the stomach. "Don't say it. Don't say such cruel things to an old man." He burst into tears, sobbing and clutching himself.

Rosita went to him, patted his back, and said, "It's hard to be loved in such a way. I know. Crying helps."

"Shut up both of you," Carmen said, her voice husky.

The man with the pistol appeared confused, and he began to blot his eyes on his shirt sleeve as he looked from El Loco to Carmen. The corners of his mouth turned down, his fierce eyebrows wilted into misery, and he began to blubber. He sniffed a couple of times, put his thumb over one nostril and blew a mist out of the other, then said in a voice that cracked, "We need to go. The people will be waiting, and look. Rain comes."

El Loco wiped a tear from his cheek. "That was bygod gross, Simón," he said.

"Yes, rain," Carmen said. "We're lucky, for it looks as if it will rain as the day falls into night. But look at you. What a bunch of babies—all of you crying except for El Don, who is the best man here." Carmen whacked El Loco's bottom with the flat side of the machete. "March. And be assured that was the last time I ever tell a man that I once loved him. El Don, you come walk beside me. Simón, walk behind the other two, and keep your pistol ready. I don't trust El Loco because he is loco, and I don't trust the children because they are children. Shoot them if they try to run away, but shoot them in the legs."

We walked past the water hole where Carmen had dipped

clothes in the mud, followed the gully past the chaparro tree where Rosita and I spent part of a night and El Loco dug for gold, and went on toward the dark line of trees that was a river jungle. A cool wind came upon us, and I smelled the strange fresh smell that comes with rain. Dad said that smell was ozone, which he said was burnt oxygen. But it was a good odor, and clean, not at all like something burnt, a smell I always enjoyed when it came in the winds just before rain.

As we left the savannah to walk among the long shadows of palms, giant rosewood, and mango trees, I said, "Miss Carmen, I won't tell anyone to kill anyone else."

"I know. It's because you have a good heart. Say only a few words. I'll tell you what those words are."

When she told me, I was surprised. "That's all?"

"That's all. Doing the right thing is easy, El Don, once you know what it is."

El Loco snorted. "And a one-eyed, lying whore is the one who knows right from wrong." I glanced back at him. Tears had drawn lines in the dust on his cheeks, but that was the only evidence that he had cried or that such a man was capable of crying. He looked defeated and tired.

"Shut up," Carmen said. "If you must speak, do so in Spanish."

"Spanish, shit. Maresey doats and doesey doats and little laaaambsey die-vey," El Loco sang. I thought his voice sounded more sober than it did back in his camp and that it had a sad note in it.

As we moved deeper into the jungle, night came on, and the noises of the night creatures began. We walked past something with a scary bass voice said a single word: "Ralph. Ralph. Ralph." A million insects began buzzing and clicking, and whistle frogs added to the din with a continuous chorus of single high-pitched notes.

We rounded a bend in the path into a clearing beside the river, and I saw that Carmen was right—it wasn't a big river at all. Ground palms with fronds as large as those in the tall palm trees grew along the edge of the water. Though it was hard to make out in the shadows of twilight, I saw a canoe tied to a bush. If it were turned crossway to the river, you could use it for a bridge all the way across. Beyond the canoe stood a little shack of a house and several

47

lighted kerosene lanterns hung on poles. Beside the shack two groups of men milled about. The large group—fifteen or twenty—wore rough cotton pants and shirts similar to those worn by the natives in El Tigrito, along with simple alpargatas instead of leather boots or shoes. The other group seemed better dressed, but they looked much dirtier. I figured these were the men from Mara-caibo who came to the wild part of Venezuela in search of gold, the men who gave what little gold dust they found to Mamacita Moreno in exchange for pleasure. They had on khaki trousers and shirts, and they all wore boots. Among the Maracaibo men was Carlos, trying to look small and invisible, so I gave no sign of seeing him. As we walked into the clearing both groups fell silent, and I again became aware of the night sounds of the jungle.

Carmen pushed me forward and said, "Men, I present to you El Don." The poorer men wearing alpargatas cheered, and the men in boots made subdued noises of approval. "Talk to them," Carmen prompted. I felt jittery and wasn't sure I could talk without my voice cracking, so I spent some time clearing my throat. "Now," Carmen said in a harsh whisper.

"You are men of men," I said. "You know what is the right thing to do, and I support you in doing it."

The men waited for more, but that was all Carmen had told me to say. One of the men asked, "Will you make the land rich again, as your father did?"

"Before you go," I said, "I must tell you that I see one man who came with the bandits today to take gold from El Loco." I pointed. "His name is Carlos, and he struck my servant in the mouth with his fist."

Carlos began backing toward the river. Just as he turned to run, several men grabbed him and knocked him down. Three of them sat on him. "El Don," one of them called to me. "What shall we do with this goat?"

"Let's cut his throat," another man said.

Rosita took my arm and whispered, "Tie him up."

"Tie him up," I said.

"He is very young," Rosita whispered.

"He is very young," I called out as the some men brought rope and began tying Carlos's legs and arms.

"His mother is Mamacita Moreno," Rosita whispered.

"He is the son of Mamacita Moreno," I said.

"Now," Carmen said in low tones, "you children shut up." She walked among the men speaking in a shrill voice: "You heard El Don. He is only a boy and already he is a man of judgment. Go. All of you. Kill the bandits. Take their ill-gotten gold, and return our land to prosperity once again. Go now. Night falls and rain comes. The bandits have grown fat and lazy. They think you are all women, that you have no spines, so they will not suspect that you will fall upon them. Take your pistols, those who have any. Take your shotguns. Take your knives and machetes," she waved my machete around over her head, "and rush them just after the rain starts to pound upon the roof. They will not hear you come upon them because of the rain. They will not suspect anyone of attacking them on such a night. I will stay here to keep El Don safe. Return when the scourge of our land lies bleeding and dead in the very house where they once butchered El Don, the father of this young Don. Now. Go in stealth; go with heavy hearts; go knowing justice is on your side; and go knowing there is gold in the pockets of the bandits, gold that now belongs to you."

This time the men from Maracaibo cheered along with the others. Then they all rushed back down the trail we had used. Within minutes only Rosita, Carmen, El Loco and I were left standing in the flickering light of the kerosene lamps. Carlos was bowed up in a knot on the ground, trussed up like a hog. He looked in no mood to be social.

"Those men are going to kill others. That's wrong," I said.

"Maybe," El Loco said in Spanish. "Maybe not. For sure it isn't right that the bandits killed the old Don and took his house. It isn't right that they stole the eye of the one woman I ever loved and made her turn from me and all men in bitterness."

"I turn from you?" Carmen said. "You abandoned me because I was ugly and because all you cared about was gold."

"I dug gold only for you." El Loco raised his voice. "I pretended to be crazy to keep gold thieves from taking me seriously—I pretended until perhaps I became a little crazy. For you, Carmencita, I dug gold— remember what you told me? That you would never have a man who was as poor as I was? You sent me away. Then I

49

dug gold from habit, because there was nothing more for me to do. It became a game, being El Loco, finding and hoarding gold while others tried to get from me what they could not get for themselves."

"Liar," Carmen whispered and started crying. "Liar. Liar." She dropped my machete and put her hands over her face.

El Loco put an arm around her. "Yes. I have learned to tell lies," he said, then dropped his voice to a whisper. They wandered toward the shack, absorbed in each other, ignoring us.

"This is not a good place for us to be," Rosita said.

"Then let's leave. Maybe we can stand under one of those palms when the rain comes."

"We take the canoe." Rosita pointed toward the small river. It was so dark I could barely make out the shape of the bush where the canoe was tied.

"My machete." I picked it up. As soon as I had it in my hand I remembered the wheelbarrow putting blisters below my fingers.

"Good," Rosita said, her voice full of excitement. "Cut some palm fronds from the palmettoes. We will use them for umbrellas when we're in the canoe. Can you swim?"

"Yes. And you?"

"Yes." She led me to the canoe, which wasn't like any I had ever seen. The sides pinched in toward the bottom, giving it the shape of a canoe. But the bottom was flat and much wider than I expected.

"What about Carlos? What about El Loco and Carmen?" I asked.

"What about them? They're not our worry. Hurry. Get the palm fronds." She began untying the rope from the bush.

I poked around the dark masses of palm fronds and hacked at them until I had a stack of large ones. Swinging the machete wasn't fun because of the sore places on my hands. The wind picked up as I put the palms into the canoe.

"Get in, quick," Rosita said. "Before someone stops us."

"We're going to steal the boat?"

"Not steal. Borrow. Besides, I think the boat belongs to Carmen, and she owes us for telling Simón to shoot us if we didn't obey her."

"It's still stealing." The canoe didn't tip much when I stepped into it. "Do you have paddles?"

"Yes. Sit down so we can get going. Sometimes it's not so bad to steal. We'll talk about that later."

I sat on the bottom of the canoe and felt water soak into my pants. "I'm sitting in water," I said.

"Stop whining. So am I. Here, take this paddle. No, put down your machete first. Take it, and let's get going."

"Which direction?" The handle of the paddle called my attention to the blisters on my hands even more than did the machete. But Rosita had blisters, I remembered, and she wasn't complaining. I resolved to ignore the pain.

"Don, there's only one direction we can go. With the flow of the river. Now be quiet and help me. I'll guide because I'm in the back. You watch for rocks and logs."

"I can't see a thing."

"Then just try to keep us in the center of the river. We should stop talking now."

"Thanks for saying it that way."

"Thanks for what?" She sounded puzzled.

I glanced back but it was too dark to see her. "Thanks for saying we both should stop talking instead of telling me to hush."

She giggled, or I think she did, for at that moment a clap of lightening roared overhead, giving me a brief view of the jungle around us. Vines hung everywhere, and trees leaned into the water. Then the rain began, and I tried to shelter my head with a palm frond.

It was impossible to hold both the palm and the paddle, so I gave up and decided it was fine to get soaked. The rain felt cool, almost cold, and I knew that before the night was over it would be quite cool. Turns in the narrow river caused leaves to drag across the canoe, across my face. It was necessary to keep ducking and, from time to time, to use the paddle to push us away from the shore. Rain kept falling, making a hissing sound in the water and on the trees of the jungle. More thunder sounded, but there was no lightening. "Gunfire," Rosita said. "Not far away."

She was right; the sounds were not thunder. We heard only three or four blasts from shotguns and a few popping noises from pistols, then heard only the hiss of the rain. "Some men are now

51

dead that were breathing just a few minutes ago," I said.

We flowed with the river, avoiding talking, ducking under overhanging trees and paddling to stay in the center. Then I said: "It's my fault."

"It is not," Rosita said. The hiss of rain quieted and stopped. Drops plopped into the water from trees, the river water gurgled against the bank, and wet leaves kept brushing us. Then there were no more leaves to push aside and we couldn't hear the sound of water against the riverbank. Overhead, clouds parted to reveal the brilliance of the stars. "The river," Rosita said.

"I think the river ran into a lake," I said. "We should find a place to go ashore and dry off before we get too cold."

"It would be dangerous to go into a strange jungle at night. We must stay in the boat until daylight. I found a can for dipping out the water." I heard the scraping sound as she scooped water from the bottom of the canoe, then heard the splash of her emptying the can overboard. I turned around to watch but couldn't see much. She dipped and poured, dipped and poured, and the water I sat in receded. "Take off your shirt," she said. "Use it to sop up the remaining water, and wring out the shirt over the side."

I did as she told me. It felt good to take off the cold shirt. She set the can aside and in the dim light from the stars pulled her blouse over her head. "I'm cold," she said.

"Do your hands hurt from the wheelbarrow and from the canoe paddle?"

"Yes. But I don't think about it."

"I think we got all the water out," I said.

"Some will return. We must get out of our wet clothes or we'll be cold in the night." She began squirming around, taking off her skirt.

I considered taking off my soaked tennis shoes and wet jeans. "Is it all right to strip?"

"Of course. Children in Venezuela often run around with no clothes on at all."

"Small ones, yes. But we're not children,"

"No? We aren't exactly adults. Take off your clothes, Don, or you will catch a cold in the coolness of the night." She held her skirt over the side and wrung the water from it.

I took off my shoes and socks, wrung out the socks, then unsnapped my jeans and thought that I couldn't go through with it. I couldn't take off my pants in front of a girl.

"Put your wet clothes between us in the bottom of the boat," she instructed. "We'll put the paddles over them, then cover the paddles with the palm fronds you cut. Then we'll use the palms as a mat to sleep on. We'll have to lie close together because the boat is narrow, but that will be good. We will lie as we did in the candy maker's truck and keep each other warm in the night."

"Naked?"

"Yes, Don." She sounded exasperated. "It'll be cold in the night, and we would be much colder with wet cloth on us."

Take off my underwear, too? I wondered, then saw Rosita wringing out a small white garment and knew the answer to that. I took off my jeans.

The mat felt lumpy when I finally stretched out on it, and the palm fronds were scratchy. Rosita tipped the canoe some in moving so our feet would be in the same end of the boat, then she settled on the mat, her back snuggled against my front. She took my arms and wrapped them around her, "for keeping warm," she said. She shivered for a few minutes until our pooled body warmth allowed us both to relax. The canoe drifted idly in the lake, and I thought maybe she had gone to sleep when she said: "It wasn't your fault."

"No?" I had to think for a moment to realize what she was talking about.

"No. The bandits killed your father. I mean the father of the other blond boy. They robbed the peasants. They robbed El Loco. It isn't your fault that the peasants and the men from Maracaibo killed them."

"Maybe the bandits killed the men who attacked them. That would mean I sent them there to die."

"There were too few gunshots for the bandits to have stayed alive. All of them had guns, and few of the peasants and gold-seekers had guns, remember? I think the battle consisted mostly of the slashing of machetes and knives. That means the good people won."

"Is it wrong to kill bad people?"

"No. Yes. I don't know. But I do know that it would happen

sooner or later—the peasants would cut the throats of those who had cheated them of a good life. You had nothing to do with it."

"Yes I did. I told them I supported what they were going to do."

"But you didn't tell them what to do."

I thought she was right about that. Carmen told them what to do, so she was bad, then, and not I. It relieved me some to shift the blame to Carmen. "Carmen said believing something makes it true. Do you believe that?"

Rosita moved around against me and yawned. "I don't know. Yes. Ask me in the morning. Don, I'm wet and cold and lying in an uncomfortable boat. But for all that, this is a good hour. You feel warm against me, and we're somewhere in a wonderful jungle lake. I love the jungle," she said with her voice seeming to trail off in sleep.

5
Riding the River

I awoke to a rhythmic bump. Rosita and I had squirmed around in the night, and we lay nose-to-nose, our arms and legs tangled. She still slept, and in the dim light of morning I could see her mouth was open and a little trickle of saliva coming from it. Her hair was scattered over much of her face and lay in curls on the palm frond mat. One of her hands lay palm up beside her, and I could see the white skin of broken blisters, one below her ring finger and one below her index finger. I stretched my own hands, feeling the stiffness from blisters, and listened again to the bumping sound. It seemed to be coming from the end of the canoe. I pushed up to look over the side, and Rosita turned over in sleep.

The canoe had drifted to the shore, and the current was bumping us against a half-submerged log, keeping us from floating into the overhanging green of the river jungle. "Current?" I said aloud and looked around. "Rosita. Rosita, wake up. We are not on a lake."

She stretched and sat up, rubbing her eyes, and in that moment, I thought she looked like one of the tiny children of El Tigrito who run about nude. She shook the hair out of her eyes and looked at the river.

More water flowed past us than I thought possible for one river to hold. The trees on the other side looked taller than any I had ever seen. "The water," I said. "It's clear. How can it be clear and be such a big river?"

"The biggest I've ever seen." Rosita's voice was full of awe.

"We floated down the river all night. That means we're far from El Loco and Carmen. I'm glad."

"Maybe not so far." Rosita gripped the sides of the canoe and made her way toward one end. "Take a paddle and help me get the canoe to a place where we can get ashore."

"This is wonderful. I feel like a wild man from Borneo." I picked up the paddle.

"Where's Borneo?"

"I don't know. Wild people come from there, I guess. My

father used to call me the wild man from Borneo."

"Are you wild?"

"Yes. Wearing no clothes and paddling a canoe makes me feel like a wild man, a savage." Especially with a naked native girl in the boat with me, I thought, but I didn't say it.

"It's because of our clothes that we must get ashore. If we don't find a place in the sun to hang them on bushes, they'll never dry, and we'll have to remain savages with nothing on. There, look. A sand bar with some rocks. We can go ashore there."

We nosed the canoe into a tiny bay where the river seemed to stop. I could see fish darting away as I dipped the paddle. The canoe nosed up as we hit the sand, and I jumped out to pull the end of the boat out of the water. Rosita put on her alpargatas and climbed the rocks above the sandbar. "The rocks form a clear place in the edge of the jungle," she reported. "Tie up the boat while I go behind a bush."

"Are you afraid I might see you nude?" I asked.

She stopped and looked down at me. "Why am I hiding from you to get rid of water? There's no mystery about how either of us look. Still, I will feel more comfortable if I go a little way off."

I pulled most of the canoe out of the water, then tied it to a log on the sand bar, though it seemed silly to tie it up when it was mostly out of the water. Our clothes looked terrible from the dirty water that had been in the boat. I tried wringing out my shirt, but it felt gritty, so I set the clothes on a rock, took my pants, and waded out in the water to wash them. By the time Rosita got back, it was full daylight. She helped me rinse the bilge water and sand from our clothes. When I washed my jeans, I held the pocket closed that contained my Barlow and a few coins.

When we finished the washing, she said, "I'll hold the clothes while you put your shoes on."

"Without socks?"

"Put on wet socks, if you want. But you'll need shoes to walk through the jungle to the savannah. We'll have to do that to find a place in the sun for the clothes to dry. Up there by the rocks, I found a surprise for us."

"What is it?"

"A surprise." Her cheek dimpled.

"I like surprises. But what would happen if we just walked around nude, if we left our clothes here on a rock?"

"Then they wouldn't get dry because there's no sun on this side of the river, and we would wear wet clothes, which wouldn't be so bad when the day becomes hot. But tonight we will want dry clothes in order not to be so cold."

I sat on the edge of the canoe and put on shoes without socks. "I'm ready now."

"Get your machete," Rosita said. I got the machete and started climbing the rocks. "Wait. Help me carry the clothes." She handed me a dripping bundle that I tucked under one arm so I had a free hand for the machete. Vines and bushes crowded the rocky ridge we walked on, but there was enough bare rock to allow us not to have to walk in the undergrowth. Then I found Rosita's surprise.

Bananas. They grew in a little stand, holding the stalks of bananas upside down with the ends of the bananas pointing up. Most were green, but one stalk was golden. "I didn't even pick one," Rosita said, "because I wanted you to see how beautiful they are, and I wanted to eat breakfast with you."

"Breakfast?" The notion of eating wild bananas and calling it breakfast startled me.

"Yes. Put the clothes here," she set her bundle on a rock that looked as if someone had scrubbed it. Then she stepped among the undergrowth to the banana tree and reached toward the stalk with the golden bananas. "Ay-yi-yi," she yelped and jumped back.

I dropped my wet clothes and lifted the machete. "What is it?"

She scrambled back onto the bare rocks. "Araña del monte," she said.

"A spider frightened you?" I felt relief that it was only a spider, but I also felt disappointed that Rosita could be scared off by a spider.

"Not just any spider. The biggest one in the world."

"Hah. I've seen some big spiders. In Texas we have tarantulas big as a fuerte. Bigger." I started toward the ripe bananas.

"No. Don't get close to it. My father told me a poisonous spider can kill you."

I ignored her, making a show of being tough, though I was a little worried about being naked and having certain parts of my body exposed while I approached a spider. "I don't see it." I poked around on the stalk of bananas with the machete. A black shape leaped out of some dark spot onto the end of the machete. It was huge and had hairy legs that wrapped around the blade. "Yikes," I squeaked and swung the tip of the blade up. Doing so flipped the spider, and it sailed like a bat through the air, over Rosita's head, and landed with an audible rip of leaves in the trees behind her. "That spider is as big as a bird," I said and retreated from the banana tree lest other spiders jump out at me.

"Yes. My grandmother said the jungle spider eats birds. It's big and dangerous." Rosita picked up her bundle. "Get the clothes. I say we forget about eating those bananas." She walked up the rock ridge toward the dense canopy of trees. I picked up the clothes, made a futile attempt to knock the dirt from the side where they hit the ground when I had dropped them, and followed her.

Rosita walked with the grace of a cat, and I liked watching the movement of her muscles on her legs and hips. When we reached the undergrowth, she turned and said: "You go first with the machete to help push our way into the forest floor.

"Will there be spiders?"

"Not likely. My grandmother said the jungle spider is rare even in wild jungles. Still, be watchful." We made our way through a patch of undergrowth into the thick shade of giant trees. Almost nothing grew on the ground between them. We moved close together, arms touching, and looked at the trees.

The trunks were so big that it would take a while to walk around just one tree. They had fins on them like rockets, and many sent roots running half submerged across the surface of the ground. Their branching started high, so high that climbing one was out of the question. The leaves, far above us, matted to look like a green tent, and no direct rays of sunlight penetrated the canopy. "Never have I seen such big trees," I said.

"Nor I. My grandmother said once such trees grew along El Tigre river close to our village. But men cut them down."

"Which way is the savannah?"

Rosita turned and pointed. "The river is there, through those bushes and small trees. That means the savannah is that way," she pointed the opposite direction, "for the trees follow the river."

"All I see is more trees. If we go into this jungle, we'll become lost. We might find the savannah, and we might find the river again, but we might never find the place where we left the canoe."

"That's right." Rosita looked perplexed. "We must mark a trail."

"I'll chop some twigs from the undergrowth we walked through. We can stick them in the ground to mark where we have gone." I handed Rosita the clothes and set to work.

When I had an armload chopped, she gave all the wet clothes to me and said, "You carry these. I'll mark the trail."

"But carrying clothes is woman's work. Marking the trail is man's work."

"Then it's a good thing we're only children." She headed into the forest and I followed, not at all happy about carrying the laundry. She stopped and tried to poke one of the twigs into the ground, but it was too rocky. The twig fell when she released it.

"I'll do it," I offered.

"No. You got to chop while I held the clothes. I'll do it." She wedged the twig between two roots running along the ground. We continued for what seemed forever with her wedging twigs to mark the way back until we could see sunlight ahead. "The savannah," she said. We walked into the sun where trees grew farther apart and shorter. "Guava," she pointed. "And there, a cashew. We must remember these two trees as the place where we left the tall trees." Savannah grass grew sparse and low among the trees, but ahead in the brilliance of the sun stood a sea of it, bending to the wind and changing shades where breezes shifted. "We'll hang the clothes on these bushes." Rosita took some of the garments from me.

When our laundry was strung out to dry, I stepped back to admire our work. "Woman's work isn't so bad," I said.

"Try doing it all day long. Try being a girl who cannot go play by the river or explore the savannah except when your father has gone to other villages to work." Rosita turned to me with fury in her eyes. "I'll never marry a man who will do no women's work and who insists that our daughters be slaves to the house." She spun around and walked toward some bushes with brown berries on them.

I caught up with her. "El Loco said I should marry you as soon as we're grown."

She looked at me in surprise. "Why would El Loco say that?"

"He said it was because a man needs a woman with fire, and that you have plenty of fire. I think perhaps he's right."

"No. He's wrong. I will not marry you."

"No, no. I meant he's right that you have plenty of fire."

"Then you don't want to marry me?" she blazed.

"I want to be your friend."

Her face softened. "Yes. We'll be friends. What did you tell Carmen? That we are best friends? That's better than being married and not being friends at all, just husband and wife." She looked at the bushes with brown berries. "We must change the color of your hair."

"Why?"

"Because out here in the wild part of Venezuela, everyone thinks you are El Don, and it's because of your golden hair. We'll make it brown with those berries. Help me pick them."

"And put them in what? Our pockets?" I pretended to put my hand in a pocket on my nude hip.

"Give me the machete. I'll make a pocket while you pick berries. Put them there, on the ground." She pointed.

While I gathered berries, she chopped some grass, sat down and began to weave the long blades. In only minutes she had an elegant basket. "It isn't very strong, but it'll hold until we get back to the river." She handed me the basket and I filled it with berries. "Could you have made such a little pocket?"

"It never occurred to me that anyone could make a basket like that."

"All women in our village can do that, even the tiniest of girls. But men can't do anything but hack up wood and chop bananas with their machetes."

"I wish I had one of those bananas," I said. "Can we eat these berries?"

"No. They might give us cramps. It's our bad luck that mangoes are not in season and there are no fruit on the cashew tree. Perhaps we can find more banana trees?"

We put the basket beside our laundry and went toward a green stand of brush that Rosita said might have something in it we could eat. I kept glancing over my shoulder to make sure I could see our laundry, figuring if I kept it in sight, we wouldn't get lost from the trail of twigs that would take us back to the canoe.

When we got near the brush, we saw the banana trees, but no sign of anything yellow. One tree had a stalk of gigantic green bananas. "Topochos," Rosita said. "We can't eat them unless we find a way to cook them. But look. Papayas. One of them is ripe."

The papaya looked like a miniature palm tree but greener. It held its fruit high in a clump just below the broad leaves. I made a step for Rosita by interlocking my fingers, and she kicked off her apagato and put her foot in my hands. That way she was able to brace against the tree, step up on my shoulder, and reach the ripe papaya. When she got down, she clutched the papaya to her breast and hopped around putting her apagato back on. The fruit was a creamy yellow and shaped like a gigantic pear. "It's warm from the sun," she said, "like your shoulder. We need to get clothes on you or you'll soon sunburn."

"Let's eat the papaya first."

"No. Haven't you ever prepared a papaya?" She spoke in surprise, and I felt embarrassed to admit that I'd never had much to do with papaya except to eat the ones my mother prepared. "Then I'll show you what must be done with these wild papayas." Rosita took the machete and scored the papaya from stem to bottom in at least a dozen places around the fruit. White liquid started oozing from the cuts. She held the papaya by the stem, watching the white stuff gather and drip. "You must bleed the rubber milk from a papaya or it will be too bitter to eat," she said. "Cut two of those topochos. Maybe we can figure out a way to cook them. Have you ever eaten a topocho?"

"No."

"They taste something like a potato but sweeter and slimy. Raw they're hard and not at all good to eat."

I cut the topochos as instructed. They looked like ordinary green bananas except that they were almost as long as my arm. I clasped them to me, liking the warmth of them, and we walked back to the bushes where we hung our laundry. Rosita set the bleeding papaya on some grass and felt the clothes. "They're dry," she announced. "We can get dressed now."

"I don't want to get dressed."

Rosita looked at me in surprise. "Why not? You're sunburning."

"I don't know. It's more fun this way, riding with you in the canoe, then walking through the jungle with nothing on. Do you want to get dressed?"

She plucked her blouse from a bush, shook it, and looked at me. "Maybe not. There is a wild kind of freedom in being nude. But we should wear clothes."

"Should? Should? Says who?"

"Grownups. I wouldn't want a man to see me like this."

"I'm a man."

"Yes. I mean another man. A grown one."

"There aren't any around."

"There might be. One might appear at any moment, and I would feel, I would feel . . ."

"Feel what?"

"I don't know. Vulnerable. Wouldn't you feel vulnerable if Carmen and Mamacita Moreno walked up to us right now?"

"That won't happen."

"But if it did. What would you do? Tell the truth."

I considered it, imagining those two women coming out of the canopy of gigantic trees and spying us. They would rush over to us and Mamacita would make clucking noises with her tongue and tell me what a naughty boy I was for being naked in front of Rosita. Carmen would bulge her eye at me and shake her head and snap at me to get dressed. "I wouldn't like it if those two women found us here, naked," I admitted.

"Nor would I. Maybe it isn't just that I don't want men seeing me or that you don't want women seeing you. Maybe we don't want any grownups seeing us without clothes."

"I hate clothes, though. Except for shoes. Shoes are a good idea. Why don't we stay naked until we come to a village, and then get dressed?"

"We would both burn in the sun. You worse than I."

"Then we should at least not dress until we get back to the canoe. We'll be in the shade all the way through the forest."

Rosita tilted her head and seemed to be judging me in some way. "When we slept in the canoe with nothing on, you didn't try to

62

touch me in the wrong ways. So far this morning you haven't stared at me too much or made me feel in any way wrong for being nude. And it does feel free and fun to be without clothes. I liked it when I climbed in your hands and on your shoulders to get the papaya. I looked down at you and thought your blond hair and fair skin were as beautiful as the golden papaya. More beautiful, even. We'll carry our clothes back, though we must get dressed before getting into the canoe. Do you suppose Evita ever walked through a jungle nude?"

"Who?"

"Eva Perón. The saint who died. Do you suppose saints ever walked nude in jungles?"

"I don't know anything about saints. And why should we get dressed to get into the canoe? I liked feeling like a wild man from Borneo when we paddled the canoe together, nude."

Rosita looked at me in exasperation. "Because of the sun. Because we will burn without clothes." She spoke as to a small child. "And because we'll surely soon see some people, and they will not understand why we're naked."

It was easier to carry dry clothes than wet ones, for we draped them over one shoulder. And it was easy to follow our trail of twigs back through the forest with me carrying the basket of brown berries and two topochos and Rosita carrying the machete and the dripping papaya, holding it by its stem. We pushed through the barrier of underbrush near the river, walked past the golden bananas, and stopped on the rocks above the sandbar where the canoe was beached.

"First," Rosita said, "we have breakfast. Then we dye your hair brown."

"I always wanted brown hair."

"Why? I would love to have hair of gold like yours."

"No." I put down the basket and placed my clothes in a neat pile on a rock. "Your hair is one of the first things I noticed about you. It's exactly right for you, falling on your shoulders in black curls."

"That pleases me."

"You should never want blond hair. It wouldn't be right for you because your black hair matches your eyes. Besides, too many people like to come up to me and touch my hair. Most people in Venezuela have never seen someone with white hair like mine. It makes me mad to have strange people touching my head and making a fuss about my hair. They would do that to you, too, and I doubt you would put up with it for long."

"Your eyes and your hair don't match. They might if you had blue hair." She watched me cut the papaya into two pieces with the machete, then she raked the seeds out with her fingers. We sat on the rocks and looked at the river while we ate, scooping up chunks of the orange fruit with our fingers. It was warm and sweet, and the juice of it ran down my arms. "I don't ever want to leave here," I said.

Rosita nodded. "We're having a good adventure, you and I. But we must go home."

"I think we crossed to the wrong side of the river. Will we paddle across, then try to find a road back to El Tigrito?"

"There are no roads here. We'll follow the river until we come to a village large enough to have roads that connect it to places such as our village. Then we walk back."

"Riding the river is better."

"Yes, we're lucky that it runs east. We can ride the river for a while, and it'll be fun." She stood and cast the skin of her half of the papaya into the water. Some fish splashed around it. "Now we bathe and dye your hair. We don't want more people trying to get you to become El Don and me to become your servant."

We took a splash-bath in the shallow water beside the canoe, washing away the sugary fruit and having a fine time knocking water on each other. Rosita said she wished for soap, especially for her hair, which she scrubbed with her fingers, bending over in knee-deep water so the hair fell in glistening black curls before her.

Then she dyed my hair. She found an indention in one of the rocks where she used a stone to pound the berries into brown mush. She instructed me to carry water in cupped hands to the berry mush, which she stirred with a stick. Then she told me to lie on the rock with my head on the edge of the indention that held the dye. She soaked my hair with berry juice and told me not to move until the dye soaked into each hair. While I waited, lying on the rock, she returned to the water to wash her hands. It took her a long time to be satisfied with her hands. She dug handfuls of mud from the river to scrub them with, then spent much time rubbing them with leaves. Finally she told me to go rinse my hair. "You will be a new person," she said.

The water where I dipped my head turned first brown then blue. I did as thorough a job as I could, then Rosita came to me with leaves and mud and rubbed my neck and forehead. "Some of the dye tried to stick to your skin," she explained. "But I think I got it all off. Now rinse your hair again and let me look."

I did as she said, again turning the water a strange blue, and I kept rinsing until the water remained clear when it ran from my hair. "So how do I look?" I asked.

Rosita chewed her lip. "I hope you won't be angry with me. I can make you a gorrito from grass, and perhaps we can get a cap for you in the first village we come to."

"Is something wrong?" I tried to see my reflection in the water, but the surface wasn't still enough for that.

"Somehow I made a mistake," Rosita said. "Your hair isn't brown. It's bright purple."

6
Human Skulls

We angled across the river so we could watch for a village on the left bank. I figured it wouldn't be long before we found people living beside the river. But we drifted for hours with only an occasional dipping of paddles into the water to keep the canoe straight with the current, and we saw no sign of anyone. The edge of the river was alive with birds and, in places, monkeys, and flocks of parrots flew overhead. We scooped water from the river with our hands when we needed a drink. It was much more fun than drinking out of a rain barrel, and the water tasted as good as what we had dipped from the candy maker's Gott can. Every time the water around us seemed calmer than usual, I leaned over the side to try seeing a reflection of my purple hair, but not much came of it. I would get a wavy glimpse of color now and then, and not much else.

"We must go ashore soon," Rosita said when the sun stood almost directly overhead. "Maybe we can find a clear place to build a fire so we can cook the topochos."

"What will we cook them in?"

"I don't know. Maybe we can roast them. Also, I can gather the grass to make a gorrito for you."

"I don't want a cap. We've got on too much clothes as it is."

"People will see your purple hair. I'm not sure what they'll do."

"I told you. I like purple hair. I don't care what people do."

"They could think you are a brujo come to cast evil spells on them. They could drive you away or try to kill you."

"For having purple hair?"

"I don't know. Maybe." Her voice became thin and she blinked back tears. "And I'm the one who caused you to have purple hair."

"Then we won't go ashore. Ever."

She gave her head a shake and cleared her throat. Something about her seemed to change. "That's silly. We need people, especially ones who can show us the road to take to get to El Tigrito." She spoke with assurance and without a trace of the tears she almost shed. "For now, we need to find food or else try to figure out how to

67

roast the topochos. Look, some animal is floating in the water." She turned her paddle and steered us toward what at first glance looked like a tree trunk.

"It's huge. A horse, maybe?"

"Caimán," Rosita said.

I worked my paddle to get us closer to the creature. "It's longer than our canoe," I said in amazement.

"Yes. Don't get close to it. That is a black caimán. The most dangerous animal in all of Venezuela. My father said the black caimán likes to attack canoes, that it can snatch a person right out of a boat or even bite the boat in half."

"That one is dead—look. It floats belly up." I took us closer. Part of it had been eaten by fish, and it smelled bad. Not terrible like something dead for days, but bad enough.

"There might be others." Rosita looked around. "They like to stay in swampy inlets, my father told me, where they lay their eggs and eat fish. I don't think we should try to go ashore here."

"From the looks of it, that caimán has been floating for several hours. I would say that whatever killed it did so way back up the river. Maybe close to where we bathed this morning."

"Don't say that." She turned the canoe away from the dead animal.

We began watching the shore for two things—signs of a village and signs of black caimanes. "They like to stick their noses out of water when they swim," Rosita said. "And their eyes."

"Like the baba in El Tigre river?"

"Yes. Exactly like the baba, but the nose of that black caimán is bigger than the entire body of a baba.

We were so intent on watching the surface of the water for the nose of a caimán and for an inlet where a caimán might go to eat fish and lay eggs that we didn't see the hills until we were nearly upon them. As we rounded a bend in the river, the hills seemed to pop up like blisters from the jungle. "They're mostly bare rocks," I said.

"Yes." Her voice had a note of excitement in it that I found contagious. "If we can find a way to put ashore among those hills, I want to climb one of them. We could see for many kilometers from up there."

"What about the caimanes?"

"We watch for those, of course. Look, some rocks jut out into the river. We must be careful."

As we passed the rocks, the current spun us around and pushed us into a pool of crystal clear water similar to the one where we had bathed earlier. The edge of this pool was lined with a tiny beach and gray rocks. "It doesn't look very swampy," I said.

"No. I doubt a black caimán would want to live out in the open like this. Look, perhaps we can climb that rock? And there—a place to pull the canoe ashore. I'll do it this time."

Before I could object, she hopped out of the canoe into the shallow water, holding up her skirt in one hand and guiding the boat toward a strip of sand with the other. I saw a small fish dart from the rocks on our left, knock against Rosita's ankle, and vanish back into the shadows of the rocks. Rosita yelped and ran out of the water. "Something bit me." She stood on one foot and held the other in her hand. A trickle of blood appeared on her ankle.

"It was a fish no bigger than my hand," I said. "I saw it."

"Carribe," she said, hopping around, inspecting her ankle.

"What is carribe?"

"The cannibal fish."

"Do you mean a piranha nibbled on you?"

"Yes. The same fish. In Venezuela we call them carribe. I think it bit a mole off of my foot. It's nothing." She walked back into the edge of the water, took the bow of the canoe, and pulled it onto the sand.

I picked up the machete and stepped out of the canoe onto the shore. "You're still bleeding. Why did you go back into the water? Weren't you afraid the blood would attract more cannibal fish and that they would eat away your foot to the bones?"

"No. If there's enough cannibal fish to do that, they would have attack me when I was first in the water. We would have seen them as the canoe drifted into the calm spot. My grandmother told me that seldom are carribe plentiful enough to be a danger. They live in the river beside our village, but not in great numbers and only occasionally does one bite a person. Come. Let's see if we can find a way to climb one of these hills. Perhaps over there?" She pointed.

"And the topochos?"

"Leave them for now. But take the machete and hand me my alpargatas."

She slipped on her sandals then searched through the vegetation growing among the rocks, selected a leaf, and dabbed at her ankle until the blood stopped flowing. She crumpled up some other leaves, mashing them into a green pulp, and attached them to her ankle under a single broad leaf that she tied in place with a stringy-looking vine.

Small trees and bushes grew in fissures in the rocks, along with an abundance of finger-thin vines. We climbed over a ridge and found a rock bowl of soil in the hill about fifty meters across where many broad-leafed plants grew, and a few small trees. Tiny birds fluttered among them, emitting squeaks and chirps, and a flock of parakeets took flight as we approached, their wings clapping and some of them squawking their anger at our presence. "Breadfruit," Rosita said with excitement. She took the machete from me and cut a large, olive-colored fruit from the a tree. "This will be food enough for us until we find a village on down the river. But first we must build a fire to roast the breadfruit."

"I'm hot," I said. "I don't want a fire."

"Yes you do, if you want to eat. Let's build a small fire, roast the breadfruit, then find some shade for our picnic." She sat crossy-legged, put a split piece of dried wood in front of her with some dried leaves crumbled up on it and picked up a piece of wood that might pass for a snare-drummer's drumstick. She put the end of the drumstick among the crumbled up leaves, held the stick between her palms, her fingers outstretched, and pushed her hands back and forth, twirling the stick and pushing down on it. Every few seconds her hands worked down close to the leaves and she reset them at the top of the stick to twirl downward again. It didn't take long for a wisp of smoke to curl out of the dead leaves. She spun the stick several more times, then leaned forward and blew on the smoking leaves. Tiny flame leaped out of them, and she dropped more leaves into the flame. "Put some dry sticks here." She pointed.

The swift way she made fire amazed me almost as much as her setting the breadfruit in the fire. When she pronounced it ready, I rolled it from the coals with a stick, and she sliced it open with the machete.

After the breadfruit cooled enough for us to eat, we sat in the shade of the breadfruit tree. "Boiled would be better," Rosita said, "but this is good. Tastes like bread."

It didn't taste at all like bread, but I didn't argue. It was more like a partly-cooked potato. When I had eaten all I wanted—maybe all I ever wanted of breadfruit—I stood and took my shirt off.

"I always wanted to do that in the heat of the day," she said. "At home it wasn't possible to strip down in the heat. My cousins could, but they are males."

"So take off your blouse. There's no adults around here."

"True." She pulled off her blouse. "Do you know what I like most about being in the wild part of Venezuela?"

"Jungle spiders and cannibal fish?"

"Freedom." She ignored my attempt to be funny. "Freedom to eat when I want, go where I want, do what I want. It's better than having my father go to work at a remote village. Even my mother made too many rules to suit me, though those rules were more sensible than the ones my father insisted upon. Here we make our own rules. I like that."

I tied my shirt around my waist. Rosita watched, then tied her blouse in the same way. "We'll sunburn," she warned.

"Maybe. I just made a new rule: it's all right to risk sunburn by going without a shirt if we're going to get too hot from climbing that hill."

"We'll try that rule. And if we burn, I'll make a poultice from papaya bark to sooth the pain. But first, we'll wrap what's left of the breadfruit in leaves and carry it back to the canoe."

As we left the canoe, she picked up the machete.

"If you're going to carry the jungle knife, then you need to cut me a stick so I can use it for poking around in the brush and to lean on when I climb."

"Jungle knife?" Dimples appeared on her cheeks. "Why not? Jungle knife. I like that." She hacked a straight limb from a plant growing beside some elephant ears, stripped the leaves from the limb and lopped the end. "Will this do?"

"That's perfect." I hefted the stick, liking the feel of it, liking that it was a bit longer than I was tall. "Sharpen the thick end?"

She knelt and chopped the end to a point as symmetrical as the end of a top while I turned the stick. Then she stood and pointed with the jungle knife. "That direction. I think I see a way to climb the taller hill of rock." There seemed to be an ancient trail carved into the side of the hill, but I decided it was just an accident from whatever forces formed the hill.

Or I thought that until we found the cave. The trail split, part of it going up and over the entrance to the cave, the other, clearly a foot path at that point, leading into the dark opening in the rock. Vines hung over it, making it difficult to see until we were almost upon it, and small birds jumped here and there among the leaves of the vines. "People made this trail," Rosita said.

"Yes. But look around. There's no sign of people now. The trail is a thousand years old. Two thousand."

"Maybe. I want to go into that cave."

"What if some animal lives in it?" I asked.

"Like what?"

"I don't know. Some jungle beast. A tiger, maybe."

"It would scare the birds," she pointed out. "Do you not want to go into the cave?"

"I wouldn't consider not going. But I'll worry about a jungle tiger."

Rosita chopped some vines from the cave entrance and I pulled them to a drop-off on the river side of the cave mouth to throw them into the jungle below. She ducked and entered. "It's not a cave," she said, her voice seeming to echo. "It stops just three meters into the hill."

I joined her, straining to see in the dim light. Beyond the entrance we were able to stand upright. Inside it was cool and damp. "I like it in here," I said. "It's much better than being out in the hot jungle." The ceiling was far above us, too far to see at first. The entrance seemed like a yellow furnace, and I turned from it so my eyes could adjust.

"The walls," Rosita said. "They're black with soot. People have cooked in here, but that was a long time ago." She felt along the back wall. "This isn't all to the cave. There's more behind this rock. I can feel a cool breeze coming from the left."

I felt along the floor with my stick, then along the back wall when the floor ran into another wall. About waist high the stick slipped into empty space. "Here," I said. "The cave goes deeper right here." We stood at the opening and tried to see into the cave, but it was too dark. A putrid odor came from the cave. "You stink," I said to the darkness. It sounded as if I were talking into an empty rain barrel.

"I want to go in there," Rosita said. "Will you come?"

"It smells bad in there."

"Bad, yes. But not terrible."

"You want to go into the dark?"

"We'll make torches. Will you go with me?" She sounded excited, and I could feel tension in her body as we leaned together, looking into the stinking cave.

"Yes. What makes the bad smell?"

"I don't know. Many things can smell bad. Stagnant water. Rotting plants. We'll find out, maybe. Let's get started on the torches." She took my hand and pulled me back toward the yellow furnace where we entered.

The area around the entrance to the cave had nothing suitable for a torch, so we descended to the bowl of greenery where Rosita had found the breadfruit tree. She prodded her way through assorted bushes and small trees until she found a branch that forked several ways in one place. "This is what we want to hold the light," she told me. "Cut this piece and find as many more as you can like it. I'll go to the edge of the rocks and start another fire, this one for the torches." She handed me the machete.

"It amazes me that you can make a fire without matches."

"Did you not know how to make a fire from dried bark and sticks?" She seemed surprised.

"I was never good at that."

My brother Todd and I once tried to start a fire by rubbing sticks together, but we didn't get far. The sticks got warm, but not warm enough to catch on fire. We worked at it for the better part of an hour, taking turns rubbing the sticks, then gave up. Todd said there was some trick to it that we didn't know.

I wandered off, hacking around in the brush and keeping an eye out for jungle spiders. By the time I returned with four more branches much like the one Rosita had found, she had a small fire going. She knelt and blew on the flame while dropping dry leaves and twigs onto it. I set the torch sticks beside the fire. "Those are wonderful ones," she said. "Much better than the one I found. Now we need dried palm fronds or stringy bark."

"There's not any palms or palmettoes here," I said.

"Then I'll find something else. You tend the fire while I go find something. Don't let it go out. Did you see any snakes?"

"You didn't warn me to look out for snakes. I did watch for jungle spiders, though. There aren't any here."

"Always watch for snakes. Most are harmless, but some can hurt you. I'm especially afraid of rattlesnakes." She went into the bushes, prodding them with the machete.

I picked up my sharpened walking stick in case a snake came by. Then I saw one crawling up the side of the rock hill about ten meters away, a big one. If I killed such a snake, Rosita would be amazed, I thought. She would show me how to skin it and we would roast it for a meal. Then we would make something neat out of its skin. A belt maybe, or some headbands. We would look like wonderful savages with snake skin headbands.

"But could I kill it?" I asked aloud. Hadn't I told Rosita that I would rather starve than kill an iguana? Hadn't I told Dad and Uncle Ray that I wouldn't hunt quail again after seeing how they flopped around when Dad shot them?

A snake is different, I argued, still wanting the savage head bands. A bird or an iguana will leave you alone, but a snake will try to kill you. Especially a rattlesnake. I began stalking the snake, though it seemed unnecessary since it hadn't moved much since I spotted it. When I got close enough to have a chance to hit it with my walking stick spear, I looked for its head. Getting it in the tail would only make it mad, and maybe it would come after me. Its head seemed to be tucked among some brush growing out of a crack in the rock. The snake writhed about on the rock a bit, and I sneaked closer, spear ready.

Then the snake solidified into a vine. Had I seen it writhing? It seemed so when the vine was a snake. Disappointment swept over me until I figured that I could use the vine as target practice. That way when a real snake came along, I would be ready. I threw my spear at the vine's head, just below where it ran into the bush.

74

The spear missed by a hand's breadth. I retrieved it and tried again, and again I missed.

It took about thirty throws before the spear hit the vine. Just as I was reveling in the flush of success, Rosita called me. I went after my spear without looking around, not wanting the savage girl to ruin the hunt. When I turned, she stood, hands on her hips, and she was not happy about something.

"The fire," I mumbled. "Crap." I pretended to look around. "There was a snake," I called out. "I nearly got it with the spear you made for me." I sauntered back, cocky, the spear on my shoulder like a wild man on a hunt.

"You let the fire go out," she accused.

"I saw a big snake."

"I'll make another fire."

"That's amazing," I said.

"It doesn't take long, and usually I don't mind making a fire this way. But my hands are sore from pushing El Loco's wheelbarrow and from the canoe paddle."

"The blisters that popped. I forgot. I'm sorry, Rosita."

"You have them, too. Come, put more twigs and bark on the fire. Be careful not to smother it. We need to get that branch burning so we can carry it up the hill to the cave and use it to light the torches. You work on the fire and I'll prepare the torches."

I did as she said, though it sounded like more fun to get the torches ready. Trouble was, I didn't know how to make a torch. As the fire blazed up, I watched her tie woody-looking things into the forks of the torch sticks. She used some sort of green fiber as the string. When she finished the five torches and I had the branch going as she instructed, we climbed the hill toward the cave, I carrying the fire and the torches, she carrying the machete and my walking stick.

When we reached the cave, Rosita cleared a spot on the rocky entrance, removing all leaves and vines she had chopped from the mouth of the cave. "For the fire," she said. "Put the burning stick here. We'll build a larger fire so if our torch goes out we can come outside and light another."

"Why didn't you just make the fire up here?" I asked.

"We could have. But I thought it a better use of time if we both worked, and making the torches is a one-person job." She lit a torch. "Get the others. It would be better to light only one until we see how long we'll be inside the cave."

"But I want to carry a torch."

"Here." She handed the lighted one to me. Flame crackled in it, and it gave off much heat. I liked carrying it into the cave, liked holding it up to the wall, then into the darkness of the smaller cave.

Even with the torch, all we saw was a tunnel about a meter around that led into darkness. "Do you want to go in first, or shall I?" Rosita asked.

"I'll go. Hold the torch while I climb into this small cave. Can you get into it?"

"Yes. Go ahead."

I got into the tunnel, took the torch, and crab-walked forward with Rosita right behind me. The putrid odor seemed to get worse. Not far in we found the bats. Rosita and I both yelped when the first one fluttered by us. The bats seemed to hate the heat and light, and started flying in and out of the small tunnel, coming so close that I could have snatched one out of the air with no difficulty, if I took a notion to do so. I was watching out for the bats when I fell nearly a meter into a larger room, dropping the torch. It felt as if I had fallen on a wet mat, and I rolled around in something cool and slick. The torch hissed and the flame went out. I managed to get to my feet, but it was hard to stay balanced standing in the dark on a wet floor.

"Are you all right?" Rosita sounded alarmed.

"Yes. Be careful—" Before I could finish the warning, she shrieked and tumbled into the bigger part of the cave, slid across the wet floor, and knocked me down again. "Did you get hurt?" I asked.

"No. What's this wet stuff on the ground?"

"I don't know, but it stinks." We held on to each other and tried to stand but managed only to slip around in the wet.

"Look," Rosita said. "I can see the embers of the torch. Maybe we can get it going again." She began to scoot toward the faint glow about a meter from us. I crawled with her. She felt around the embers until she found the handle of the torch, picked it up and blew on the glow until flame leaped out again. "Nasty," she said and looked at the floor.

I looked down as she began scrambling to stand up. The floor was covered with black ooze, and scurrying around in the ooze were thousands of tiny creatures. Some were roaches, sick-looking whitish ones, and others were wormy with more legs than any crawly thing should have. "Ai-yi-yi," Rosita said.

"Did one sting you?" I forced myself to my feet, brushing myself as I did so.

"No. There are worse things in here than bugs. Look." She held the torch high and I looked where she pointed. On a shelf that appeared to be carved into the side of the cave were hundreds of bones. The shelf nearest to us held human skulls. They grinned at us, and in the flickering torchlight their empty sockets appeared to have eyes in them.

"Let's get out of here," I said in a shaky voice. Rosita and I reached out for each other and somehow slipped. We both fell, knocking ourselves against the cave wall. Rosita managed to hold the torch so it didn't go out. We scrambled to our feet, using the wall to brace us, and I felt the edge of the tunnel that led to the outer cave. I put my hands on the ledge and heaved myself onto it. Rosita thrust the torch into my hands and joined me. It took only seconds for us to get through to the outer cave and less time than that to dart out into the white tropic sun.

We stood blinking at one another. "You look like a tar baby," I said.

"Thanks. You look like a mud pie."

I looked at myself, found some roaches crawling around in the black stuff on my tummy, and flicked them off with a fingernail. "What made this nasty mud, anyway?"

"Don't you know?" She busied herself thumping tiny cave creatures from her arms.

"No."

"Bat droppings."

"No."

"Yes. Bats were all over the ceiling. I glanced up just before we climbed out of there, and I saw them, thousands of them—moving about on the ceiling. Some of them were watching us. I could see their eyes."

"I'm covered with bat poop? I need a bath."

"I thought you said you didn't like to spend so much time bathing."

"I never said that. I love to bathe."

Rosita eyed me in a disbelieving way and began scattering the fire to put it out. I picked up my spear and started down the hill. She joined me, carrying the machete. "I hate that place," I said.

"Yes," Rosita said. "So did I. But there's something you ought to know. I'm going back in there."

I stopped walking and stared at her, amazed but not doubting for a moment that she meant it.

7
A Cloud of Bats

"You're a bit funny to look at." Rosita laughed.

"Because I'm covered with poop?"

"Yes. Your skin looks white as the sun compared with the bat droppings you're wearing, and your purple hair makes you look like the strangest wild man ever."

I tried to figure out how I felt about her description and her grinning way of looking at me. "Let's go bathe," I said, deciding that she wasn't making fun of me and deciding I liked being called a wild man. As we climbed down the hill, I took some of the black from my pants and drew lines on my forehead and cheeks, then hefted the spear to be ready for an enemy attack. Rosita looked back at me and nodded, and I could tell she liked how I looked even if she might not like what I used for war paint.

While we bathed, I kept an eye out for carribe and caimán, though Rosita said it was unlikely either would be interested in a meal covered in bat crap. We tried bathing without undressing in order to wash our clothes but gave that up fast and stripped, bathed, then did as good a job as we could washing the black stuff out of our clothes. Rosita wasn't happy with the results, but we got the clothes clean enough to suit me.

"We must tie the canoe to a tree or a rock," Rosita said.

"Why? You pulled it up on the sand. It can't float away."

"Not now. But the rains have begun, and when that happens, sometimes rivers have much more water. This river could come up fast and snatch away the canoe if a big rain fell even many kilometers upriver." She took the rope from the canoe and tied it to root of a tree that looped out of the ground among the rocks.

We carried our wet laundry back to the rock basin where the breadfruit tree grew. Rosita wore only alpargatas and I had on only my tennis shoes. "When are we going back into the cave?" I asked.

"You don't have to go." She began spreading her clothes on a rock in the sun.

I did the same with mine. "If you're going, I'm going. So when do we go?"

79

"I don't know. When the sun dries our clothes. I don't want to go in there nude because if I fall, I want some protection from the bat droppings and the little animals that eat it."

"They eat that poop?" The idea astounded me.

"Of course. Why else would they be in there?"

"Bugs that eat poop." I marveled at the idea. "Then they poop out some of it, and maybe there are smaller bugs with legs that eat the bug poop, and of course the smaller ones then crap out some of what they eat so that some really disgusting teensy little things can eat—"

"Don, you think of such odd things."

"I think of odd things? What about you? You planned to go back into there even before we washed the bat poop off of us."

"I'm not going back for the bat droppings."

"That cave is spooky and nasty. Why go in there at all?"

"Come. Let's go sit there out of the sun." She led me to some rocks in the shade of the hill. I thought her hair, slicked with water against her head and back, looked like a solid piece of shimmery velvet. She began twisting her velvet hair, wringing drops of water from it onto the rock beside her. "How long ago was it that we climbed into the back of the candy maker's truck?"

The question startled me. I hadn't been thinking about time, and somehow it seemed as if Rosita and I had been together for weeks, months even. But that couldn't be true, I thought, counting the nights we spent together. "Two days," I said. "But it feels like more."

"Yes. Many more. And why did we climb into that truck?"

"To come here." Even as I said it, I knew how stupid it sounded, so I was quick to add: "But we didn't know. We thought he would take us to El Tigre so we could see the bones . . ." I fell silent.

"Yes. Yes. The bones of Indios. We found them. It took longer than we planned, and we didn't exactly find them in a shop with a shrunken head, but we found them. I think those bones are very old. Hundreds of years. Maybe thousands."

"Why do you think that?"

"Because of the jungle. No one has been here for a long time or we would find evidence of their eating from the breadfruit tree and making trails and building fires for cooking. Also, there is the floor of the cave where the bats live."

"That nasty floor with all the nasty roaches and bugs. And the smell."

"But did you feel how the floor gave when we fell on it? It was like a thick layer of leaves on the jungle floor."

"Leaves?"

"Like leaves, a little. And the bones? They were on shelves carved by the Indios. The floor of bat droppings curved down by the wall of bones, and some of the bones were half buried. I think that floor is very thick with what the bats put there. I think they have been doing it for so long that many shelves of bones lie buried under it. And I think we are the first people to go into that cave for a long, long time. Do you know what that means?"

"No."

"It means the bones are old, maybe a thousand years old. Nobody would care if we took some of them because there are no relatives alive to worry about the bones. Probably there is no one else alive who even knows the bones are there."

I looked at the rock bowl of not-so-tall jungle plants that had chosen to live on the layer of dirt gathered in the basin, and I tried to think about a thousand years. Columbus lived when? I counted. Nearly five hundred years ago. Half a thousand. When Indios put those bones in that cave, my grandmother, who was older than anyone I knew, wasn't even a little girl yet. She would have to wait for Columbus, and then wait another five hundred years just to get born. And in a thousand more years, grandma would be dead. That idea made me feel sad. Her bones would be lying somewhere for a long time before a thousand years were through with them. Somebody might come and find them, someone like Rosita, and she might want to take some of them home to show to friends. Grandma's finger bones, maybe. I flexed my fingers and watched them move, glad to have bones in my hands, good bones. The idea that someone like Rosita might want grandma's finger bones cheered me up some.

"I'll make a basket." Rosita stood and surveyed the plants in the basin.

"Why?"

"For carrying things we find in the jungle. We could keep this machete in it, if you want."

"Things like bones?"

"When we find a village, the people will be angry or frightened if we come to them carrying human bones. Especially since you have purple hair. A basket would hide the bones. Also, I think I know what to do about your hair."

"I told you, I like my hair."

"You might not if you could see it. Before we bathed, the black from the cave covered the purple of your hair on one side."

"You want me to wear bat poop in my hair? Is that one of the reasons you want to go back into the cave—to get some of that nasty stuff to put in your basket? I suppose you want to carry around terrible-smelling bat poop full of bugs that are crawling around in there, eating each other's poop, until we see a village, then scoop some out and glob it on my head. I won't allow it."

"River mud is black, and it smells clean. We could dab some of it in your hair, then cover most of your head with a gorrito woven from grass."

"No mud. No bat poop hats, and no gorrito. Besides, I like the idea of scaring people with my purple hair. I could hide behind one of their grass huts and jump out and say yah, yah and make faces and shake my purple hair at them."

"No mud, then. Don't get so excited. How would you feel about spending the night here close to the breadfruit tree?"

"I thought you said it wasn't a good idea to spend the night in a strange jungle."

"It isn't. But we have hours to get to know this area. We can find a safe place to sleep. That would give me time to make a basket and for us to explore."

"We could climb to the top of that hill." I jumped up and brandished my spear. "We could make camp and I could guard it and fight off any jungle animals that tried to come eat us." I stabbed at a vine growing across a rock. "I could kill some snakes and chop them up and we could make headbands from their skins. You could dye the headbands purple to spook the villagers even better than I could with purple hair."

"That would be fun," Rosita admitted. "But perhaps not so

82

smart. So do you want to spend the night here?"

"Yes."

"Then we need to make a shelter. We should do that soon because it might rain again later this afternoon."

"First let's climb that hill. From up there we can look across the jungle to the savannah, and maybe see all the way to El Tigrito. Maybe all the way to the Caribbean Sea."

"We couldn't see that far."

I stabbed the vine a couple of more times. "I know that," I said.

"We'll climb the hill, then. But we need to stay in the shade as much as possible." She started up the trail that led to the bat poop cave, and I followed, spearing the heads of a few vine-snakes along the way.

When we came to the cave, we took the trail to the left that led us to an expanse of flat rock in front of what at first looked like another cave, but we soon found it was just a shallow indention in the rock about the size of my bedroom back in El Tigrito. The ceiling of the rock room was black—from soot, Rosita said. "But nobody has been here for years. That little cave would protect us from the rain, and I could sit right over there to make a basket. We could camp here, if you want."

I could tell by the tone of her voice that she wanted just that. From the rock ledge we had a good view of the river, including the place where we bathed and the place where the canoe was tied. We could see across the river and over the giant trees where the savannah stretched to the horizon.

The final climb wasn't easy. Perhaps it would have been impossible if someone hadn't chipped into the rock places for our hands and feet. When we made it to the top, we both were out of breath. Rosita's face was flushed with pleasure, and I felt as if I were standing above the entire world. I lifted my spear and did a little victory dance. Rosita clapped when I finished, and I felt like the best wild man ever standing nude above the caves of dead Indios with a naked savage girl to applaud my dance and a river below me cutting through a jungle. "I like the wild part of Venezuela," I told the savage girl, and she laughed in a way that felt good to hear.

We surveyed the jungle to the north. "There seems no end to

it," Rosita said, then, suddenly, she pointed and added, "There, you can see a strip of another river glimmering in the sun. I think the river joins ours, and the jungle around it makes it seem that there is no savannah. Do you know what that means?"

"That our river will become larger?"

"Yes. It means we will have to cross that other river and maybe some others. It means we'll go through more jungle. It means more adventure. I dreaded walking across nothing but boring savannah to get back to El Tigrito. Other rivers mean more adventure on the trip home."

When we got back down the hill, I was delighted to find our clothes too wet to wear, though Rosita worried that I might be getting a sunburn on my shoulders. She took the machete and went in search of reeds for her basket. My job was to find something to sleep on. "Big leaves to make a mat would be good," Rosita had told me. "Palmetto fronds would be all right, though banana leaves would be better because they would be softer. Find as many as you can for a cushion."

I took the Barlow out of the pocket of my wet jeans and went down the river from our canoe to a patch of palmettoes. But they were too tough to cut with the Barlow. A little farther on was a stand of leafy plants that looked as if they ought to be banana trees but were not. The Barlow sliced right through their stems, and I cut enough of the almost banana leaves to make what I figured would be the best sleeping mat in the entire wild part of Venezuela. I took them up the hill past the bat poop cave to our camp. The trip up was sweaty work, though I did enjoy the clean smell of the leaves. After smoothing off a spot in the rock room, I arranged the leaves into a mat and tried it out. It felt cool and smelled good but was a bit lumpy and hard, so I went back to the river to gather more. When I returned to camp, Rosita was there with a pile of reeds.

"Our clothes are nearly dry," she announced.

"I don't want them."

"You will in the night. And you ought to be wearing them now on account of the sun." She surveyed my work with the mat. "That looks good, better than I thought we would have. I wish I had some cotton string to make us a chinchorro."

I looked around. "There would be no place to hang it."

"I know. But it would be nice to sleep in a proper chinchorro instead of on the ground."

Rosita carried our clothes and more reeds. I brought a breadfruit and some dead wood for a campfire, though Rosita said it wasn't likely we needed a fire. "Cave men have fires," I told her. "They keep away wolves and bears." I raised my hands to stop her protest. "I know, I know. There are no wolves in the jungle and not many bears. But other big toothy animals might come to check us out."

Clouds came just before nightfall, bringing the sweet smell of tropic rain and a cool breeze. Rosita put on her clothes. "Stay naked, if you want." She pulled up her skirt. "The sun can't hurt you now." She stood, silhouetted against the last red streaks from the sun, and I lay on the mat of leaves.

Suddenly a thin, dark cloud popped up from the cliff below our camp, leaping into the sky and growing thicker as I watched. The cloud made a sound like wind in leaves, and Rosita spun around. "Bats," she said.

I stood beside her, and she clutched my arm in excitement. Their wingbeats became louder when the hill we stood upon emptied its bats into the evening sky. As they flew downriver like a fog of dense black smoke, a rain cloud came from upriver, pushing ahead of it the odor of rain and a cool wind. We stepped out of the rock room to watch the bats vanishing in one direction and the rain cloud coming from the other. The cloud dropped bolts of lightening as it came, and thunder rumbled through the jungle. "You'll want your clothes soon," Rosita said.

Within minutes it was dark, and the rain hit, spewing upon the river and the trees in a loud hiss. We retreated into our room, and I fumbled in the dark to put on my clothes because of the cold. My pants and shirt were stiff from drying on a rock, and they had a musty smell to them instead of the clean smell that freshly-laundered clothes have. Rosita and I bedded down on our mat of leaves, lying close for warmth.

The sound of rain and the cool of it and the fresh smell had always made for good sleeping. During the rainy seasons of the past, Todd and I liked to open our window enough to allow a fine mist of rain into the room. Todd said that the sound of the rain on

85

the roof made him want to hibernate like a bear. I thought of Todd lying in bed alone, no doubt worrying about how I was still missing. The rains might hit there in the night, also, and he would open the window for the mist. With my eyes closed, I could see him in our bedroom, settling down to hibernate like a bear. I imagined June in her bedroom, reading by the light of a kerosene lantern, looking up from time to time because she was thinking about my being out there in the rain. Mom and Dad would be worrying, too. But maybe tomorrow they would get my letter, and they could stop worrying because they would know I was on the way home.

"I'm glad I tied up our canoe," Rosita said.

The statement brought me back to the rock room, to the sound of the rain on leaves and on the rocks, to the spattering of water running from the hill above us and falling across the entrance of our rock room. Our canoe, she said. Ours. But, I wondered, is it our canoe? Whose was it when we found it tied up in the small river where Carmen had gathered the natives so she and I could send them to kill bandits? I doubted it was Carmen's. Wasn't she just a washerwoman for the men from Maracaibo? A stab of guilt hit me as I thought about telling the natives that I approved of whatever they did. Probably one of those men owned the shack by the small river, and he might have owned the canoe. Would he approve of whatever I did? Would he be disappointed that EL Don stole the boat and turned out to be not the son of the Old Don at all but just a common thief who sent some of his friends to die?

"We stole it from those men," I said.

Rosita turned toward me, rustling the leaves so they sounded as if the rain were falling inside our rock room. She brushed my face with her fingertips. "No. We took what we needed from men who would have given us anything we asked for because you are El Don."

"But of course you and I know I'm not El Don, that I'm just a fake one, especially now that my hair is purple. We know that nobody gave us permission to take the boat, so when we took it, we were like the bandits who take whatever they want."

"We are nothing like the bandits. Carmen said that the men believe you to be El Don, and she said that believing makes it true."

"I asked you about that last night, and you told me to ask you

86

later. Do you think that if you believe something, it becomes true?"

"Yes. I don't know. Perhaps." She turned over again and moved her back against me. "I'm cold."

I put my arm around her wondering how anyone could be cold where we were. The air brought by the rain felt cool to me, but my clothes were plenty to keep me warm. "I'm not El Don," I said, "but it's not because I don't believe it that I'm not. It's because I'm not, and that's that."

Rosita settled closer to me and patted my arm. "Do you believe in ghosts?"

"No." It was a quick easy answer, one I knew for the absolute truth. "I don't believe in invisible people of any kind."

"When we were in the cave today and we saw the skulls look at us in the torchlight, did you feel a shiver in your back and on your scalp?"

"Yes."

"I felt the same thing. I think perhaps you and I both believe in ghosts, and that the ghosts of those dead Indios knew it, so they came to watch us."

A clap of thunder close by made us both jump, and we clutched each other. The rain seemed to increase in its frenzy of pounding the rocks and the jungle. "You think there were ghosts in that cave, waiting for someone like us to enter so they could trip us and make us wallow around in the bat poop?"

"There were no ghosts in the cave until we saw the skulls. Then they came. We made them come into the cave with us, don't you see?"

"I don't see." I remembered the skulls grinning at us, and their grins weren't friendly ones. "If you think there are ghosts in that cave, why are you going into it again?"

"Are you afraid to go back?" she asked.

I replayed her question in my head, looking for signs in her intonation that she might be taunting me. She wasn't. "No." I heard the lie in my voice.

"I am. I think maybe you are, too, just a little. It's all right to be afraid of ghosts. They're scary things."

"Yes, then, maybe I am a little afraid. But I'll go back."

"So will I, and I'll be afraid. But not terrified. Those Indios

87

died so long ago that they don't care what happens to their bones. They'll know that I know that, and so my ghosts will merely be curious. They'll watch us walk through the bat droppings and select some of the bones to put into our basket, and they'll find that odd, maybe, but they'll do nothing to us."

"How do you know?"

"Because I believe they won't."

"And you think believing something makes it true."

"Maybe. Sometimes. Yes."

We fell silent, listening to the rain, and after a while I drifted off to sleep, lulled by the comfort of Rosita pressing against me, by the clean smell of jungle rain, and by the sound of the water. Perhaps it was the stopping of the rain that awakened me. More likely it was Rosita's crying.

She didn't make much sound. I heard the wheeze of her breath and felt her chest heave a few times. For a few moments I pretended still to be asleep, letting her finish crying. I did that sometimes—cry to myself at night—and it never lasted long. I always did it as quietly as possible so no one else in the house would know and ask me questions I didn't want to answer, especially while I was still crying. When she settled to normal breathing, I said:

"Why are you sad?"

She gripped my arm. "I thought you were asleep."

"I was. But your sadness woke me up." It was the right thing to say, I could tell, even though it made her whimper a few more times.

"I was thinking of my mother. She'll be so afraid for me because I've been gone for three nights now. She might think I'm dead or stolen by some bad men."

"Maybe my letter arrived today, and my parents have already told her that you and I are on our way home."

"Your letter will never make it to El Trigrito. There isn't any mail delivery out here on the high savannah and among the river jungles in the wild part of Venezuela."

"I think there is, now. Didn't you hear Mamacita Moreno say that she would give my letter to some men who came in trucks? I'll bet they already came and she gave them the letter and they have delivered it to my father and he has gone to your house to tell your mother not to worry."

"You're a good person, Don. But I think it unlikely Mamacita will give the letter to anyone, and even if she does, the men she gives it to won't know what to do with it."

"I believe it will get to them. Perhaps by believing it, it will become true."

She patted my arm again. "You are the best purple-headed wild man from Borneo ever to come to the jungles of Venezuela." She meant what she said, I could tell.

8
Stealing Bones

It had been some years since I was a dumb enough little kid to believe in invisible creatures like the tooth fairy and ghosts. Why, then, I wondered in that half-awake stage of early morning sleep, was I dreading going into the cave again? It wasn't the bat poop. I didn't like the stuff, but I had been dirtier with worse things. It was those grinning skulls that gave me such a fright and filled me with dread there on the mat of almost banana leaves while the morning noises of the jungle came to me.

I could identify several sounds: parrots flying over and talking to each other in their specialized parrot squawks, frogs down by the river speaking in foghorn notes, fish splashing here and there, the watery sound of the river. Other noises ran together in a blur of bird calls and insect buzzes. Another faint sound came to me—a rattling sound like wadding up paper but more rhythmic. I reached for Rosita but felt only the mat. "Rosita?" I sat up.

She was perched on a rock by the entrance of our cliff house, folding something upon itself. Behind her the intense green of tree tops across the river, the bright olive savannah beyond that, and the powerful blue sky threw so much light into my eyes that she looked almost like a shadow on a screen. "Good morning, Don." Her voice had a cheerful sound to it. "I saw the bats again."

"Bats?" I joined her, blinking against the brilliance of morning. She fashioned a handle on a basket that had been a pile of reeds when I went to sleep. The handle was a good one and long: you could slip it over your shoulder to carry the basket on your back, if you wanted. The top of the basket had a wonderful lid tied down with fiber of some sort.

"The bats came back just before the sun arrived. I was already at work on the basket when they returned. They came from three directions in great flocks that joined into one and seemed to spin down like a black dust devil into the cave below us. I thought about awakening you to see it, but you slept with such peace on your face that I did not. Do you like our basket?"

"That's the best basket I've ever seen."

91

"Hardly. But it is tight and secure, and the reeds are strong. It'll hold many bones. Not that I plan to take many. A few will be enough. We'll have a long way to carry them once we leave the river. And there is one other matter."

I walked to the edge of the cliff and looked down. The canoe was still there, but it looked different somehow. "What other matter?"

"A surprise. A rabbit came to nibble the grass at the edge of our house. I was sitting still, watching the bats when the rabbit arrived. It took little hops and kept stopping to wiggle its nose. When it got right there," she pointed almost at her feet, "I got it with a stone."

"You got it? You mean you hit it?"

"Yes. In the head. It fell without making a sound. We'll have rabbit for breakfast, if you want."

"You killed a rabbit?" The idea astounded me. I tried to imagine doing it: letting my hand drop in stealth to the ground to pick up a good chunking stone, all the while watching the rabbit come closer and closer, mistaking me for a rock or a tree; I imagined lifting my arm with the slow movement of a tree limb pushed by wind, then coming down with sudden violence to crush the bunny's skull while it munched on a blade of grass, innocent and cute. Could I do that?

"I want to take it to the river and clean it, then impale it on a stick and bring it back here to roast it over some of the dry firewood you carried in for us. Too bad we don't have any salt. I prefer meat with salt. But the rabbit will be good to eat without salt. What do you think?"

I told her I thought it was a fine idea, and it was, too, until I watched her take a machete to the rabbit.

She carried it by its ears down the hill to the river. I got ahead of her so I wouldn't have to see the rabbit dangling that way. We walked past some good snake-looking vines that I had enjoyed spearing the day before, but I didn't have the heart to gig any of them right then. When we got to the river, I saw why the canoe had seemed different from the edge of our cliff. The river had risen almost a meter, and the canoe floated above what had once been a sandy beach. The root Rosita had tied it to was now in the edge of the water. Some water had seeped into the canoe, though not enough to cover the topochos, the two giant bananas that we thought we might eat but had no need for after finding the breadfruit tree. Rosita didn't seem surprised by the way the river had risen, but I sure was. "It's a good thing," I told her, "that you tied up the canoe."

She nodded with her jaw set and her lips a grim, thin line, then she set about cleaning the rabbit. I got into the canoe and bailed out the bilge water, telling myself that I wouldn't watch what she did to the rabbit. But something made me watch as she spread the rabbit on a flat rock and used the machete to open it from its tail to its chest. She reached inside and pulled out a big glob of bleedy-looking innards and flung them into the river. They floated for a while with little fish popping the water around them until something really big snapped them up in a sudden splash. It happened so fast that I didn't see what did it. A big fish, maybe? I wondered. A baba? I got out of the canoe and started back to our camp when I got a glimpse of Rosita pulling the skin from the rabbit, her hands dripping red. Maybe, I told myself, I would never eat meat again.

When she walked into camp, she carried the machete in one hand and in the other the rabbit skewered on a stick. It looked pink and bald and not much like a rabbit, though the head and the way its legs resembled those of a running dog made it clear that this was once a living creature. Rosita glanced at me from time to time as she prepared the fire. When the skewered rabbit sat above the flames, each end of the stick resting on a rock, she came to sit beside me on the mat of broad leaves. "Some parts of food preparation that are less than pleasant," she said. "Have you never prepared an animal for cooking? A chicken, maybe?"

"Never. What you did to the rabbit looked so terrible."

"You must not think that way. If you think of the rabbit's death the way my grandmother explained such death to me, you might understand better. Grandmother said that the food animals we raise or find in the jungle and savannah give their lives not gladly but willingly that we might live. She said that we must say a prayer as we kill the animal, and that we must eat its flesh with gratitude."

"Do you believe your grandmother?" I asked.

"Yes. Anyone who eats meat must be content somehow with

killing an animal. Grandmother told me Evita Perón grew up a poor girl, just like I am, so it seems to me that she once killed chickens and ducks, perhaps even rabbits. And she was a saint. I said a prayer as my stone found the rabbit's head, and I butchered the rabbit with reverence."

"You prayed? To some invisible people, maybe?" I thought of how I used to pray to the likes of Santa Claus back when I was a dumb little kid.

"Not to invisible people. To the rabbit. To myself."

Until she said that, I was about to tell her how silly it was to pray to invisible creatures that didn't exist anywhere in the world. But her statement stopped me completely, and I tried to figure it out. As I did so, she went to the fire to turn the skewered animal, and the delicious smell of the cooking meat filled the air. At that moment, I decided maybe it wasn't such a smart idea to give up eating meat. "It smells good," I said.

"Yes. It's no longer a rabbit. It's food, and food is good, especially if it gets cooked properly, which I know how to do."

After breakfast of roasted meat and breadfruit, after we wrapped what remained of our food in some of the broad leaves from our mat and carried it to the canoe, we made preparations for going again into the bat poop cave. This time we each carried a lighted torch. "We won't need others," Rosita said, "because we'll get in there fast, select the bones we want, and get out."

"Will we hurry because of the ghosts? I don't believe in them, even if they scare me." I leaned the machete against a rock beside the cave entrance.

"We'll move fast because of being scared, yes. And I want to hurry because of the smell and the bats and what they might drop on us even if we manage not to fall in it this time." We entered the outer chamber with our torches flaming, the basket strapped to my back.

"I didn't think about them pooping while we're in there. On our heads. On our clothes. It'll be falling in there like black rain." I climbed into the tunnel that led to the bats and bones and got a whiff of the bat poop. "In there, the rainy season comes each day when the bats hang on the ceiling and get rid of what they ate during the night. What do you think they eat?"

Rosita climbed behind me and we crawled toward the larger cave. "In this part of Venezuela, some bats are vampires and drink the blood of cows and other animals. Some eat bugs," she said. "Others eat fruit. I don't know what these bats eat."

It took only a split second to decide about the kind of bats in our cave. "They eat only fruit," I said, certain that I would rather be bombarded with poop that once was fruit rather than cow blood or dead bugs. I held the torch into the larger room and saw the bones, some of them grinning at me, and a thrill of fear shot through me. A few bats whiffed past, fanning the stink into my face, but I didn't let them spook me into falling. I glanced at the grinning skulls as I lowered myself to the thousand-year mat of bat grunt where disgusting bugs ate each other's poop. The skulls watched in amusement, and one of them seemed to open its mouth to laugh. I gripped the rock wall and braced against the sound of mad laughter, but the only sounds were the creak of the basket on my back, the scraping noises Rosita made lowering herself beside me and the faint hiss of our torch flames. I glanced up at the writhing ceiling a few meters above us and saw the spooky glimmer of eyes. "They look like vampire bats to me," I said. My voice came out high and squeaky.

"You're worrying about bats when those dead heads are looking at us?" Rosita moved against me. "Hold my hand while we walk on the snot."

"Snot?" The novelty of the idea almost made me forget the vampires above me and the ghosts looking at us from their empty eye sockets. "Snot?"

"You be steady, now," she commanded, "and walk slowly. The bat droppings are already running over the soles of my alpargatas, and I think I can feel things crawling on my feet."

"Something just landed on my nose. Those bats are pooping vampire blood on us. Maybe we should leave?"

"These bats are not vampires. Forget I mentioned them." She urged me toward the wall where the bones were shelved.

"I think one of them just bit me on the back of the neck. Only vampires bite people on the neck."

"Don't whine so much," she said, her voice sounding high and whiny. "That was just some bat droppings. At least it doesn't have insects in it like the ones on my feet. Would you hurry?"

95

"I thought you told me to go slow so we wouldn't fall."

"I did. But go slow just a little faster. It's taking all my courage not to run out of here. If I try to run, stop me."

"Stop you?"

"Yes. So we won't fall down in the lake of bat droppings. Look. There's a hand bone. I want some fingers."

"Will the owner mind?" I wondered if my grandmother would mind a couple of kids stealing her bones if she ever died and got shelved in a cave.

"No. This Indio has been dead a thousand years. I told you that." Rosita moved close to the place where the floor slanted into the wall. "Hold on to me, now. Here. Take the torch."

"I can't hold onto you with one hand and hold my torch in the other hand and your torch in the other. I don't have a third hand."

She turned to me, her face looking ghastly in the flickering light. "We're saying crazy things, did you know that? But never mind. Your torch is enough." She leaned her torch against the wall where it flared in the face of a dead Indio, making its eyes look close together. "Now hold my hand while I pick up some of her fingers." She braced her free hand against the wall for a moment then started fumbling through some bones. It sounded as if she were playing checkers, clicking them around on the board.

"How do you know those are bones of a woman?" I asked.

"Hush. I know." She fumbled with the basket hanging on my back, and I heard the fingers thumping against the reeds as they tumbled into the basket.

"I want some toes," I said.

"Over there." She took my arm and pulled me down the wall. The torch she abandoned began to slip, making the shadows in the room dance in a frightening way. "I see a leg there, and my guess is that there are toes at the end of the leg. Do you want a leg?"

"No. Too big."

"Maybe just the lower part of a leg? It'll fit into the basket since that bone came from a short woman."

"Or a short man," I suggested.

"No. Definitely a woman. Do you want a leg or not?" She sounded querulous.

"All right. A leg. I want a leg. Mind you, though, pick a short

96

person." I again held her hand while she leaned against the wall and picked up more bones.

"I have the toes you want." She slid back to me and dropped them into the basket. "Now for the leg."

When she retrieved it, I was amazed at how short it was. "Maybe it's not a leg," I suggested.

"It is. A short leg, like I said. What else do you want?"

"I want a head, but I'll get it, Rosita. You're getting to pick up all the bones."

"I'm sorry. Here, I'll take the torch for you."

I gave her the torch and reached for a skull. It looked as if it might bite my hand, so I gripped it by the top. "The jaw fell off." I passed the skull to Rosita so she could put it in the basket on my back.

"Get it. We will tie it back together."

"Do you want me to get another head for you?" I picked up the jaw.

"No. One is enough. We can both look at it." The abandoned torch fell the rest of the way to the floor where it sputtered in the crack between the thousand-year mat of bat poop and the wall. "Did you knock over my torch?" Rosita asked.

"No. It fell of its own accord."

"Nothing falls of its own accord. Somebody or something pushed it."

"No," I said, not at all sure I was right. "It just fell."

"Let's go now." She took a quick step and slipped. I grabbed her in time to make us both fall. We landed on our bottoms and Rosita dropped the torch. It sputtered out on the wet floor and the light level in the cave dropped to almost nothing. The torch that something had pushed over continued to give a weird flicker of indirect light. We helped each other stand.

"I'll never get my skirt clean, even if I manage to get out of here alive."

"We go that direction," I said.

"Hurry, before what's left of the other torch dies."

"Dies? You didn't have to say it that way." We gripped each other and took sliding steps toward the exit. Just as we reached it, the other torch went out. "Hop up on the ledge," I said, though it

97

was hardly necessary. She was on it before I finished telling her to get there.

"Come on," she urged. "Maybe it was a man after all."

I climbed to the entry tunnel, feeling a surge of relief wash through me, feeling I had somehow won and the cave lost. "Maybe what was a man?"

"The ghost who owned the bones a thousand years ago." Rosita's voice came from down the tunnel.

"Ha," I laughed. "He's dead and doesn't mind." I laughed again and shouted into the cave, "DO YOU MIND?"

The shout broke the bats loose from the ceiling, and from deep in the cave came an answer: "MIND, IND, ind, ind, ind."

"Ay-yi-yi," Rosita said.

I crawled down the tunnel as fast as possible while bats flapped all around me. There seemed to be a solid wall of them, all trying to get out of the cave and mad that I was in the way. Some got caught in my clothes and hair. I had to shut my eyes and scramble to get out. When I made it into the sun, I ducked under the insane flight of bats and ran to Rosita. Something flapped on my head. "A bat is in your hair," Rosita said in horror. I slung my head around and tossed the bat against the side of the hill. It slid to my feet and lay on the ground, stunned, while I stood, stunned, looking at it.

"I want a bath," I said.

"Yes. A bath. But not now. The spirits in the cave are angry. Come." She took my hand and started down hill.

"Wait," I shook free of her. "My machete."

"Leave it."

"No." I hurried back to the entrance of the cave and picked up the machete, dodging for fear of getting another bat in my hair.

It took only minutes to get to the canoe. "The water is too deep for bathing, " Rosita said. "And there's no time for that, anyway. We must leave." She began untying the canoe from the root. I shoved the machete into the basket of bones, then pulled the boat close and tossed in the basket before getting in.

We paddled into the center of the river and paused to look back. Bats flew about in small, confused clouds. "What did you say to the ghosts?" Rosita asked.

"There's no such thing as ghosts." I took off my shoes and began taking off my pants.

"No? Then why were you talking to them?" Rosita took off her skirt.

"I don't know. I just did."

"And the cave answered."

"Not the cave. That was an echo of my own voice."

"What made the echo?"

"The walls of the cave. When the sound of my voice—"

"Then the cave answered. Don't explain an echo to me, Don. I'm not a baby."

"I'm sorry. I didn't mean to make you mad."

"It's all right. I'm not angry, not like the ghosts in the cave."

"There are no ghosts."

"Then why were we so afraid of them?"

I had no answer for that. We watched the bats begin to spiral back into the cave and I glanced at Rosita. "You have bat poop on your blouse."

"Yes. And on my feet and in my hair. So do you." She turned around to look at me, her face aglow with excitement. "I'll tell you something about me if you promise not to laugh."

"Have I ever laughed at you?" I asked.

"No. But promise, anyway."

"I promise."

"I liked going into the cave. I liked stealing bones from ghosts, knowing that they were watching from dead eyes. I liked the delicious fear that came when the torch fell and when your shout made the cave speak and bats jump out of the cave like fleas."

"Did you like the vampire bats dropping their blood poop on you?"

"Are you laughing at me?"

"No."

"They're not vampire bats." She leaned over the side and swished her skirt in the water. "This won't work. We need to find a place to stand in the water for washing our clothes." She stripped, looking at the black stains on each article of clothes and shaking her head. When I took off my shirt and underwear, she said, "You'll sunburn."

99

"Yes. But I just made a new rule that says it's better for me to be sunburned than to wear clothes with bat poop on them."

"I think I must be obeying that rule. We'll see later if it's a good rule or a bad one. You turn around now, because I'm going to make this end the back of the canoe."

I turned to face what would be the bow of the boat. Rosita spun the canoe around with a few splashes, and we both paddled in silence for a while, then I said: "I liked it, also."

"Liked what?"

"Being scared in the cave. That's why I shouted to the ghosts."

"I know."

"I want to ask you something now, if you're not still mad at me."

"I never was angry. Stop saying that."

"Why did you insist that the bones we took were from a woman and not a man?"

"I don't know," Rosita said. But I thought she did, so I kept quiet while we paddled down the river. Finally she said, "Maybe women aren't so punishing when people do things they shouldn't do."

"Then we shouldn't have taken the bones?"

"Of course not. It's wrong to disturb the dead. Would you take the bones of Ramón's mother, if you found them?"

I didn't reply, but it wasn't necessary, for she knew my answer. We kept the canoe in the center of the river and floated past two more hills rising from the jungle, bald and gray. Then there were only gigantic trees, the ones on the left bank throwing green shade on us. A bird flew past us, then came back, skimming the water and dipping its beak into it to leave little punctuation marks in its passing. A flock of parakeets, green as the jungle, flapped over, close enough for us to see the yellow around their eyes. When the line of tall trees moved back from the river, making room for shorter trees along the bank, Rosita brought the canoe close to shore. "Maybe," she said, "we can find another place shallow enough to bathe and wash clothes."

The sound of the river seemed louder somehow, but I saw no reason for it since the water along the bank seemed to go no faster than before. When the boat came too close to the trees hanging over into the water, she used her paddle to push us away from them. I turned around to watch her while keeping the tip of my paddle in the water to steer the front of the canoe out of the overhanging branches. "Look." She reached for an odd-looking tree that seemed devoid of bark, "I've never seen such leaves before."

As soon as she touched the tree, ants began leaping on her hand and arm, hundreds of them. It was as if the branch exploded, shooting out ants. "Ay." She jerked her hand back, but by that time they were on her face and shoulders. "Ay." She stood and batted at her face while I paddled us away from the tree. "They sting," she said, and jumped into the river, surfacing more than three meters from the boat. I could see ants floating in little piles. She splashed about, raking her fingers through her hair, rubbing her face.

Then I heard another splash and looked around. Something large had gone into the water from the bank down river not thirty meters away. When it surfaced and I saw the shape and size of its snout, I shouted, "Caimán, Caimán. Get in the boat, quick."

The black caimán swam toward Rosita in an almost leisurely way. She began a frantic swim toward the canoe, and I saw that she wouldn't make it. I looked in the boat for something to throw at the caimán but there was nothing that could hurt it. Certain it wouldn't help, I snatched up the leafy bundle that held the remains of our breakfast, pulled out the roasted rabbit, and threw it toward the nose of the caimán. The creature snatched the rabbit and rolled, exposing its lighter underside for an instant. Rosita reached the boat when the caimán reappeared, heading for her. I threw the breadfruit, then the two topochos, and the splashes distracted the animal long enough for Rosita to get into the boat, tipping its edge dangerously close to the water as she did so. The caimán bumped its nose against the boat, then veered off. I started to dip the paddle for a hard push to get us away, but Rosita hissed, "No. Put it down. Get down—hide in the boat and make no noise.

I lowered myself to the dampness of the boat's floor and found my face close to Rosita's. Her face looked bumpy and red from ant stings, and her eyes, upside down to mine, had a weird curve to them. "Thank you, Don," she whispered.

"Will the black caimán bite our canoe in half?" I asked.

"I hope not. I think not. What did you throw to it?"

"What was left of the rabbit. Then I threw a breadfruit and those two huge bananas."

"I hope the caimán enjoyed them." She kissed my forehead.

"Can we get up now? I think the river makes more noise than before."

"I don't know if it's safe to let the caimán see us. I keep thinking of the story my father told of a black caimán leaping out of the water and snatching a man from a canoe. It took the man's leg before the others could pull him out of the water. Men in another canoe killed the caimán with rifles, and they tied a rope to it and pulled it ashore. Inside its belly they found the man's leg."

"That's a terrible story."

"I should not have jumped into the river."

"But the ants—"

"They stung like fire, and I could do no thinking. It was my legs that did the thinking for me. I would not have jumped if my legs had consulted my head before jumping me into the water like that."

"Your legs did the thinking." I marveled at the idea.

Suddenly she tensed. "We're moving faster. And that noise." She sat up. "Don, get the paddle, fast."

I sat up as the canoe went around a bend where the river ahead of us roared and splashed. Not far ahead the river fell into a wall of white smoke. "To that bank," I shouted and grabbed the paddle. "Try to make it to that bank."

We both struggled with the paddles, but it was no use. The boat spun around, out of control, and I knew we were going over the falls.

9
Over the Waterfall

"Jump," I yelled, but my voice was lost in the sound of crashing water. I sprang out of the canoe in a crazy attempt to jump back up river. The air seemed to catch me like a feather, and I drifted above the water, turning in a slow arc so I saw the trees of the jungle on the bank, the water mist from the falling river, then Rosita in the canoe as it tilted at a strange angle with her clutching its sides and moving also like a slow feather drifting over the edge. Water tugged my feet and legs as I entered it, lying me down as into a bed, feet pointing toward the mist and head upriver where I wanted to jump. Then the world went white, and I knew I was under water with the entire river falling on top of me, holding me under.

Don't breathe, I thought, feeling myself tumbling and rolling in the white: don't breathe. Wild images flashed through my mind. The candy man driving his truck into the night, the dust. Rosita on the ground with a bloody mouth after Carlos struck her. My own inward whisper like El Loco's maresey doats chant, "don't breathe, don't breathe, don't breathe."

But I had to. Air, my lungs demanded, I need air, and as I gave in to the demand, I hit the bottom of the river with my knees, then my chest, and I inhaled even while telling myself not to breathe. The breath came easy and I gulped again and again for air and getting it, getting it, not on the bottom at all but on wet sand and pebbles and leafy things against my cheek.

I coughed and coughed and rolled over and the sun struck my eyes and my hand came up to block the sun like maybe someone chopped it off and set it on my face. Are you still with me, hand? I asked, telling fingers to move and they did, they moved rough and watery against my eyelids. The hand worked, then, and so was still part of my arm. I sat up, looked at the hand and laughed, glad to have a hand and frightened by the sound of my own laughter.

"Rosita," I said aloud. "Rosita." She went over the falls. I saw it—she drifted over slow and easy without uttering a sound to vanish into the mist while moving water laid me down and tucked me into the white. "Rosita," I called and sat up. The river had become wide and shallow with rocks and islands of flattened grass. I stood and found myself on one of those islands, some distance from the falls. "Rosita?"

She was nowhere in sight, not in the water and not along the banks. Maybe, I thought, the river is still holding her under water, and I'll have to find a way to get her out. I started toward the falls, wading into a channel that fast became so deep and fast-moving that I had to back out. If she is still being held under water, I told myself, then she has drowned. The idea was too vast to hold for long. The river washed her out of the falls, I told myself, pinching her like I pinched watermelon seeds to see them fly. It had to have done that, it had to, and Rosita would be down the river, on the bank or on an island such as the one where I washed up.

But she wasn't. I jumped from island to island and waded in shallows where fish moved like underwater bats at my approach. The pebbles ground at my bare feet making me wish for shoes. One channel I tried to cross grabbed me and dunked me and slammed me many meters down river before I found bottom and fought out of the water. Wedged into rocks and brush at the edge of a tiny island was a stick exactly right for bracing against the kind of current that had grabbed me, and beside it clinging to a broken tree limb, a sock fluttered in the current, my own sock stained with bat poop. I picked it up, wrung it out, and hung it around my neck thinking if the sock was so easy to find then maybe I could find my shoes. Maybe even the canoe—but later after finding Rosita.

I used the walking stick to help me cross the river to a rocky sandbar where trees dipped their leaves into a shallow pool. From there I surveyed a long piece of the river where it was wide and bespeckled with islands. But there was no Rosita. I sat on a rock, put my face in my hands and remembered jumping from the boat and watching Rosita and the canoe slide over the falls. The bat poop sock around my neck had a clammy, dirty feel to it, and I knew I deserved the filth of it, deserved much more poop to be heaped upon me than was in the stained sock, deserved a whole river of it to slide over me and crush me with black. Birds flew close by, squawking and flapping—maybe parrots, I thought, or parakeets, but I didn't look up at them or at the rattle of leaves on the bank beside me. It seemed like too much effort. I had jumped. Jumped like a coward out of the canoe, leaving Rosita to go over the falls alone where the canoe bashed against her and the river fell on her in a mean way instead of pinching her out like a watermelon seed to put her on a sandbar as it had me. I should have stayed in the canoe and died with her, I thought, because by jumping I caused her to stay and drown. Tears ran through my fingers and I heard myself crying.

Something tickled my shoulder but I ignored it as I had the parrots and the sounds on the bank, but the tickle became pressure and more insistent, and Rosita said, "Don?"

I stood in a sudden motion, whirled around and grasped her arm. "The river—the river flipped you out like a watermelon seed."

"Don? You look strange. Stop pinching my arm and let me hug you."

I thought of a skinny guy in a movie that my brother Todd and I watched in San Tomé, of how a pretty woman and the skinny guy would dance when they were happy, dance in sudden places without musicians in sight to play for the dancing, though there were always violins when they embraced. With a quick shift of arms, I turned Rosita's hug into a dancing position, our left arms held out straight, my other arm around her waist, and our cheeks together. Hers felt gritty, or maybe it was mine, and her hair, wet and wonderful, touched my face as I twirled her around and said, "ta-ta-dum-ta dum" to add to the music that always came. In that moment we were the grandest dancers in the world and certainly the grandest along the wild river with the sounds of water, wind in the trees, and the cries of parrots for an orchestra. Or we were the grandest until we fell.

"Here." She said handed me something as we sat up. "The sock fell from your neck."

"I don't want it. I'll never wear clothes again. Neither will you."

Rosita stood and brushed sand from her side. "We might not. They're gone. The river took all our clothes except for your one sock. Did you get hurt in the waterfall?"

"No. But look, your face is bruised and your arm scraped and red-looking."

"That's where the ants got me when I touched their tree. The river rocks or maybe the canoe hit me here." She pointed to a place on her arm. "It'll be a bruise and turn as purple as your hair."

"Does it hurt?"

"Not much, but it did when I first came from the water." She walked around me, inspecting me from head to foot. "No bruises. The river likes you. Oh, Don, I was so afraid for you. I searched the bank where I thought you would go, then found you." She blinked a bunch of times and cleared her throat. "Sitting here, crying for me." She blinked some more.

"Well. Maybe. I have a great walking stick." I pointed.

"Walking. Yes." She looked up and down the river. "We can walk for a while, until the river becomes narrow again and swallows the sand and rocks. Then we must go into the jungle, and that could be hard with no trails to follow. Perhaps we can find some of our clothes, more than this one sock?"

"I won't look for clothes." I picked up the walking stick and followed Rosita through some shallow channels.

She tied the sock around her wrist. "I'll look, then. You look for shoes. Will you at least agree to that?"

"Shoes. I'll do it. But no underwear. No shirts or pants. Nothing but shoes. Do you actually want to get dressed again?"

"Don," she stretched out my name in annoyance, glancing toward the sun.

"So we'll burn. You can make some medicine from papaya bark. You said you could."

"Only if we find another papaya, and even then it'll be hard to do without a knife to strip the bark. The machete is lost with the canoe."

I stopped and whacked the water with my stick. I hadn't thought about the machete or the Barlow in the pocket of my pants. Stupid river, stealing my Barlow. I whacked the water again. "Maybe, maybe I'll look for my pants, but only because of the Barlow. I won't wear the pants if we find them."

"Barlow?" She gave me a strange look. "Never mind. I'm glad you'll look for the pants. We can cut them up and make them into shoes, if we don't find any shoes."

We zig-zagged across the river, looking in piles of brush and in the still pools, looking at tree branches dipping into the water along the banks. For hours we continued the search, finding only rocks and brush and sand. Then we looked for bananas, papayas and breadfruit, but the jungle was too dense with underbrush on one side of the river. On the other side, the jungle offered no fruit. The sun dipped behind the trees casting shadows into the river, and we had still found no clothes and nothing to eat. "This is bad," Rosita said, her face drawn with worry. "We must eat soon. Maybe we can catch a fish?" She pointed to the zippy shadows moving about in the pool we stood beside. The fish were hard to see because of the ripple of the current through the pool.

Hefting my walking stick like a spear, I stood rock-still until several fish stopped darting about. They looked wavy from the wavy surface of the water, but at least they stayed still like Rosita said the rabbit had become that morning just before she got it with a rock. I threw the spear like a fish gig. It sank into the water with a satisfying pluke of a sound, then popped back out, the handle end toward me. The fish scattered, again reminding me of bats. "This will take some practice," I said and hefted the fish spear that once was a walking stick. After a couple more throws, the fish were so agitated that we had to try another pool. Rosita watched with growing consternation on her face as I tried and missed, tried and missed.

"Maybe with a stone?" She picked up several good round ones and went to another pool. Why not? I said to myself. She had clobbered a rabbit with a stone earlier in the morning.

"Will we eat it raw?"

Rosita stood beside a narrow strip of the river, her arm cocked for throwing. "Eat what raw?"

"The fish you're going to get with those rocks."

She glanced at the sky. "The evening rain is coming, and we have no shelter and no food." She threw a rock. It went into the water, trailing a white streak of bubbles, and missing the fish. She tried again. "We could eat raw fish, if you want. Or we could roast it."

"Like the rabbit. But how will we get the fish's head off and the guts out without a machete?"

She threw the rest of the stones, shook her hands to get the sand off, and bit her lower lip. "I can't get one. I can't." She sounded on the verge of tears.

107

"At least we had rabbit and breadfruit for breakfast," I said.

"I wish we still had the rabbit."

"I don't. I'm glad the black caimán ate it instead of your leg." I tried for another fish with the walking stick, but it moved too fast for me.

"Night will be here soon, and rain, and we'll have to go to sleep without eating, if we can sleep in the rain. Then morning, and still no food." She sat at the edge of the pool and hid her face in her hands.

"In the early morning, we'll hunt rabbit. Maybe birds. We'll knock a parrot right out of the sky and eat it. Two parrots. Ten. I'll gather throwing stones right now, then we'll sleep on one of these islands, close to the bank where we'll find the rabbits and birds in the morning. We'll build a fire with some of the brush and hold palmettoes like umbrellas."

Rosita sniffed a few times and looked at me with raised brows. "The river might rise fast and wash us away. Rainy season is underway now, and the river will grow large and angry. We should climb a tree in case there are snakes that come around in the dark."

Climbing a tree sounded good to me, as good as anything except food could sound at the moment. I began scanning the banks for a proper tree. It wasn't easy to do. Most trees near the river were too spindly to climb. Rosita said it was because they get washed away every year and had to grow back, that only the big trees farther from the river survived from year to year. But they were too big to climb, for they branched too high up, and without branches, the trunks had no hand-holds.

We limited our search for a suitable tree to the area between the huge trees and the river, a strip of rocky land thick with brush. The sky darkened and rain began with a sudden rustle of leaves, the drops, slow at first, became so thick the air looked as white as the river at the waterfall. We moved into the big trees where rain didn't reach us, not at first, then it came in big drops that gathered high in the canopy, rolling from leaf to leaf before falling in drops the size of marbles. At the edge of the tall trees we looked at the area where there were some smaller ones. When we found a tree that we could climb, it was so dark that we couldn't make out exactly how tall the tree was, though it seemed plenty high and had low enough branches for climbing.

The tree stood too close to the water to suit Rosita, and it didn't afford much protection from rain. We found a place where the trunk forked in enough directions that, by bending some of the branches upon themselves, we made a tree house with a floor of sorts. "You will have to be there," Rosita leaned close to my ear to speak so I could hear her above the sound of rain. "And I will be here so we both have sturdy branches beneath us. We can't cuddle for warmth." She sighed. "If we did, one of us might fall."

I struggled with the branches to find a safe way to lie down that wasn't too uncomfortable. Rain pounded our tree, and the leaves above us gathered it to dump upon us in large, cold splats. "We should have cut palmettoes, like you suggested." Rosita almost had to shout for me to hear over the roar of rain on the river and on the jungle leaves.

The rain sounds reminded me of rain pounding on the corrugated zinc roof of my home in El Tigrito, and I thought of my sister, trying to read by candle light, of Todd, of Mom and Dad looking out the window. Probably they were wondering where I was on such a night, and probably they worried, though not too much on account of having read my letter on those tiny pieces of paper I got from El Loco. I wanted to tell Todd about the neat things I was doing, about the bones in the cave and the black caimán trying to eat Rosita's leg, about going over the waterfall and having the river shoot me out of the falls like a watermelon seed, about fishing with a spear, about being naked in the top of a jungle tree with a naked native girl like two wild folk from Borneo. I chuckled out loud at the thought of his jaw dropping to hear such stories. But I wouldn't tell him about stealing a canoe or trying to dance like the skinny guy in the movie and falling down or about how it wasn't possible to find bananas or papayas. I wouldn't tell him about losing the Barlow and the machete and about not being able to spear a fish. I wouldn't mention how my stomach hurt from being empty or discuss how I was cold in the rain up in that nasty tree but too afraid of snakes to climb down in the dark to find a place out of the rain. Wild men weren't supposed to be cold and hungry and afraid. I was so stricken with the unfairness of my situation, so hungry and cold, that I started crying.

Drops kept falling on us a long time after the rain stopped. I kept shifting around to find less uncomfortable ways to lie in the crumby little tree house we made, but it was no use, and sleep was out of the question. No matter how hard I tried, it wasn't possible to avoid having a branch gouging me and fearing I would fall to the jungle floor where the night snakes would get me. Then it happened: a branch slipped and I drifted out of the tree like a leaf floating to the leaf mold below. The drifting felt good like floating on my back in a warm swimming pool, and the ground met me softer than a pillow. The cushion of the turf felt so good that I drifted off to sleep as I couldn't while lying in the tree branches, and a big snake came out of the water to bite me with its hypodermic needle teeth, stunning me into being still, then about fifty smaller snakes slithered out of the brush and started nibbling on me—I saw them in little spotlights from the moon stabbing through leaves up high where Rosita slept. The snakes bit off chunks from the bottoms of my feet and from my toes and fingers and chewed them up, sounding like El Loco smacking as he ate panbread, and the sound was so disgusting to Rosita that she woke up and growled to the snakes to chew with their lips closed.

Her growling at the smacking snakes got louder and louder until the sound awakened me. It was a bit startling to find myself still draped upon the tree branches we bent into a nest for sleeping. The bottoms of my feet still hurt from where the snakes bit off chunks of them, except that it made no sense for snakes to nibble on a person that way—and besides, I wasn't on the jungle floor. The sound of Rosita's growling wasn't complaints about snake smacking at all but a soft kind of talking, like someone had climbed the tree and settled down beside her for a chat. I listened for meaning in the words but couldn't make out much: "Aveh María, madre . . ." mumble, mumble. It took me a while to understand that she was praying.

But to what? I knew for a fact that the Easter bunny and Santa and the tooth fairy were made-up stories. Surely she knew the story parents told native kids about the three wise men filling shoes with gifts was a hoax, so she wouldn't be praying to them. I had a fair notion that the other three guys that Mom insisted were real were in fact just more invisible people and no more real than the tooth fairy, though maybe Rosita didn't know they were fake. I listened some more and again heard the name Aveh Maria and the words madre de diós. So Aveh was the mother of some god. That was a strange notion, one I had to think about some. I had never wondered if Santa had a mother, back when I believed in him, and then I got too old to think such silly thoughts. But what about the three invisible guys that somehow got rolled into one? Did they have a mother? If so, perhaps Rosita thought Aveh was the mother of those gods. Mom claimed she believed it was just fine to pray to any of the three because they teamed up to be some powerful folks and weren't three anymore. If Aveh was mother of the three that had become one, then she had to be important enough in the grand design of the world that she could do anything her sons could do.

My sister June claimed one of the three invisible guys counted the hair on your head, which made no sense to me at all. Why would anyone waste the time it took to count all those hairs? And what would he do with such useless information? But it was still impressive that he could do it—if, of course, you believed that he was real, which I didn't. Rosita seemed to believe in Aveh or she wouldn't be saying her name so often. Carmen said believing something made it real, I remembered, and Rosita thought Carmen was on to something there. So if Rosita could believe Aveh into being real, and Aveh had magical powers like the tooth fairy used to have back when I was a little kid or like the guy who counted all the hair, then maybe Aveh could grow us a few banana trees with ripe bananas somewhere close to our tree, or maybe change some of the worthless brush into breadfruit or papaya trees or something else useful. The pain in my stomach made me wish I could help pray Aveh into being real so we could put her on the job of getting us some food. But it seemed like a stupid waste of time for me to pray to someone I didn't know well enough to believe into being as real as the tree that held us off the jungle floor.

Rosita kept on with her mumbling chant of a prayer, and she became slower and more quiet until she trailed off into sleep leaving only the night sounds of the jungle for me to listen to. Not that the jungle critters had gotten cranked up yet on account of the rain. But they were warming to the idea that the dark belonged to them, or the bull frogs were, and some of the insects had begun to peep and chirp. As the drops from leaves slowed to a halt, night critters in the jungle put up such a din that I wanted to shout, "Would you please shut up," but didn't on account of not wanting to awaken Rosita. When the birds got into the act with their gurgles and yodels—if it was birds that made those odd sounds—I was ready to yell at the jungle even if doing so knocked Rosita out of a sound sleep.

Just when I thought I would shout at the entire wild part of Venezuela to be quiet, dammit, and let me sleep, Rosita awakened me with a nudge. "Don. Don. You're twitching so much it must be a nightmare. Wake up. It's morning. Also, I think I have a surprise for you."

"You killed another rabbit?" The notion astounded me. "From up here in this tree?"

"I found something we couldn't see in the dark last night. Look, that way, just back from the river."

I stood on a branch to see where she pointed. "Banana trees?"

"Why are you standing in that strange way? Do your feet hurt?"

Rosita didn't seem to miss anything. I didn't even know I had been standing on the branch in an odd way. "Maybe from the snakes nibbling on them in the night."

"What snakes? Oh. That was a joke. The same snakes must have nibbled on my feet, too. If the snakes didn't do it, then it must have been the rocks along the river that hurt our feet. It isn't good to go barefooted, even if it might be fun not to have to wear other clothes. Today I make us some shoes. But first we eat." She untied my sock from her wrist and offered it to me. "Put this on. It will give some protection for one of your feet."

"I don't want clothes. Ever again."

"Not even something to keep your feet from feeling as if snakes have been biting them?"

"Shoes, maybe. But not that stupid sock."

She shrugged. "Then I'll wear it."

We left the tree and made our way to the stand of banana trees, walking gingerly on account of having sore feet. Rosita looked strange wearing my sock, the heel pulled up to her ankle and bat poop stains on the upper part. I would prefer to see her with nothing at all on, but it made sense for her to try to protect at least one of her feet. Rosita walked in front of me as we headed toward the banana trees, and I admired the grace of her brown body even if her having the sock on didn't seem right for savage jungle people that we had become.

There must have been twenty big, leafy trees, one with a purple banana flower, but none with bananas, green or ripe. I felt like crying, especially when Rosita looked so disappointed. She didn't cry, though. Her disappointment seemed to last only a few seconds, then she set her mouth into a determined straight line and told me to pick the banana flower.

10
Carribe, the Cannibal Fish

"It would be wise," Rosita said, "to poke around on the banana flower with your walking stick to make sure a jungle spider doesn't jump out."

After establishing that no huge spiders were going to leap out at me, I broke the stem of the flower, which wasn't an easy task. "Why do you want this thing?" It didn't look much like a flower, more like a big purple insect pod, rounded on one end and the other coming to a point.

"Have you never eaten a banana flower?"

"Eaten one of these?" I handed her the flower. It felt tough and pulpy to me, the surface having much the same feel to it as the leaves of the banana tree.

"Break off two leaves from that tree," she pointed at a young banana plant. "We'll use them to sit on while we have breakfast." She began to peel layers of purple while I got some broad leaves. As we headed toward the river, I watched her work on the purple pod that could ripen into bananas if we had left it alone for a few weeks. It was like shucking corn except that the layers became lighter in color as she pulled them off. "This layer," she said, "is about the color of your hair, which means it's too tough to eat. The flower would be better cooked, but when I get down to the yellow part where it's tender enough, we can have something of a meal."

We had walked down river in the semi-darkness and had paid little attention to it while we looked for a tree to hold us above the night snakes of the jungle. I half expected to find the water bunched up again into a single stream, but it was still broken up into little channels with islands among them, and it was a long way across to the trees on the other side. We shared the banana flower while sitting on a rock at the edge of a shallow channel, the broad banana leaf feeling cool and slippery against my bare bottom. "It tastes like lettuce," I said. "Maybe lettuce with perfume. I like it. Do you believe Aveh put the banana flower there in the night?"

"What?"

"And if she did, maybe she messed up some by not making

115

some ripe bananas instead of just giving us the flower."

"Don, whatever are you talking about?"

"In the night I heard you praying to Aveh Maria for some bananas."

"I did nothing of the kind. I prayed. That's all."

"I didn't pray. It occurred to me that I ought to help you try to pray Aveh into becoming real enough to make us some breadfruit trees or a papaya, maybe, but I didn't do it. I couldn't believe in her and it seemed useless to fake it. Maybe if I had been able to believe even just a little, the two of us could have convinced Aveh to do better than one little banana flower."

"You don't understand. I didn't pray for fruit. I was cold and lonely and hungry and a little scared, and it was hard to go to sleep. So I prayed."

"For what?"

"What do you mean for what? I prayed for comfort."

"I used to pray for a bicycle. We always had plenty of food, so it never occurred to me to pray for anything to eat."

"You did it wrong, then."

"Did what wrong?"

"The praying. You're not supposed to pray for a bicycle or for food or anything like that."

"Then what's the point of praying?"

"For comfort. I asked that she comfort me. I also asked that she comfort you. And her name is Maria, not ave. That's just something you say as part of the prayer."

"You didn't ask Aveh, I mean Maria for bananas?"

"No. I asked for comfort. I told you that." Her voice became a little testy.

"Did you get it?"

"Yes. I felt the spirit of the holy mother with me, and the fear left with the loneliness, and I forgot about being cold and went to sleep."

"That's it? That's all you prayed for?"

"Yes. Stop asking me that same question."

"If she would give you comfort, why wouldn't she give you a stalk of bananas or another ripe papaya?"

"That's not the way prayer works. My grandmother told me

never to pray for something like money or even for flowers. You're supposed to pray for comfort."

"I don't understand."

"No, you don't. To get food, we must go looking for it and earn it."

"I would have prayed for bananas. Ripe ones. That is, if I believed in invisible people enough to pray to them. The banana flower is good, as far as it goes. But there's not much to it."

"It'll help to eat the flower, but we'll have to find some real food soon. You're right, bananas would have been better, if we had found some."

"Maybe some of those fish?" I pointed at the fish lazing around in the shallow stream beside our rock. "I wish I had a fishhook and some twine." It seemed wise to get off of the subject of prayer for a while. Rosita didn't understand what I was trying to tell her, and she seemed to be put out with me, though I didn't understand why.

"A fishhook?" She stood and tossed the pulpy remains of our breakfast into the water. The fish rose to inspect it, and one of them took an experimental nibble, then they drifted back toward the rock. "I think I can make a fishhook."

"Out of what?"

"Thorns, maybe. Perhaps from a small tree limb with a fork in it. I could shape it by rubbing it on this rock."

"What about string?"

"I could get that from stripping lines of bark, if the proper kind of tree grows nearby. I'll try to do it. You can catch the bait while I look for the right tree. But first, we need something on our feet." She scanned the edges of the river. "There. Down there are some grasses that will do for shoes."

"Grass shoes? Won't they wear out fast?"

"Yes, but better the grass than our feet. Help me gather it."

She seemed relieved not to be talking about prayer anymore, and I decided it wasn't something to discuss, especially when we were both hungry and a little edgy. I followed her to a spot where the river had deposited a bunch of fist-sized stones. Rosita picked up one and dashed it against some larger stones, shattering it. Then she looked among the pieces, rejecting one then another until she found one that fit her needs. "See this edge?" She held the stone sliver for me to inspect. "It'll cut better than any knife, except for being so small. This one is yours. I'll find another, and the two of us will cut enough grass for shoes." She sorted through the broken stones again until she found another sharp piece.

"How will you turn grass into shoes? Have you ever done that before?"

"No. But my grandmother told me she used to make grass shoes before all the stores in El Tigrito began selling alpargatas. Grandmother said it wasn't hard to make shoes, though I'll probably not make very good ones, not at first."

I thought that if they weren't as good as alpargatas then the shoes would be plenty bad. Alpargatas were slabs of old tires cut into the shape of the bottom of a foot. They had cotton string woven to a mesh and shaped like a sandal sewed to the slab of tire, and they made your feet black to wear them.

When we had plenty of grass, Rosita went to work and I watched. She wove the grass stems much as she had done the baskets, doing it fast and neat, only this time instead of a basket, she made little rectangles. It was necessary for me to keep putting my foot on one of them until she was satisfied with its size, then she made another. The final task was to wrap a mat around each of my feet and tie them on with more grass. "How does that feel?" she asked.

"Weird." I took a few steps. "Crunchy."

"They look strange, but they'll help keep your feet safe." She began work on more mats for her own feet. When she tied them on, she kept my bat poop sock on one foot. I thought that I looked weird enough wearing funny little baskets instead of shoes, but she looked even stranger with one basket on and another over a dirty athletic sock. But I didn't say that. She took several steps in her new basket shoes. "The crunching ought to stop soon. Likely we'll wear these out fast, but it'll be easy to make another pair. I could make us each a kind of skirt to tie around our middle."

"Why? In the jungle, who is to see us except us? It's a bit silly to worry about covering up any part of us, except for our feet.

"I agree. But when we find people, we'll have to have something on. Grownups won't understand. We've already talked about that." She bent down to adjust her new shoe. "I'll bet wild men from

Borneo wear grass bands around their waists instead of pants or skirts."

"You think so?" The idea of being dressed like a wild man sounded good to me. Maybe clothes wouldn't be so bad, if Rosita made them from grass and we could go around looking like savages. "I'm willing to try some Borneo wild man clothes. Maybe we can find a snake to make some snake-skin headbands?"

"Maybe. But first we get some food. That banana flower wasn't much. You catch some bait while I try to make a hook and some string."

"Catch some bait? Where?" I looked around.

"Check on the underside of leaves. Bring us a grasshopper or a bug of some kind. We'll meet on the rock where we ate the flower and try to catch the fish in the puddle beside it."

Catching bugs turned out to be easy. There were a zillion of them among the leafy plants on the edge of the river. My favorites were the butterflies, though I didn't try to catch any of them. They were too beautiful. For some reason they liked to light at the edge of the water and prod the wet ground with a long black tooth that curled into a spring when they weren't poking around the ground with it. I sat under a fern and watched what I thought of as a flock of butterflies looking for whatever butterflies look for when they uncurl that black tooth. Maybe, I thought, it was a covey of butterflies, and I wished I knew the right word for a bunch of them. June would know the word, and it made me sad that I couldn't run into the house and ask her to teach it to me.

I established that there was more bait on the bank than fish in the river and that holding the bait in one spot was harder than catching more if some got away. Rosita took her sliver of rock and started scratching on one tree, then another, while I sat to watch the butterflies.

"The shoes worked well," she said, sitting beside me. She had a twig with thorns on it and a bunch of stringy fiber from a tree trunk. Using the shard of stone, she carved on the twig until it was only a thorn attached to a piece of wood, and I thought it looked very like a fishhook. Then she knotted the fiber together for a long string and tied one end to the fishhook. "Get me some bait," she said.

I grabbed a fat, green grasshopper from a fern beside us and held it while she stuck it with the thorn. It moved its legs fast and produced some brown spit. Todd once called grasshopper spit "tobacco juice." Rosita held the bark-string so the grasshopper dangled on the thorn.

"This looks good," she said. "When I pull the fish out of the water, you whack it with a rock. Don't try to pick it up because the chances are those fish are carribe, and they have teeth like razors. The fish could flop around and bite you."

"I'll do it," I said, eager to clobber a fish with a rock, more than ready to eat it, maybe raw. "It's fun to be a savage."

Rosita raised one brow and looked at me, then busied herself with the line. It seemed smart to get a rock ready, so I picked out a stout one while Rosita stood beside the pool and tied the string on her wrist. It looked as if the fish were watching her, as if they expected her to feed them or maybe wade into the water so they could bite more moles from her ankle. She tossed the grasshopper into the water. As soon as it hit the surface, one of the fish snatched it up and Rosita squealed in surprise. Her line jerked tight and ripped the water, then broke, and all the fish vanished under the rock. "Carumba." She inspected the broken fiber. "I thought it was stronger than that. I'll have to braid some of it to make it strong enough to hold the fish. That means stripping more." She turned to me. "You watched me make the fishhook. Can you make another?"

"Yes."

"Then come. I'll show you the thorn bush. You make a hook while I get us some stronger fiber. Perhaps you should make several hooks."

Making the hook was harder than it looked when Rosita did it. I kept stabbing my fingers with the thorns, and I nicked myself a couple of times with the sharp rock. My fingers shook, probably from being hungry, and my stomach was starting to hurt again. Rosita had the line ready about the time I finished making a hook. Mine didn't look as much like a real fishhook as hers had, but she seemed to think it would work.

She threw the hooked grasshopper into the water while I hefted a stone, but this time the fish stayed under the rock. After a couple more tries to entice them out, we went to another river pool. When she dropped the baited hook into the water, a fish struck nearly as fast as before, and this time it stayed hooked for a little longer. I thought the line broke again, but when she pulled it in, we saw that the fishhook had broken. I felt myself wilt. "Being a savage is more work than I thought it would be," I said.

"Don't worry. We're new at being savages, and we're learning. The line didn't break this time. All we have to do is make a stronger hook."

We both started on another hook. I found the biggest thorn on the bush and made a big hook with it. "This one," I told her, "will be strong enough to bring in a black caimán."

Rosita kept nodding her approval at my work while she trimmed up a tough little branch with a fork in it. "Maybe," she said, "thorns break too easily. Maybe this hook will hold together since it isn't a thorn." She held up a little V-shaped piece of wood with one sharp point. It didn't look much like a fishhook. "We'll try your caimán hook if this one breaks."

Her wooden hook worked well. She dragged a carribe out of the water, I knocked it in the head a few times with stones, and we set about building a fire on one of the sandbars. While we ate roasted fish, Rosita said, "We solved the problem of food. But it created another problem for us."

"Savages don't have problems." I sure didn't, anyway, not in that perfect moment. We sat on sand covered with banana leaves, a crystal blue sky above us, and we had trees tall enough to shade the entire river. Flocks of parrots flew overhead, birds fluttered among the ferns on the shore, flashy blue-and-green butterflies poked black teeth into the sand beside us, and we ate the best-tasting fish anyone ever roasted. The feel of the cool air and its tease of heat to come with the climbing sun, the green smells of the jungle, the raucous call of parrots, the taste of roasted cannibal fish, and the wonderful colors of the butterflies made that moment the best ever. Also, I had on a great pair of savage jungle sandals, and I sat, otherwise naked, beside another savage who knew how to make fishhooks and string and build a fire with her bare hands and some twigs. "I could stay here for years, whacking carribe in the head with stones and sitting on banana leaves to eat roasted fish."

"No you couldn't. In a few days, this river will rise enough to cover the spot we're sitting on."

"You know what I mean."

"Yes. I feel the same way. But we have to go home sooner or later."

"Later would suit me just fine."

"The problem we've created is that we must stay close to the river in order to catch the fish we must have for food. But we need to get out on the savannah in order to walk home."

"We don't know which road to take out there."

"There aren't any roads, not around here. That's another problem. We need to find a village, a big enough one that has roads going toward home. That means we have to follow the river, which is another problem since the river might be taking us farther from home. For a while we can walk on sand in the riverbed, but when the river becomes narrow or when rains fill up the wide parts, we'll have to go through the jungle. It won't be easy."

"With your fishhook and line and with some bananas and other fruit we'll find along the way, it'll be fun and not hard at all. We'll find people long before I'm ready to give up being a savage."

"I thought you said being a savage was more work than you wanted." Rosita's cheeks dimpled. "But never mind that. We need to start down the river as soon as we finish our fish."

When we got started, Rosita carried a piece of driftwood onto which she had wrapped her fishing line, and I carried my walking stick. We hopped puddles and waded shallow channels, our new sandals squishing with water on the rocks and sand. I kept trying to spear fish with my stick, pretending they were black caimanes that had to be killed to keep them from biting off our legs. I did manage to whack one fish enough to make it swim crooked for a while. Rosita waited while I threw and retrieved the spear, and she seemed thrilled when I whacked the fish.

"Look," Rosita said while I was trying to spear a fish in a wide channel, "our canoe."

It was caught among some brush where a tree leaned into the river's edge to snag driftwood. At least most of it was caught there. One side had been ripped away, leaving the bottom and the other side more or less intact. We walked around it and I prodded the bow a couple of times with my stick. "If we had a board, we could nail it on the side," I said, "if we had nails and a hammer."

"Perhaps we can find the missing side?"

"I doubt it."

"Can we try to pull it out on the bank, just in case?" Rosita began tugging on the end, trying to free the boat from the tree and brush.

I waded into the water and pushed while she pulled from the shallows by the bank. When it broke loose, Rosita gasped. I thought she was surprised that we got the remains of the canoe unstuck, but she had released the boat and stood pointing at the place it had been stuck. "The basket, the basket. Get it, quick. Do you know what that means?"

"Yes," I said, delighted to recover the bones we had worked so hard to get from the bat cave. The basket was waterlogged and sunk, caught on some driftwood and among the branches of the tree that hung into the river. It was hard to get it unstuck, much more difficult than was the canoe. As I labored to extricate the basket, Rosita managed to pull the remains of the boat part way on the shore. When the basket broke loose, it was so soaked in water that I had a hard time dragging it ashore.

Rosita immediately began opening the top—to check on the condition of our bones, I thought. She reached inside, and I expected her to drag out the skull or the leg, maybe. Instead she pulled out the machete. "Yes, Yes, Yes." She ran her fingers over it where the blade had begun to rust. "With this, we can make shelters. It'll help us get food. Getting the canoe back would have been nice, but this. This. This is a miracle." She waved the machete around over her head much as Carmen had when she cajoled the peasants and miners to murder the bandits.

"I wish I had put my Barlow in the basket," I said.

"Barlow? What is this Barlow?"

"My pocket knife."

"Oh, that." She waved her hand, dismissing the importance of the Barlow. "Today when the rains come, we'll be ready for them. We'll sleep warm and dry on a mat of leaves high in the safety of a tree. This," she held out the machete, "will be the key to comfort." Her eyes blazed and her cheeks dimpled, though she didn't seem amused.

"What about the boat?" I pulled it farther onto the bank and tied the rope to a small tree. My sandals almost squirted out water with every step. Rosita took the bones from the basket and set them on some grass to dry. The skull didn't look at all spooky sitting there on the live grass and in the full light of day. I sat and examined the jaw, the leg, the toes and the fingers. "What great bones," I said.

"Yes." She scooped some sand from the basket. "Help me empty the sand and wash this out. I think the basket is still usable with only a little repair."

After we washed the basket and set it beside the bones to dry, I returned to the problem of the canoe while Rosita chopped some reeds and did some work on the basket. The canoe looked hopeless. "Even if we find the missing side," I told her, "I doubt we can stick it back on well enough to keep water out."

Rosita glanced up from her weaving. "I was afraid of that. Take the machete and cut the rope from the front of the boat."

"Why?"

"For tying up things. It'll be good for building a shelter."

I severed the rope, saving as much as I could. "Finding this canoe was useless, except for the rope."

"It led us to the basket," Rosita pointed out. She picked up the leg bone. "This is definitely the leg of an ancient woman. If it had been a man, he would never have let us find the basket."

"The boat led us to the basket, not some woman's ghost."

"Yes," Rosita said. "That's true, also."

Was she making fun of me? I cut my eyes toward her. She sat, legs crossed, folding reeds into the water-logged basket, her face looking as pretty as usual and not at all sarcastic or amused in any kind of mean way.

I looked back at the canoe and felt a touch of anger at it for being broken. It seemed unfair that we had to steal the canoe and then it broke on us so there was no way to give it back when we were done with it. El Loco probably wouldn't be mad at me for stealing the canoe. He would probably say that we did what we had to do, because he believed that he always did what he had to do, even if it wasn't what he wanted to do. Maybe the canoe did what it had to do, also, when it went over the falls. It couldn't help what the river did to it when the current grabbed it, and it couldn't help breaking apart when it crashed at the bottom. It would be lucky for me if the canoe belonged to El Loco, though that seemed unlikely. Probably it was Carmen's. Or maybe it belonged to Carlos, who for all I knew was still lying on the ground near where his canoe used to be, his hands and feet tied up. Carlos would be angry about the loss of the canoe, if he ever got untied. Carmen might not be so happy about it, either, if it were hers. If praying would do any good, I thought, I'd pray that the canoe belonged to El Loco.

We spent much of the day toting a wet basket with bones in it, along with the machete and a rope, and I kept an eye out for my pants, hoping to get my Barlow back. Around noon we caught another carribe, a big one, and cooked it up. We had to retreat to the bank to find shade while we ate, and we sat on a long root that snaked along the ground from what Rosita said was a strangler fig. Some rattling in the leaves of a nearby tree made us look up. Two monkeys stood on a limb regarding us. "This is good luck," Rosita whispered.

"Monkeys are lucky?"

"Yes. They know where to find fruit. All we have to do is follow them and we'll find some good fruit. Maybe."

"For sure," I said with enthusiasm.

"Not for sure. Sometimes monkeys eat leaves."

"Not those. They look like fruit eaters to me. Let's follow those two."

"Not now," she said. "Where you find a couple of them, you'll find others. I think we ought to finish eating this fish. I wish, though, we had caught a catfish this time."

"Don't you like carribe?"

"It tastes good enough, I guess. I just don't like to think about what it eats."

"What does it eat?" Even as I asked, I remembered the dead caimán floating belly up with part of it eaten away by fish, probably carribe, the cannibal fish.

"They eat anything that moves in the water, sometimes. One ate a mole from my ankle. If there's enough of them and a monkey fell in the river, carribe would eat it. My father told me he once caught one of the terrible fish, cut it so it would bleed, and threw it back.

Another carribe bit it where it bled, and it turned and bit the one that bit it. Others came for the blood, biting one another, until the river turned red with the frenzy of the fish eating each other."

"Maybe." I tried for a skeptical look. "Maybe not."

"What do you mean?"

"My father told me that same story, only he said he was fishing in the ocean close to a place called Padre Island. He said he caught a shark, cut it, and flung it back so another shark could bite it, and it bite back, and soon the water was red from shark blood with sharks everywhere gobbling each other up. What I mean is, maybe the story of mean fish eating each other is one that grownups like to tell because it's gross and scary. My brother and I liked the story, and Dad seemed to like telling it. He told it more than once, and each time it was bloodier than the last."

"Men might do that." Rosita took another hesitant bite of the cannibal fish.

"Yes. Grownups seem to enjoy lying to kids."

"Not grownups. Men. Has your mother ever told you such a story?"

I thought about the tooth fairy and the other invisible creatures Mom used to lie to me about. "Yes," I said, uncertain if the stories Mom told were as bad since they weren't bloody and gross like the shark story. Then I added: "Maybe Mom's lies weren't about fish."

11

The Palmetto Igloo

The monkeys vanished while we ate, and not long after that, clouds rolled in, fast and dark. "We've been lucky so far," Rosita said. "The rains have come only in the evening and at night, and they haven't been hard rains. Today the clouds are more serious." She led us to some ground palms and set me to gathering fronds while she went looking for a place to make a shelter.

It was easy to cut them: one whack on the stem where it turned into leaf did it, if I managed to swing the machete at the proper angle. I had a stack bigger than I could carry when wind and rain hit at the same time. A thunder clap seemed to turn the rain on like throwing a switch. Water fell at a slant to ride the wind, and the drops stung my skin. A cloud curtain dimmed the sun into twilight while I stacked the palmettoes, and I welcomed the cool of it. Even rain felt good at first, except for the sting of striking my skin. It sounded wonderful the way it thumped the palmettoes, bending them down as if they kneeled before the clouds, making it easier to whack the stem in exactly the right place. Rain hissed in the trees and splattered on the river. I imagined the sound as voices in a choir humming different notes to blend into a song of water. The only sound louder than the rain was the occasional growl of thunder.

By the time Rosita returned, I had a huge stack of fronds, and I was soaked. She clenched herself to show she was cold, pointed to the stack of palmettos, and indicated the direction we needed to take them. I put the machete into the basket, shouldered it, and picked up as many palm fronds as I could carry. She hoisted an even larger stack, set them on her head, and led me to a ridge of rocky ground covered with bushes. "Hurry," she shouted above the sounds of rain, and she threw down her load. I set mine beside hers and looked at her with uncertainty. She mouthed something else, then made chopping motions. I set down the basket, took out the machete and handed it to her. The rain began falling straight down. Rosita did some chopping under the bush, and I pulled out the branches she lopped. Then she began wedging the palm fronds into

127

a tangle of bush limbs, overlapping them until she had a green igloo. I handed her the palms until I caught on to the design, then began placing them as best I could. As soon as there was enough of a shelter, she dragged the remaining palmetto fans inside and continued to weave the sides of the shelter from within. She leaned close to me and said, "Make us a floor from the dryer ones on the bottom of the heap."

I tried to find dryer ones, but that seemed like a hopeless cause. We worked squatting down on account of the low roof of our igloo, and we soon had a shelter that shed the water from us and had a floor that, though scratchy, was a bunch better than the bare and rocky earth.

The green igloo sang with the rain, adding its own wet voice to the choral hum of the jungle and the river. It was so loud Rosita and I had to put our heads close together to be heard. "I'm cold," she said. "Help me get the water off of some of these palm leaves and we'll use them like a blanket." She picked up a frond, held it close to the edge of the igloo, and created a fine mist by shaking it.

It seemed impossible to me for palmetto fans to make much of a blanket, but then I was amazed to see them become an igloo. I helped her mist the air around us by shaking some fronds. "Move close," she said into my ear. "Sit beside me, our legs together." When I did so, she began covering us, feet first, with the stiff fans. Soon we were lying down with a weird green covering that, with imagination, could pass for a blanket. Her body felt cold as a frog as she snuggled against me, her wet head on my shoulder.

"This is the best jungle house in Venezuela," I said.

"It's just a thatched bush. I was lucky to find such a bush on a place where water won't run across our floor."

"The house doesn't leak water on us."

"It will, if we stay here long enough. There's only a couple of layers of palm leaves."

"I think we ought to make a new rule."

"I don't like rules." She waited for me to explain, then asked, "What new rule?"

"A good one. I think we should stay here until the thatched bush starts to leak, then move on down the river."

"We need to get home."

"Sometime. But not today. Would you go home right now if all we had to do was walk down a short trail that took only twenty minutes?"

"Yes. No. What I mean is, maybe. You're warming me up."

"Don't change the subject."

"I'm not."

"You are," I said.

"Am not."

"After you get warm, then, and the rain stops, and you could get home in just a few minutes. That's what I mean. Would you go?"

"No."

"Then when? Tomorrow? The fact is, Rosita, I love the jungle and the river—even the rain. I like lying here under this green blanket that isn't a blanket but almost works like one. I like trying to warm you up when you're cold as a frog. I like eating roasted fish that have all those scary teeth in their mouths."

"Frog?"

"I like having grass shoes and a reed basket of spooky-looking bones and a fishing line made from fiber you stripped from a tree."

"Cold as a frog?"

"And having the machete is nice because it allowed us to make this great little jungle house that doesn't leak even in a rain that looks like someone is pouring the entire El Tigre river on top of us. I like it that we fell on the bat poop even if we got nasty bugs on us, and I like—"

"You liked falling into the bat droppings? That's disgusting. That's like a pig who loves to wallow in stinking mud."

"I didn't say it was good to roll around in the bat poop. I said I liked it that we did so to get dirty enough to take off our clothes. If we hadn't done that, then the river wouldn't have snatched away our clothes when the waterfall grabbed the canoe. What I mean is that maybe best of all I like walking down the river with you, nude like proper savages, looking for fruit and trying to spear fish, even if I never got one. Our hunt along the river is much better than when we pretended to hunt for tigers and lions in the savannah when we lived in El tigrito. Hunting for food is a real hunt, and since the river took our clothes, we really are naked savages, not just kids with our shirts tied around our waists. What we played at

129

doing in the savannah close to our village was only make believe."

"Pretending to hunt tigers wasn't dangerous," she said.

"No. But we haven't sunburned yet."

"Carmen told Carlos to shoot us. That was dangerous. The ghosts in the cave nearly got us. The caimán nearly ate me. The waterfall nearly killed us both. And you're worrying about sunburn?"

"We stay in the shade most of the time, so sunburn isn't a problem."

"What about all those other dangers? Weren't you afraid?" she asked.

"I don't know. Maybe. I guess it would be smart to go home if we could walk there in twenty minutes. But I still wouldn't do it. There's Todd who can do anything better than I can. There's June who knows more than I'll ever know and likes to remind me of the fact. There's all those dopey rules my parents make up, not to mention the stories they tell each other at night when they think I'm sleeping but I'm not and I get so scared that sometimes I can't sleep from thinking about what they said. There's houses that have to have iron bars in the windows to keep people from stealing. Did you know that back in the days when Mano de Goma was president of Venezuela, police used to chop off the hands of anyone caught stealing? We both would lose a hand for taking the canoe. We would have had to make this jungle house with only one hand each because of stupid rules that grownups like to make. I never want to go back there."

We lay still under the scratchy blanket, her wet head resting on my shoulder, her arm over me, and we listened to the rain drumming on the green igloo, and I thought my use of never might have been a slight exaggeration. But I was in no mood to admit it, not right then.

"I like it that you're not afraid of snakes," Rosita said.

"Maybe I am."

"You tried to kill one with just a sharp stick."

Guilt washed over me. "I have to tell you something, and you probably won't like me much anymore. I let the fire go out for no good reason at all."

"You think I might not like you? Not like you?" She sounded

astonished.

"There wasn't any snake. I lied. There. Now you know."

"What are you talking about?"

"When I let the fire go out. You remember. I told you I couldn't help it because of the snake that came along. It was a lie. The snake was a vine. I thought it was a live snake at first, but it turned out to be just a vine, then I got to throwing the spear at it and thinking about the neat head bands we could make from a snake skin and pretending I was throwing the spear at a dangerous snake. But it was just a vine."

"For a while there was a snake, if you believed there was. So it doesn't matter. The fire going out was nothing. We made another. Also, I think maybe I'm not a frog anymore."

"Frog?"

"You warmed me up. I don't know how you stay so warm when I'm so cold. I don't even know why I get so cold in this jungle. I never got so cold around our village, even in the rain—but never mind that. You fed topoches to the caimán so it didn't get me when the ants made me jump into the river."

"You're not mad because I lied about the snake?"

"I lied about your letter going to the president of Venezuela."

"Does that mean you'll stay here until the jungle house starts to leak?"

"Now you're changing the subject."

"I am not. So will you or not?"

"If that's what you want, yes."

"I do. But you need to want to stay, also."

"Until the thatch leaks. We'll do it." She spoke with such enthusiasm that I hoped the thatch would never leak. "We'll find people soon, I think. If we keep following the river and it keeps going east, there will be villages, maybe big ones. We'll need clothes. While we're waiting for the thatch to leak, we can go out to the savannah to gather grasses for weaving clothes. What I'll make won't be very good, but at least we'll be covered when we walk into a village, and grass will be better than reeds since reeds are too stiff. Staying here for a while will allow me to make us clothes."

When the rain stopped drumming on our igloo, Rosita made a little door on the river side of the house and we crawled out. The clouds still roiled around down river, dropping rain and lightening. The river, louder than ever, had filled in from bank to bank. The sandbars where we had stood to catch our lunch in a small channel of clear water had vanished under murky waters. "The river will rise much more," Rosita said.

"It might flood our camp?"

"Our thatched bush is too high for that. But high waters might make it harder to follow the river."

We scouted out the area around our camp and found a swamp just a little way into the jungle. "It's a new swamp," Rosita said, one that comes only in rainy season." We followed the edge of the swamp down river. Trees dropped water on us, and Rosita shivered, though I didn't feel too cold. Strange-looking plants appeared along the edge of the swamp—spiky ones that looked like century plants but weren't. The century plants growing around El Tigrito had thorns on the edges of their broad leaves, and on the tip of each was a thorn the size of my thumb. Todd told me they were called century plants because they bloomed once every hundred years.

The ones Rosita and I found didn't have thorns. I was looking at one when Rosita shouted. It wasn't a frightened sound—more like she found something good that I ought to see, so I didn't stop looking at the weird plant. In the center where the leaves unfolded and spread in all directions was a little cup of water. Just a little farther on was another of the weird plants, and a big one. The center of it looked as if it could hold a liter of water. Rosita called again.

She had found more banana trees than I had ever seen growing in one place. "The two monkeys." She pointed. "probably come here for food. Look, ripe bananas and many stalks of green."

"These are tiny bananas." I prodded the ripe stalk with the machete and no spiders jumped out, so we broke some off and ate them. The inside was almost as yellow as the peeling.

"Small bananas are the best," Rosita said. "These are manzanitas."

"Little apples? Why are these called apples? They don't taste like apples."

"Smell the underside of the leaves." She tore a leaf and handed a piece to me. The underside was almost powdery white. I held it to

132

my nose.

"Apples," I said. "But don't all banana leaves smell like this? Many in our village had this odor."

"Then they were manzanita banana trees."

I examined the stalk. "The monkeys haven't found this bunch of bananas yet. There's no sign that they have eaten any of them."

"That means there are many others ripe and ready. Don, we picked a good place for our camp. I want some leaves for our bed tonight."

I lopped a bunch of leaves while Rosita picked bananas to take back to our green igloo. She bundled them in a leaf for carrying and I picked up a big bunch of leaves. "We'll look for a good tree on the way back," she said.

"A tree? For what?"

"To sleep in."

"We have a place to sleep. A good one that will keep us dry if it rains in the night."

"It's on the ground."

"So?"

"So snakes might find us and bite you on the bottoms of your feet, like in your dream."

"That was just a dream."

We got back to the little jungle house without finding a suitable tree. They were all either too tall or too skinny. "We should keep looking," Rosita said.

"But I want to go fishing."

"Then go. I'll find us a tree."

"I think we ought to sleep in the house we already have."

"You go catch a fish. I'll worry about a tree house."

The current moved so fast that my fishing line zipped down stream and floated on the top of the water. After watching it dance about for a while with nothing showing signs of taking the chunk of banana I used for bait, I gave up and returned to the palmetto igloo. Rosita was nowhere in sight, and I didn't want to find her because that meant I'd have to help find a tree to climb for the night. Sleeping in the igloo sounded much better to me. I spent some time covering the floor of the green igloo with banana leaves to make it softer and perhaps more appealing to Rosita.

But she might still insist we climb a tree. I looked around, trying to figure out what to do that would allow her to be more comfortable sleeping on the ground. Then it hit me. A fire.

Didn't savage people build fires in front of their tents and caves to keep away wild animals? And weren't snakes wild? If I were a jungle snake and had never seen a fire, I'd stay away from it. I looked around for firewood.

But everything was wet. Everything. I found a tree that had died but hadn't fallen all the way to the ground on account of hitting other trees, which held it up at an angle. The tree was rotten, so it was easy to pull off dead limbs. But they were wet. Still, those limbs were the best bet around for firewood. I broke some and stacked them close to the entry of our jungle house. Maybe, I thought, we could make a small fire to dry out the wet wood enough to burn it, and the burning would keep away snakes.

12
Jesus Frog

"I can try." Rosita eyed the stack of wet firewood. "But we'll have to find some drier wood. Maybe we can find a dead tree that hasn't fallen yet?"

"Those pieces of wood came from such a tree," I said.

"Then we'll have to do without a fire. I found a live tree that will hold a good tree house, but we have to start soon because it will be dark before long, and I think it might rain again."

"Rain? In that case, we should stay in the jungle house we already built."

"That's not safe."

"Don't snakes climb trees?"

Rosita looked startled. "Some do."

"Then we need a fire in the tree to keep the snakes away."

"In the tree? Impossible."

"This looks bad. We can't build a fire on the ground and it's impossible to build one in a tree. Since things seem equal, I say we save the work of making a tree house and stay on the ground."

"You aren't reasoning properly. Some snakes don't climb trees, such as rattlesnakes."

"But some do. Besides, we haven't seen a snake yet, with or without rattles. The snake I saw changed into a vine as soon as I got close to it. Check inside the house we built."

She bent down and looked. "Banana leaves. Those looks comfortable. How did you get so many?"

"Try it out. When I tried it, I thought it was like lying on a bed perfumed with sweet apples."

She crawled into the green igloo. "It does. I smell manzanitas all around me."

"Then it's settled. We sleep here tonight."

"I still don't think it's a good idea. You were supposed to gather these banana leaves for our tree house." She came out of the jungle house.

"We can try for a catfish for dinner. There's still enough daylight to catch one and cook it up."

135

"True. You build the fire and—"

"Fire. I forgot." I felt foolish. "Then we'll explore some more. There's a plant by the swamp that has a cup of water in the center of it."

"I've seen those plants in the jungle by our village. Sometimes there are frogs that live in the water."

"Frogs?" It seemed unlikely to me that a frog would choose a little cup of water when there was an entire swamp to hop around in and do whatever froggy things it needed to do—but then Venezuelan frogs seemed to live in odd places. Some long, skinny green ones liked to live in trees.

"There's enough daylight left for us to go through the jungle to the savannah. We can gather grass for me to weave us some clothes." She saw that I was about to object and added, "But of course we won't wear them unless we find a village or have to walk much in the sun. We should take the basket for carrying back the grass."

"Grass clothes," I mused. I wondered what a wild man from Borneo would wear. Certainly not jeans and tennis shoes. Grass sandals, maybe, and grass pants. Back in Texas, Todd and I used to wear grass or straw hats when we went to Padre Island with Dad to fish in the ship channel. Those straw hats smelled like the sweet weeds from a vacant lot.

Rosita emptied the basket on the ground beside our hut. When she turned the basket up, out tumbled the canoe rope along with bones we stole from the ghosts in bat poop cave. "No reason to carry the head and the legs or even the fingers and toes all the way to the savannah and back," she said.

The way the top part of the head and the leg fell close together gave me an idea. "What if," I took the machete and began digging in the soil beside the entry to our jungle house, "what if we made a wild decoration for the front of our hut?" It took some effort to pry out a couple of rocks and a divot of soil, making a hole deep enough to hold the end of the leg. I set it in place and wedged it upright with the rocks and some dirt, then put the skull on top so it seemed to stare at anyone who came by.

"That's a little scary." Rosita shouldered the basket and picked up the machete. "Maybe we'll take it down before we go to sleep?"

"If you want." I was pleased by her reaction. The bones did look scary set up like that. "We'll say that the hut belongs to a couple of head hunters. Ones who can shrink heads if they chose but don't always so they can have heads to decorate their house. Maybe there are a dozen or so inside the hut, and a pile of them lying on the ground out back, grinning at the jungle." I picked up my walking stick and followed her toward the swamp.

"Let's try that way," she said. "Maybe there's an easy way to walk around the boggy area."

I wanted to find the plant that looked big enough to hold a liter of water, but Rosita took us in the wrong direction. We had gone just a little way when we saw an even bigger water-holding plant than the one I had hoped to find. "Maybe that one has frogs in it?" I said. We walked around it, prodding among the leaves with machete and stick to spook out any snakes and jungle spiders. When none emerged, we pushed among the long, rubbery leaves for a peek in the center of the plant.

"Minnows," Rosita said.

I thought she was pulling a trick on me, then I saw one. "A plant with minnows in it? That doesn't make sense."

"I've seen tadpoles in smaller plants like this in the jungle beside our village."

"Tadpoles, yes. A frog could hop up here and lay its eggs. But I've never heard of a fish that could climb out of a river, jump into a bush and lay eggs." A couple more minnows ventured into my range of vision. The center of the plant was like a bowl, a big one. "So how did the minnows get there?"

"Sometimes it rains minnows," Rosita said.

I had heard that story before, back in Texas. Minnows appeared in the ditches in our front yard after a big rain, and some kids in the neighborhood said the fish had come with the rain, that they fell out of the sky. I thought about fish falling from the sky for a couple of hours before telling Todd about it. It didn't make sense to me that a fish could find enough water in the sky to live. Besides, how would they get up there in the first place? But there were the minnows in our front yard, swimming around in a ditch far from any rivers or lakes. There was no other explanation: minnows had to have fallen from the sky. Or so I told Todd.

He took me to a culvert that ran under the street a couple of blocks from our house. "There's always water in that culvert," he said. "Fish live in there, little ones, anyway. The rainwater washed some of them down to the ditch in front of our house."

"How did they get into the culvert?" I wanted to know.

He had no answer for that. So we asked Dad, who told us that ducks swim around in lakes where fish lay eggs, and they get fish eggs on their feathers. Then they fly to little puddles of water and ditches, and the eggs wash off, putting fish into water that had none before the ducks arrived. Todd seemed satisfied with the answer, so I accepted it.

Or I did until Rosita and I stood beside the weird jungle plant with minnows in it and I remembered Dad's explanation. Ducks didn't ever swim around in culverts, at least not in our neighborhood back in Texas—a fact that slipped by me back when I was a dumb little kid. So how did the minnows get into the ditch? While I pondered the question, a tiny frog with large feet jumped onto the water, then jumped again. It landed on the water and hopped as if it weren't landing on water at all but dirt. In a flash I knew what it was. "A Jesus frog," I said in English.

"What?"

I pronounced Jesus the way people say it in Spanish: haySOOS, a common name for boys in our village.

"You call that frog Haysoos? Why?"

"I didn't name it. Uncle Ray told me he had seen the Jesus frogs in the jungles out west, and he said people called them Haysoos because they can walk on water."

"That's silly. The frog hopped on water. It didn't walk."

"Hopping is close enough, for a frog, anyway."

"Jesus didn't hop on water. He walked."

"I've heard that story, too. If he really did walk on water, how do you think he did it?"

"He was God. He can do anything he wants to do. Anything."

"I wish I could walk on water, especially if you could, too. We would run up and down the river together. We could get going really fast and then slide for a long way because water is bound to be slippery when you walk on it. It would be my luck to trip on a wave in the river and fall in right on top of a whole school of hungry

138

carribe. They would bite all the moles off of my body before I could get up and run down the river."

"Trip? On water? Slide?"

The frog hopped across the water again, leaving tiny rings where it landed and jumped. "Clever little Jesus frog," I said. It was smart enough to hop around on the plant's bowl of water instead of the river where carribe would snap it up faster than biting a mole off an ankle.

We wandered beside the edge of the swamp, finding more plants that held water. Some had minnows in them, and in some were the little water-hopping frogs. But we found no way around the swamp. Rosita was disappointed. "We'll try downriver." She stopped and stared at the gray hulk of a tree. It had died long enough ago to have lost its bark and for its branches to have fallen away. "Something lives inside that tree." The way she spoke, low and tense, gave me a shiver along the spine.

A black, triangular hole gaped from the base of the tree. "The den of a jungle tiger?" I asked.

"Look inside the tree, at the floor."

"Floor?" I liked the idea that a hollow tree could be so large that it had a floor inside. We walked closer. "That black stuff? And the smell. I'll never forget that smell. Do you suppose there are little bugs in there eating each other's poop?"

"Mainly they'll be eating the bat droppings."

"Do you want to go inside?"

"Don! Inside the tree?" She shot me a horrified glance, decided that I was ribbing her, and managed a tiny smile. "Why would you even think of such a thing?"

"It's a kind of a cave, isn't it? Don't you have a fondness for caves—especially ones with bats? Maybe there are some bones of Indios in there."

Rosita walked around the tree, put her ear to the gray trunk and knocked with the machete. "Bats are in there. I made them flutter and move around."

I put my ear to the tree. "There must be a thousand. Two thousand." Our noses were close together as we leaned against the tree. "I'll bet the wood isn't thick right here. That means there are bats crawling around just a few millimeters from our ears, maybe gnawing at the wood. They could come popping through at any time and get into our hair, like that bat did when I yelled into the cave."

She jerked away from the tree. "I hate bats. Come on. We need to go downriver to find a way around the swamp."

Cupping my hands against the tree, I put my lips close to the trunk and yelled, "Hello, bats." My greeting set them to fluttering.

"Come on, now. Let's leave before you make them fly out like you did in the cave of the bones."

As we walked back the direction we came, we heard thunder and decided it was time to get to our jungle house. "Why," I asked, "would those bats want to live in an old hollow tree when there's a perfectly good cave not far up the river?"

"Who knows the ways of jungle animals?" She shrugged. "Maybe they're fruit bats and like living close to the stand of bananas."

When we reached our hut, Rosita worked at not looking at the skull atop the leg bone. It seemed to me like a good idea to leave the bones standing where I put them, but Rosita said she would have a hard time sleeping with them there. She wouldn't let me put them back into the basket, either, because she wanted the basket in the house with us, and she didn't want to have to worry about bones lying so close to us. Just before the rain hit, we settled upon placing the bones at the base of a tree and covering them with leaves. The day was nearly gone when we heard the first rattle of rain striking the trees. We hurried inside the hut.

Within minutes, the jungle was again singing its wet song of the rainy season, but this time we were dry and had a comfortable bed of perfumed leaves to lie upon. Still, the air became cool from the wet, and we scooched close together, covering ourselves with banana leaves.

"When I told you minnows fell with rain," Rosita said, "I could tell that you didn't believe me."

"Some things aren't possible, things like building a fire in a tree or making fire with wet wood, or fish living in the sky." It made me feel as clever as Uncle Ray to connect up such a list of impossible feats, and I must have sounded pretty smug because Rosita sounded a bit irritated when she said:

"It's impossible for us to make fire from wet wood, but it isn't impossible for God to put fish in the sky and make them fall into the center of the jungle plants."

"I don't believe in God."

Rosita got quiet and still, which scared me some. I thought of how upset June and Mom had become when I told them that I had figured out that Jesus was on a par with the tooth fairy. When Rosita spoke again, she no longer sounded irritated. She sounded worried, like I had a bad sunburn and she needed to help me with the pain of it. "It's all right. My grandmother said that people sometimes get angry at God, but she forgives the anger."

"Your grandmother forgives?"

"No. God."

"Then you meant he."

"No," Rosita said. "If you're brave enough to tell me that you don't believe in God, then I'll be brave and tell you that I figured out God is a woman."

"That's silly. God is a man."

"But, Don," Rosita giggled, "I thought you didn't believe in God."

"I don't. But if I did, he would be a man. Everybody knows he is."

"I suppose it would be possible. She could be a man, if she wanted, since she can do anything."

"Or a boy, maybe? Like me. Or a girl like you?"

"Yes. God can do anything."

"What would it be like to be God? I think I would hate it."

"Don, don't say such things."

"Why not? It would be fun to be able to walk on water. But if you could do anything, nothing would be a challenge. You want a meal? Reach into the river and pull out a fish. If you got a carribe, then change it into a catfish. A cooked catfish. You want to go home to El Tigrito? Just step from here to there. Or else change this place into El Tigrito. Our jungle house could become my bedroom, and the tree where we set the bones could become the water tower out back. You don't like my purple hair? Make it blond again, or change it into savannah grass or turn my hair into yellow snakes. Anything could be anything with no effort at all, and I would hate it. Life would be so boring. God must be very bored if he can do anything."

"She."

"Okay, she, then. I would hate to be God."

"You make me think such strange thoughts. Hair turning into yellow snakes."

"You're the one with the strange ideas, and they startle me. God as a woman? Now that's strange."

"If God became bored, she could make herself not bored."

That one stumped me. It didn't seem possible for God not to be bored, that is, if there were a God. "Maybe she can't do anything, after all," I ventured.

"No. She can do anything."

"Can she make a mountain so big no one could lift it?"

"Easy. No one can lift a mountain, anyway."

"Not even God? Can she make one so big that even she couldn't pick it up? If she could, then she couldn't do everything, and if she couldn't then she couldn't do everything."

"Go to sleep, Don." Rosita sounded annoyed.

It seemed to me that I was being plenty clever again, though it wasn't a good idea to sound smug about it. I wanted to talk more about why Rosita thought God was a woman and about her problem with a mountain she couldn't lift, but it didn't seem like a good idea to keep talking right then. So we listened to the rain.

When it stopped pouring down and turned into the splat and plop of water falling from leaves, the whistle frogs over in the swamp got tuned up. I loved their sharp little whistles and imagined them to be conversations: "Who? Me. No. Us. Look. Jump. There. Here." Having to communicate with one little shrill word had to be as limiting as I felt with writing the letter on paper chopped up for El Loco's cigarettes, but I figured the frogs were up to the task, especially if their smaller cousins could walk on water.

"The frogs," Rosita said. "I forgot about them. With that many, there are bound to be snakes all over the place."

As soon as she mentioned snakes, I heard the frogs talking about it: "Snake. Run. Jump. Teeth. Bite. Ouch. Ouch. Ouch." Every frog in the swamp seemed to be yelling about snakes. I laughed.

Rosita gave me an angry shove. "Don't you laugh at me for being afraid of snakes."

"Not at you. At the frogs, at the way they're talking about the snakes."

"Frogs don't talk."

"They do if you listen in the right way. It's sort of like writing on cigarette paper."

"Cigarette paper?" Rosita sounded bewildered, then her voice went back to the certainty she usually spoke with: "I know what you're doing. You're trying to make me think about something else so I won't worry about snakes. You're a good person, Don." With a rattle of banana leaves, she gave me a quick kiss on the cheek. "You can stop distracting me now and talk to me about the snakes."

It felt unfair that I got credit for doing something I had not done, but I didn't want to give up the credit with an explanation. Besides, I figured I would sound stupid explaining how I imagined whistle frogs squeaking out short words about snakes biting them. "What if," I said, "we decided that there were no snakes for twenty kilometers? Fifty, maybe."

"But there are. Listen to all the frogs. Snakes will hear them and gather in this part of the jungle.

"Snakes can't hear because they don't have ears."

She remained quiet, no doubt thinking about snakes' ears. "Frogs have ears," she said.

"I've never seen a frog with ears."

"And I had never seen a Jesus frog until today, but that didn't mean there weren't any. Whistle frogs are bound to have ears—or else why would they do all that whistling to each other? I think their ears are so tiny we never noticed them. Or maybe they fold their ears up somehow and tuck them away during the day when we look at frogs, then pop their ears out at night when it's time to whistle. Snakes are probably the same way. That means the snakes down by the river are listening to the frogs, maybe with their snake ears popped out, and thinking about how good frogs are to eat, and a thousand snakes are about to go into the swamp for a snack. When they do that, some of them are bound to crawl right through our thatched bush, into the banana leaves with us." Her voice became higher as she talked about snakes in the banana leaves.

"Maybe we could believe them out of existence?"

"What?"

"Like the ghosts. You said that if we believed in the ghosts, they

143

would appear in the cave, remember? And Carmen said that believing something makes it true. So if we believe there are no snakes, maybe there wouldn't be any."

"I don't think belief works that direction. Only the other direction."

"Believing has directions?" I asked.

"If that cave was just a cave full of bones and the bones are only things like chips of wood or rocks, and that's all there is in the cave for hundreds of years, except for the bats and those nasty bugs, then there's no ghosts in there. But we come along and believe there are ghosts, so the ghosts become real. Real to us, which is the same thing. That's one direction. The other direction is what you want to do. We might believe the cave has no bones in it, or no bats, maybe. But the bones and bats are already there, so there's nothing our belief can do about them. Believing they are gone won't make it true."

"So if there are no snakes, and you believe there are snakes, then they appear and might bite you. But if there are already snakes, then not believing in them won't make them go away. Is that what you mean?"

"That's close enough. And the jungle is full of snakes, especially around here with all the little Jesus frogs and the whistle frogs for them to eat. We should be up in a tree right now."

Her logic made sense to me, and I was wishing we were up in the tree she had found. But I didn't want to admit to wishing that since I had insisted we sleep in the green igloo. "If I were a jungle snake," I said, "I would want to slither over to the swamp and make a dinner of the frogs. Even if I happened to crawl through a jungle house and found some kids in there, I wouldn't have any interest in them because they're too big to eat. Don't snakes swallow whole animals? We're too big to swallow. So if I were a snake out to eat those frogs, I would ignore big animals like us and go right through the green igloo to the swamp."

"Green igloo? Are you trying to make me think of other things again?"

"No. I'm trying to think like a snake, and snakes are too little to be interested in us."

"Anacondas aren't too little. My dad said he saw an anaconda once, and it was bigger around than he was and longer than a stalk of sugarcane. He said an anaconda could gulp down a child like I gulp down an empanada. Anacondas live in the rivers out in the wild part of Venezuela, which is exactly where we are right now. That means there might be some in the river close to us."

I had heard of anacondas, and they scared me plenty—but I hadn't thought about them since arriving in the candy man's truck. "Would they eat frogs?" I asked. "A frog is so tiny that an anaconda would have to scoop up a thousand of them to get one bite."

"We aren't frogs."

"No. But why would an anaconda climb out of the river to go after the whistle frogs? It wouldn't, so no anaconda will find us."

"My dad said an anaconda is too big to crawl around out of water. I just remembered that. He said they are fast as a carribe in the water, but are slower than turtles on the land. We don't need to worry about anacondas—just the smaller snakes."

We stayed awake worrying about snakes, but not for long. At least I didn't. After we stopped talking, I slipped into sleep and didn't wake up until Rosita shook me and said, "Listen. I heard a voice. It sounded like a chant."

13
Vampire Bats

The first dim light of day broke into the jungle. We stood beside our hut in a mess of shadows, Rosita clutching herself from the cold, though I thought the temperature was fine. I moved close to her to share my warmth and to savor the savagery of the moment. Night sounds of the jungle dimmed, stars faded, and we stood on a rise between our hut and a wild river where carribe swam and black caimanes prowled about, looking for legs to bite off. Best of all, I had the cleverest native girl in all of Venezuela leaning against me, the two of us naked like wild animals—except for our grass slippers that only a savage would wear. We listened for the sounds of drums and the battle chants of headhunters wearing war paint purple as my hair and brandishing blowguns loaded with poison darts, men good enough to shoot a monkey right out of a tree so that it hit the ground dead, only this time instead going after monkeys in the green twilight the headhunters danced and chanted to work themselves into the primitive frenzy necessary for war. I shivered with the thought. "They'll shrink the heads they take," I said.

"Listen," Rosita whispered. "I think I heard her again."

"Her? Her?"

"Yes. Be quiet."

"Do you hear the savage drums?"

"Not drums. Just a chant. There. Listen."

The voice came, faint and soprano, a steady and rhythmic song in some unintelligible language. "Maybe she's singing for the men before they go to war. But I don't hear the drums."

Rosita gave me a smat with her palm. Be quiet, the smat said, and don't be so silly, it said, punctuated as it was with an exasperated sigh. We leaned together, listening, as the sun leaped into the sky and the short tropic twilight turned into morning. "She's done with the ceremony of dawn," Rosita said. "I wish I could meet her. She's somewhere on the other side of the swamp, right through there. Maybe we'll find a way through to the savannah today."

"I want to catch a catfish."

She patted my arm and stepped away, turning to look at me. "I'll find a way through while you catch a fish. But your leg. Look. You have a cut on it." She knelt and examined my calf. A thin trickle of blood ran to my heel, then puddled on the ground.

"I don't feel a thing. I must have scratched it on our walk last night."

"No." She reached inside the hut and pulled out a strip of banana leaves to dab at me. "If you had cut yourself last night, there would be a scab right now. It keeps flowing." She held the leaf against my leg. "I'll have to make a bandage of something less slick than this banana leaf."

After getting the machete from the green igloo, she went about hacking on trees and bushes. I glanced at my leg, amazed that the blood wouldn't stop. "Probably," I said, "I scratched myself on one of the palm fronds. It's just a tiny scratch." I busied myself with looking at the fishing twine and the wooden hook Rosita had made.

When she returned, she carried some pulpy-looking stuff and some woody string. "It's still weeping."

"Ignore it," I said. "It's just a scratch."

"Do as I say. My grandmother said never to ignore a scratch when you're out in the river jungle because it can fester. She said to put a proper poultice on it. Come on, now."

I presented my leg as instructed. "You didn't make a fuss over the mole you lost to a carribe, and you bled plenty."

"Stop whining. I'm not making a fuss over this, either. I did, if you remember, treat the fish bite to keep it from festering." When she finished, I had the neatest-looking wild bandage attached to my leg—a broad leaf holding the pulpy stuff against the scratch, and the leaf tied on with strips of bark string.

When we went to the stand of banana trees for breakfast, we found a tribe of monkeys already there. They were wonderful little creatures who vanished into the trees as soon as they saw us. "This is good luck," Rosita said.

"Do Venezuelans believe that monkeys are good luck?"

"No, no. We're lucky that the monkeys came before we did because they are clever enough not to go near jungle spiders or poisonous snakes. We can have breakfast without worrying that something bad will bite us."

We gathered bananas, Rosita selecting ones with a greenish tint to them and I picking only the deep yellow ones with dark spots. Rosita lopped banana leaves to make a picnic blanket for our meal. She cleared away enough leaves to reveal an old log beneath the trees. "Firewood," she said. "That old tree is a bit rotten, but look how the leaves kept it dry. We can cook fish today."

"The water got too high to find puddles and channels with fish."

"But the fish are still there. Maybe you can catch us a catfish?" We sat on the banana leaf blanket to eat, and Rosita watched me peel a speckled banana. "Those are too ripe," she told me.

"These are sweet. You picked green ones that are tough and not as good to eat."

"What do you know about bananas? You're a north American."

"Bananas grow in North America." I spoke without certainty.

"They do not."

"Do, too. Big ones. Sweet ones. Maybe not as sweet as these little apple bananas, but plenty sweet, and the best ones are yellow with speckles."

"My father likes bananas that are too ripe. Maybe men have no taste. If you want to use a banana for bait, you should use a greener one. Catfish like green bananas."

"Catfish and girls have something in common, then."

"Hush. You said that the current carried your hook to the surface. Try tying a stone the shape of your finger to the string. That will make the hook sink to the bottom where catfish like to live."

I stood, eager to try her suggestion. She frowned. "Where are you going?"

"To catch a fish."

"Eat first."

"I'll eat on the way." I picked up some bananas.

"But you will have to do it by yourself, and I'll have to eat by myself. What's the fun of a meal if you have to be by yourself?"

I sat down again, resigning myself to fishing later. She watched me with amusement, and we ate in silence. Finally she said, "You can go."

"Aren't you coming with me?"

"No. You go find us a large catfish. I'll take the machete and find a way through the swamp so we can meet the woman who chanted to the sun this morning."

We agreed to meet at noon, when the sun cast no shadows beside us.

The river had risen more, though not as much as I expected. I found a finger-shaped stone, tied it to the braided bark string, hooked a chunk of green banana to the wooden fishhook, and dropped it into the river. The current took the string off to my left, but not very far. Squatting on a rock, I looped the string around a wrist and leaned toward the water, imagining a catfish as long as my arm taking the bait.

But nothing happened. I drew the hook in to make sure it was still baited and dropped it into the water again. What if a caimán took the bait, I wondered. I would drag it to the surface, and we would look at each other in the eye, both of us knowing that if we got into a wrestling match, I would ride it like a gator tamer wrestled alligators in East Texas, straddling it and pulling its mouth open so wide I shattered the bones in its jaw. The caimán would swim around, unhappy at the prospect of being humiliated by Don Seal, the world-famous gator tamer. It would spit out the bait and maybe bite the wooden hook into a couple of useless pieces then splash me with water from its tail before trying to swim away. But I'd be too fast for it and leap on its back to get my legs locked around it for the death struggle.

Just as I was about to break the monster's jaws, something tugged on the fishing line, and the scene of my wrestling a black caimán vanished. I wrapped the string around my wrist a second time and waited.

The line went stiff with a sudden jerk. I tried to pull back, but there was no give in the line. A catfish bigger than Rosita surfaced at the end of the string, then dove, jerking me from the rock into the water. I struggled to get the line off of my wrist while the fish dragged me downriver. At first I scooted along with my head above water a little like the way I had wanted to slide down the river if I could walk on water like a Jesus frog, then the monster fish pulled me under. It took me a long way, or so it seemed, before pausing enough for me to get untangled from the twine. I popped to the surface like a cork. After gasping for air a couple of times, I swam to the shore, grabbed some branches dipping into the water, and pulled myself ashore among bushes. The rock where I had squatted to cast the line into the river was only a few meters away, a fact that disappointed me because I fancied that the catfish had pulled me under water for at least five minutes.

My grass sandals were gone, as was the bandage on my leg. I inspected the cut and found it scabbed over. My wrist had a bruised place on it in the shape of a bracelet, but other than that, I suffered no injury. Having lost the twine, I knew fishing for the day was over—at least until Rosita came and made some more string. I told myself that if I had my Barlow or even the machete, I'd strip some more bark, braid it into line strong enough to hold the biggest catfish in Venezuela, then catch a fish so big it could feed a village. But that was a lie, and I knew it: the fact was I had no idea which tree to whittle on, even if I had a knife.

While waiting for her, I busied myself with cleaning out the hut where I had bled in the night. It was necessary to replace the banana leaves stained black from my scratch. While I was at it, I looked for the palm frond that put the scratch there, but I didn't find it. One palmetto fan had a prickly-looking stem, and I removed it from the hut. It didn't look sharp enough to scratch me, but as it was the most likely suspect, I threw it into the river.

Rosita returned well before noon, carrying two lumpy-looking green fruit. "Guava." She set them on some leaves. "There's no easy route around the swamp, but I did find a guava tree so we don't have to eat only bananas."

I rubbed my wrist. "The swamp goes on forever?"

"It curves into the river in a place where the water comes ashore shallow and wide. It's in such an inlet that my father said the black caimán likes to live. As soon as I saw that, I came back. Did you catch a fish?" She looked around as if expecting to see dead catfish lying all over the place.

"Not exactly. A catfish nearly caught me, though. It snapped the bait and jerked me into the water, then pulled me half way across the river."

"Where is it?"

"It got away."

"Big ones always do, to hear men talk." She gave me an amused smirk. I held out my wrist. She dropped the machete and took my hand. "Don, it's true, what you said, and not a game. Look at what it did to you. And your bandage—washed away. Your cut." She knelt and looked at my calf, then stood again. "You could have died. I shouldn't have gone to the swamp." She gave me a fierce hug. "It was a caimán who took the bait, no?"

"No." Her hug startled me, but I liked it. "It was a catfish. I saw it—a catfish bigger than you, bigger even than I am. I'm sorry it got away. And I lost my grass shoes."

"No matter. They were worn almost to nothing. I'll make you some more."

For lunch we had guava, after Rosita peeled and quartered them. They tasted like woody apples and were sort of fun to eat though not nearly so good as Rosita seemed to think. I wanted to see the place where black caimán lived, but Rosita said it was too dangerous. "They can run on the ground fast as a horse," she assured me. "We would become lunch."

I had to settle for seeing the spot where we might cross the swamp if we didn't mind wading. But before going there, Rosita made me another pair of shoes, this time from vines that looked like string. They were better than grass shoes because of the little leaves on the tops and sides, like shoes just my size grew on a bush and all we had to do was pick them like picking a banana. "These are beautiful," I said when I put them on. "No purple-haired wild boy ever wore such wonderful shoes."

"They're not as smooth or soft as woven grass, but they'll do until we get to the savannah, where I'll make you a better pair."

"These are better," I said, though they did feel lumpy and uneven to stand on.

Frog-and-minnow plants grew in abundance near the place where Rosita thought we might wade across. A ridge, if you could call it that, ran part way into the water, then vanished under the mirror-slick surface. Trees and old stumps protruded from the swamp, and birds hopped around in the branches. Some of the trees held orchids, tiny ones that added spots of pink and yellow to the green jungle.

"Perhaps," Rosita said, "we should get our basket, put the rope and bones into it, gather some bananas and guava, and cross the swamp this afternoon?"

"The jungle hut didn't leak in the night."

"I knew you would say that."

"Besides, I want to catch that giant catfish and eat it."

"The thatched bush might leak tonight. Snakes might crawl into it."

"Snakes stayed away last night," I said.

"Maybe." She led us back toward our hut, pausing to whittle some bark string from a tree.

I carried the machete while she began braiding the string into something stout enough to hold the meanest catfish. When we were nearly to our camp, I said, "What did you mean by 'maybe?'"

"I think one might have scratched your leg with its needle tooth."

"The stem of a palmetto did that. I found it and threw it into the river. I also replaced some of the banana leaves."

Rosita gave me a smile that said thanks, then circled our hut, inspecting it. "It will be my luck for the thatch to last another night," she said.

With a new wooden fishhook and new jungle twine, I caught a catfish less than half a meter long. It put up enough of a tussle that I was convinced I had one much bigger, but Rosita said it was plenty large for a good meal. She knocked it in the head with the blunt edge of the machete, chopped off three spikes, one on either side of what would have been a neck if it were a land animal and the third spike sticking out of its back. Holding the fish against the rock where I had stood while fishing, Rosita sliced open the fish's belly and dug out some disgusting-looking guts. Then she threaded the fishing twine through its gills and tied the fish to the trunk of a tree. "Go get the firewood from the stand of banana trees," she told me. "And bring some bananas. Make sure mine aren't too ripe." She used the machete to score the skin at the base of the fish's head, then began to strip it from gills to tail.

"I'll need the machete," I pointed out. "You're using it to peel the catfish."

She made a couple more cuts and handed me the machete. "You might want to wash it first."

The machete smelled of dead fish, even after I washed it, but I forgot the smell after a while. By the time I dragged back enough

153

firewood, Rosita had the fish skewered and suspended over a circle of stones she had carried from the river's edge. She built a fire with the same quick efficiency that went into the making of the fire in front of our cliff house above bat poop cave. When the fire crackled and licked at the catfish, she put green leaves into the flame to make a thick, white smoke, and tented a banana leaf over the fish. She declared it done as evening clouds gathered. I dragged some spare banana leaves out of the hut to cover our unused firewood. By the time rain swept into the jungle, we were sitting cross-legged in our hut, each holding a banana leaf plate of fish.

The rain hit the palm fronds with even more fury than the night before. I was certain the roof would spring a leak, but it remained water tight. The fish was the best I had ever eaten, its flesh thick and firm and shot through with smoky taste. Following Rosita's example, I tossed the green plate of bones into the rain and wiped my hands on a banana peel. We held our hands in the downpour to rinse them, Rosita withdrawing hers fast and shivering. I enjoyed letting the water splash pure and cool over my hands and wrists.

We settled back, heads together for hearing each other over the drum of the rain, and Rosita said, "Since the minnows didn't fall with rain such as this one, where did they come from?"

"What made you change your mind about it raining minnows?"

"When we washed our hands just now, I tried to remember ever seeing minnows on the ground after a rain. But I never saw such a thing. And yet there are fish in lakes that are not connected to other waters."

"What about my Dad's idea that ducks carry fish eggs on their feathers?"

Rosita considered the explanation, then asked, "Do you believe that?"

"Maybe. For some lakes."

"But not for the plants with water, right?"

"No."

"Never have I seen ducks swimming in the middle of a water plant, not that one could even if it wanted to because of the tiny amount of water."

"That's right," I said.

"Then there's no other explanation. She put them there."

154

"Who did?"

"God. She can do anything she wants—and don't try to trick me again with the question about a heavy mountain. If she wanted to make a mountain so big she couldn't pick it up, she would. Then if she wanted, she would pick up the mountain and move it somewhere else."

"That isn't logical."

"That's right. It isn't logical. It's just true."

I tried to look at her, but sometime during the rain, the sun had dropped into night, and we sat in complete darkness. It seemed that if I could see her face, I might figure out how to argue with her, but it was no use. Maybe the problem was all the fire inside her, like El Loco said. When he told me never argue with a woman who had a fire in her head, he could just as easily have added that it was also useless to argue with a girl who had a fire in her head. Right then Rosita seemed plenty intense from the fire inside, even if she had moved close to me for warmth, and her skin felt cooler than mine. "I thought my idea concerning the heavy mountain settled the matter about God's ability to do anything."

"It settled nothing. She's everywhere and can do anything."

"I still don't believe it. I don't even believe she is a woman. God is supposed to be a man."

"It doesn't matter what you believe. If you tried to believe away the minnows in the water plants, they would still be there. Snakes would still crawl into the swamp after whistle frogs even if you believed they didn't."

Sometime in the night, a rustling around my feet awakened me. Rain had stopped, and the night was filled with frog whistles, insect noise, and other strange sounds. And there was something rattling around, faintly, in the leaves close to my legs. A snake, I thought, and felt fear chill through my scalp and spine. If I moved it would bite my toes off. I felt it there, slithering around on my toes with wispy touches of its coils. But I couldn't just lie there and let it make up its own mind about biting me to death. I had to take control, to do something. It tickled me again, this time on my calf near where I wore the wild jungle bandage before washing it off in the river. Maybe it was a snake after all that had cut my leg. Maybe it had come back to finish me off.

155

I jerked my legs up, flipped up on my knees and pounded a fist on the spot where my calf had been when the snake tickled it. My fist connected with something that was neither banana leaf nor palm frond. I pounded again and again, hoping not to get the snake in the head if it happened to have its mouth open and its needle teeth sticking out. Something flopped around in the hut, something large enough to brush my hair, and I figured I was a goner. Any snake big enough to keep part of its body on the ground while the rest of it reached high enough to touch my head was also large enough to swallow me. Maybe an anaconda was in the hut.

"Don? What are you doing?"

At least, I thought, the snake hadn't swallowed Rosita. Yet. "Trying to drive away an anaconda."

"You're having a bad dream. Go back to sleep."

"Something was crawling all over me." I batted the air around me but felt nothing.

Rosita squeaked and got to her knees. "I felt one. A snake. Our house is full of snakes."

"I think they're gone. Besides, it was only one. A tall one, maybe."

"We need to get outside."

"I chased the snake out of the hut. It might be out there in the dark, waiting for us." I felt around where I had whacked at the snake, touched something and jerked my hand back. When it didn't rattle the leaves with movement, I figured it was dead, so I touched it again. "Maybe it wasn't a snake after all. Are there rats in the jungle?"

"Yes."

"Then I think I killed a rat."

"Probably not. Rats are too smart to get themselves killed so easily."

I picked up the dead thing. It felt light as a leaf, though it filled my hand. The thing felt warm and furry. "Here, touch it. I have the animal I smashed to death right here in my hand."

"No. Quick, Don, throw the nasty thing outside. Maybe you only stunned it, and it could wake up and bite you." Her voice had a frantic sound to it. She rattled around with the palmetto fans we used for a door, and I tossed the creature outside.

"It's gone now. But I'm sure it's dead."

"Then we'll inspect it in the morning. Sit here beside me. We need to stay awake in case the thing that came in after us returns."

I settled beside her, and she clutched me. I put an arm around her and braced the other against my leg. That's when I felt something slippery—in the same area where I had worn the bandage until the catfish got it. "I think my leg is bleeding again."

"It's time to get out of the hut," she said. "We'll make a fire, if the wood you covered stayed dry enough."

Outside there was a faint glow from the moon and stars filtering through trees and reflecting from the river. The jungle whistled with a million frogs, and other things made noises in the night. I stood beside Rosita as she knelt to uncover the firewood and feel around for the right materials to start her fire. Soon she moved in a rhythmic way, and I heard the swish of the fire stick. Only the bare outline of her was visible, but from the sounds she made, I knew what she was doing. Soon a red glow appeared and Rosita blew into the heat. The glow vanished and she muttered something that was lost among the soprano sounds of the jungle. I heard her resume working with the stick. The glow appeared again, then vanished. "Carumba," she said, and again spun the fire stick. When red appeared again, she managed to coax it into a tiny tongue of flame, then another. Soon she had a fire going, and she told me to turn so she could see my leg.

"I think I'm still bleeding."

"You are. Not much, though." She picked up a stick, held it in the fire until the end of it was aflame, then turned, holding the burning stick like a torch. "Where's the rat you killed?"

"I threw it over there."

She crouched, holding the torch away from her, and we both searched the ground. "There," she said. "It is a rat. Stop that. Don't pick it up."

I held the creature between finger and thumb. It unfolded. "A bird," I said, amazed that some sort of night bird would come into our hut.

"Not a bird," Rosita thrust the torch close to it. "A bat. A vampire bat."

I dropped the vampire and stepped back. "But it didn't bite me

157

on the neck. It's just a regular bat."

"My grandmother said such bats once lived in the jungle close to El Tigrito, back when she was a girl and the village was small. People killed them. She said they liked to find a donkey or a cow in the night, bite it enough to make it bleed, then gather around the wound and lap blood like dogs lapping water."

"That's disgusting."

"Yes. It means there were many of them in our house, crawling around on your leg to get at the blood. My grandmother said the bats liked to return to the same animal night after night and reopen the same wound. It's quite disgusting."

"They took me for a donkey or a cow. That's the disgusting part."

"We need to leave this area of the jungle as soon as it's light enough to see."

"Our hut didn't leak. I'd like to stay here for a while longer and catch one of the giant catfish."

"You would stay after being bitten by vampires?"

"Why not? I've had worse things happen to me."

"What could be worse than that?

"Once I got worms in my head. Maggots. The kids in San Tomé called me 'maggoty headed,' which made me mad at them."

"That was merely a jungle fly that stung you to lay its eggs. That isn't as bad as being attacked by a flock of blood-licking bats."

"The bats made only a tiny scratch, one that didn't hurt at all. We can patch up the hut, make it tight enough to keep the bats out, and stay a few more days—until the hut starts to leak, like we agreed."

"The hut leaked already. It leaked bats, which is worse than leaking water." Her voice seemed thin, and suddenly I realized she was on the verge of crying.

"Leaked bats? That's true. Then we must leave in the morning."

"Yes." She sniffed a few times. "Now. Come with me so I can put some ash on the place where the vampire bats bit you."

14
Quicksand

We kept a fire going to scare away the vampires. "If we had some garlic," I said, "we could tie it around our necks to keep vampires away. A crucifix would work, also."

"Whatever are you talking about?" Rosita demanded.

We sat beside the fire to await the coming of the sun. I poked embers with a stick. "Vampires. The kind that turn into men and bite you on the neck."

"You believe that?"

"Not exactly," I hedged. "But since seeing a movie with a spooky-looking man named Bella Lagoosie, sometimes I get scared in the night. He had long teeth, and he liked to bite people on the neck."

"Why would you think garlic would keep away vampire bats?"

"I saw it in a movie one Saturday night in San Tomé."

"I've never seen a movie. They have movies in cities, I've heard. In Caracas. My father said he once saw a movie in Puerto La Cruz. He said the wheels on the wagon moved in the wrong direction—they spun backward when the wagon went forward, and everyone in the movie house laughed. But there are no movie houses in the villages. I don't ever want to see a movie if they lie about how wheels move and if they're about men who bite you on the neck."

"Not all movies are about vampires. Some are about people who like to dance in the rain." I wanted to explain about the wheels, but it was a problem that stumped me, also. Todd said the wagon wheels only seemed to move the wrong direction, that going around backwards was a trick the movie maker pulled, though he didn't know why a movie maker would want to pull such a stupid trick.

"Dance in the rain? Whatever for?"

"I don't know. My brother and I usually go to the pickup to watch for falling stars when there's too much dancing. He likes the comedies about clever mice who know how to burn up cats and skin them and mash them flat, but I would rather watch for falling stars."

159

"Mashed cats and stars that fall? I don't understand movies."

"Who does?" I shrugged, realizing the gesture was lost in the darkness and that I couldn't explain movies to a native girl who had never seen one. Movies didn't seem so mysterious to me—except for the wheels that spun wrong. Movies merely seemed wrong, like the mouse that tortured the cat. Or stupid like the skinny man who danced too much to music that came out of nowhere. The best thing about a movie was the popcorn, but I found that I couldn't explain that to Rosita, either.

"Do you think a crucifix would keep the little bats from biting your leg in the night? I don't. A crucifix is just something people use to help them think about God. It's a piece of carved wood—or plaster, sometimes. Bats would take no notice of either wood or plaster that you might have lying around. They would fly in, land near your leg and make it bleed, then sip the blood. Garlic wouldn't help, either, I don't think."

"In the movie, a crucifix works. So does the garlic, but not as well. Movie vampires are different from jungle vampires." I wanted to stop talking about movies, so I clammed up. Rosita seemed through asking about them, which was a relief since she didn't seem to understand anything I said.

Morning came sooner than I expected, and with it the voice of the wild woman chanting. "Probably," I told Rosita, "there aren't any headhunters over there."

She gave me a curious look. "Don't talk. Just listen." We listened to the chant, faint and strange, until morning flooded the jungle with light and shadows, and the voice stopped.

Rosita examined the place on my leg where vampires lapped blood. She smeared some more ash on the scratch and said she would make a bandage later. "We must load our basket with bananas and guava."

"And bones."

"Yes, those first. Also the rope from our canoe. Then we hike to the guava tree, then to the banana trees. After that, I plan to kill some vampires."

"You have to drive a wooden stake through a vampire's heart to kill it," I warned.

"No you don't." She retrieved the basket from our hut.

"Yes you do. A stake in the heart is the proper way to kill a vampire."

"Where did you learn that?"

I wanted to say from a movie, but it didn't seem like a good idea to bring up that subject again. "I just know it. That's all."

"Then you can use wooden stakes, if you want. I plan to go about it differently."

"Vampires hide in coffins during the day. We'll never find one."

"Coffins? Oh. You're talking about movies again. Remember what you said: jungle vampires are different from movie vampires. There won't be any coffins around here."

"Then where will you find the vampires to kill?"

"In the hollow tree. You remember."

"Those were just bats."

"Vampire bats. We're going to kill them."

She moved about with a determination that convinced me not to argue. I followed her to the guava tree, which wasn't a tree so much as a bush. She found only four guavas that satisfied her, picked them and put them into the basket, then led the way to the stand of bananas, where we ran the monkeys into the trees and took the bananas we wanted. She looked under banana leaves until she found another dry, half-rotting log. "Help me carry some firewood," she said.

"Are we going to catch a fish and cook it for breakfast?"

"No. We'll eat breakfast on the other side of the swamp. Right now we're going to take care of that nest of vampire bats."

"Burn them to death?" I wasn't sure I wanted to burn up the bats. As we carried wood toward the hollow tree, I imagined myself turning into a bat like Bella the vampire man in the movie and flying into the hollow tree. People with torches came after me in the night, their eyes red from the flickering light and scary music getting louder and louder as they approached my tree. They set the tree on fire and the flames shot up the inside of the tree, coming after me. I managed to fly through the fire, though it singed off my eyebrows and toenails. Out there in the dark they were waiting for me with sharp stakes and hammers. One man swatted me out of the air with rocks tied to a string. As I fell to the ground, all the villagers jumped on me, Simón in the lead with a hammer the size of an axe and a stake so sharp its point glinted in the firelight. "We'll bury his body in the jungle," he said as he put the stake to my heart and pounded on it with his sledge hammer. Black blood spurted like a fountain and someone said, "Now there's one less thief in the world." The people drew back in horror as I changed from a bat to a boy with purple hair.

"I don't think we should burn the bats," I told Rosita.

"Yes we should." She spoke with such conviction that I fell silent, replaying the scene of the villagers and the fire, and this time it was Rosita who drove the stake into my heart, her long hair cascading around her face as she looked down at me and her nude body glowing bronze in the flicker of torchlight.

She stopped abruptly and I nearly ran into her. "I'll make a fire while you stack the wood over the entryway to the tree."

I threw down the wood. "No."

"No?" She looked at me, her head tilted at an angle like dogs tilt their heads when they almost understand you but don't quite.

"They're just little bats trying to make a living out in the jungle. They don't even have a regular cave. It's wrong to kill them."

"You killed one already. Was that wrong?"

"It was an accident."

"You slugged it to death with your fists, and that was an accident?"

"I thought it was a snake come in the night to bite me to death. If I had known it was a bat, I would have shooed it out of the hut instead of killing it."

"It bit your leg. It drank your blood."

I jutted out my jaw. "It's wrong."

"You caught a catfish and helped me kill it. You didn't think it was wrong when I killed the rabbit."

"We ate them. I don't plan on eating roasted bats."

"They're vermin." She set about making a fire. "They might come after you again tonight. They might drink all of your blood and leave you like a dead stick or a dried-up sack of bones. We're moving out of their jungle neighborhood. They'll have to find other donkeys for their midnight snacks."

"We're not moving if we don't find a way across that swamp. And I am not a donkey."

162

"Donkeys are stubborn." She got a small fire going, then piled all the wood we brought over the entrance to the bat tree. I could tell by the set of her face and the tension in her shoulders that she was angry, but I still wouldn't help burn up the bats. She carried burning sticks to the bat tree. "Killing vampire bats isn't wrong. I'll bet if Evita Perón were here right now, she would help me set this fire to rid the jungle of them."

"And Evita is a saint?"

"Yes."

As soon as the first wisp of smoke went up the hollow of the tree, bats started fluttering around inside, knocking against the tree. I moved farther back so I wouldn't have to hear their death agony. Rosita let the fire burn for a while, then threw green leaves into the flames as if she were cooking another catfish. The fire changed to white smoke that flowed like heavy fog into the tree, then leaked out of it, running up the outside of the tree. She picked up a stick that looked about the right size for driving into a vampire's heart and scattered the firewood.

"Did you change your mind?" I asked.

"No. I don't want to set the tree on fire because it might spread to other trees in the jungle. The bats are dead from the smoke, so there's no reason to keep the fire going."

I thought about being one of the bats inside the tree when all the smoke fogged around me. The other bats started making little hacking sounds that bats make when they cough, and they started dropping. It was like being under water only worse because the river water didn't sting my eyes that much when the waterfall dunked me under or when the giant catfish dragged me deep into the river. I could breath inside the tree, but it wasn't air, and I coughed some bat coughs, then fell to the floor of the tree on top of the other bats, who were all dead. I started changing from a bat into a purple-haired boy inside the tree as Rosita began scattering the fire.

"These vampires won't ever bite your leg again," Rosita said. "Come look."

"I won't look at them." I told myself a couple of more times that I didn't want to see the corpses of the bats, but it didn't do any good because even as I told myself that, I was walking over and bending

163

down for a look. Bats filled the bottom of the tree, though they didn't look much like bats. They looked more like dead leaves with ears.

"Come on, donkey boy. Pick up the basket and let's wade through the swamp. Bring your stick in case we find snakes, and I'll carry the machete."

I shouldered the basket, picked up my stick, and followed her, feeling numb. Rosita whittled and hacked on trees along the way, and she gathered some leaves, but I didn't pay much attention to her. She was doing native things, mysterious things, things that killers of bats liked to do in the jungle. I mainly kept my eyes on my vine shoes, trying to recapture yesterday's enthusiasm for the leaves on them and trying not to think about the dead bats that turned into leaves with ears. When we got to the place where a small ridge protruded into the swamp, Rosita said:

"Stand still for a moment. I need to put a bandage on your leg, one that won't wash off in the swamp." She dropped to one knee and started tying leaves and a poultice to my leg, using strips of bark that would work as catfish twine if it were braided. I held the basket of dead Indios on my shoulder and watched her work. The anger was gone from her face and shoulders, and she didn't look so hard and metallic as she had when she drove the stake into my heart and the torchlight glinted on her skin. In fact, the way her hair fell around her face was beautiful. "Are you still mad at me?" she asked.

"Why did you call me donkey boy? Because the bats mistook me for a donkey?"

She stood, her job with the bandage complete. "Donkeys are stubborn, and you are one stubborn purple-haired kid."

"And you're not?"

"No. My hair is black. But stubborn? Yes. You may call me donkey girl." A faint smile played along the edges of her mouth. "Are you ready to cross the swamp?"

Before, when we had no plans to wade into it, the swamp looked like a lake of slick water. It seemed harmless, even pretty with its trees and orchids. But as we stood beside it the waters seemed to be black with shadows, and I noticed more tree stumps than live trees protruding from the water. "I wish we could be Jesus frogs for a while," I said.

"Then we would hop across the water, do you mean? I would carry the machete in my mouth and you would carry the basket on your back. We would hop fast so nothing in the swamp could catch us."

The water seemed to get blacker. "Black caimán live in the water," I said. "We'd better have a couple of bananas handy to toss to them when they come looking for a leg to bite off."

"I think not. Caimán like swampy inlets with fish. They like to live closer to the river." She waded into the edge of the water.

"What about our jungle shoes?"

"Keep them on. Mine are nearly worn out and yours are not good ones. I'll make us some more on the other side."

"If a caimán comes after us, I'll jump on its back and wrestle it better than Mamacita Moreno wrestles drunk men that try to hurt girls."

"Come on. Hold my hand so we can steady each other." She held out her hand. I took it and we started toward the heart of the swamp. "Don't splash much, and keep your stick ready." She held up the machete as if she expected some monster to come popping out of the black water at any moment.

The water looked dark, but it was crystal clear, like that in the bowl held by the plants where minnows lived and Jesus frogs walked on water. The dark mat of leaves covering the bottom reminded me of the bat poop we walked on to gather ancient bones. We went a long way in water not much deeper than our ankles, past trees and stumps and an occasional bush that didn't look too happy about having to live in such black water. I didn't worry much until the water became deeper. As we walked, it crept up to our knees in a slow tickle.

A row of turtles stood like statues on a half-sunk log. When we approached, they slid into the water and vanished, only to reappear a few meters away, their heads seeming to float like sticks. "Some turtles like to bite," I said.

"They're afraid of us." Rosita's response had a reassuring certainty to it.

Still, I found myself remembering turtle stories, none of them good. "A snapping turtle will grab you with its sharp beak and won't let go until it thunders."

"Did you learn that from a vampire movie?"

"You can't tell the size of a turtle from looking at its head, and that's all you can see when it comes up to breathe. Some turtles get as big as washtubs. A turtle that size could swim right up to us."

"If one does, we'll catch it and tie it up with the rope from the canoe and drag it to the savannah with us. There we'll cook it up and eat it."

"Eat a turtle?" The notion seemed weird to me, though it made snapping turtles less scary. The water became deeper, well over my knees. "Here comes a turtle," I pointed, "Swimming directly toward us."

"That turtle has a long tail." Rosita released my hand and took the machete in both hands, holding it up as if she planned to behead someone. When I looked again at the swimming turtle, it had become a snake longer than my arm, and it seemed to be interested in Rosita. She waited until it was less than a meter away before bringing down the machete. The blade sliced into the water with barely a splash. Black snake coils churned the water for a few seconds. When the snake became still, it seemed suspended below the surface, two pieces of it, and the water turned pink around it. "If this were the river," Rosita said, "that blood would attract cannibal fish. But this isn't the river."

She took my hand again, and we gave the dead snake and its pink water a wide berth. "A baba." Rosita pointed at a log.

It took me a few moments to see the alligator since it wasn't much longer than my foot. It looked like a toy with a glittering black eye. "If there are baba here, then there will be other alligators. A giant black caimán, perhaps."

"No," Rosita said. "There are plenty of babas in the river beside our village, but there are no caimanes like the one that came after me when the ants made my legs jump into the river."

"Electric eels, then. Don't they like to live in swamps?" I remembered Dad telling me that they lived in the still part of the river, among reeds. A quick glance around confirmed what I already knew: there were no reeds in the swamp. The presence of trees we walked among indicated the swamp was dry only days before the coming of rainy season.

Rosita ignored my question about electric eels. We waded on, the water coming up to our waists. "This isn't good," she said. "I thought the water would be shallow. Soon we will be swimming, and I'll have to put the machete into the basket in order to do that."

An animal with a head shaggier than a dog's swam toward us, and Rosita moved closer to me. The creature looked something like pictures of beaver I had seen, but it couldn't be a beaver, I thought. Beaver like to live in icy places. "Will it bite?" I asked.

"That is a capybara, a large one. My grandmother said the capybara is the king of rats, though it doesn't behave much like its nasty smaller cousins. Mestizos like to eat capybaras."

The animal veered off when it got close enough to look us over, and I was glad for that since it looked as if it might weigh nearly as much as I did, and it swam much better than I ever could. "I don't want to eat a capybara," I said.

We pushed on, the water becoming more shallow and the bottom softer. Black water bugs zipped around in circles like miniature speedboats, and spindly-looking bugs with spider legs ran like Jesus frogs on the surface. As the water level dropped to our knees, we could see the other shore of the swamp. Rosita gripped my hand and whispered, "A family of deer. They're beautiful."

They stood at the edge of the swamp, nosing the water then looking up, regarding us with huge eyes: one adult with antlers, the other without, and the baby wearing speckles on its sides. We waded on, the swamp becoming shallower, and we were watching the deer when we stepped into the sucking mud.

The squashy bottom grabbed my feet. I managed one small step before being unable to lift either leg. "Quicksand," Rosita said in a thin voice.

But that didn't make sense. Close to us stood a tree, and it showed no signs of being sucked into quicksand. Beside it was a broken stump of a tree with jagged edges of trunk sticking up around a hollow center—and it, too, stood firm. How could we be in quicksand that close to ground solid enough to hold a tree and a stump?

The water climbed up over our knees as we struggled. "Trying to step out makes it worse." I heard fear in my voice.

"The rope," Rosita said.

I took the basket from my shoulders, opened it, and pulled out the rope. Then I secured the lid and threw the basket into the center of the hollowed-out tree stump. "Take one end," I directed. "Let's try to loop the rope over part of that dead tree." We each held an end of the rope and tried to flip it as if we were beginning to swing a jump-rope. It caught in the water behind us and barely cleared our heads, falling short of the stump by half a meter. We continued to sink. Our second try was worse.

The mud or sand kept sucking us down, or maybe we were sinking into it from our own weight. Water rose above our waists, so it was necessary to hold our arms high in attempting to toss the rope. Again the loop fell short. I gathered the rope in my right hand, holding one end in my left. "When I throw, lean as far as you dare," I said.

"Hurry."

Good advice, I thought, given the rate we were going down. It would be our last chance to throw the rope before we went under. I threw the central part of the rope and we leaned forward, each gripping an end. The rope caught on one of the jagged teeth of the stump.

"Lie forward in the water," Rosita said, "and pull steady but not hard. Don't jerk the rope." The bog tugged us deeper into itself, and water reached our chins. We pulled as Rosita said we should, and leaned, and I felt the mud letting me slide out of it. Our movement was slow, too slow to suit me, especially when the tooth of the stump began making cracking sounds. "If that breaks," Rosita said, "we'll be pulled under."

"We'll die."

"Don't say it. Don't even think it." Her voice carried command and power, and I thought maybe her voice alone might be enough to get us out of the bog. The tree cracked some more, but we kept pulling, moving hand-over-hand along the rope. Mud still had a grip on my feet when the stump splintered and the rope went slack. I began to slide back into the bog. "I'm nearly out," Rosita said. "Give me a push."

I released the rope, put my hands under her arms, and pushed her toward the stump. Doing so sank me to my armpits, but it freed her. She kicked up to the surface, swam to the stump and climbed into its hollow center. Her body looked black and slick, like the fur of a black dog emerging wet from a lake. "Spiders. There must be a hundred of them in the middle of the tree." She pulled on the rope, found it slack. "You let go of the rope," she said in alarm. "Here, catch it."

When I caught the rope, only my head and arms were above water. She leaned back, bracing herself, and began a steady pull. "I hate spiders," she muttered again and again: "I hate spiders."

I moved toward the stump and felt the bog with great reluctance releasing its grip. Bubbles came up behind me as the sticky part of the swamp gave up its attempt to consume me. I dog-paddled in the shallow water to the stump and pulled myself, with Rosita's help, into the center of it. "There's spiders all over the place in here." I climbed out on the shore-side of the stump.

"I told you." She picked up the basket and joined me. The bottom felt spongy, but it held. "You're covered in mud," she said as we waded ashore.

I looked at myself. Almost my whole body was slicked over with mud, slimy and black. Rosita looked even worse. "Pigs," I said. "We look like a couple of pigs."

15
The House of the Jungle Witch

"The swamp," Rosita said, "is beautiful. The colors in the trees, look at them. Different shades of green and all of them so intense. On this side, the jungle is a garden. Did orchids grow in the trees on the other side of the swamp?"

"Yes. But they were smaller and not so pretty." I looked into the shrubs where the deer had gone. The area there had none of the gigantic trees we found on the shores farther up river, but the smaller trees were the best ones I ever saw in a jungle. The underbrush looked inviting rather than impenetrable. I glanced at Rosita. "You look wonderful."

"I'm covered with mud."

"Good mud. Clean mud—not like the mud in the bat cave."

"You're right." She walked around me, inspecting the mud that slicked most of my body. "What terrific mud. We can wear it instead of clothes. I don't have to chop grass and weave a covering for our bodies since we're covered already."

The sound of her laughter seemed pure music. Even the swamp, so sinister just minutes ago when the bog tried to eat us, was lovely. How could I ever have thought it an ugly place? I stepped back into the water, taking care that the bottom felt solid, and sat down. "On this side the swamp is a clean place—except for that bog beyond the tree stump."

Rosita settled in the water beside me. "I didn't put the machete into the basket, did I?"

"No."

"Then the bog has it."

"The bog swallowed the machete? Better the jungle knife than either of the wild kids from El Tigrito." I began rubbing mud from my legs.

"I'll help you." She splashed water on my back and rubbed. "It comes off easier than I thought."

We washed each other until we had removed all of the bog mud. Then we splashed as if we were in a swimming pool. Suddenly she became still. "Stop playing," she commanded. "Someone

171

watches us."

"Who?"

"I don't know."

We stood close together, dripping, and looked at the shore. "I don't see anyone," I said.

"Perhaps it was my imagination." She tried for a smile. "Remember the bandage I said wouldn't come off your leg? The bog got it."

"So it ate the machete and the bandage. Oh—and our shoes. We can do without those things."

She moved some strands of hair around on my head. "Even your purple hair looks good to me right now."

"Your black hair is wild and good." I shifted a lock of her hair from her forehead.

"I must make another bandage for your leg. When I rubbed the mud from your leg, I saw that the place where the vampires bit you is still trying to bleed." She took my hand and led me out of the water. "It'll be less easy without a knife. You must help me. See those leaves?" She pointed to a bush. "Gather about ten of them and crush them up. I'll strip this vine." She plucked a string-thin vine from another bush and began pinching away its greenery.

I gathered leaves and wadded them up. "It's just a little scratch. I say we leave it alone."

"We can't ignore a jungle scratch. Remember what my grandmother said?"

"This isn't a jungle anymore. It's a garden. You said so."

"The most beautiful garden in the world. And yet we must still tend to wounds." She picked a broad leaf with green and red ribs. "This will do for the covering. Give me the crushed leaves." She knelt beside me, held the leaves against the vampire scratch and bound them in place with the vine she had stripped. "That isn't so good, but we won't be wading in any more swamps for a while."

"Not ever. At least not in ones that like to swallow people."

"Would you like to eat breakfast now?"

"Eat?" I looked at the basket and the canoe rope beside it. "Bananas and guava. Maybe not right now? I don't feel hungry."

"Neither do I."

"Then let's explore."

"I should make us some clothes. People live close to here. At least one person does—the woman who sang to the morning sun."

"I don't want clothes."

"I know. Neither do I. But we'll have to put some on sooner or later."

"Later suits me just fine." I picked up the rope, coiled it, and put it into the basket. The sight of the bones and the fruit tumbled together gave me a start. "One of the little bananas is sticking in the eye of the dead Indio. Maybe we shouldn't eat fruit that has been stuck in a dead person's eye." I remembered Mom saying that bones of the dead can give you diseases. "Maybe we shouldn't eat any fruit that has been rubbing against dead fingers and toes."

"We'll throw the fruit away, if you want. But we ought to keep it until we find something better."

I shouldered the basket. "The bog also ate my walking stick."

"We'll watch for another. The jungle garden will be full of good sticks."

We surveyed the jungle, looking for the least dense place so we could head for the savannah. "That almost looks like a trail going up the side of that hill," I said.

"Perhaps it is a trail." Rosita took my hand and dropped her voice to a whisper. "Someone is there. Maybe something. I don't know."

"Where?"

"I don't know."

We climbed the hill, walking on what seemed to be a trail, ducking under lianes and broad-leafed bushes hanging over us. I kept an eye out, searching among ferns and bamboo for whatever Rosita felt was out there. A cat, maybe. A big one of the type that my neighbors in El Tigrito said ate some little kids from another village out west. Little kids, I repeated to myself, remembering what Dad had said about my being too tough and stringy for a jungle cat to want to eat. Still, it would be good to have a weapon of some kind. I tried without success to break a stick of bamboo. "Leave it," Rosita said. "The leaves will slice your hands."

"I would rather cut my hands than have a jungle cat eat me."

"What?" Rosita looked at me, puzzled.

I was about to explain when the trail leveled off and we came to a small clearing with a tree that had fallen. On the tree sat a naked woman. She smiled. Two of her front teeth were missing, and her eye teeth gleamed white and sinister. Also, she had enormous tetas. Rosita stepped closer to me, almost in front of me. "You're a sign from heaven," the woman said.

"You're naked." I tried not to look at her eye teeth. When she closed her mouth, she looked good, for a wild woman. She caught me looking at her breasts and smiled again. I stepped back.

"I saw you emerge from the swamp, naked and black with the afterbirth of the swamp's womb. It seemed best to receive you as you come to me, without clothes."

"Are you the one who sings to the morning sun?" Rosita asked.

"Afterbirth?" I said.

"You heard my prayers, then. I stood above the new waters of the swamp and asked the heavens for a sign. You heard and came." She smiled again, and this time I saw that she did have front teeth. They were stained and hard to see, unlike her eyeteeth. I was glad to see them, though, for they make her look less spooky. With the appearance of her teeth, the rest of her began to look more normal. Her hair, like Rosita's, had a black sheen to it, though it was more curly and much longer. I liked her crystal brown eyes, the color of a raw cashew, but clear. Likely Dad would have described her nose as Negroid, a term he always applied to people with darker skin than the naked woman had. She had full, round lips, big ones, and hollows in her cheeks that almost dimpled when she smiled.

"We should have on clothes," Rosita said.

"You should be just as you are, beautiful and innocent and without sin. Will you be guests in my home?" The woman stood, and I was astounded to see a dark triangle of matted hair below her navel. When I looked again at her face, she seemed amused. "You have never seen adults, have you?"

"Yes. But never, uh, never with such hair." My cheeks felt hot.

"I meant nude adults, of course. Your mate will have such hair in time. You blush." The woman sighed. "I'm sorry we live in a fallen world. Sorry and glad. Would it comfort you if I put on clothes?" She picked up a gray cloth, soiled and old, from the log where she had been sitting. It seemed as if she snatched it by some magic out of the gray bark of the log. With a quick motion she wrapped herself in the cloth, tying it under her breasts.

"Perhaps," Rosita glanced at me and said, "You should tie that over your breasts."

The woman chuckled and retied the cloth, covering most of her chest. "I am no threat to you and your mate." She held her hands out to us. "You will call me Sylvia."

"Rosita. I am Rosita. This is my friend, Don. Not El Don. His name is Don. We should be wearing clothes."

"No, we shouldn't," I said.

"He is from north America, and he has some strange ideas. But he's good. He is the best."

"Don who is not El Don wears a bandage. I watched you make it, Rosita. You have the gift of healing, I can tell, and someone has taught you well. I could teach you even more. You knew I watched from the covering of the jungle, and you knew not to be frightened. What caused Don's wound?"

"Rosita and I are glad to meet you, Miss Sylvia. We will now be going on our way." I took Rosita's hand and tried to get her to go with me down the path. She resisted.

"Bats. Vampire bats came to him in the night."

"A colony of them lives somewhere in the swamp, and they are a bother to the cattle of the villagers. But none will hunt them down because they are afraid of this part of the river, especially when the swamp comes, bringing the black caimán. Will you be guests in my home for a day or two?"

"We're trying to find our way home," Rosita said. "Perhaps you can direct us?"

"Where is home?"

"Our village is El Tigrito."

"It's far away, but I've been there. I can help you return. Will you be my guests until you must depart?"

Rosita looked at me. "I would like to go with her, Don. Not for long because I'm worried about my family. But we need to agree on what we'll do."

"Our adventure in the jungle is over, then." I sighed. "And it's time to go home."

"Not yet," Sylvia said. "There are good adventures for you here, before you must leave."

"Adventures with adult rules. Clothes to wear. A house to sleep in. We'll have to go back to pretending to hunt lions, Rosita. It makes me sad."

"Not here, you won't have to pretend." Sylvia put her hand on the knot holding the gray cloth around her. "And if you wish to go without clothes, that is just fine with me. I'll do it, too, if you want."

"No," Rosita said. "It isn't right for adults to go naked. Where's your village?"

"I live with my daughter farther down the river. Right now I'm visiting some people near here because they have need of my services. I am a curandera."

"A bruja," I said. A witch. I had heard there were witches out west. "Wow."

"Oh, Don," Rosita said.

"It's all right, Rosita. Many people call me bruja. Perhaps I am—but if so, I'm a good one. It's my job to be healer to the people who need me. My job here is almost finished. Stay with me two days, and we'll travel together as far as my regular home. We'll help each other."

"Will you stay, Don?" Rosita asked.

"In the jungle house of a bruja? Yes."

"We will, then. But we must have clothes before going into the village."

"The curandera's house isn't in the village. I think the people have always feared me and my kind. Years ago, they built a house out of sight from their village for the curandera to stay in when she comes. It once was my aunt's house when she visited the village. Now it's mine. The villagers will leave us alone. None come except when they're sick and in need of healing. I doubt they'll even notice your presence, so you can dress as you wish around my home. Or not dress, as you like." She led us up the trail.

"A secret house with a witch," I whispered to Rosita. "This is great."

"Why do you invite us to your home?" Rosita asked.

"Because you must be the sign I prayed for. If I can understand why the spirit of the sun sent a purple-haired white child and an angelic mestizo, then perhaps I'll know what to do with a certain man who troubles me."

176

"Did you understand that?" I whispered to Rosita. She shook her head.

Sylvia's house stood in the dense shade of mango trees, their large leaves brushing the thatch and hanging over several of the windows. Beyond the house a thicket of bamboo shot four meters into the air, forming an effective fence. Rising beyond the bamboo fence were palm trees and rosewoods. Likely the village was that direction, toward the river, I thought. Off to the left stretched the savannah, rolling and vast, all the way to the horizon. Wisps of grass and low shrubs with wrinkled and colorful leaves grew around the house, some of them sprouting from the thatching on the roof. Walls of the house had been patted into place with red mud and grass, and the windows and door looked rounded and too small. "A gingerbread house," I said. Rosita glanced at me with arched brows, but she remained silent. We followed Sylvia through the door into the cool, dark interior, stepping down as we had done in Mamacita Moreno's place when we went on the bean run for El Loco. The dirt floor felt cold to my bare feet, and it was as solid as cement.

The interior was much larger than I expected. Several chinchorros hung on one wall, folded to be out of the way. A table with three chairs stood beneath one of the windows, all rough-hewn from jungle trees and bound together with bark fiber. A kind of wild divan covered with a grass mat sat beside a cupboard with drawers. There was no other furniture. "We sleep in here," Sylvia said, "in the chinchorros. Sometimes when villagers come to seek my help, you will stay in the next room. There is a loft," she pointed above a wall, "accessible from a ladder in the other room. Out the back door is a well with good water, and the toilet is just down the hill beside a wall of bamboo. In that cupboard are bread, eggs, and bananas. I'll make some cookies for you this afternoon and keep them in the cupboard. You may eat when you're hungry, and you may have whatever is in the house. Or you may find fruit in the jungle. Right now there are guavas, bananas, and some papayas. Mangoes, of course, are not in season." She opened the cupboard. "On this side are my medicinal herbs. Do not eat these. Some are dangerous if not prepared in the right way. Look at them, if you want. Explore anything in and around the house as if it were your own. There are no rules here, and we'll live together as equals for the short time the

177

heavens have put us together. Do you have any questions?"

"Wow," I said. "No rules."

"We need clothes," Rosita said.

"Need?" Sylvia seemed amused. "I think not. But if you want clothes," she opened a drawer in the lower part of the cupboard and took out a red-and-white cloth, "tie this around you. I'll sew some pants and a simple shirt for Don in case a villager comes and he wants to dress. But it might be better if you stayed out of sight until we can decide what to do about your hair."

"I told you the hair would be a problem," Rosita said.

"What's wrong with my hair?"

"Nothing," Sylvia said. "It is exactly as it should be. But the villagers will be frightened, especially finding you here in the home of the curandera. For their sake, we will either dye your hair or cover it with a cap."

"I thought there were no rules."

Sylvia shrugged. "Leave it, then. If the people are frightened, so be it. There is one man who is unpredictable. We'll have to watch him."

"Is he dangerous?" Rosita asked.

"Yes. But not as you might imagine. He thinks he's here to teach the people about God, but he knows little of God. He is a white man from the north, and he calls himself a missionary. This man hates me, though I don't know why, and he also wants something from me. Perhaps you two will help me come to some understanding of him and what to do about him."

"You will help us find our way back to El Tigrito soon?" Rosita looked worried.

"I'll calm your worries about your family. Perhaps tonight."

For the remainder of the morning, Rosita was content to make clothes for us. I watched her for a while as she used scissors and thread to make a simple dress, then endured her laying black cloth across my back and bottom to make me a weird pair of shorts with a single black suspender running over one shoulder. While she worked, I examined the contents of the witch's cupboard, but found it disappointing. Mostly it was dried sticks, mushrooms, twigs, and leaves.

Sylvia went outside to build a fire under a griddle, then

178

returned to mix flour and water and other powdery things. Her notion of baking cookies was to cook them like Mom cooks pancakes. For a witch, she didn't do particularly witchy things. Or she didn't until the man came to have his son cured from losing his soul.

By that time, we had eaten the best pancake-cookies in all of Venezuela; we had dressed in Rosita's strange sewings, and we checked out the rest of the house, including the loft. It was an area no bigger than my El Tigrito bed, made from rough-cut timber, the cracks smoothed with adobe. A woven lattice of sticks running from the top of the wall to the thatching of the roof separated the loft from the living room. Rosita and I found we could lie on the floor of the loft and peek into the witch's main den without being seen on account of the lattice work. We could barely sit up because of the roof being so close, but that was okay by me since the tight quarters gave me the sense of hiding in a tiny tree house. Sylvia sent us to the loft when she saw the man coming with his son. "Remain quiet," she warned us. "Watch and learn."

Lying on the loft with Rosita beside me and watching through the woven sticks reminded me of how we had hidden in high savannah grass, peeping out at El Loco and the bandits who came to tax him out of his gold. Below us stood Sylvia and a man wearing clothes made from flour sacks. His son sat on the divan looking wild-eyed. His jaw was open and twisted to one side. Spit dripped from the corner of his mouth, stringing down to his shoulder and making him look moronic. "Julio went to the cemetery last night," the man said, "with some other boys. They peed on a grave and laughed about it. Then a ghost put his hand on the shoulders of the boys. An icy hand, they said. All of them ran back to the village except for Julio, who tried to look at the ghost. You can see what happened to his jaw. He cannot close his mouth, and he cannot speak."

"He suffers from loss of soul," Sylvia said. "But his soul isn't gone. It hangs suspended in the air beside him, part of it still hung in his mouth. It leaped from his body in fright when the ghost touched him. I'll conjure his soul back into his body." She sat beside the boy, who looked at her with his frightened, wild eyes. He seemed to be about my age, perhaps younger. Sylvia the witch began humming a tune I had never heard. She sat Julio in her lap, though he was almost too large for that, and her humming turned into a chant as she drew his head to her shoulder. As she chanted, she rocked and patted Julio, and some of her words became clear.

"Relax my sweet my child and sleep and dream sweet dreams of Mary. Relax my child my sweet and feel the love of heaven." Sylvia hummed and chanted and rocked until I almost went to sleep watching. Rosita drew closer to me and rested her cheek on my arm. She did go to sleep, I could tell from her regular breathing. Just as I was about to doze off, Sylvia stood and handed the boy to his father. Julio's mouth looked normal, and his eyes drooped in fatigue. "Take him home." Sylvia patted Julio's head and said some more words in a chant, then addressed the father again: "Let him sleep, if he wants. When he awakens, feed him warm bread, and do not punish him for going to the cemetery. He has been punished enough."

"Should we give him herbs?" the father asked.

"No. Give him hugs. Tell him that he is the best son anyone could have."

"The white brujo from the north will not be pleased. Mr. Marlin wanted to give Julio laxative, but the boy couldn't swallow anything. He also wanted me to beat him to knock the devil out of him."

"Julio has no devil in him, and he needs no herbs."

"Mr. Marlin will not be pleased."

"Are you pleased that I have conjured Julio's soul back into his body and restored your son's jaw? Are you pleased that he sleeps in your arms with the sleep of an angel?"

"Yes."

"Then don't worry about Marlin." Sylvia patted the man's shoulder and ushered him out the door.

"Sylvia is the best curandera ever," Rosita whispered. She yawned. "She knows good magic."

"Magic?" I considered the notion. "Was that magic?"

"Yes."

"All she did was hold him and rock him and sing to him."

"Yes."

"Do you believe Julio's soul jumped out of his mouth?" The

180

idea was so comical to me that I had to stifle a laugh.

"Why not? You saw his jaw."

"But jumping out of his mouth? That's funny."

"It is, but I think we shouldn't laugh right now. Let's laugh about it after we leave here so Sylvia won't see and hear. We can hoot and howl with laughter, if we want. Later, though. Is that all right?"

"Be amused now, laugh later? That's funny, too."

"It is not. Not so funny, anyway."

16
Becoming a Parrot

Sylvia took us to El Tigrito after dinner. I became a parrot, Rosita turned into a cat, and Sylvia went along as a cricket.

For dinner, we ate fried topochos and white cheese. I remembered June telling me that in the States, we called such big bananas plantains. Sylvia cut the plantain into woody-looking slices and pounded them with the handle of her knife. Then she dropped them into sizzling grease where they popped and snapped into a golden brown. They tasted like potatoes, sort of, and the white cheese she sprinkled on them became soft and rubbery.

As the sun dropped into the jungle, Sylvia lighted some candles. I thought she would hang up the chinchorros for us to sleep in, and I looked forward to that. Dad bought a chinchorro and hung it under the chaparro tree for us to try out. Todd called it a hammock, but June said a proper hammock was made of canvas, not netting made from cotton string. It wasn't easy to get into the chinchorro and even more difficult to get out, and it wasn't possible to use a pillow when lying in it. I had no idea how natives managed to sleep in a sling like that, all bowed up and without a pillow. But since sleeping in a canoe and on various mats made from jungle plants, I thought a chinchorro would be easy to sleep in, maybe even comfortable.

Sylvia prepared a tea for the three of us to drink. "The taste isn't so good," she said, "but the tea is necessary if we are to see your families tonight."

"See our families?" I grinned, waiting for the punch line.

But she seemed dead serious. "Rosita, you and Don lie down on the couch. Put your heads at opposite ends. I'll sit on the floor beside you. But first, finish your tea."

We drank the tea, and I kept waiting for her to tell us her joke. The tea had a musty, wooden under taste that was almost covered with cloves and sugar. The three of us drained our cups and Sylvia put them into the cupboard. Lying on what passed for a couch in the witch's house, I put the bottoms of my feet against Rosita's, and we pushed against each other in a way that would have made me laugh if it weren't for the odd tricks the candles were playing on me. The flames became huge, then tiny, then huge again. "Closing your eyes will help," Sylvia said.

Her voice filled the room. "How could you best travel to El Tigrito if you could become any kind of animal you wanted to become?"

"First there's the river to travel," I said. "A fish, maybe?"

"Frog," Rosita said.

"Go, then, each of you. I'll come along as a water bug on the surface."

The world became a river and I a silver fish, and a fast one, long and skinny like the needle gar I used to watch in the water beside the Tee Head in Corpus Christi Bay. I could dart from shore to shore, if I wanted, but it made sense to go east with the flow of the river. Above me Sylvia ran on the surface. I could see her tiny legs, dozens of them, moving in a blur as she kept up with me. "You're doing it right," she told me, and her voice came distant and dim through the water. Rosita was a great, leggy bullfrog, drawing in her legs to look like a green mango with eyes, then kicking out huge feet in a way that shot her past me until the force of the thrust was spent and she slowed, again becoming a green mango. I wanted to tell her how amusing she was but didn't know the language of a frog. A school of cannibal fish loomed like a cloud, all turning to eye me as I swam past. They bared their teeth and started for me, but I flipped my tail and left them far behind. "Don't go too far," the water bug warned. "You must leave the water and cross the savannah soon. What will you be on the savannah?"

"I'll leave the water as a baba," I said.

"Yes," Rosita-frog said, and I regretted not talking to her since even as a frog she used Spanish, same as always. I saw her turn into an alligator. My own alligator feet sprouted from fins, and my gar nose grew dark and toothy. I climbed out of the water. "Sylvia?" the baba that was Rosita said.

"I'm here. I'll go as a cricket, a small one but sturdy and fast. No one but you and Don will see me." Sylvia-bug became blurry like Dracula did in the movies when he changed into a bat. Her features reassembled into those of a cricket, a brown one the exact color of her crystal cashew eyes. "What will you be now?" the cricket asked.

"A parrot," I said, my voice already sounding like one. I grew long wings, and my snout turned into a beak with a blue tint on the area of my nose holes. A male parrot, then, I noted with satisfaction. It took only a couple of parrot hops to leap into the air and start flying. Rosita was a bird behind me and to the left. Sylvia flew beside me with her cricket wings. "How did I get so many feathers?" I asked. I meant to ask how I got to be a bird, but the words came out jumbled.

"You are what you are," the cricket assured me. "Can you find the village? It isn't far now."

"There, far below. See the water tower? That's my house. How do I see it in the dark?"

"Is it dark?" the cricket asked, its wings abuzz.

"No. How did it become day? And my arms aren't even tired from flying," I said.

"Wings, you mean," cricket said.

"I'm glad to be a parrot because parrots can talk, and I want to talk with my family. There they are." I glided down into the chaparro tree and looked them over. Dad and Todd sat on the cement base of the water tower, making a home-made knife. June and Mom sat in canvas chairs, June reading volume seven of the Encyclopedia Britannica, Junior. She kept glancing up at what Dad was working on. Mom clicked her needles together, making on a doily, string dancing around in her fingers and becoming knots much finer than those of a chinchorro.

"You could talk to them even if you were not a parrot," Sylvia-cricket said.

"Don?" June called out. She was looking right at me. How she found me so fast among all the big leaves of the chaparro tree was a mystery. "Don, get down out of that tree and join us."

"Where have you been?" Mom asked.

I fluttered to the ground and walked toward them in the funny waddle of parrots. My dog Ginki stood up, lifted her fur to a point all along her back, and growled at me. "Shut up, Ginki," I snapped. I sounded strange, like the parrot that our next-door neighbor, Amos, had taught to speak. Ginki whimpered, turned around three times, and settled to the ground, watching me with one brow raised. "Didn't you get my letter?" I asked Mom.

185

"Yes. Why did you write it on such small paper?"

"It's all El Loco had."

"El Loco?" Todd became interested and set aside the black wad of steel wool and the shiny blade he was working on. "I thought the bandits killed him."

"Did they, Sylvia?" I asked the cricket.

"Don't talk to me, Don. Talk to your family. Besides, you know the answer to your questions."

"No," I told Todd. "The miners chased the bandits out of the gold country, and El Loco plans to get married to Carmen. He said he wants to marry her because she has a fire in her head."

"I'm glad you're back," June said. "But I do wish you would be a kid again instead of a parrot. I never liked parrots much."

"It's all right for him to be a parrot," Dad said. "Better a parrot than a thieving little kid."

"Try getting into the San Tomé camp after dark as a parrot," June said. "The guards will just laugh. The mean kids on jefe hill will squirt you with water."

"Yeah," Todd said. "And they'll put a hot pepper in your beak." He frowned. "Some of the kids over in San Tomé say you've gone native."

"Is that true?" Mom asked. "Have you gone native, Don?"

"Sure he has," June said. "He's been running all over the wild part of Venezuela without any clothes on."

"No kidding?" Todd looked envious.

"With a native girl beside him. A naked one." June set her jaw in a disapproving way.

"Son, son, son." Mom clucked her tongue and shood her head.

"Simón told me you stole a canoe," Dad said.

"Simón is a liar," I said. But the way I said it in a high, squeaky parrot's voice sounded like a lie, and they all looked at me, knowing I was guilty and that I ought to have a hand lopped off. "I don't have a hand right now." I stood on one leg and held up the other to show it was a parrot foot and not a hand at all.

"A foot, then," June said. "Mano de Goma decreed that parrots who steal will have one foot cut off."

"I couldn't stand up. I couldn't hold parrot food in one foot and stand on the other. I'd starve."

186

"There'd be one less thief in the world," Dad said.

"Simón and El Loco would bury your thieving body in the jungle," Todd said.

"I guess nobody is worrying about me around here." I felt huffy.

"Nope," Todd said.

"We got your letter," Mom said. "That's enough for me."

"When you do get back," Dad said, "I want you to stay away from the bones of dead people."

"Where's your Barlow?" Todd asked.

"In my pocket."

They all laughed. "A parrot pocket," they said. "A feather pocket." More laughter. "A green pocket." The sound of their laughter stabbed me like needles.

"I've seen as much of my family as I can stand," I told the cricket.

"Do you feel better now?" the cricket asked.

"No. I feel worse. I want to go back to the jungle with Rosita."

"The jungle is dangerous."

"Not as dangerous as laughter. Mean laughter." I spread my wings, took a little run, and flapped past the chair June sat in. It was a temptation to bite her nose as I went by, but I didn't. "I'll fly all the way back," I told the cricket. "There's no need to become an alligator or a fish again. It's much more fun to be a parrot."

"Are you glad we went to El Tigrito to see your family?"

"Yes. And no."

"Families are like that," the cricket said. "You love them and you hate them. You want to be around them and you want to run away from them. Most children know the truth of that. When you're an adult, you'll remember your family as loving and kind."

"Where's Rosita?"

"She's returning, also. She talked with her brothers and sisters. Also her grandmother."

I flew to the witch's house as night closed in again, and I landed in the window beside a candle, hopped onto the dirt floor, waddled up to the crude wooden couch, and climbed upon it. I closed my eyes.

When I opened them again, Sylvia was no longer a cricket. She sat on the floor with her legs crossed, her clear brown eyes soft in the candle light. Rosita lay with the bottoms of her feet against mine. She moaned and stirred around. I sat up. "How did you do that?" I asked.

"I didn't do anything. You did it all. You and Rosita. Are you still in a hurry to get home?"

"No," I said.

"Not so much as before," Rosita said. "Nobody is worried nearly as much as I had thought." She sat up beside me. "I hear someone coming."

Sylvia looked alarmed. "This isn't good. I'm vulnerable from the tea, so he shouldn't come in here. Can you find your way to the loft in the dark?"

"No," I said.

"Yes," Rosita said.

"Then do it. Hurry. I'll try to get him out of the house. Don't talk while he's here. I don't want him to know about you."

Rosita took my hand and led me into the room with the ladder. I kept stumbling and felt dizzy. She put my hand on the ladder rung and whispered, "Climb. I'll be right behind you."

"I might fall."

"No. Parrots don't fall when they climb ladders."

"I'm not a parrot anymore."

"Part of you is. Climb."

As I settled on the floor of the loft and Rosita came beside me, we heard steps outside the front door.

"May I come in?" A male voice asked. It sounded foreign, blocky.

"No."

"No?" He chuckled, low and almost mean. Then he came in. Sylvia stood in the center of the room, hands on her hips, her eyes flashing white in the candle light, her eye teeth gleaming. The man stood before her. "I need to see you," he said.

"Not here. And not tonight."

"Your beauty draws me."

"Are you courting me, Marlin?"

"I burn with strange fires in your presence. I should not, but I do."

"Then why seek me out?"

"My love of you is great. You ignite vast fires within me."

"But Marlin, I light nothing. The fire is in your own heart."

"Your hair, your eyes, the heat of your soul draws me from holy work into the night. It's this strange and dark country that causes me to stray. If I could go home—even for a week, a day, an hour—I could purge the darkness of the jungle from me and be whole again. But God has chosen to thrust me out here." He sighed heavy and sad.

Sylvia put her hand on his shoulder. "If you went home, you would take yourself with you. You would still be Marlin, and you would still burn for the touch of a woman."

"No. Never was it so in America. This strange land stands me on the edge of such soul fires as I never knew existed. The green of the jungle draws me. The silver flash of the river in the morning draws me. The seduction of the darkness draws me and repels me and frightens me. The witchery in your eyes more than anything in the wild jungle melts my will, and oh, Sylvia I become so afraid. I want to go home and reclaim my soul, and yet I yearn to strip the missionary vestments from me and cast them into the leaf mold of the steaming jungle to rot. I want to swim in the river, nude, and bask in the sun. I want to vanish into the deep pools of your eyes, to ignite and explode like a star in the vast tropic night."

"You frighten me."

"I frighten myself. What powers do you have, Sylvia, that they so captivate my soul?"

"I am curandera, the woman who cures and brings comfort. I know nothing of the torment you speak of. I serve the people. And yet I am a woman, and what you say about me stirs the woman within me. You have come to court me, but in such an odd way."

"I've come to teach you about God." He tried to take her in his arms. She slipped past him and out the door. Marlin spoke in English: "Forgive my sins for wanting this woman, Father. I know I'm worthless. I know I'm a base sinner and deserve all of thy fires."

"What did you say?" Sylvia spoke from outside the house.

"I spoke English." He joined her outside.

"I know. If you want to be around me, speak so I can understand."

"May I kiss you?"

189

"No. Not now. Come. Let's go for a walk in the moonlight."

"There's no moon."

"Not yet. But she is on her way. Perhaps she will give us her blessing."

"Blasphemous," he said in English.

"Speak your foreign tongue again and you will have to go for a walk without me."

Their voices faded into the night. Rosita nudged me. "What did he say?"

"He talked to his father, I think," I said. "He said he deserved to be put in a fire."

"That doesn't make sense."

"No? You tell me what does make sense around this weird house. I turned into a fish and Sylvia became a water bug. You swam beside us as a bullfrog."

"No. I was a Jesus frog. I hopped on the top of the river while you swam on the bottom. You were a catfish with long whiskers."

"No. I was a zippy silver fish with a long snout, not a catfish at all. You hopped on the top of the water?"

"Yes. Then I became a jungle tiger, sleek and fast, and I ran all the way across the savannah to El Tigrito."

"You were a bird. I saw you."

"You were the bird. Not I. I was a cat. I talked to my family when I was a cat."

"Cats don't talk."

"I did. No one was surprised when I came home as a cat."

"Rosita, whatever is going on around here? Did we dream we were animals? Did the witch make us have a strange dream?"

"She was a cricket, right?"

"Yes."

"I saw her as a water bug, too, then as a cricket. How could we dream the same thing at the same time?"

"I don't know."

"I do. It was magic."

"I don't believe in magic."

"Even when it happens to you? You were a parrot, Don, and you had great white plumes."

"Green. They were green. And my family wanted to cut off one

190

of my feet."

"No."

"Yes. Because they thought I stole a canoe."

"We took the canoe but we didn't steal it."

"I didn't like the way my family talked to me."

"I believe you. My brothers and sisters weren't nice to me, either. Nor my mother. But my grandmother was. She told me to learn from Sylvia."

"Did they get the message I gave to Mamacita Moreno on El Loco's cigarette paper?"

"Not exactly. But your father got the letter and he told my mother about it, so she isn't worried about me. I didn't like talking with her, though. The only thing I did like was being those animals. It was fun to be a Jesus frog and hop on water. Did you enjoy being a catfish?"

"I wasn't a catfish. But yes, it was fun to push myself along in a thick, almost silent world with a tail that made me speed through the water. Being a baba was fun, too, but it didn't last."

"You were a baba? I wish I had been one."

"You were. I saw you."

"No. I'm certain I was not a baba."

"Best of all was being a parrot—that is, until I got home and everyone was rude to me. Flying as a parrot was fun."

"Running as a cat was fun. I stretched my legs and grabbed the ground with great paws." She hooked my ribs with her fingers to show how she ran with her claws out. "I would like to become a cat again. A big cat. It was good magic."

"Do you believe in magic?"

"I have always believed in magic. And I think you believe in it after what happened to us tonight."

"I'm not sure what happened. Maybe I had a dream."

"A magic dream. Maybe our whole trip is a magic dream, starting with hiding in the candy man's truck."

"That was real."

"And now that it's past, it's a dream, like the one-eyed woman who sang about doves. Like the canoe."

"Do you think we stole the canoe?" I asked.

"Borrowed. And the bat cave, and the ghosts of Indios—all are dreams we remember together."

"Real, all of it. I can prove it. I carried the basket you made into this house. Inside the basket is a head, some fingers and toes, and a leg. All from ancient Indios. None of that was a dream."

"It is now. Perhaps it was then. A good dream." Rosita sighed a sleepy sigh. "I believe we took those bones, so they're in the basket here in Sylvia's house. Carmen said believing something makes it true. Do you believe you became a parrot?"

"I was a parrot. Belief has nothing to do with it. I was, though now it seems that I couldn't have been."

"I think we should go to sleep."

"I didn't understand that man, Marlin. He sounded like El Loco with all that talk about fire inside people."

"He likes Sylvia."

"So do I."

"You do?" Rosita's voice took on a worried tone. "Is it her tetas?"

"Whatever are you saying? What do tetas have to do with anything? All I said was that I like Sylvia. Not in the same way as I like you, but I like her. She's kind and gentle. And she does such odd and interesting things, like taking us to see our family."

"I like her, too." Rosita sounded relieved. "But I don't understand her. She said Marlin frightened her, yet she went for a walk with him in the dark. Today has been too tiring." She yawned again. "Let's talk about all this tomorrow."

When Sylvia returned, Rosita was snoring in a quiet way. I nudged her awake, and we felt our way down the ladder. We found Sylvia hanging the chinchorros. "How are you feeling?" she asked.

"Weird," I said.

"Fine," Rosita said.

Sylvia watched me struggle with the netting of the chinchorro. She helped me settle into it, turning me so I lay in a slant. I had been trying to put my head and feet toward either end of the chinchorro, and that bowed me up like the curl of a banana. But lying in a slant to the ends made the strings spread exactly right to hold me out as flat as if I were lying on a bed. Rosita climbed into her chinchorro with no effort. Sylvia pinched out the candles, and a shaft of moonlight appeared on the floor from the window, speckled with the shadows of leaves. I could make out Sylvia's outline as she untied the cloth she used as a dress, folded it, then slipped into the chinchorro hanging beside me. She was close enough that I could feel the warmth of her and smell the sweetness of topochos and cheese upon her.

"Being a parrot was a kind of dream, wasn't it?" I said.

"No," Sylvia said. "You did what you did. I was with you, remember?"

"You were a cricket. A beautiful one the same color as your eyes. How did you do that?"

"Become a cricket? It was easy. You helped me, as I helped you become a parrot. You were a fine parrot, Don. I saw you with purple feathers, like your hair, though you probably saw the feathers differently. Green, perhaps."

"Green. I was green, not purple. Did I really fly all the way to El Tigrito and talk with my family?"

"Yes."

"It isn't possible."

"That's right. It isn't."

"Then I didn't do it."

"You did. I was with you, remember? You asked me about a man named El Loco, but of course I didn't know him."

"How can it be true that I became a parrot and at the same time for it to be true that it is impossible for me to become a parrot?"

"I don't know. It just is. The impossible often happens. Rosita seems to understand that. Don't you, Rosita?"

"Yes. I understand it but I don't understand it. I was a Jesus frog."

"A Jesus frog?" Sylvia sounded astonished. "This is true?"

"Yes. I ran down the river in big hops, landing on the water with a smat and making rings where I hit, then jumping again. Don and I saw a tiny Jesus frog in the heart water of a jungle plant. I became a big Jesus frog. You were a water bug."

"Don was below me in the water. He was a carribe."

"No. I was a fish shaped like a needle. I don't understand any of this."

"You do. You understood what your family had to say to you,

for what they said was already inside you. You understood how to fly as soon as you became a purple parrot. Nobody had to teach you."

"Green. I was a green."

"A green parrot, then. You understood how to find El Tigrito and the house with the water tower. You have within you all understanding. All you have to do is look for it in the right ways."

"I don't understand what you just said."

"Are you comfortable?"

"Yes. This is a wonderful chinchorro," I said. Rosita giggled.

"Then you understand more than you know," Sylvia said.

"Go to sleep, Don," Rosita said.

"We must all work at understanding, and we must help one another," Sylvia said. "I remain puzzled by Marlin, but you will help me know his heart." She yawned. "Tomorrow, perhaps."

17
The Curandera at Work

The next morning Julio came with cassava and onions. He stared at my purple hair.

I stood on the edge of the hill, trying to see the swamp down in the flowering jungle. At Rosita's insistence, I had put on the black shorts with the single shoulder strap. Sylvia and Rosita were up by the house, doing something with a fire and corn. I didn't hear Julio behind me until he spoke: "Are you one of the witch's spirits?"

I turned around, startled. Julio wore cut-off khaki pants remade from someone much larger. He had on alpargatas, and he carried a wheel of cassava in one hand and onions, braided together, in the other. "Good morning, Julio," I said.

He took a couple of steps back, and his eyes rounded. "Where did you come from?"

"Down there," I pointed.

"You're a swamp demon, then."

"No. I came down the river on a canoe."

"A water demon." He seemed to be measuring something about me. "Did you once wear blue pants?"

"Blue jeans. Yes."

"Did you have a knife in the pocket of the blue pants?"

"My Barlow. You found it? I sure would like to have it back."

"Is that the name of your knife? Barlow?"

"Yes. My father gave it to me. Where is it?"

"Mr. Marlin took it from me. He said a boy shouldn't have such a knife. But I think he wanted to keep it for himself. You don't talk like a water demon."

"I'm not a demon of any kind. How does a water demon talk?"

"I don't know. But you know my name."

"Sylvia told me. She said a ghost tried to grab you in the cemetery and it made your jaw stick. She said she cured you."

"She's the best witch in the world. I don't know your name."

"Don. Not El Don. Just Don. It's my name. I came from The United States."

"In the north. I've heard of it." He looked disappointed. "Maybe you're not a demon, then?"

"Maybe not. But last night I was a parrot."

"No!"

"Or I thought I was. This morning I've tried to become one again. I'd like to fly over the river and look at it from high in the air. But it's no use. I can't be a parrot anymore. Likely it was only a dream. Can you go down to the swamp with me? We could cut some cane for spears."

Julio glanced at the cassava. "I have to give this to the witch for putting my spirit back into my mouth. My father said he watched her gather my soul in her hands. He said she rolled it up into a thin little tube, and inserted it into my mouth, and that's what made my jaw get right again." He worked his jaw from side to side. "It's still sore from the way she pushed my soul back inside me."

"Your father said he saw her do that?"

"Yes. He told me not to stay here, just to give the witch the onions and cassava and leave."

"You can't go to the swamp with me, then."

"There are black caimanes in the swamp. And you might be a demon."

"I'm a boy, like you." I pointed at the bandage on my leg. "A vampire bat bit me when I was sleeping down by the river. Would a bat bite a demon? Would the demon bleed and need a bandage? And there are no caimanes in the swamp. I waded across it, so I know."

"My father said to take the gifts to the witch and hurry home. He said Mr. Marlin would be unhappy if I stayed around the home of the witch. But he also told me not to be afraid of her because she is a good witch." Julio turned toward the house.

"I have some finger bones of ancient Indios," I said.

Julio turned back. "Where did you get them?" He looked amazed.

"From a cave. My friend Rosita and I found them in a cave up the river. The cave was full of bats and had bat poop all over the floor. I have extra fingers, if you want one."

"The finger bone of an Indio. That would be a treasure."

"Is there a chance you can get my pocket knife back for me?" We began walking toward the house.

"If you're not a demon, how did you get so white? And why is your hair purple?"

"My whole family is white like this. And many boys from the United States have purple hair. What about the pocket knife?"

"I'll try." He sounded dubious. "Mr. Marlin keeps it in his own pocket."

Julio took his gifts to Sylvia, and I went into the house. The basket was still where I had put it, behind the ladder to the loft. I opened it and fumbled around among the bananas and guava. When I got back outside, Sylvia was admonishing Julio not to tell anyone about me and Rosita. "You're not afraid because you're smart enough to see that my new friends are children like yourself. But others might be afraid. I would rather they not know."

"I won't tell," he said.

"I believe you. Tell your father thanks for the onions and cassava."

I handed off the finger some distance from the house, taking care that Rosita and Sylvia didn't see. Something told me neither would approve of my giving Julio an ancient finger. Besides, I felt a vague sense of guilt for sneaking the bone out like that and giving it away. But Julio was delighted.

"This is better than a pocket knife. Never have I seen the bone of an ancient Indio."

"Try to get my knife back."

"I will." He hurried toward the cane brake, clutching the finger in his fist.

Later in the morning, while we were hanging the chinchorros back on the wall and Rosita swept the dirt floor, I told Sylvia about the Barlow. "He found your pants in the river?" She seemed confused. "How did you lose your pants?"

"The river took them. After the ants got on Rosita and the caimán tried to eat her leg, we hid in the canoe so the caimán wouldn't leap out of the water to get us. We didn't see the waterfall until it was too late. That's when the river took my pants."

"The river pulled your pants off?"

"I took them off because of bat droppings. We fell in the bat droppings in the dark of the cave, so we took our clothes off. We planned to wash them, though it's hard to get bat droppings out of cloth. So we were nude when the ants jumped Rosita's legs into the river and I had to throw a rabbit to the caimán, a rabbit and some topochos, then like I said we hid in the canoe, lying down so we didn't see the waterfall. We heard it, though. By the time we understood what it was, the current had us."

"This is true?" Sylvia turned to Rosita.

"Yes. We didn't much like wearing clothes, anyway, so we didn't miss them. Don wanted his pocket knife, and I wished for our shoes. But those things were small loses. After we went over the falls, I feared Don was dead, but I found him in a river puddle, crying because he thought I had drowned."

"I didn't cry," I said. Rosita and Sylvia stared at me. Rosita put her hands on her hips, dropping the broom. "Not so much, anyway," I hedged.

"You've told me so much astonishing news." Sylvia took a cup from the cupboard, dipped her fingers in it, and sprinkled water on the floor.

Rosita picked up the broom and thrust it into my hands. "It's your turn to work," she said.

I swept where Sylvia sprinkled the water, and the broom gathered small bits of dirt from the hard-packed floor. "I was so happy to see her that we danced." I twirled the broom around to show how we did it. "But we fell. Dancing is harder than it looks—" I started to add "in the movies," but it occurred to me that Sylvia had probably never seen a movie, either. Besides, I felt a little silly about dancing with the broom. I resumed sweeping.

"What were you doing in a cave with bats?"

"Gathering bones of Indios," I said.

"It's best not to talk about the bones, Don," Rosita said.

"You can talk to me about anything. What became of these bones?"

"They're in the basket we brought with us," Rosita said. "The basket was the only thing we found after we went over the falls."

"Yes," I added, "and the rope from the broken canoe. We used the rope to pull us out of the bog."

"May I see the bones?" Sylvia made her request sound like a formal command.

I brought the basket from beneath the ladder in the other room.

"It still has guava and bananas in it that we found on the other side of the swamp." I handed Sylvia the basket.

She opened it and looked inside. "This is a treasure. Did you know you had a wonderful treasure? The bones are ancient ones, perhaps bones of my ancestors. It was the bones that protected you in the river. They kept you from drowning. These are bones of good luck. The bones kept the vampire bats from harming you very much. The bones kept the bog from sucking you down."

"No," I said. "It was the rope from the canoe that kept us from sinking in the bog. The rope and the old stump with spiders in it."

"Spiders? You had spiders to help you?"

"Yes," Rosita said. "But I didn't know they helped until now."

"They didn't help at all. They scared Rosita, but not so much that she couldn't pull me out of the bog with the rope. Those bones had nothing to do with anything."

"Bones and fruit." Sylvia looked into the basket. "You children are amazing and wonderful creatures—children of the river and the jungle and the swamp. Were you ever afraid?"

"No," I said.

"Yes," Rosita said.

"Maybe a little," I admitted. "When I had to throw the rabbit to the caimán, I was afraid. And when Rosita chopped the snake into pieces with the machete. That scared me, but not a lot."

"I didn't know the snake frightened you," Rosita said. She looked at me with such intensity that I resumed sweeping. "I was so afraid that my fingers trembled on the handle of the machete, and I was afraid I'd miss the snake and it would bite us." She spoke in a soft, almost puffy voice.

"You like him," Sylvia said, also soft and low. "Have you ever kissed him?"

"Yes. When I found him beyond the waterfall. And another time, a kiss on the cheek. He's good with the broom, don't you think?"

"Yes."

"I could never marry a man who wouldn't sweep our house."

"A kiss of joy." Sylvia put the cup away. "And the other kiss, the one on cheek. A kiss of innocence?"

"Yes."

"Why are we talking about kisses?" I asked, annoyed.

"Woman talk," Sylvia said. "But that's enough of it since you won't be interested for several more years."

"I gave Julio a finger bone." I spoke with defiance. It was a relief to admit to having given away one of the bones.

"Why?" Rosita demanded.

"Because I wanted him to get my Barlow back from Mr. Marlin. Because he found my jeans. I don't know. Because I wanted him not to think I was a demon."

"You gave him a human finger bone," Sylvia said, "so he wouldn't think you're a demon? This was not good thinking, perhaps?"

"They're my bones, some of them anyway, and I can give them to anybody I want."

"It's all right, Don," Rosita said.

"The bones won't mind," Sylvia said. "Julio is lucky to have such a bone as saved you from the river and the swamp."

Later Sylvia went into the village, returning with two pairs of alpargatas. "Your feet look about the size of mine." She handed us the sandals. "Besides, the alpargatas are forgiving and don't demand feet be an exact size. Try them on."

They fit exactly, the mesh over the toes and around the heels holding well to my feet without pinching. I liked having alpargatas even if they looked less savage than the grass shoes Rosita had made for us.

Two more people came from the village to seek help from the witch. Rosita and I hid in the loft and watched. One was a man with a gray moustache. He said he was worried about having a limp rope, that he feared his woman would laugh at him. "Has your woman ever laughed at you for having a limp rope?" Sylvia asked him.

"No. Not that I could see, anyway."

"Having a limp rope isn't something to be ashamed of. It happens to all men, and women understand. My guess is that your woman has been very tender and loving with you."

"Yes. But I fear her leaving."

"No woman ever left a man she loved because his rope was limp." Sylvia took a jar from the medicine side of her cupboard. "Chew two leaves of this plant in the afternoon, and by evening, your rope will no longer be limp."

"Two? Only two?" The man with a gray moustache looked skeptical. "For my rope, it will take four leaves."

"No. One leaf will probably do it. Two will make any rope in the world into a stout sugarcane pole."

After the man left, I told Rosita that the man was a dope. "A rope is supposed to be limp," I said. "If the canoe rope had been stiff, we wouldn't have been able to use it to loop over the stump in the swamp. The bog would have swallowed us. It isn't such a good idea to make a rope into a piece of sugarcane."

"Do you suppose Sylvia meant it when she said chewing the leaf would make his rope into sugarcane? How could that be?"

"How could Sylvia become a cricket? How did I turn into a parrot? I don't know. Sylvia is the trickiest person I've ever seen."

"Perhaps," Rosita said, "she was talking about something else and not a rope or sugarcane at all?"

"No. They both said rope. We heard it."

"My grandmother told me, when I went to her as a jungle cat, that I should learn from Sylvia. But I don't understand much of what she does." Rosita dropped her voice to a low whisper when another person entered the witch's house.

This one was a woman, not so old as Sylvia, but much older than I. She wore a hibiscus in her hair, and her cheeks were too white. Her lips were dark blue with a black line around them, and the skin under her eyes was black as a raccoon's mask. "My sister," she told Sylvia, "is much more beautiful than I."

No kidding, I thought, looking at her blue lips and sugar-white cheeks: a lizard is more beautiful. Maybe even a bat.

"There's no one in the village more beautiful than you," Sylvia said.

"My sister is. She's two years older. She has tetas so large the boys all watch her when she walks by. Her face is without a blemish, her teeth are white as river sand, and she has lips the color of roses. My tetas are small, my face rough as palm bark, my teeth are stained, and my lips are more pale than milk."

"What do you want of me?"

"Make me as beautiful as my sister."

"Some women would have me make their sister ugly."

201

"She deserves her beauty. I wish her no harm. I want only to be less ugly."

Sylvia took a cloth from the cupboard, dipped it in the water cup she used for sprinkling the floor, and dabbed at the woman's face. "Hold still. You have flour on your cheeks. It makes you look like a ghost. No wonder boys look at your sister and not you. And your lips. How did they become blue?"

"I put juices on my lips to make them red."

"Don't use so much, then. Blue lips look like dead lips." Sylvia scrubbed on the woman's lips but without noticeable results. "Stand up." The woman stood. "Take off your blouse." She pulled her blouse off over her head. Sylvia walked around her. "Your tetas are young and firm, high and rosy, like pomegranates. They are beautiful."

"They're small."

She stood with her back to us, and I wanted her to turn around so I could see her pomegranate tetas. I imagined them to be bright pink with little cells of juice clustered all over them. But she didn't turn. Sylvia tugged at the cloth she wrapped around herself, pulling it down to expose the tops of her breasts. "Wear a dress like this one. Wear it low, but not so low as to show your nipples. Promise with the low dress, but don't deliver on the promise. It will drive the boys wild."

"But you have such magnificent tetas. Men talk about them. Boys would never notice me and my small ones, even with a low dress."

"They'll notice. And it's a curse to have breasts like melons. When you're young, they get in the way, and when you're old, they'll sag past your navel. Also, women attract men with what they have, not by painting themselves or covering themselves with flour and fruit juice. Try cleaning your face so it looks natural. Try teasing with your wonderful tetas. If you do that, even for one day, boys will look at you even more than they look at your sister. And there's one other thing you might think about doing."

"What? I'll do anything."

"Ignore the boys. If they're interested in you only for tetas and rosy cheeks, then they're so shallow that you're better off without them. Ignore them and their stupid ways and wait for a real man to come along. That is, if you want a man."

"I don't like that advice. Every girl wants a man."

"Not true. Men can be more trouble than any animal in the jungle."

"Boys and men are trouble to me only because they ignore me. I hoped you would have some magic herbs to make them notice."

"All the magic you need is inside you. Look to what you have, and you will find life will give more than you want."

"I'm not magic."

"Oh but you are. You have more magic inside you than there is in all the herbs of the jungle."

Later when we wandered outside beneath the mango trees and felt the air grow damp from the coming rain, I asked Rosita what Sylvia meant by saying men are like animals.

"They're just as Sylvia explained," Rosita said.

"But animals? Jungle animals?"

"Take that man who pulled my hair the night we got out of the candy man's truck. He was an animal. Or the man who pointed his pistol at us when Carmen wanted us to go with her to the river jungle. Or the bandits who killed the old Don. Animals, all animals." She held out a hand, testing the mist coming from the low clouds.

"Is Marlin worse than an animal?"

"Yes. He confused and frightened Sylvia, and she's more wise even than my grandmother."

"Do you think I'm worse than a jungle animal?"

"No. You're a boy. You're my best friend." She thrust a finger in my face. "Just don't you dare grow up to be a man."

I thought what she said was the dumbest thing I had ever heard. What else did she expect me to grow up to become? But I didn't say what I thought since it seemed like a good idea at the time to get off the subject of men.

The mist became large drops and we went inside. Water poured down white and furious so it wasn't possible to see the cane brake from the front door. Whoever put the thatching on Sylvia's house did a good job, for water ran off of it and out of it, but none got into the house except for the mist that came in the window. The rain spattered with a faint drone on the roof instead of with the roar it caused on the corrugated zinc roof of my El Tigrito home. As Sylvia hung a cloth over the window to catch most of the mist, she told us a man would come, this one after dark, and she said as she lit candles that we should hide again in the loft. "Try to go to sleep up there. If I blow out the candles, it's a sign that Marlin and I are going to spend the night together, so you should get some sleep and not worry about us."

"Spend the night with a man?" Rosita said, her eyes wide. "I thought you said you had a daughter down river. Doesn't that mean you have a husband?"

"It doesn't mean that at all. I have a daughter who is wonderful. I don't want a husband. Ever. Now up the ladder with you. Take this in case you get cool in the night." She handed Rosita a piece of cloth that could pass for a bed sheet.

When we got to the top of the ladder, we took off the clothes Rosita had made, and she folded them. Mr. Marlin arrived not long after the rain stopped. We had settled on the floor of the loft, lying on our stomachs to watch through the lattice work. Sylvia poured him some tea. She also held a cup, but she drank almost nothing. "Sit on the couch," she told him.

"With you, yes, on the couch." Marlin sat. "The candles flicker so bright. Where did you get candles with such large flames?"

"Lie down, please."

"You will lie with me." He did something to the knot tying the cloth over her breasts, gave the cloth a tug, and pulled it from her. "You are magnificent." He put a hand on one of her breasts.

She leaned toward him, pushing him onto his back. "Close your eyes," she said. "The candlelight will be less harsh. You said last night that if you could go home, you could learn to put out the fire that drives you to me. Would you like to see if it's true?"

"Go home? How could I go home?"

You could go as a parrot, I thought. Or a cat. I clutched Rosita's hand in excitement, for we were about to watch some of the magic of the witch—the same magic she used to take us to El Tigrito. That is, if it was magic and not a trick.

"Home, yes. You have within you the power to go there any time you want. I'll be your guide tonight, but it will be a trip you take. If you want, I'll go with you, but I won't appear to any of your family or friends there." She removed his hand from her breast and set it on his chest. "I'll stay right here, beside you." She spoke in a mellow, smooth voice, then began singing:

"When baby slept in a green palm tree
all jungle creatures came to see—
a capybara from its lair,
wildcats and monkeys all were there,
snakes with snake skin gold and brown,
parrots in their feathered down,
piglets with their mother pig
and savannah moles that love to dig—
all came to watch the palm tree keep
the baby safe and rocked in sleep."

She stroked his hair. "How would you get home if you were to go there right now? By airplane? By boat?"

"I would walk next door, to my house," Marlin said in English. His voice sounded like that of a child, a young child.

"Perhaps, Marlin, you shouldn't be so young when you return home? Perhaps you should be as you are now? Perhaps you should speak Spanish so I can help you if it becomes necessary?"

Marlin continued in English: "They sent me to play with Brenda and Ralphie so they could talk in loud, mean voices. Sometimes I peek at them through the window. Today I'll go into the house to see them. Through the screen door, holding it soft and trying not to let it squeak. The porch is gray and black. Into the big door and past the fridge. They're in the front room, and they're yelling again, especially mommy. She yells too much. At me. At Daddy. Daddy is strong and hits her when he thinks I don't see. I would hit mommy when she yells at me, but I'm too little."

Sylvia patted his hand. "Speak to me in Spanish, if you can. Tell me what you see."

"A red rug," he said in English. "A ball on the kitchen floor. In the front room, listen. Daddy and mommy in the other room. Their voices scare me."

"Can you speak Spanish?"

"No. Mommy is crying because she isn't strong." He became quiet, then he shouted in a deep voice, a man's voice that didn't sound much like Mr. Marlin: "What is this shit, woman?" As he spoke, his voice shifted to a throaty voice of a woman, then to the deep rumble of the man. "Don't do that again, Frank. Don't hit me like that, not now. Look, the baby is watching. Shut up you sniveling woman. I'll take my belt to you again. There. Kneel down. Down, I said. No, Frank, I won't, not this time. Don't make me do it, Frank. Ha, you don't have the guts to use that. I'll take it away from you and ram the barrel up your ass until you beg me to use the belt again. No, Frank. Not this time, no. Get back. Get back." Mr. Marlin twitched around on the couch, making coughing and retching sounds, then became still. When he spoke, it was in the voice of a child: "Daddy? You can get up now, daddy. Come on, daddy. Get up. Mommy, daddy won't get up. Make him get up, please mommy." He began to cry, but it didn't sound much like a grown man crying.

Sylvia lifted his head, slid her legs under it to hold what she could of him in her lap. She put her breast against his cheek. Tears ran down his face, and he continued to mew like a child crying. She guided his lips to her nipple and sang:

"The palm tree bends with wind and rain
but holds the baby safe again,
holds the baby safe and warm,
rocks the baby safe and warm.
keeps the baby safe and warm
high above the jungle floor
in the blue of father sky
in the arms of mother palm."

She hummed and stroked Marlin's hair and rocked him for a long time. He seemed to sleep, then his eyes fluttered open. "I had such a dream," he said.

"It was no dream. You found truth inside you where truth always lives. This one was a painful truth."

"You were there."

"Yes."

"You saw."

"Yes, but not as you saw. You spoke words I do not know. But I understood the feeling of them. I saw with my heart. Your father is dead."

"Yes and mommy, she—" Marlin's voice cracked. He sniffed and looked at her breast. "You suckled me."

"Yes."

"Lie with me now."

Sylvia slipped off of the couch, took several steps around the room, and pinched out the candles. A dim shaft of moon came through the window again, enough for me to see the shadows on the couch, to understand that Marlin was taking off his clothes. Rosita gripped my hand and I heard her intake of breath. She put her lips close to my ear and spoke in a plosive whisper: "We cannot watch." She drew me to her and away from the lattice work at the end of the loft.

18
Marlin's Shotgun

A rattling sound awakened me. Rosita lay beside me, one arm thrown across my chest. She breathed in quite whistles. The rattling came from directly in front of my face, and for a moment I thought it might be rain, then dismissed the notion because rain didn't sound like that on the thatching. A bat, maybe, I thought, and opened my eyes, half expecting to find a vampire bat crawling around on the palm thatch above me. But it wasn't a bat at all. It was a mouse.

I figured the sun was about to spring over the jungled horizon because enough light came into the house for me to see in a dim way, but not enough for it to be full morning. The mouse seemed to be making its way through the thatching in some mouse tunnel with holes for it to peer through every few steps. It rattled for a while, then stuck a twitchy nose out for some sniffs, glanced at me, and went a few more steps. The mouse delighted me, and I was tempted to awaken Rosita so she could enjoy it, also. Then I saw the ants.

They walked in a curving black line, like a living crack on the underside of the thatching. They were tree ants, doing whatever tree ants need to do when they've made a mistake and climbed into a roof instead of a regular tree. A couple of beetles walked around on the roof just down from the mouse. Maybe they were the breakfast the mouse was looking for when it stuck its twitchy nose out of its mouse tunnel. They made a tiny amount of noise, more than the ants but less than the mouse. The whole roof seemed alive with bugs and ants and beetles, and I realized for the first time that in Sylvia's house I had been sleeping beneath a wonderful world of living creatures. It made me wish Dad would rip off the corrugated zinc roof from our house in El Tigrito and put on thatching. I was trying to count the tree ants when Mr. Marlin began mumbling.

I lifted Rosita's arm from my chest, and she turned over, still asleep. As quietly as possible, I scooted to the lattice work at the edge of the loft and looked into the living room. Marlin kneeled beside the window, a fervent face turned toward the greenery of mango trees and his hands clasped under his chin. ". . . for my sin,

209

oh Father," he was saying in English. "Forgive the weakness of my flesh with this witch and purge me of evil that I may serve thy will."

Sylvia sat on the couch, nude, watching him. "God understands Spanish as well as English." Her voice sounded soft and warm.

"Filth and corruption dwells within the soul of the woman witch," Marlin mumbled. He stood, and I was startled to realize that he, too, was nude. He turned to Sylvia and addressed her in Spanish: "How did you give me such a false and evil vision last night?"

"Last night, Marlin? Last night we loved, you and I. You were so gentle."

"Lust, filth, and corruption. You call that love? You conjured evil spirits to show me the false vision of my mother murdering my father."

"Was it false, Marlin? Look within your heart for the truth. The vision came from within you. I had nothing to do with it."

He took two quick steps across the room and slapped her, knocking her back against the wall. I scooted down the ladder, grabbed the broom, and ran into the room, broom handle held like a knight might wield a lance. Marlin turned, his eyes round in astonishment. The broom caught him on the shoulder and spun him around. I wanted to knock him down, but all I did was stagger him. He snatched the broom from me. "One of your familiars," he said in English. "I'll snuff him out." He brought the broom down to strike my head. I bent forward and it hit my back, knocking me to my knees. He lifted the broom again, holding it as Rosita held the machete when she struck the swimming snake. I dived to escape the blow.

That's when Rosita hit him in the stomach with her head. I rolled over, prepared to spring upon Marlin, but it wasn't necessary. Rosita must have run into the room, her head down to drive into his midsection as he had his arms raised to strike me. Air went out of him with a whoosh, and he crumpled to the floor, gasping..

Sylvia, her cheek red and a drop of blood running from her nose, knelt beside me and inspected my back. "It doesn't hurt much," I said.

She helped me up, hugged me and drew Rosita into the hug. "My two wonderful children of the jungle and the swamp," she said, "came to rescue me from this troubled man. Look at us." She stepped back, her hands on our shoulders. "All nude as if just cast from the divine garden, bruised with this man's hatred. Marlin, you're lucky you didn't hurt my children. If you had, I might forget that my mission is to cure." She helped him from the floor. Bent almost double and still struggling for air, he allowed her help in settling him on the couch. His eyes bulged red and angry.

"Your nose bleeds." Rosita looked with alarm at Sylvia.

"He struck me from his own pain. It had nothing to do with me. We must forgive him. I forgive you, Marlin, and I turn my other cheek."

"But you'd better not strike it," Rosita said in a dangerous growl.

"I forbid," Marlin said, still struggling for air, "I forbid you to forgive me."

"These words make sense from a man of God?" Sylvia said, her palms up.

"This is a nest of demons, evil. Evil."

"Marlin, I didn't murder your father."

"My father?" He seemed surprised. "He killed himself while cleaning a pistol. A stupid accident. My mother had loaded the gun, and he didn't know." He began straightening out, rubbing his stomach and wincing. "Must you all be here with no clothes on? Have you no shame?"

"You're as naked as we are," I said in English.

Marlin sprang to his feet, standing on the couch and backing away from me. "Back, get back you purple spawn of the devil."

"Don't speak English to him, Don," Sylvia said. "It frightens him."

"You slapped Sylvia, and she never did anything bad to you." I stepped toward him, liking the effect of my using English. "You struck me with a broom. You said you were going to snuff me out. You are a bad, bad man, Mr. Marlin."

"My clothes, witch. Where are my clothes?" He leaped off of the couch, bent low, held his stomach where Rosita rammed him, and coughed.

Sylvia handed him his pants. He snatched them, grabbed his shirt, socks and shoes from the floor, and scrambled out the door.

"Corruption," he said as he fled toward the cane brake: "filth and corruption."

Rosita followed him to the door and watched him. "He runs like a wounded rooster," she reported. "There, he dropped a sock. And another. It's funny to watch him, if you think about it—running away from a woman and two children, barefooted and naked. Good. He stepped on something sharp and is hopping around. I hope it was a big thorn."

"Rosita!" Sylvia stifled a smile.

"Now he's gone. We're rid of him."

"He'll be back. I think today is the day we should go down river. My work in this village is almost finished, anyway."

"Should we get dressed?" Rosita turned from the door.

"Does it offend you that I'm nude?" Sylvia looked from me to Rosita. I turned to Rosita, deferring the question to her, thinking it best for me to remain quiet in that discussion.

"No," Rosita said. "You're beautiful. Don is beautiful. There's no shame in this house, as Mr. Marlin thought."

"Perhaps we're still in the divine garden, the three of us. Being fallen is a condition within people, after all, not a place. Still, those who see us wouldn't understand. I think we should dress before we go outside today. In the house, wear what you please, and wear nothing at all, if that pleases you. Don, I have something that I think is yours. If it's not, we'll send it to Marlin."

"What is it?"

"There," she pointed, behind the couch, "on the floor. I found it in the night and thought to save it for you."

I looked where she said. "My Barlow."

"Are you sure it's yours, Don?" Rosita asked. "Many pocket knives look alike."

I snapped the knife open. "It's mine, all right. Here's the initials Dad scratched at the base of the blade so Todd and I could tell ours apart. Thanks, Sylvia."

"Now I have to sew a pocket in your new pants," Rosita said.

"No. I'll carry it with the bones in the basket."

By the time Julio came, we were all dressed. Sylvia had sent me to find firewood so she could cook pan de mano as provisions for our trip. She sent Rosita to bring a hand of bananas from a stand of banana trees just beyond the cane brake. We had just returned when Julio arrived, sneaking toward Sylvia's house, glancing back as if fearing someone might be following him. I stacked firewood beneath Sylvia's griddle, and Rosita set aside the bananas to help Sylvia pat the cornmeal into proper shape. Julio handed me a roll of blue cloth.

"My jeans." I unrolled them. "Someone washed the bat droppings out of them. Thanks, Julio."

"I couldn't get your knife," he said.

"That's all right."

"You must leave." There was a note of urgency in his voice. Sylvia lifted one eyebrow and glanced at him. "Mr. Marlin, he is saying that you are an evil witch, that you have mated with the devil and mothered two demon children, one with purple hair. He and some of the villagers will be here soon. Mr. Marlin has a shotgun." Corto, he called the shotgun: short or sawed-off. "Some of the men carry hoes and picks. I didn't cause them to come. I didn't tell anyone. I didn't. I must go now." He went slinking toward the cane brake.

"Thanks, Julio," Sylvia called after him. "You're a good person." She picked up a cloth to wipe the cornmeal batter from her hands. "We must go without packing anything."

I dashed into the house and came out stuffing my jeans into the basket Rosita had made.

"The good luck bones," Sylvia said. "You did well to remember. But nothing else. Come this way and hurry. There's a smaller trail around the village where we can get my canoe. Marlin and the village men will be on the main trail. Come."

Rosita and I followed her on a trail that wasn't much of a trail. Ferns, broad-leafed plants and grasses reached across the path to wet our legs with last night's rain. Where the path widened beside some castorbean bushes, Sylvia stopped us. "They'll find us gone and divide up. Some will come this way. Give me the bones."

I handed her the basket. She took out the skull and the leg bone. "Hold this," she gave me the skull, then squatted and jammed the leg bone into the topsoil in the center of the trail. She set the skull on the leg bone so it looked up the trail, much as I had done with it in front of our green igloo down beside the river. "This will scare them so bad their belly buttons will fall off. Let's get going."

It would be fun, I thought, to hide among the castorbean bushes and watch the natives lose their belly buttons. Not smart—but fun. We went down a hill, through some high cane and among tree ferns, getting glimpses of the thatched roofs of the village. Then I saw the river. It looked swollen and muddy. Behind us we heard a shout. "They found the skull," Rosita said with satisfaction. "They sounded scared."

"They now have no belly buttons," I said.

"Like Adam and Eve after the fall," Sylvia said.

"The bones will stop the villagers," Rosita said. "But if Mr. Marlin is with them, he won't stop."

"We'll hope he went with a group toward the savannah," Sylvia said. "There, beside that tree. That's my canoe."

It was turned upside down and looked far too big for the three of us to carry to the river. We rocked it and flipped it over. Rosita picked up two paddles and put them inside as Sylvia began sliding it on the grass toward the water. With the three of us pushing, it took only minutes to get the canoe into the water. "Get in, quick," Sylvia said. Rosita and I got into the canoe. It had a broad, flat bottom similar to the canoe we borrowed from the miners, so I guessed it would be quite stable in the water. The end Sylvia was pushing seemed clear of the bank when Marlin stepped into view from the tree ferns.

"Stop," he shouted.

Sylvia got into the canoe, but her weight caused the end to jam into the bank. She took a paddle and began pushing, sliding us into the water. She was turning around to sit down when Marlin fired the shotgun.

It sounded like a thunder clap just meters away. Sylvia spun around, her face speckled with blood and her chest caved in. She fell into the water. "No!" Rosita screamed. I was about to dive in after her when Rosita caught my arm. "No, Don, no."

Blood stained the water around Sylvia as she surfaced, face down, and the cannibal fish were already at her, the water splashing and popping from the frenzy of their fins. I turned toward Marlin, who stood on the bank, his face grim, his mouth set in a straight line, the short-barreled shotgun hanging in the crook of his arm.

"You killed her," I shouted. "You murdered Sylvia. You murdered her."

"Sit down, Don." Rosita's voice came to me as muted and distant, reminding me of Sylvia's voice when she was a water bug and I was a needle gar beneath the river. "Sit down."

What was left of Sylvia sank from sight leaving a red stain on the water and an occasional splash of a carribe. I sat in the canoe. Rosita was already paddling us out toward the center of the river. On shore, people from the village gathered, women and children, to stare at Marlin. I glanced at him.

He knelt in the grass with the barrel of the shotgun in his mouth. I wanted to shout to him not to do it, but I sat in the boat, stuck in place, unable to utter a sound, watching as he reached toward the trigger. When he pulled it, I saw the hammer moving, heard the oily click of it. The hammer seemed in slow motion though I knew it was not, and I heard the villagers shout. I ducked down in the canoe as the gun roared again. The shouting of the people changed to keening, high and full of pain, and in the bottom of the boat I heard the lapping of river water against the side of the boat, the splash of the paddle as Rosita, sitting behind me, pushed us away from the village; I heard Rosita's crying and soft grunting sounds each time she dipped the paddle into the water. I sat up, wanting to help her.

We pushed the canoe. Dip, drag, lift, dip again. On and on. Spots of Sylvia's blood stained the side near the front of the canoe where she stood when Marlin's gun roared and she spun into the water. But I won't think about that, I commanded. Dip, drag, lift, dip again. We seemed to be flying across the surface of the water, rushing faster than the current, and the jungle on the far shores seemed to be a green blur. Dip, drag, lift, dip again.

"You can stop now," Rosita said. I scarcely heard her. Dip, drag, lift, dip again. And again. And again. "Don. Please stop now. Please talk with me."

We put ashore where the jungle dripped with green water shaking ferns and bamboo. The large drops knocked palmettoes into nodding their heads like green dogs with imbecile faces, flat and blank. A rock, warming in the morning sun and streaked with lime fuzz, provided a place to sit and a tree offered a branch for tying the canoe. Rosita sat, her knees drawn up to her chin, hugging herself and rocking. I sat close to her, leaning against her, wishing I could say some words of comfort, but none came. The image of Sylvia spinning around with her breast caved in and her face measled from the spray of shot kept coming to me and coming to me until I grabbed my head. We sat, huddled together in silence with the river swirling at our feet and the jungle dripping from leaf to leaf, and I heard the river and the drip but somehow neither seemed to be there in any important way. Something happened with time, some braking and stopping as if the garden jungle, river, sky, and rock we sat upon were set into a giant chinchorro in a dark place for sleeping. I don't know how long we sat on the rock or what signal caused us both to rise and free the canoe, to set it again in motion with the river, using the paddles only to keep us out of overhanging branches close to the edge. Sunlight seemed thick with heat, especially on my shoulders, and I sought ways to keep the canoe flowing with the river where trees leaned toward the water to offer shade.

We ate once that day, maneuvering the canoe into shade of a bent tree and peeling bananas that had been bruised from riding among bones. I peeled and cut the guavas with my Barlow, gouging out the black spots. We said almost nothing. When evening and the threat of rain came, we tied high branches into a platform for sleeping above the jungle floor, and we made a roof of palmetto fronds to keep the evening rain from soaking us. I carried my jeans up the tree for Rosita to wear if night air made her shiver. When the rain hit, just before dark, the tree shifted and groaned, but our platform held, and the palm fronds, which had been so much work to cut using only my Barlow, kept most of the water off of us. It wasn't until she settled against me that Rosita discovered the heat in my shoulders. "You sunburned." Her voice carried a note of alarm. "Tomorrow we build a canopy in the canoe to shield you from the sun."

Hours later, after rain turned into residual drips from leaves, the din of insects and birds made the nighttime jungle sing round and mournful notes. I had thought she was asleep when Rosita said, "I should have taken the paddle and helped push the boat into the river. Maybe his shot would have missed."

216

"The boat stuck in the mud, and he was too close. I angered him in Sylvia's home. I frightened him with English and with my light skin and purple hair. He thought I was a devil. I frightened him so he came back to kill Sylvia."

"He struck her before you ever spoke to him. He was a bad, bad man, yet I don't think he meant to kill her."

"Of course he meant to do it. He shot her."

"But did you see how he did it? He called to her to stop, then swung the gun up from his waist and fired. He didn't put it to his shoulder and aim down the barrel. He just fired. I think he was surprised when he hit her. His face showed surprise."

"He deserved to die." I was a bit startled by the fervor of my statement, for I wasn't at all sure Marlin deserved to die.

"I don't know. But I do know I hate him for taking Sylvia away."

It wasn't easy, but we both managed to sleep. The next morning Rosita directed me into whittling sticks for holding up our canopy. It was slow work with the Barlow, and I found myself wishing for the machete that the bog had swallowed. To connect the sticks into a grid, she used the rope from the canoe we had wrecked at the waterfall, the rope that pulled us from the bog and that we had used to tie our tree house together. As we put broad leaves on the top of the grid, I said, "He did it like uncle Ray killed the monkey."

"What?" She turned to me, her face streaked from dried tears. She held a sheaf of leaves for the canopy in one hand and used the other for gripping the grid of sticks to balance herself in the boat.

"He didn't mean to shoot the monkey. He raised the rifle and fired without aiming. That's when the monkey fell to the ground."

"And started putting leaves and twigs in the hole in its side to stop the blood. I remember your story now."

"Uncle Ray felt so bad that he got rid of the rifle and never again hunted large animals. Mr. Marlin felt so bad that he put his mouth over the shotgun."

Rosita said nothing. We finished the canopy, and as we used paddles to shove away from the bank, I said, "I called him a murderer."

"You were right. He murdered our Sylvia."

"But, Rosita, don't you see? I called him that when he felt bad for shooting her because he just pointed and shot, like Uncle Ray

217

did. If I hadn't said what I did, maybe he wouldn't have put the barrel of the gun in his mouth."

"You said he deserved to die."

"Did he?"

"I think perhaps no one deserves to die."

"Maybe he could have done what Uncle Ray did. If he hadn't died, maybe Marlin could have thrown the shotgun in the river or buried it in the swamp and maybe like Uncle Ray he would become a better man than he was."

"Maybe. But I doubt it."

"Uncle Ray never hunted again. I'm glad he didn't put the barrel of the rifle in his mouth after killing the monkey."

"Shooting a monkey is different from killing Sylvia."

"Yes. But still. I told him he was a murderer at the wrong moment. I helped cause his death."

"He chose what he did. You sat in the boat while he chose."

"Yes. And I was quiet. I wanted to yell at him not to do it, but I didn't. I wish I had yelled."

"It wouldn't have mattered, not then."

"It would matter to me now. It matters that I sat there and said nothing."

We rode the river, huddled together in the center of the boat beneath the canopy of leaves, saying nothing. On the shore, trees grew to impossible heights in places, while in others monkeys in lower trees leaped from branch to branch, chattering to one another and ignoring us. Orchids grew in profusion, and parrots flocked into branches, talking in soprano squawks. We floated past swampy inlets where caimanes like to live, though we saw none. An occasional fish splashed the water, reminding me of how I had become a needle gar and swam down this very river with Sylvia the waterbug running on the surface close by. It seemed impossible that the river and jungle could be so beautiful and so indifferent to Sylvia's death, impossible that so much life could go on and on and take no notice of what had happened. But it remained strong, this jungle and wild river, strong with its orchids and birds, its bamboo and ferns, its dripping leaves and dark waters. We rode the currents, awed by the life around us, and we said little until we saw the anaconda.

19
Sam Dean from Abilene

First we saw the deer, a small one, standing on a grassy place similar to the one where Sylvia had left her canoe. The deer drank from the river, its nose to the water, and didn't see us. I pushed with the paddle to bring us in for a closer look. Rosita whispered, "She's beautiful," and the two of us sat still, taking in the soft, girl-like features of the deer, so we were quite startled when the anaconda struck.

The head of the snake and a long piece of its body came flying out of the river to attack the deer, knocking it into the water. "Ay," Rosita said. The deer struggled and thrashed about, and the snake threw coils of itself around it, drawing it underwater in seconds. "So sudden." Rosita spoke with a shaking voice.

"It was bigger around than I am at my waist," I said. "It was as long as the canoe." Then I looked at the water around the canoe, drawing my hands and the paddle into the boat. "There might be others."

"The anaconda hunts alone." Rosita began paddling us toward the center of the river.

We rode the current in silence, and I eyed the waters and the shore. With the floods of the rainy season came carribe from up river, and they came in numbers to do more damage than bite a mole off an ankle. The black caimanes lurked in swampy areas, now abundant from high water, and a snake larger than a canoe had showed itself. "Perhaps," I said, "it's time to leave the river and find the nearest road back home."

"Yes," Rosita said. "The deer was about the same size as you. If an anaconda saw you, it might strike like lightening, leaping from the water to drag you down and crush you and swallow you."

"Or you."

"Or me. Has the jungle become an evil place since Mr. Marlin murdered Sylvia?"

Her question made it true: the jungle was evil. After she said it, the rocks along the bank seemed to become jagged like teeth, and vines in the trees looked like hungry snakes. Even the dark places beneath the trees looked scary, like mouths waiting to bite. "We must put ashore, push through to the savannah, and look for a road," I said.

"Or a village. Yes."

"What will we do when we get thirsty?"

"Wait for the rain. We should not drink from the river again unless we want to become a meal for an anaconda." Rosita began steering the canoe toward the left shore. "We'll climb those rocks, and we'll do it fast before something in the water tries to catch us."

"What about Sylvia's canoe?"

"It's ours, now."

"She has a daughter. Perhaps we should stay in the canoe until we come to the village where her daughter lives."

"Too dangerous. We'll give the canoe to the river. Maybe someone will see it and give it to Sylvia's daughter."

"Maybe." I didn't think it likely.

Rosita bumped the front of the canoe against the rocks. I ducked from under our canopy, picked up the basket, and jumped to a flat place. Rosita joined me, and the current took the canoe. We backed away from the river's edge and watched the canoe drift down river. "I hope we made the right choice," she said.

I cut cane walking sticks, sharpening the ends so we could use them as weapons if attacked by jungle beasts. As I carved a point between two joints of the cane, I wondered what kind of jungle beast could possibly attack us. A big cat, maybe. Or a snake—though not an anaconda, for they were water animals, too big to move well on land. Rattlesnakes frightened Rosita but not me. They were too small to spook me, and they liked to give warning with their tails. Boa constrictors seemed more dangerous. Todd once told me that boas of a certain kind liked to drop out of trees on small animals, wrap around them to crush them to death, then swallow them. A big boa, Todd thought, could drop out of a tree on a person, not realizing the person was too big to eat. "Boas have tiny brains," he said, "and might not know a big animal like a person from a small, edible one." After it fell on you, he figured it would coil around your neck and pop your head like a pimple. Boas seemed to be the greatest danger, or they did while I carved points on our walking sticks.

We walked through the trees toward the savannah. Wrinkled-leafed plants grew along the ground, some with tiny yellow flowers, others with leaves more colorful than most blossoms. As we neared the savannah where trees stood less tall, we found many types of orchids. Pink ones grew in trees, others, blue as the sky, sat on long stems that grew out of the leafmold turf. Birds whistled and chirped overhead, and great flocks of parakeets flew above the trees. We wore the alpargatas Sylvia had given us and the clothes Rosita had sewn from Sylvia's cloth, and neither of us suggested taking them off, though the flowers, birds, and colorful plants made it seem safe enough to do so.

Rosita carried the basket on her shoulders because carrying it on my back bothered my sunburned skin. When we reached the place where savannah meets jungle and the trees thinned, she said, "The greatest danger here seems to be from the sun. I'll make a grass cape for you to wear to keep the sun off of your back."

"Grass will scratch me where I'm burned."

"Then I'll make a parasol. You can carry your own shade with you when we leave the protection of the trees." She found some shaggy branches that had died and fallen from high palm trees and told me to use my Barlow to strip the thin ribs out of them. "Boys use these as sticks for their kites," she said. "Pretend you're making many kites while I gather grasses."

From the palm tree gleanings and from the grass she pulled, Rosita made an umbrella, using the cane walking stick I had cut for her as the handle. "This won't stop rain, but it'll keep the sun from burning your light skin," she said.

Rain clouds gathered in the afternoon not long after we found cashew nuts. They grew on a bush-like tree that had bell-shaped fruit, red and yellow. On the ends of the fruit were the cashews, encased in thick hulls. Rosita ate some of the fruit, but I thought they tasted like kerosene. While I gathered nuts Rosita built a fire. When it burned down to charcoal, we put the nuts against the glowing remains of wood until the husks cracked open from the heat. Then we scraped the nuts onto broad leaves to cool. It wasn't too hard to break the shells with a stone and get out the roasted cashew. "I wish we had some salt," Rosita said.

"These are perfect as they are. They don't need salt." I thought

221

the cashew meal was the best one we had in the jungle since Rosita roasted a rabbit.

We ate in the shade of a mango tree and watched the clouds build across the savannah. "When it rains," Rosita said, "we'll catch water with a big jungle leaf and get a drink. We'll need to drink enough to last until tomorrow."

"We could go to the river for water. One of us could drink while the other watched for anaconda."

"We stay away from the river. Right now we need to build a shelter from the rain. It might as well be in a tree where we can spend the night."

The mango that provided shade for our cashew meal had a place where large branches went all directions. It was easy to climb to, though Rosita thought it might be too close to the ground for safety.

"What could possibly reach us there?" I asked.

"I don't know. I'm just worried about being safe."

"The chaparro tree we slept in after we first arrived in the wild part of Venezuela was even lower than this mango."

"Yes. But that was before this place became evil."

"Since we left the river," I said, "we've been safe. I've even considered going without clothes again."

Rosita looked worried, but she said nothing else about it while we gathered branches from smaller trees to build a floor in our tree house. There were no palmettoes in sight, so we wove a kind of roof with branches that had fallen from tall palms. "This isn't so good," she said as we finished.

As the clouds thickened and rain began, I stripped off the black pants with the weird shoulder strap, left them and the alpargatas in the tree shelter, and stood in the open with a broad leaf for catching a drink. Rosita joined me after leaving her clothing beside my pants. At first the cool rain felt good on my burned skin, and the two of us got soaked while getting our drink. Rosita's black hair matted against her head and clung to her neck, reminding me of the blue-black sheen I had seen on some blackbirds. Water beaded on her skin, and she soon began to shiver. We climbed into our tree house and raked water from our bodies with our hands, flinging it away with our fingers.

The palm roof leaked some, as Rosita said it would, but the broad leaves of the mango carried away most of the water before it hit our inadequate roof. We settled on the branches that made up the floor, lying close for warmth, and Rosita covered with her dress. Not long after that, night came and the rain moved on to another part of the river jungle and savannah.

I heard her crying in the night.

The next day we walked along the edge of the jungle, staying in the shade where grass was short for better walking. It took three days of walking to find anyone—three days of foraging for fruit and cashews, of becoming so thirsty that we were tempted to go to the river before rain came. I wore my jeans because Rosita feared my legs would sunburn, and I carried the umbrella she made. Each evening for three days we built tree houses and slept close together on prickly branches. On the fourth day, when my shoulders looked like a chalk map on brown paper from water blisters forming, breaking and peeling, we climbed from a chaparro tree on the edge of the savannah and walked for an hour in search of breakfast. We had just spotted some papaya trees at the edge of the jungle when we heard the sound of a truck .

"It has a hole in the muffler," I said. "Maybe the candy man has come back."

"It could be the candy man, though I doubt it." Rosita sounded excited. We forgot about the papayas and headed toward the sound, but we weren't quick enough. When we found tire tracks on what might have been a road in the past, it was easy to follow the truck, though the sound of it receded until it was tiny with distance. Then the sound stopped, and Rosita seemed to wilt in disappointment.

"At least we have tracks to follow," I pointed out. "The truck is bound to go somewhere near people."

"It will lead us to people, yes." She didn't sound cheerful, though.

We walked until about mid-morning, wishing we had gone for the papayas but unwilling to leave the tracks until we had to. Then we found where the truck had stalled out.

A wash area, dry most of the year, cut through the savannah with a trickle of water about a finger deep and three meters wide. The wash had caught the pickup, bogging its right front wheel in sand, and the driver, rather than trying to rescue his truck, had made camp. He had stretched a couple of ropes from a chaparro tree to his pickup and attached a tarp to them for shade. When we found him, he knelt beside the trickle of water, washing a frying pan.

From a distance, the first thing we saw was an odd platform mounted on the truck. Someone had bolted stout timbers to the corners of the pickup bed. These held up a flat platform even with the top of the cab of the truck. Above the platform stood more timbers holding a roof that looked like something a circus might erect for a show. The top of the roof was painted red and decorated with a series of staffs, each of which had black snakes coiling around and facing each other. The decorations were hand-painted and ugly, like maybe a child with no artistic talent had done the job. The pickup looked so top-heavy that I imagined it falling on its side in a sharp turn, though it was something of a stretch to think the old truck taking a corner fast enough to be dangerous.

"I once saw some water men," Rosita said, "get their truck bogged down in wet sand like that. They got it unstuck using only a shovel and a machete."

The truck driver swished his frying pan around in the stream and stood, his back to us, so we didn't see the patch over his eye until he turned around. "You idiot of a crick." The man sounded angry. "You call this gold? If this is gold, then God's a possum." He turned around as he flung wet sand from the pan. "You kids going stand there looking like something the cats drug in and the dogs wouldn't eat, or are you going to help me get the truck out of that pus-hole?" He regarded us from a single eye so blue you might figure a drop of the sky had leaked into it. His hair was red as a rooster, and freckles covered his face except for where the black eye patch sat with its thick string running across one cheek and up at a slant over his brow. The patch would have made him look mean like maybe he was a pirate but for the boyish shape of his face, so that instead of a pirate he looked like a teenage boy trying to disguise himself as a pirate, or he would if you took a quick look at him without making the effort to see lines around his eyes and worry lines on his forehead. The lines and the few red whiskers on his chin were clues that he had left boyhood behind some years ago.

"What did he say?" Rosita whispered.

"I said," the man switched to Spanish, "that I'm pleased to meet you, especially since you're here to help get the truck out of the sand. I said that your Kraut friend has the best-looking head of purple hair south of Dalhart. I said that I cooked some pan biscuits but you got here too late to get them while they're hot, but that even cold they beat eating after the buzzards. I said my name is Sam Dean from Abilene, though that's a lie based on an old joke that wasn't funny the first time it got told."

Rosita lifted her brows and looked at me. "That was Spanish, but I didn't understand much of it, either." She seemed amused.

"I'm Don," I said in Spanish, "and this is my friend Rosita. We'll help you get the truck out of the sand, if we can." I looked at the truck, thinking that there wasn't much we could do that would free it from the grip of the wash.

Sam Dean from Abilene turned away and shook a fist at the sky. "I told you to send me some English-speaking help," he said to the clouds, "not Little Orphan Annie with eyes and a freaky Kraut boy who looks American but speaks like a dad-blasted native." He turned back to us with a shrug. "But what the hay, he sent someone, though this ain't so hopeful for getting the ox out of the ditch."

"What did he say?" Rosita asked.

The man snapped his fingers. "Of course," he said in English. "You do talk English, boy, else this little queen of the savannah wouldn't be asking for a translation. My brain is slower than molasses in a blizzard." He glanced at the sky. "Thanks, though you might have sent someone with more muscles."

"He said his ox laid down in a ditch," I told Rosita.

"Close," the man said. "But you don't win a cigar."

"Cigar?" I said.

"Say something in English," the man commanded.

"It snows in Dalhart." It was all I could think of to say. Dad liked to tell a story about being caught in Dalhart during a blue norther back before the war.

"I knew it. My name is Henry Winchester the First. In Texas they call me Hank, and in this desolate land I imagine some Americans might call me Tex."

I turned to Rosita. "He said his name is Enrique Weenchestar.

225

People in Tejas call him Jenk. He said—"

"I'll say what I said, if you don't mind. But first I'll get some food. You kids need to beef up some if you plan to help me with the truck." He rolled his eyes heavenward and muttered, "What could you have been thinking?"

Rosita looked at the truck. "It'll take much work, but we can get it out of the wet sand. Please call me Rosita, and he already told you his name is Don. Not El Don. Just Don. What should we call you? Mr. Weenchestar, perhaps?"

"No. Sam. Call me Sam. It's my middle name and the only good one I have. My daddy named me Henry Winchester the First as a bad joke, and the man upstairs let him do it. If I ever meet the nasty little Irishman who was once my father, I expect to hold him accountable for naming me after a rifle. I've already had it out with the other fellow over the matter."

"What other fellow?" I asked.

Sam laughed, glanced at the sky, and handed me the frying pan. "Wash this. Scrub your knuckles while you're at it. You, too, my little queen of baby roses—wash the prairie dust off your hands. We'll have breakfast under the tarp, or at least you will, and we'll talk about your notion of hard work."

After we washed up, Rosita and I sat, as directed, on the running board of the pickup with the tarp flapping above us and Sam fussing around a low table made from a board set atop two apple crates. He put a huge iron skillet with a lid on the table, two metal pie pans and a jar of yellow stuff. "That is sour dough biscuits." He pointed at the skillet. "Beside it is orange marmalade, the best in the country even if I'm tired of the stuff. Eat hardy." He lifted the lid from the biscuits.

Rosita was of the opinion that the biscuits were spoiled, though still edible. I put so much of the tart jelly on them that I couldn't tell what they tasted like. Sam, sitting across from us on a folding stool, said the sour taste was from his starter and that he reckoned children with their young mouths might not like it. "Took me weeks to concoct that sour dough starter," he said. "I got it working away in a jar behind the seat of the pickup. Doctor Bee-Bee said it made the best dang fast bread on this side of the Atlantic."

"Why do you wear that black thing over your eye?" Rosita

asked.

"Because I lost my eye."

"Lost it? Did it fall out like a marble falling from a hole in your pocket?" she asked.

"I lost it to the tip of a bull's horn in San Angelo, back when I rode the rodeo. Why aren't you afraid of the evil eye? Nearly everyone who sees me with this patch thinks I'll get them with the evil eye."

"I don't believe much in the evil eye," Rosita said.

"You're a cowboy?" I asked.

"Yes. From Bushland, near Amarillo, though I lived most all over Texas."

"You speak strange Spanish," Rosita said.

"I don't speak Spanish at all."

"Sure you do," I said. "You're speaking it now."

"No. I speak Tex-Mex. I learned it in the Rio Grande valley. It isn't Spanish, but it's close enough for me to get along here."

"Why did you come to Venezuela?" Rosita asked. "Why do you drive such a strange truck?"

"Diamonds. I came for the diamonds, but it turns out that there aren't many to be had, at least not by me. A man in Africa told me you could scoop rocks out of river beds in Venezuela and get a can full of diamonds. But he was lying. You kids are full of questions. How about if I ask you some for a while? Why do you have purple hair? Why are you wandering around the prairie alone? Where is your home?"

"I dyed his hair because people thought he was El Don, and the bandits wanted to kill him. But I got the color wrong. Our home is in El Tigrito, and the candy man brought us out west in his truck."

"That makes everything clear." Sam winked at me.

"If you laugh at me, I'll stop talking to you," Rosita warned.

"I'm not laughing." He held up his hands as if to ward off an attack. "I came to Venezuela for diamonds, but I'm willing to settle for gold, though there's not enough lying around for me to find. I shipped out of Houston aboard the Santa Veronica, a rusting old trash barge of a ship that hopped all over the hot part of the world, including Africa and on to the South China Seas where all the pirates live, then came to Venezuela. I jumped ship in Puerto La

Cruz where I traded my belt buckle for this junker of a truck and its supply of colored medicine."

"Belt buckle?" Rosita looked puzzled. "Your story doesn't make sense."

"And yours does? Please remember you said the candy man brought you. That makes about as much sense as saying you were found in the cabbage patch."

"Cabbage?"

"Let's talk about something else," I suggested. "Let's talk about getting your truck out of the sand."

"That's what you kids are here for, to get that maggot of a wheel unstuck. I bargained with the old boy upstairs, and you're what he sent."

"You still don't make any sense," Rosita said.

"No. None of us do. How were the biscuits?"

"Good," I said.

"I already told you. They were spoiled." Rosita sounded annoyed. "Don likes anything, and I was hungry enough to eat even spoiled bread."

Sam stood, folded his stool, and picked up the iron skillet. "You cleaned me out of biscuits faster than soldier ants strip a rose bush."

"Bachacos," I said. "In this country the big ants that are the color of your hair are called bachacos."

"A kid with a purple topnotch is in no position to josh me about the color of my hair." He glanced at Rosita, then translated what he had said into Spanish, sort of.

"I wasn't making fun of it."

"See to it that you don't. Take those pie plates to the creek and wash them. Then tell me how you plan to get the ox out of the ditch."

"Ox?" I said.

"He means truck," Rosita said. "Do you have a shovel, Sam?"

"Yes. I bought it in Cantaura on my way out west because I figured I would shovel me up a bunch of diamonds instead of scooping them up with a coffee can. But the old man keeps playing tricks on me."

"While we wash the plates, you start digging behind the stuck wheel."

"That won't do any good. I tried that."

"Did you put sticks in the hole before trying to back out? Did you put grass behind the other wheels?"

"Sticks? Grass?"

"I thought not. If you want my help, go start digging behind the tire."

While we scoured out the pie pans with sandy water, Rosita said, "I like Sam."

"You do? I thought he annoyed you."

"He does."

When we got back to the truck, Sam was muttering while he dug wet sand from behind the stuck wheel: "First you stick me with Doc Bee-Bee, then you make me lose my bull-dogging buckle. And don't call it an even trade because this heap of junk ain't worth mouse droppings. Then you drag me out here to show me diamonds that ain't there and gold that ain't gold before burying the wheel in this here crick. And when I ask for help getting out, who do you send? Jerry Todd and the waltzing hen."

"What did he say?" Rosita asked me.

"He said—"

"I said," Sam switched to Spanish, "that the old man doesn't count the hair on your head unless there's a joke in it for him. I said sand chiggers gnaw on me if I sleep on the prairie, no-see-ums bite me if I stand in the shade of one of those fake fig trees that grow in strange places out here. I said it's a pain in the big toe to scoop up rocks and get no diamonds and to pan for gold and have to use tweezers for gathering gold specks that never add up to anything worth having. I said the old man let me find those few diamonds in South Africa so I'd have a hunger for the white stones that you can't get wet with water, stones that you can trade for enough money to go half way round the world to find more. I said I didn't think digging out this wheel was worth the effort because it won't get me unstuck, but if the old man sent you then maybe there's something to this digging. I'll try it."

"Did he say all that, Don?"

"No."

"I thought not. Sam, do you have a machete?"

"Everybody in Venezuela has a machete. Why should I be an exception?"

"Good. Give the machete to Don. Don, you go cut some branches from that chaparro tree. Cut small ones so it won't take so long. Bring the branches over here."

Sam leaned the shovel against the side of the pickup and headed for the tail gate. "What will you be doing, my little princess of baby roses, while we work? Here, Don, is the machete. Well?"

"I'm jefe, and the boss works with her head." She tapped her temple.

"Fair enough." Sam got back to his shovel, and I went to the chaparro, glad to have something to do that might help.

When I had a dozen or so chaparro sticks, Rosita put me busy cutting savannah grass. "Lay the grass like a highway behind each of the other wheels, especially that one." She pointed at the right rear tire.

"Why that one?"

"Because it's the one the engine turns, and we don't want it to get stuck in sand while it struggles to pull the front wheel out."

"The drive wheel," I said, remembering what Dad called it. I did as she said, and she directed Sam in putting the chaparro sticks in the puddled hole he had dug.

"Take down the tarpaulin shade," Rosita told Sam. "Load up everything that you want to take with us. Then back the truck out of the sand and water. Go slow. Don't spin the back wheel, and when you start moving, don't stop until you're on dry savannah."

"Yes, boss lady." Sam saluted and started taking down the tarp. "If this works," he muttered in English and glanced at the sky, "I owe you one. Not a big one, and we ain't even by a long shot. There's still the matter of the belt buckle and the rocks that ain't diamonds, not to mention that no-good Irish garden slug you selected to be my daddy."

"What did he say?" Rosita asked. "And don't you tell me, Sam. You always lie."

"Lie? Lie?" Sam appeared to be offended.

"He said he owes someone for turning his daddy into a garden slug." I shrugged. "I didn't understand him so well."

"Close enough," Sam said.

20
A Magic Box

With Rosita standing to one side, hands on her hips and lips clamped into a determined frown, the creek didn't dare keep its grip on Sam's tire. The truck rolled strait back on the chopped grass an beyond. "Hot dog," Sam shouted over the roar of the damaged muffler. "You kids get in the truck and we're out of here."

Inside the cab of the truck, Rosita said, "Go to the right of the place where the sand caught the wheel, and go fast. If you stop, we'll get stuck again."

"You're the boss for now." Sam gripped the wheel with one hand and pushed the floor shift forward to make a grinding sound. He drove through the creek with no problem, the truck producing a cloud of white smoke behind it. "Forgot to check the oil, but I'll do that later. This goat of a truck drinks oil so fast I have to keep pouring it through the engine." He glanced at me and switched to English: "Don, my little purple-headed Kraut, when this jewel sitting between us gets growed up, you better nab her and marry her before some good-looking peasant with a moustache lays claim to her. She's going to be a real looker, but the world is full of lookers, and what a man needs is a woman with brains."

"A man up the river already told me to marry her, but he said it was because she had a fire in her head. I don't plan on getting married to anyone, ever, regardless of brains or fire."

"You two are talking about me," Rosita said. "And it's getting me angry. You'd better speak Spanish because I don't think you want to get me angry. What did you say, Don?"

"Spanish it is." Sam slapped the steering wheel.

"I'm sorry, Rosita. He said good things about you. He said you know how to look and that you have brains."

"Is that true, Sam? Is that what you said?"

"Yes. And Don said that—"

"You're about to tell a lie. Don, what else did you say about me?"

"Nothing. Sam said I should marry you, and I said I'm not one to think about marrying anyone. But I did say I like you and if I

231

married anyone, it would be you. But of course I'll never get married."

"You didn't say that. Did he, Sam?"

"Yes he did. He also said that you have the most beautiful eyelashes on any girl in the southern hemisphere. He said yours is a face that launched a thousand ships and burned Troy to the ground. He said—"

"Stop it. Just stop it, both of you. Boys. And speak Spanish from now on."

"But Rosita, I've been talking Spanish since jumping ship in Puerto La Cruz. Even to Doctor Bee-Bee because he knew only four phrases in English. I get a headache when I talk Spanish too much. Besides, I have a life-long habit of speaking English to the man in charge."

The truck bounced along, its roar muted in the cab, the circus-looking structure attached to the back causing us to lean more than we should with each bump. We drove so slow that some of the white smoke from the exhaust came into the cab when the wind shifted directions. I hung my elbow out the window and Rosita sat back with her arms crossed on her chest. Buzzards circled off to the left, high above the savannah, and flocks of parrots flew as green spots above the river jungle to our right. Sam appeared to be following a faint road where savannah grass grew less tall. Maybe, I thought, he's heading for the village where Sylvia's daughter lives. I hoped not because I didn't want to be the one who told her what Mr. Marlin did. We seemed to he heading east, which according to Rosita was the proper direction for getting to El Tigrito.

"I won't either," Rosita said.

"You won't what?" Sam glanced at her, curiosity on his face.

"Get married. Ever."

"If I came back in ten years, which I won't ever do—but if I did, I would remind you of what you said. You would be standing outside a cute little house with a purple-haired baby on each hip and some pan de mano cooking inside the house and your husband gone away for the day, working for an oil company. You and I would have a good laugh about what you once said about marriage and—"

"Where are we going?" Rosita demanded.

"Let me finish."

"Where are we going?"

Sam sighed, rolled his eye upward, and said in English, "Why don't you send me one this feisty who isn't just a baby? You know I don't have time for her to grow up."

"Spanish. You'd better talk Spanish," I warned.

"I told you, Rosita," Sam said, "that I have this life-long habit of talking to the man in English, and I'm not likely to stop."

"What man?" I asked.

"I think he means God. Is that what you mean?"

"Yes. But I don't like the word god so much, in English or Spanish."

"You're praying, then?" Rosita looked at him, round-eyed.

"I wouldn't call it that. It's more like a dialogue, and I do more fussing at him than asking for anything. The old boy is a trickster. I have to keep reminding myself that I need to forgive him, though it isn't always easy. And we're going wherever this nothing of a road leads us. I hope it takes us to a village soon, preferably one with a lot of people in need of medicine and entertainment so I can make some money. You two will help me. We're on our way out of the diamond and gold country, out of the primitive parts toward the coast. If I stay out here much longer, the rainy season will bog me down in a place where not even you can get me out until the rains stop. East. That's where we're going. Toward El Tigrito, if you want, since it's sort of on the way. I went through El Tigre on my way out west back when I thought I was going to scoop up a coffee can of diamonds and dig up a ton of gold, back before I found out that diamonds are rare as rattlesnake lips and before discovering how tiny flakes of gold show up in the panning to keep you at it with a joke of a promise, flakes that glitter and make you want to gather them with tweezers but you never get enough to be worth anything. I plan to sell all of Doctor Bee-Bee's medicine and maybe make enough to get back to Texas."

"How will we help you?" I asked.

"You'll see when the time comes."

The time came that afternoon, after we drove slow through the violence of a rain storm, the wipers on the truck clicking and moaning to leave streaks on the windshield, the tires of the truck sliding in puddles, and rain beating the truck's cloud of white exhaust out of the air. The time came on the edge of a village where Sam set up his show.

At first Rosita and I said we didn't want to be a part of it. But Sam told us how much fun he had with the show and that he made money from donations as well as from selling medicine.

"People donate money to pay for the entertainment of the show, and they never complain when they drop coins into my magic box. Besides, it's good medicine they buy from me. It helps people with pain, and many believe the medicine cures them. And I'm here to tell you that thinking they're cured makes it true."

No one gets hurt, he assured us. Everyone benefits: the natives get medicine and have fun, he gets Bolivars for his efforts, and we get a ride home as well as the fun of being part of the show. So we agreed. Sam parked far enough from the village to be something of a mystery, he said. With oleanders and castorbean bushes as a backdrop, he set up his stage.

Before the little kids wandered over to gape at us, he took a glass eye out of the glove box in the pickup, turned his back to us, and made some grunting sounds. When he turned around, his patch was gone and he looked at us from two blue eyes. "This one gives me a headache if I wear it for long. If people hang around longer than they should, I might have to put in my green eye. It's smaller and has to be held in place with tissue paper. But I cannot appear with my eye patch or people will assume I'm here to put a hex on them with the evil eye."

He painted Rosita's face with colored chalk: maroon on her eyelids up to her eyebrows, black on her brows to make them longer and thinner and slanted at good angle, black at the corners of her eyes, and a thin line of black around red lips, reminding me of the girl with pomegranate tetas and berry-stained lips. He lightened Rosita's face with tan and white and worked some subtle lines into her forehead, making her look like a grown woman of startling beauty. With brown chalk, he darkened my face and hands. He also colored my feet in the white strip where neither jeans or alpargatas hid my white skin. I had to wear one of his long-sleeved shirts and a straw hat so big my ears fit inside the hat band. Just after he finished chalking us up, the little kids arrived—seven or eight of them, ragged and dirt-smeared and not much older than Fatima, the candy man's daughter.

They wanted to peek in the bed of the pickup, in the area that Sam called "the substage," but they were too small to see over the side of the truck, and Sam wouldn't let them climb up for a look. He pressed a loche into each of their hands and told them to come back when he made his truck sound like a cow with a stopped-up nose. "It will moo three times," he said. "That means you need to come back with all your friends and family to see the magic medicine show. The loches I gave you are payment for telling the people about the show. I will perform great magic."

The boys eyed Rosita with awe, and when Sam dismissed them, they scampered away clutching their copper coins. Some older kids stood at the edge of the clearing to watch us. They were boys, but one girl with two long braids stood among them, and she looked a bit strange. Her face seemed too small and her neck looked more maroon than brown. With only the few curious older kids watching from a distance, the three of us worked on the stage. We hung a canvas backdrop over three sides, leaving one side exposed to the grassy area where the villagers would stand. Sam hung canvas over the area between the walls of the pickup and the platform, and he showed me and Rosita a trap door in the floor of the stage. "You two will climb this little ladder to join me on stage when I call for you," Sam explained. Then he gave us some other instructions.

I didn't much like what I had to do with the magic box until he showed me the handcuffs. "If this box isn't cuffed to your wrist, some of the natives will try to make off with it. I know, because it used to be my job to show the box, back when Doc Bee-Bee ran this show." Sam produced a silver Bolivar from his pocket, and we watched through the glass side of the box as he dropped the coin into a slot. We heard the coin clunk as it fell in, but we didn't see it in the box. The coin vanished as it went through the hole.

"How does the box work?" I asked.

"It's real magic." Sam chuckled.

"There's no such thing as real magic," I said.

"There is, too," Rosita said. "But I doubt the box is magic."

"Oh you of little faith," Sam said. "This box has special magic. It changes their money into my money without them ever complaining about the matter, and that's magic. Mostly they drop loches into it, but little coins add up, and some people drop in a Bolivar, so it's worth the effort."

"But how does it make the coins disappear?"

"You figure it out, boy. You have a good head. Just don't you pry up the lid and don't let anyone get after it with a machete to see what's inside."

"It's a trick," I said.

"Maybe. But because the trick is so interesting and so like real magic, no one complains. The people always think it's magic, and if they believe it is, then it's true."

"Believing something makes it true?" I gave Rosita a significant look.

"Not in that way," she said. "Carmen wasn't talking about a trick. Neither was Sylvia. They were talking about real things. Real."

"Who are Carmen and Sylvia?" Sam asked, but he didn't want an answer. He bent over and muttered, holding his hand over his glass eye. "Ding nab it, fellow, why did you have to let that dirtbag of a bull jab me in the eye with his horn? Then you sent me a doctor trained by the Nazis to make a glass eye so big it gives me a headache. You ought to wear this glass ball bearing for a while, see how you like it."

"What did he say?" Rosita asked me.

"He's talking with his god again."

"God is everybody's god. What did he say?"

"I said," Sam spoke in Spanish, "that one of the tricks the old boy pulled was to give me two glass eyes. One that matches the real one in color but causes headaches. The other that is the wrong color but is too small. I have to roll up toilet paper and stuff it around the eye to keep it from falling out."

"Did he say that, Don?"

"No. He said something about gnats training his doctor. I didn't understand him."

"Gnats," Sam said. "You're exactly right. Gnats. No-see-ums. Heh-hens, the natives call them. Oops." He glanced at the storm building in Rosita's face and switched to Spanish. "Don't expect me to translate when I talk to the man upstairs." With an angry glance at the sky, he turned and got into the passenger side of the pickup cab, opened the glove box, and started doing something with his

236

glass eye. When he got out, one eye was green, though you'd have to get up close to tell for sure, and it didn't seem to look at the right things.

Sam was busy in the substage with colored pieces of cloth and a cotton rope that he took out of the trunk when the maroon-necked girl came over to us. Some of the boys wanted to follow her, but she stopped them with a few words and a gesture of her hand. "I'm Juanita," she said to us.

"I'm Rosita."

"I'm Don. Not El Don. Just Don. It's my name."

Juanita looked at me as if she were about to laugh, her face conveying joy in her amusement, not hostility or criticism. The illusion that her face was too small came, I decided, from the maroon splotch on her neck and from her tiny chin and huge mouth. She didn't look grotesque—just strange, and pretty in an odd kind of way. Maybe it was her full lips and her large, wide-set eyes, black as the truck's tires, that caused me to think of her as pretty. "The one with hair like the sunrise," she gestured toward Sam, "is only the second white man I have ever seen."

"He isn't white," Rosita said. "He's pink."

Sam glanced at us. "I'm white," he said. "My mother said I'm cotton-mouthed Irish."

"What does that mean?" Juanita asked.

"I never found out. Mama told me to ask my daddy, but I never got the chance."

"I understand," Juanita said, "about not being able to talk to your father. Some fathers seem to stay angry all the time."

"Tell your family to come to our show," Sam said. "When I make the truck sound like—"

"I heard what you told the little ones." Juanita turned to me and Rosita. "I would bring you some empanadas dulces, if you would like."

"Thank you," Rosita said.

"I would pay you for them," Sam said.

"No you won't." She leaned close to me and whispered, "It would be nice to have you and Rosita as cousins." Then she left, and I noticed how the maroon splotch spread around to the back of her neck and up into her hair.

Sam put a box covered with black velvet on the stage for holding his cotton rope, the magic box and other items. He also got pills out of a trunk, huge clear bottles of them. The pills were all about the same size and shape but were different colors. Some bottles contained red ones, and in others were pills that were white, blue, green, and brown. "Red sells best," he said, "because I advertise them as aids to the pain of lost love. It seems everyone has lost someone and needs help with the heartache of it. All pills go into these paper packets." He produced a shoe box full of packets made from cut-up newspapers. "People sometimes value the packets almost as much as the pills because they believe there are magic words on the packets. I don't tell them that. It's something they figure out for themselves."

"Do you have other medicines?" Rosita asked. "Something for cuts, perhaps. Ointments?"

"No. Doctor Bee-Bee had all kinds of junk like that, but I streamlined the operation. I sell only these pills. It keeps the business simple. Besides, I don't know a thing about medicine—except for these pills, of course. And I keep the price simple: ten pills for one Bolivar. Doctor Bee-Bee priced them out in different ways based on the color, but I calculated that he would come out about the same with one price, so when he took my belt buckle and I took the pill business, I changed the prices. Ten pills. One Bolivar. Remember that."

When he was ready for the show, he bribed the older kids to go spread the word in the village. Juanita was nowhere in sight. Rosita and I got in the bed of the pickup, under the stage, and Sam handed me a wet cloth to scrub the brown chalk from my face, hands, and feet. "Put on those funny black pants you carry around in the basket," he said. "And you, Rosita, don't take the makeup off. You'll have the title of Princess of the Western Jungle and maybe some others as they occur to me. The crowd will love you."

He closed the tail gate, dropped canvas over the back so the area beneath the stage became dark, and he tooted on the pickup horn three times.

"It does sound like a cow with a stopped-up nose," Rosita said.

The sudden darkness that fell on us when Sam closed in the substage reminded me of how dark it had been in the candy maker's truck as we left El Tigrito. And, as in that other truck, bits of light began to appear as our eyes adjusted. "I've been on stage, but only once," I told Rosita.

"Once I helped with an Easter play in the village church. I was an angel standing over the tomb of Jesus. But I didn't have to say anything."

"Who played Jesus?"

"Father Martinez. My grandmother said that Father Martinez came back from the dead better than any priest she had ever seen."

"I played Rumple Stilskin in a play at Elizabeth Street School in Corpus Christi. Was there an Easter Bunny in your play?"

"Bunny? Like the rabbit we ate near the cave of the dead Indios?"

"Yes, but I was making a joke."

"That was a joke? Perhaps you could explain it to me. I'm not good about understanding jokes. And what is a Rumple Stilskin?"

"Not a what. A who. He was a dwarf who exploded into pieces because the fairy princess found out his name."

"You had to explode in front of people? How did you do that?

"It was a trick. Most of what happens on stage is a trick, like the priest dying and coming back to life."

"He pretended, yes. But to explode?"

Sam stamped on the stage above our heads. "You two be quiet down there. The villagers are arriving."

"I want to come out and see them," Rosita said.

"Be quiet. You'll ruin your grand entrance. I'll signal you to come soon. But Don is supposed to come up first."

"I'm coming now." Her voice sounded cross.

"Wait. I'll call you first, then Don afterward. Please be quiet."

Rosita and I listened to the noises outside: footsteps in the grass, people coughing and whispering. "It's a quiet crowd," Rosita said. "Like in church."

For a few minutes Sam paced upon the stage, then he started talking: "Men and women, boys and girls, people of Venezuela, please forgive my Spanish. I learned to speak in a Spanish school in Tibet."

"He did not," Rosita whispered.

"My teacher was David Crockett, a great magician who lived on

239

top of Mount Vesuvius, the tallest mountain in the world."

"Is Mount Vesuvius in Tibet?" Rosita whispered.

"No. I think it's in Nebraska." I kept my voice low.

Sam took a couple of extra hard steps to tell us to hush. He cleared his throat, and I knew he was trying to make it sound natural to the crowd and angry to us. "My teacher taught me the art of bringing wonderful people here from far places. Earlier today some of you children probably saw Nefertiti, the child queen of Egypt. She likes to visit me when I come to a new village. Right now she's floating down the Nile on a boat made of waddles and scarabs. But she'll come if I call her sweetly and use Master Crockett's magic sheet. Nefertiti, sweet angel of the Ganges River and Queen of the Nile, come to us and share your wisdom." He stamped on the floor and kicked the catch to the trap door. It fell open and Rosita climbed up the ladder. She paused before going on up and whispered, "Don't you explode on this stage." I got a glimpse of Sam holding up a sheet as Rosita drew the trap door closed.

"Mount Vesuvius is in Nebraska," she told Sam in low tones.

I heard Sam flip the sheet and the audience gasp. "The princess says she is pleased to be here instead of on my teacher's mountaintop, for the winds there blow colder than in Nebraska, which is ten kilometers from the north pole. Look at her. So beautiful. But when I first found her, she suffered from a pain in her heart so powerful that she had decided to end her life by allowing a deadly snake to bite her on the neck." The audience gasped, and some cried out no, no. "Yes, yes. She held a deadly aspen close to that divine neck, and the snake, its jewel eye glittering and tongue flashing about, had opened its mouth to taste her sweet flesh when she came across the world to appear beneath my master's magic sheet. Back, you foul serpent, I cried and flipped the sheet upon it. When I withdrew the sheet, the snake was gone, banished into the jungles of Borneo from where it came. This queen looked at me with such pain in those beautiful eyes that I knew she was dying from a tragic love. So I gave her one of these red pills." I heard two quick steps across the stage, the sound of a jar lid being unscrewed, and the rattle of pills.

"One. That's all it took. For a child queen, as for any person about her size, one is all it takes. More than one can be dangerous.

240

To help babies who cry for unknown reasons or no reason at all, break the red pill twice and give the baby the smallest piece. How do you feel now, oh my lovely and tiny queen?"

"I thought Borneo—"

"You see? She is over her tragic love and now thinks about her pet snake, deadly though it was. One red pill did it. Never take more than two at once, and always wait until half a day has passed until you take more. You, boy. Yes. You eating a banana. You like bananas?"

"Yes sir."

"And if you eat one banana, it makes you happy?"

"Sometimes."

"What happens if you eat twenty bananas?" Laughter rippled through the crowd. "I'll tell you. Your stomach hurts. One banana is good. Too many bananas hurt you. So it is with the red pills. So is it with all medicine. A little is good for you. Too much becomes harmful. Ten red pills for one Bolivar, my friends. This is a bargain you won't ever see again. My supply of red pills comes from a medicine factory in a Chinese city, just across the border from Ireland. After my last shipment, the factory burned to the ground. Yes. And it will be years before I get another shipment. In the big cities, these red pills would bring five times what I'm charging you. In Caracas, they pay it, too. Yes. A silver fuerte for ten pills, and you can buy them here from me for only one Bolivar. Little Queen, will you help the people get their pills? These are good for pains of the heart caused by loss of love. They are also good for other pains in the chest—any kinds of pains. Buy ten and watch the child queen of Egypt count them out for you. She'll wrap them in paper made in Bombay, just down the river from Cairo, and printed with prayers and other magic words."

"But you told us that you didn't—" Rosita sputtered.

"Right you are, my queen. I told you I haven't had a single heartache since taking the red pills." He dropped his voice. "Take the packages and sell some pills." Above me, I could hear Rosita settle at the edge of the stage, no doubt beside the bottles of pills. I heard the clink of coins and knew the red pills were a hit.

"As amazing as the queen is, I'll conjure someone even more amazing. He'll come to us from the distant mountains surrounding the famous city of Bushland. This is a mestizo boy whose parents took him from Mexico City to the dry mountain air of West Texas because he suffered from headaches. These terrible pains came upon him when he was a small child, and the agony they brought made his skin pale and his hair turn purple." Several in the audience laughed in a way to show they didn't believe Sam. "Yes. See for yourself. I'll hold the Crockett receiving sheet and mutter the right words and he will appear before you, El Don, heir to the riches of his family. They own the Empire State Building in Dallas, not to mention the famous pyramid of Cheops outside Mexico City."

The trap door fell open and I scrambled up the ladder, pausing to draw the door closed behind me. When I stood, Sam still held the sheet. He winked at me with his blue eye and continued his line of bull while the crowd began whispering and laughing. "I suspect his skin has regained some of its color. When I first found him, he was white as a dry-season cloud, and his hair was more purple than a sunset." He flung the sheet aside with a couple of dramatic flaps, and the crowd fell silent.

Appearing thus to the villagers was even better than I had imagined when I daydreamed about leaping out from behind their huts, shaking my purple hair to scare the pee out of them. I strutted about on the stage, enjoying their stunned silence. Rosita gave me a poisonous look and got back to stuffing pills into paper packets. Sam spoke to me in English. "Don't try to say the wrong things like your friend did. Remember that this is just a show. Okay?

"Okay," I said.

Then he reverted to Spanish. "El Don just told me that he has fewer headaches than in the past. When you do have a headache, which pill do you take?"

Sam had told me which one was for the head, but I forgot. I pointed in the general direction of the pill jars and said, "That one."

"The white. Yes. One white pill for a boy. Anyone much larger than El Don here should take two, but never more than two. Remember about eating twenty bananas. More than two of my pills can cause problems. Look at his hair, my friends. Have you ever seen such terrible evidence of the ravages of a headache? And his skin. It looks better now, though he's still disgustingly white. When the headaches had El Don in their grip, his skin turned white as the belly of a snake. But now he is recovering, and look at him. Soon he will appear healthy and brown again, like his father, the Prince of Monaco."

"Mexico," I corrected.

"Yes. His father is from Mexico, but he married the daughter of the Sultan of Turkey, who gave him the island of Monaco as a wedding gift. I bring you royalty, my friends—the offspring of the great and famous. This boy is so grateful for my curing his headaches with the magic white pills that he has agreed to come here and help you buy them. Ten white pills for one Bolivar. A true bargain."

I joined Rosita at the edge of the stage. She handed me a stack of paper packets, and I opened the jar of white pills. They smelled vaguely of vinegar. "Aspirin," I whispered in English. "Sam is selling aspirin."

"What?" Rosita said.

I started to explain when I spotted Juanita in the crowd, staring at me and Rosita, her large mouth open as in surprise. Before remembering that I was the son of the Prince of Monaco and not the brown boy with a hat over his hair Jaunita had met earlier, I nodded to her. She closed her mouth and made her way to me. "Don," she whispered, handing me a packet tied in banana leaves, "What happened to your skin and hair?"

"We'll tell you later," Rosita said.

"Thanks for the empanadas," I said.

Juanita stepped back, nearly tripping on the alpargatas of an odd-looking man who had a continuous eyebrow running across his face. She glanced up at him and winced, perhaps because of his angry frown, and she fled to the back of the crowd.

"While they help those who are prone to heartaches and headaches, I will show you my magic rope." Sam held the cotton rope up to show how solid it was. I counted pills and traded packets for Bolivars, dropping the coins into the box of paper packets. Sam amazed the crowd by cutting the rope with a pocket knife, then dragging it through his hands and pulling out a rope that had been magically mended. It was an old trick, one that Todd and I read about in a book of magician's tricks, and I knew how it was done. But I never could make it work properly. Sam did a good job of the trick. Then he stuffed colored pieces of silk cloth into his ear, pulling them out of his other ear, and they were all tied together like he had made the knots inside his head. The crowd clapped and laughed and kept coming to buy the white pills from me and the red ones from Rosita.

One fellow wasn't amused, though, nor was he buying anything —the man who scared Jaunita with his frown. He stood, lean and discontent, his arms folded across his chest, his chin down, and he glared at Sam from beneath that heavy eyebrow running across the top of his face. The brow edged down above his nose to accent his mean scowl, and I thought that I wouldn't like to have such a fellow angry at me.

21
Brandishing the Glass Eye

The eyebrow man watched with his odd frown, and I figured maybe he had understood Sam's lie about Nebraska being at the north pole. Sam pumped the crowd up with all kinds of horse marlarky about the heartache and headache pills, amazed them with some tricks, then got the magic box with the handcuffs dangling from it. "This box holds any money you put into it," Sam said, "but it doesn't like anyone to see its coins. So it makes them invisible. I'll drop this Bolivar into the slot to show you. Look through the glass side and you can see everything inside the box except for the coin." He made a show of holding up the box and clinking in the coin. "You can rattle it around." With a quick shake he rattled the coin inside. "But the box has already hidden the coin from sight." He approached the edge of the stage, bent down, and showed the box to those close enough to see. I noticed that the eyebrow man uncrossed his arms and leaned forward to get a better look. Sam handed the box to me and I snapped the handcuffs onto my wrist. "The amazing El Don, he of the purple hair and light skin from a thousand thousand headaches, will demonstrate the box to anyone interested. Just drop a coin into the box and watch it vanish. Be warned that the box will not return your coin. Bolivars are best, but the box will hide any coin you put into it."

I turned the sale of aspirin over to Rosita the Queen of the Nile and got on with the business of the box. People came up to the edge of the stage, and I leaned down to let them peer into it. Mr. Continuous Brow pushed up close. "Shake the box," he said.

I did so. "It's still in there, but I can't see it," I said. "This is the strangest box in Venezuela."

"Let me hold it," a boy asked. "I'll feed it a loche so I can watch it eat the coin."

"I'll hold it for you." I made a show of the handcuffs. The boy looked disappointed but only for an instant. He dropped in a coin.

"It's gone," the boy said with awe. "I watched through the glass as I dropped it in. The coin vanished."

"I don't believe it," Mr. Eyebrow said. "Hold it down here."

I held the box for him, and he put a Bolivar halfway into the slot but didn't let go of it. "Drop the coin," Sam said. "Watch the box make it invisible."

The man pulled the coin out of the slot and pushed it in again, keeping a grip on it. "This is a trick. Half of the coin seems to disappear, but the part in my fingers is still visible." He experimented more with the coin.

The boy who had dropped the loche into the slot pushed up close again. "I want to see," he said and gave my arm a tug. This caused the man to lose his grip on the Bolivar and the coin clinked into the box. "It vanished, the same as my loche," the boy said.

"My Bolivar," the man said. "Give it back. I wasn't going to drop it."

"I don't know how to open the box," I said.

"I do." He grabbed the box. I jerked back, and the cuffs pulled the box out of his hands. I moved back from the edge of the stage. "You thief," the man said in a low and dangerous voice. "I won't be tricked."

Sam chuckled. "I warned you that the box wouldn't give back coins."

"Fake." The man grabbed the edge of the stage, put a foot on the rear tire, and vaulted onto the platform. "You said Mount Vesuvius is in Tibet, but I know that it's in Australia. You're a liar and you sell poison medicines and you tricked me out of my money." He took a swing at Sam.

It was a fast punch, and Sam tried to duck, but he was too late. The man's fist caught Sam's head, and his eye popped out. The crowd gasped, and the man watched in horror as the eye bounced on the stage and rolled toward me. For a split second I thought maybe I caught a glimpse of blue on the eye, which meant the man knocked Sam's good eye right out of his head. I grabbed up the eye, half expecting it to be rubbery and moist, and turned it so I could see the color.

Green. I sighed with relief and held it up for Rosita to see in case she, too, thought Sam had lost his good eye. The man seemed to believe I was reaching toward him with the eye. "No." he said, throaty and low. "No." He stepped back and fell off the stage but managed to roll and spring to his feet when he hit the ground.

I stood, brandishing the glass eye, making it stare at the crowd. They seemed locked in place, like someone had handcuffed their ankles to the ground, and they stared at me. Then someone pointed at Sam and said "Ay-yi-yi. Mira." The toilet tissue he had stuffed into his socket to hold the eye in place had come unraveled and was hanging down his cheek like a white worm. "The brujo is weeping snakes," someone shouted. People seemed to remember that their ankles weren't manacled to the ground, and they started backing away, slow at first, then picking up speed, especially when a voice cried out, "The evil eye and the snake of perdition." Everyone fled, or nearly everyone, knocking against each other as they left. In a matter of seconds, we were alone on stage with the grassy place where the audience had stood looking trampled and the jungle beyond growing black shadows in spots of gold from the evening sun. The one villager who had not run approached the truck, her lips tucked into a line to make her chin appear even smaller and the splotch on her neck glowing.

"He left frightened," she said. "But soon he'll remember feeling embarrassed and humiliated, and he will return with friends."

"Mr. Eyebrow," I said.

"Yes. You should get into the truck and go. Quickly." Juanita started to leave, then turned back. "The empanadas dulces are still warm."

"Thanks," I called as she left.

Sam produced his eye patch from a pocket, set it in place to make him look like a little boy playing at being a pirate, and said with disgust, "You really ripped it that time."

"Don't you blame Don," Rosita said.

"I'm sorry," I said.

"I wasn't talking to you. I was talking to that mean trickster in charge of this mess."

"God?" Rosita said, astonished.

"You really owe me one for this." Sam shook a fist at the sky. "We'll settle accounts on this later." He turned to us. "Those people left here frightened. Doc Bee-Bee told me that scared folk can turn into mad folk, and that if I ever got people scared to leave and leave fast. That little native girl was right in her warning." He started rolling up the canvas on the back of the stage.

Rosita gathered pills, jars, and paper packets to take down the ladder into the bed of the pickup. I handed Sam his green eye. "Thanks." He stuffed it into a pocket. "I won that eye in a crap shoot with an Iban fellow near Kuching." Sam got back to rolling up the canvas, and I helped.

"Where's Kuching?"

"Borneo. The Iban are reformed headhunters, though judging from the baskets of heads they hang in their longhouses, they haven't been reformed for long. James Nudong was the Iban who bet me the glass eye against two silver dollars. I won."

"Do you suppose James chopped off someone's head to get the green eye?" I asked.

"I thought about that, thought about a one-eyed Englishman maybe, gone to Borneo to trade the Iban out of their raw rubber with beads and other junk, and James or another fierce fellow taking the man's head when he cheated them. Then he slung the head into his family's basket hanging in the longhouse, and one day maybe months or years later the eye worked its way out of the skull and fell on the floor. Might have given the whole family a real fright. I don't know. Just in case the eye had vacationed for a while in the socket of a dead Englishman, I boiled the thing before trying it out, though I could tell from looking that it was too small to make a good fit. Getting me to win a green eye that was too small was another of the old boy's tricks."

"Were there wild men in Borneo? Headhunters, even. Wow." I thought of the shrunken head hanging in the shop in El Tigre, a string through its lips. "My daddy often talks about wild men from Borneo."

"Yes. James was one of them. Drank like a fish, that boy."

"What did he wear?"

"Wear?"

"Yeah. I always wondered what a wild man wears. Was he naked?"

"James? No. But I went with him to his family's longhouse up river and saw plenty of wild women. They wore a sarong, which is a kind of skirt they wrapped around their waists. They let their flappers hang where they would."

We dropped the canvas into the bed of the pickup and started rolling up the piece hanging over the back of the truck. Rosita stuck her head through the trap door and spoke a single word before vanishing: "Spanish."

"She sure gets riled up about us talking English."

I switched to Spanish: "She thinks we might be talking about her instead of the wild people of Borneo."

"I'd druther talk English, if I had my druthers."

"Speak what you want. I'll talk Spanish." It seemed safer that way, I thought. Let him answer to Rosita. "Did the Iban shrink the heads before they hung them in baskets?"

"No. The ones who shrink heads come from somewhere else. Africa, maybe. Or New York City."

When we got into the cab of the pickup, leaving much of the packing undone, Rosita said, "Thanks, Don, for talking so I could understand. Sam will do the same."

Sam had started the pickup, gunning the engine so it blew an extra-thick cloud of white smoke out the exhaust. He glanced in his outside mirror and muttered some nonsense in a nasty tone and began turning around with care not to brush the stage against trees. "Look." Rosita's voice carried a note of urgency.

Mr. Eyebrow and his men emerged from the oleanders and castorbean bushes. All of them carried machetes, and when they saw the truck moving, they began running toward us. "What?" Sam muttered in English. "More of your tricks?"

"That didn't sound much like a prayer," Rosita said.

"I don't ever pray. But if I did, now would be the time." Sam took off with the engine rattling and blowing smoke and the top of the stage scraping against high branches. The men with machetes fell behind, and when I looked back they seemed to be shouting, though I couldn't be sure because of the noise of the truck. Their mouths opened and worked as if they were saying plenty, and their machetes flashed in the evening sun.

Sam slowed when we hit the bumpy grass of the savannah, and he turned east to drive parallel with the river jungle. "How many packages of pills did you sell?" he asked Rosita.

"I don't know. Maybe twelve or more."

"More, I hope. Don?"

"Less than that. Six, I think."

"So that's at least eighteen, not counting the one Bolivar that fellow dropped in the box before he punched my eye out. We made a bit over six dollars, then. That's not bad, though I hoped for better."

"You were selling aspirin," I said in accusation. "It doesn't cure anything."

"I never said it would. I said it would help with pain, and that's what aspirin does."

"But you were tricking them," Rosita said. "The red pills and the white ones are the same, aren't they? Both are aspirin."

"Yes. And if it hadn't been for the mad boxer that the old man sent, I would have sold some of the green ones and some of the brown ones. And yes, they're all aspirin. But it's good medicine. It helps with pain, and that's about the best thing any medicine can do."

"You sold the red aspirin for broken hearts," Rosita said.

"I did. Broken hearts hurt worse than ordinary chest pains. The green pills are for sore arms and legs, and the brown ones are for stomach aches. And they all work just as I promise."

"They work to make you money." Rosita sounded scornful.

"And what's wrong with that? Show me a doctor who doesn't charge a fee, just one. Medical people have to make a living, too."

"Sylvia didn't charge for her work."

"She didn't," I agreed, "but people brought her gifts, which is like charging them."

"It's not the same. Also, you sold aspirin for the pain of losing a loved one. That's dishonest."

"It isn't. Half of curing is believing the cure will work. When I got the tropical runs in Kuching, I went to a medical doctor named Isahak who claimed to have studied medicine in London. He tried to get me to buy some red syrup from him, along with two different kinds of pills. I asked him which one stopped me up, and he said it was one of the pills, so I bought only them and asked why he wanted to sell me the other stuff. He said that people in Kuching didn't believe he was treating them properly if he didn't prescribe at least three kinds of medicine. That syrup and the other pills might as well have been aspirin, as far as I'm concerned. But the people there believed such treatment cured them."

250

"And believing something makes it true?" I asked.

"That isn't what Carmen meant," Rosita said. "I told you that."

The truck engine made a sudden noise like the sound of a jackhammer breaking concrete, and we came to a halt. Sam struck the steering wheel with his fist. "I should have put in more oil."

"What happened?" I asked.

"Sounds like I threw a rod."

"Say it in Spanish," Rosita said.

"This is bad." Sam popped the hood by pulling a lever under the dash. "I'll look, but I think we're on foot from now on."

"The men," Rosita said.

"Yes. The men." Sam got out and lifted the hood. Rosita and I looked also, as if we could make sense of the mechanics of the truck. He slammed the hood. "You skunk kissing son of pie-bald mule." He bashed the hood with a fist and switched to Spanish. "There's no repairing that mess. My guess is that we have about five minutes to get whatever we need to take with us before those men get too close."

I took the basket that contained my jeans and what was left of our bones, and I put Juanita's empanadas dulces into the basket. Rosita and Sam rummaged through the trunk behind the cab. She took the cotton rope and the machete. He stuffed his pocket with coins, then took out a canvas bag and began putting what I regarded as useless junk into it: the pill bottles, which he wrapped in old shirts, the box of paper packets, the sheet he got from David Crockett, the black velvet cloth. I watched him pull the blue eye out of a pocket and toss it into the trunk. "You sewer rock of a Nazi eyeball," he said.

"I want it if you don't." I retrieved the blue eye and dropping it into my basket.

"Leave that trash," Rosita told him. "We need to get moving."

"Just a few more things." Sam dug around in the trunk.

As we climbed out of the pickup, we caught a glimpse of the men on the savannah, not more than two hundred meters away. "Into the jungle, fast," Rosita said. We started toward the line of trees, now a shadowed mass in the evening sun.

"Buzzard lips," Sam said to the sky, then to us: "Try not to leave an obvious trail."

"They'll know we're in the jungle," I said.

"But not where. I have a plan to bamboozle them."

"Spanish," Rosita snapped.

"Spanish it is. We head straight into the jungle, then go back to the village." Sam laughed without humor.

"No," I said.

"Yes," Rosita corrected. "Sam, you're smarter than I thought. It won't occur to the men that we would go that direction. They'll search for us down river."

"Then they'll figure it out." I shifted the basket on my shoulder. The river jungle loomed upon us. "They'll catch us in their own village and chop us up with machetes like Rosita chopped up the snake in the swamp."

"There's canoes in the village," Sam said.

"I won't steal another canoe." The certainty in my voice was greater than what I felt.

"I will," Sam said.

"I won't get in one that's stolen. I'll stay behind."

"If Don stays, I'll stay," Rosita said.

"That way." Sam pointed.

"You go." I stopped. "No stolen canoes."

"I'll buy one, then. Come on." He started toward the village, angling in the direction of the river and the thicker jungle growth. Light dimmed as we entered the trees, and I knew it would soon be dark.

"Buy a canoe?"

"It's an idea," Rosita said. "Come on, Don. I don't trust those men."

"And we trust Sam?"

"We do."

"Thanks, kids. Now it's time to be quiet and get to the village."

We found trails in the jungle, many trails, and we knew the village had to be close. Someone shouted behind us, far back, and Sam said, "They're on to us. Now we jog instead of walking fast."

I was out of breath when the trail opened up to the village. It was a cluster of some fifty or more houses made from skinny logs, palm fronds and mud, most of them facing the river. Curious people watched but made no move to interfere while we selected a canoe from ten or so tied to tree stumps and bumping against one another in the edge of the river.

Juanita appeared from one of the huts, the maroon splotch on her neck seeming to glow. "Not that one," she told Sam when he put his canvas bag into a canoe. "It's too heavy and hard to paddle. That one." She pointed. Sam shifted the bag to the other canoe. "You were clever to come here. It would be even more clever to throw the paddles from the other canoes into the river, though if the men catch you, you must not tell that I suggested it."

"Thanks." Sam nodded to her. "Don. The paddles."

Leaving the basket on the bank, I stepped from canoe to canoe, throwing the paddles into the current. "We should pay for the canoe. Sam, pay her for the canoe."

"But I'm nearly broke as it is. You have anything to leave for the owner?"

"The blue eye." I threw in the last paddle, leaving only three in the canoe we were stealing, and went to the basket. "Juanita, look. I'll leave this blue eye for the owner of the canoe."

"The owner is my father. Or I think he is. He wouldn't like the eye. He would throw it into the river out of fear."

"Pills," Sam said. "I'll leave her a packet or two of pills. Brown ones."

"No." Rosita climbed into the canoe, opened Sam's bag. "We'll leave her a whole bottle of red ones."

"Not red. We'll need the red. Leave the green"

"Green is fine," Juanita said.

"Here." Rosita passed the bottle to Sam, who handed it to Juanita.

"A bottle of aspirin for a boat? You call that fair?" It still felt like we were stealing the canoe. "Juanita, look." I picked up a handful of small bones from the basket. "From Indios. Ancient ones. Take as many as you want."

"My father would give you the canoe, if he would only think right. But he seldom does." She looked over her shoulder. "He is leading the men who want to hurt you."

"Mr. Eyebrow," I said.

"Yes." She took two of the bones, likely toes, though I couldn't be sure. "My mother tried to cure him of his vanity, but there are

253

limits even to the power of a strong curandera."

"Get in the canoe," Sam said. "Those guys will be here soon." He sat in the back, Rosita settled herself in the bow. I closed the basket, untied the canoe, and climbed in just as we heard the shouting of the men emerging from a jungle trail. Pushing away from the other boats with the paddle, I managed to get us out where the current began to take us.

"Hurry," Juanita said.

"Your mother. Your mother. Your mother." Rosita's voice sounded so strange. "Her name was Sylvia."

"Yes. How did you know?"

Rosita stood, seeming to forget she was in a canoe, but the wobble was slight. "Juanita, I'm so sorry. The missionary. His shotgun."

"Sit down," Sam said. The men with machetes ran to the canoes, shouting, cursing.

"No." Juanita fell to her knees and tore at her braids. "No."

I glanced up from paddling and saw her neck. It seemed to fill my entire range of vision with its crimson flush, brighter than ever, and I had the absurd thought that the light of it banished all evening shadows from the riverbank. She put her hands over her face, her elbows hiding part of the blush on her neck. Rosita stood, muttering something among the shouts from Mr. Eyebrow and his machete men.

"This one isn't at all funny." Sam's voice was tense, angry. "We could use a little help now, you slug-brained mump jawed mangy son of a fly-bred trickster." He beat the water with his paddle, accomplishing nothing in our need to get down river.

"Rosita. Sit. Please. I need your help." From my spot in the middle of the canoe I couldn't do much steering, though I did manage to get us out into the main current.

With a quick jerk of her hand, Rosita wiped her cheek, then turned toward me and sat, picking up her paddle. "Sam, put that down. You're making it worse. Don, take the right side. I'll take the left and direct the canoe. Sam's end is now the front of the canoe." The canoe swung around, even with Sam punishing the water in wrong ways with his paddle, and we began rushing with the current.

"Sam, do as Rosita said. Put the paddle down." I looked back.

Shadows deepened from the sun sliding off the edge of the world. Juanita still knelt, her face in her hands. Two women stood over her; one seemed to be patting her head. Men moved about among the canoes, still shouting, though their voices were losing power across the distance and beneath the splash of our paddles.

"Twilight," Sam said. "It'll be dark in five minutes. We won't be able to see a thing."

22
God as Trickster

The river shone with starlight, and the jungle, shadowed and vast, sang its nighttime chorus. I paddled while Rosita kept us in the center of the river, heading downstream on the sparkle thrown back from stars. "We must leave the river," she said.

"There's diamonds among the rocks at the bottom of this river," Sam said. "If I could catch the river low enough, maybe I could find some of them, though I doubt there's enough to scoop up with a coffee can. Venezuela, they said in Africa, Venezuela is the place for diamonds. Ha. What a joke that was. I should have known such advice was another of the old boy's tricks."

"It isn't so safe to be on the river at night," Rosita said.

"Why?" Sam sounded not at all worried.

"There are monsters in the water that would like to eat us," Rosita said.

"When I was a child, I was afraid of monsters under my bed at night."

"I have never slept in a bed," Rosita said. "If you think the river monsters aren't real, try taking a short swim. You won't get far."

"What would get me?" Sam's tone shifted, became serious.

"An anaconda might," I offered.

"They live farther south, don't they? In Brazil and Chili?"

"We saw one leap up from the water and grab a deer," I said.

"Carribe would eat you before you got far."

"Carribe?"

"The cannibal fish," I said. "Piranha."

"We also saw a black caimán," Rosita said. "It tried to eat me, but Don distracted it with topochos and the remains of a roasted rabbit."

"This is true?"

"Yes. She jumped in the river when ants from a tree she touched swarmed on her. I saw the caimán swimming right for her, and that's when I threw the bananas and the rabbit in the water. Rosita can climb into a canoe fast when she wants to. The caimán was as long as our canoe."

257

"Alligators big and mean like crocodiles, cannibal fish, and snakes that eat deer." Sam sounded impressed. "I thought these river jungles were safe places, given the villages along the banks."

"Not safe. Not safe at all. We should be ashore right now and up in a tree. Don and I have spent many nights in a tree. But it's dangerous to go ashore in the dark."

"Then I'll make it light." Sam rummaged around in his bag, drew something out, and flipped a switch. A beam of light stabbed the night, lighting up the jungle beside us. The eyes of an animal flashed when Sam's beam hit them. A large animal. "What was that?"

"Something tall," I said.

"Probably a monkey, a small one in a tree. You didn't tell us you have a flashlight." Rosita sounded cross.

"You didn't ask. You think we should climb a tree? I say let's do it with the help of this light. But first let's put a little more distance between us and that village back there."

"We need to eat," Rosita said. "Don, take the empanadas dulces from our basket and divide them among us. Give Sam more because he is bigger and needs more food."

"No," Sam said. "Divide it equally."

With dim starlight and with the movement of the canoe to contend with, it wasn't easy to divide the empanadas, but I managed it, and I did as Rosita said: I handed Sam more than I gave to Rosita or kept for myself. Not that it mattered, for there was plenty.

"What is this stuff?" Sam said. "It's delicious. Old doctor Bee-Bee had a way of expressing himself in English, even if he knew only four phrases. One of them was 'good soup.' These empanadas are definitely good soup."

"That's stupid," I said. "These things are solid, mostly. They're not soup at all."

"No, but they are good soup," Sam said.

"Doctor Bee-Bee was crazy, I think."

"He doesn't mean they are soup," Rosita said.

"Then why say they are? Why not just say "good empanadas?"

"Maybe," Sam said, "because the term 'good soup' can be applied to anything you like."

"It can't. Soup is soup."

"It's all right, Don," Rosita said. "Anyway, I make empanadas in a different way. But these are good. Maybe it's not the best food in the world to eat as dinner, but we're lucky to have it."

"When we finish eating, we'll go ashore for the night," Sam said.

"As soon as we finish dinner, Don will count to one thousand while we paddle. It's important to get farther away from those angry villagers. We'll go ashore when he gets to a thousand."

"I'll do it. But empanadas are not soup."

I took my time with the count, repeating a bunch of numbers just in case I had missed them, and by the time I announced the completion of the task, the moon had come up, or enough of it to tip the leaves and the water ripples with its silver. Sam used his light for finding us a place to put ashore, and he found a good one, a grassy one where we could drag the boat completely out of the water. I tied the boat to a tree.

"Why are you doing that?" Sam's voice was on the edge of laughter. "Are you afraid it will drift out on the grass?"

"The river rises suddenly during the rainy season," Rosita said. "Don is wise to secure the canoe."

"The water can't rise this high over night. I have two pieces of oiled canvas in my bag. We'll put one on the grass beside the boat to sleep on and tent the other one over us in case it rains."

"No," Rosita said. "We should climb a tree."

"Not in the dark. What is there to get us on the ground, here beside the canoe?"

"High water," I said. "We've seen the river rise over night enough to put this grass underwater."

"Jungle tigers," Rosita said.

"Tigers can climb trees. That's why they live in the jungle."

"They can?" A note of fear crept into Rosita's voice.

"That makes sense, doesn't it?" I said. "Jungle cats ought to be able to climb trees. Besides, you and I slept on the ground inside the green igloo, and we were safe enough."

"You call that safe? You call being bitten by vampires safe? Why don't you go to sleep right here beside this canoe. The black caimán could come out of the water and make a snack of your leg. It might

259

eat your silly purple head."

"What did I do to you?"

"You have to ask? He has never had a carribe bite off part of his foot, never had banditos threaten him with a pistol, never fallen into bat dung or had araño mono leap out of bananas at him or gone over a waterfall or seen an anaconda or been attacked by a snake or seen Sylvia shot to death and eaten by the carribe." Her voice became increasingly shrill. "And you take sides with him against me. You. El Don, who has suffered with me and eaten bananas with me and papayas and roasted rabbit and walked among ghosts and in swamps and become a fish and a parrot beside Sylvia as a water bug and me as a Jesus frog, and after all that you take sides with this pink man who cannot use a canoe paddle."

"Jesus frog?" Sam was astonished. "Vampires?"

"I say we sleep in a tree," I said.

"Now you're treating me like an angry child," she flared.

"But Rosita," Sam said, "You are an angry child."

"You stay out of this, Sam," I snapped. Sam took a couple of steps back into the shadows. "Rosita, you and I are partners, and partners do what they decide to do. They decide together."

Rosita sat on the edge of the canoe and cried. I could tell by the way her shoulders jerked, though she made no sounds at all.

"I'll talk only Spanish all night," Sam offered. "Even to the tricky old boy who put us into this jungle."

Rosita laughed in a strange, choking way since she wasn't through crying. "I would like that, Sam. We'll sleep on the ground, if you want. But not this close to the river."

"Up there." Sam pointed with the beam of his flashlight. "The bank goes up quite a bit and levels off. I doubt an alligator would climb that high. I could build a fire to keep away other jungle creatures."

"I still say we climb a tree," I said.

"You're trying to make me feel better." Rosita jumped up and kissed me a quick smack on the cheek. "Let's put up a tent there, high above the river. Bring the basket. Sam, you carry your bag and the light. I'll take the machete. When we get up there, you'll chop some branches for the tent. We won't build a fire because everything is wet from the afternoon rain."

The noise we made climbing the hill quieted the jungle chorus, but not by much. Sam cut the branches as Rosita directed and I held the flashlight for him. We had a tent in no time. It wasn't as tight or as wild as our green igloo, and it smelled like a tarpaulin, but it would keep the dew off of us and maybe some of the rain, if any happened to fall in the night. The canvas we spread on the floor of the tent was less scratchy than palm fronds, but it smelled funny. I would have preferred to find banana leaves to sleep on like we had above the bat poop cave, but it was too dark to go looking for any.

"I'll warn you," Sam said as we settled down in the tent, "that I snore."

"So do I," Rosita said.

"And there's another thing. I'm tired of talking Spanish. Since jumping ship, it's been Spanish, Spanish, Spanish. I get a headache from it. I dream in Spanish."

"You usually talk to God in English," Rosita said. "But not tonight, not after what you promised."

"Goats and monkeys. I did promise to talk Spanish, didn't I? And I plan to do plenty of crabbing at the old boy tonight. But the only way he answers is to make things happen. I want to have a conversation with someone who'll speak back, so maybe I ought to talk only with you tonight."

The jungle night had recovered from our foreign noises, and night creatures got cranked up again. The air felt heavy with moisture, and it smelled clean as only a jungle can smell clean, stronger even the oily odor of the tent. The sweet odor of flowers drifted on what little breeze there was, and from time to time I got a whiff of the river, of the watery smell of a new swamp, and of over-ripe bananas.

"Goat-brained bugs," Sam said. I took it that he meant the night insects and birds that had resumed their full-throated chorus of night music. "I thought the savannah was bad to yell at me in the night." He sat up and leaned out of the side of the tent. "Shut up," he yelled. The sound of his voice made a small dent in the wall of jungle noise, but it filled in fast with whistles, chirps, grunts, fleeps, squawks, moans, chatters, thumps, and other sounds.

"The jungle won't listen," I said. "I've yelled at it enough times to know."

261

"I wasn't talking to the jungle." Sam settled down again near the edge of the tent, a bit away from me and Rosita.

"Then," Rosita said, "you must have been yelling again to that odd notion of a god you seem to have."

"When I yelled at him just now, I was actually saying that the old boy needs to learn some manners, that it isn't fair to dump me in this black jungle, rob me of my honest profits from my hard work, make the pickup throw a rod, then fill the night with such noise that I'll never sleep."

"Nobody's out there," I said, "making the bugs and animals of the jungle say anything. They're just singing because that's what they do at night."

"And who told them to be so rude? I'll tell you who. That same tricky old man who caused a bull in San Angelo to poke me in the eye with his horn, making it tough for me to be a cowboy because nobody ever heard of a one-eyed cowboy but plenty of people know about sailors with eye patches, so he set me up to go to sea as a merchant marine and took me to Borneo where he turned the dice so I won from a headhunter that green eye that didn't fit, then dragged me across the seas to look for a riverbed in Venezuela where I could scoop up diamonds with a coffee can, hooked me up with Doc Bee-Bee and inspired him to trade me out of my silver belt buckle so he could to back to Belgium and I would come out to this wild jungle where a maniac would punch me for doing my job. He planned it all, the no-good trickster, setting me up for tonight's sleepless night in the noisy jungle when he directed the tip of that bull's horn into my eye. Cause and effect. It's as simple as that, and the ultimate cause is the fact that the old boy is a trickster by nature."

"I think God is a woman," Rosita said.

"And I don't believe in God," I said. "Everything that happens just happens. No one is in charge of anything."

"A woman." Sam sounded amazed. "God as a woman. If you're right, then I might like her better. But if she's a woman, it doesn't change her nature. She's a trickster whether she has flappers or a flat chest. Call her a woman if you want. I'm too used to calling him a man, not that it makes any difference now that I think about it. And, Don, any Texas boy with any real sense is in atheist."

"You're from Texas," I pointed out.

"Yes. And I have no sense. I do know, though, that everything happens for a reason. There's no such thing as a coincidence. You two came along to help get my truck out of the sand. You found me stuck in the sand because you needed me to take you home. Things sort of interlock that way, though it's a wonder anything works, given the old man's love of pulling tricks."

"If some weird old guy in the sky made us find you to unstick your truck so you could take us home," I said, "it didn't work. The truck broke down, and here we are in the river jungle again with no way to get home."

"You'll get there. I'll see to that. The old trickster left me plenty of resources to see to that. The pills, for example. The magic box. We'll earn enough money to get you home."

"I don't like your idea about God, not entirely," Rosita said.

"Then get your own idea. It doesn't matter to me if you think like I do. Don can believe there's no old trickster in the sky if he wants. What do I care? Right now I have a score to settle with that sewage sucking gorilla brain of a trickster who directed the bull's horn into my eye just so he could be amused by that scene back at the village when my glass eye bounced across the stage and maybe so he could chuckle about the village men swearing over their lost canoe paddles."

"Sam," I said, "you remind me of a man we met up river, a fellow called El Loco."

"Thanks, kid."

"El Loco worked at figuring everything out, and like you he stayed plenty mad about most things. But he used the nastiest language I've ever heard. Nastier than my brother and I use when we're away from the house and can talk like we please. You say things that sound as if they ought to be nasty words, but they aren't. Sewage sucking gorillas. That sounds plenty bad."

"People think I'm crazy, too. But you're right about the nasty words. I don't ever use them. That is, I hardly ever use them."

"Do you think it's a sin to use bad words?" Rosita asked.

"No. Sin is an idea that people made up and blamed on the old trickster they named God. I doubt if he cares what we think we decide to do. The way I see it, the only one guilty of something so

263

terrible-sounding as sin is the old man himself. He makes people do mean and stupid things, and then he wants us to suffer for what we did. I decided a long time ago that I need to learn to forgive the old maggoty-headed toad, but forgiving him is tough to do when he pulls such mean tricks on us."

"Forgive God?" Rosita seemed astounded.

"It's the only way to be moral. But I'm not so good at it."

Rosita moved around on the canvas, sounding agitated. "I always thought of God as a woman like my grandmother until I met Sylvia. Then it became clear to me that God was like Sylvia, even after we saw Mr. Marlin kill her. But—"

"You watched someone get murdered?" Sam sounded concerned.

"Yes," I said. "A missionary from the States. He shot the curandera, who was our friend, then he put the barrel of the shotgun into his mouth to kill himself."

"Sylvia." Rosita whispered. "Sylvia. Juanita's mother. Juanita wasn't through with her yet. She needed her mother. The people of the river needed their curandera. I needed my new friend. And that man. That man. His shotgun."

"And you saw that? This isn't right." He switched to English. "What in the name of Pete were you doing? Those kids don't deserve to see such horror. But I forget. Deserve's got nothing to do with it, you chicken-gutted cross-breed of an armadillo and a wall-eyed skunk."

"I heard the anger in your voice," Rosita said. "Praying in anger is such a strange idea to me."

"Anger, yes." Sam reverted to Spanish. "But not prayer. I might ask the old man for something from time to time, but it isn't prayer. It's more like an idle wish. Much that the trickster does deserves our anger. Setting me up with that glass eye in Borneo, for example. He had me believing I won that eye, and that it was something of a good thing. Now I know better."

Sam muttered more curses at God, nasty ones in clean words hurled skyward with decreasing energy as he relaxed toward sleep. It was amazing how he didn't use bad words, not exactly. "The stink of your nastiness," he muttered at one point, "would knock a buzzard off a gut wagon." It seemed odd that he gave so much effort to fussing at God.

Sometime in the night I awakened to the soft sound of Rosita crying, a sound that didn't fit with the choral song of the nighttime jungle. I swam out of sleep, trying to grasp the wrong sound, and when it came to me that it was Rosita in pain, I jerked awake. When her crying became sniffing, I whispered, "I'm sorry she's gone."

"Yes." Rosita made herself stop sniffing and kept her voice low so as not to disturb Sam. "The strangeness of Sam and his weird truck, his glass eyes that don't fit and the colored aspirin and the magic box that steals coins, the way he painted my face and called me a queen, his red hair and odd way of speaking to God—all of those things directed my attention away from the sadness of Sylvia's death. Am I bad for not thinking about her until I understood that Juanita was her daughter? Sylvia came to me in a dream, her face spotted with blood, and told me it was her own fault that she died, not God's and not even Mr. Marlin's. That helped me. But there's something else."

"What?"

"When you were out exploring the jungle around Sylvia's house, I told her about the death of Eva Perón. It made her too sad because she knew of Evita. I caused Sylvia to weep not long before her death, and it hurts me that I did so."

"You couldn't know that Mr. Marlin would kill her."

"No. I couldn't. But it still wasn't right that Sylvia had to know like that, and I'm still the one who told her. That's bad. But there's something else that's been troubling me."

"Something you told Sylvia?"

"Something about me. I liked it when Sam painted my face. I liked being called a queen. But I must have known it was wrong to be so selfish and vain after the death of Sylvia, for I sneaked around where you wouldn't see and looked at myself in the pickup's mirror. I liked looking at my face with the strange chalk on it to make me seem beautiful. I haven't been so good."

"You're wrong about not being good. I'm the one who has been bad, not you. When I got on stage in front of all those people, I loved it. Even after I understood that Sam was selling aspirin, I kept putting them into packets and taking money from those people. The magic box was even more exciting. Best of all was when Sam's eye bounced on stage and rolled toward me and I picked it up. I scared that angry man right off the platform, and then I held up the eye to scare the audience, and I liked it. I liked it. That's being bad. Not as bad as when I told Mr. Marlin he was a murderer and made him hate himself just enough more to put the shotgun into his mouth, but bad enough. Nothing you've done has been bad."

Rosita rolled closer to me. "You've done nothing wrong. You were angry with Mr. Marlin for what he had done to our Sylvia. I hated him, too, at that moment. Maybe I still do, and that's bad. My grandmother told me to work at never hating anyone. Sylvia would tell me that, if she were still alive."

"You're good, Rosita. Better than anyone I've ever known."

"You like me better than I do. Isn't that strange? And I like you better than you like yourself. I'm glad that you see me as good. It makes me less sad for me."

"There's another thing," I said. "I want to be in Sam's show again. I want to scare people with my purple hair and to trick them with the magic box and watch them be amazed."

"And I want to become the Queen of the Nile again. Are we bad, then?"

"A little, yes. I think so. I am, anyway. You're not."

Rosita snuggled against me and we drifted off to sleep. It seemed only minutes later when she nudged me awake. Morning had already begun, gray and cloudy. Sam still slept. With a couple of gestures, Rosita communicated that we should get up in silence and steal away by ourselves.

We put on our alpargatas, grinning like a couple of monkeys over how we were fooling Sam by letting him sleep away the best part of the day. I took the machete, and we made our way into the tall trees where shade kept out undergrowth. When we were far enough from Sam to talk, Rosita said, "I want to pretend that the jungle is still a paradise, that we're savages like the ancient Indios who wore only what they were born with." She pulled her dress over her head.

"We don't have to pretend. We can be what we want out here where no one can tell us what to do." I came out of the black pants Rosita had made back in Sylvia's house. We stepped back and looked at each other in an appraising way, and I nodded. "Real savages."

"No. This is just pretend. The jungle would never let us live in it for long, we know that now. But it's good to wish and play."

"I believe we could live here like wild people as long as we wanted, you and I. With just you and me there will be no Mr. Marlins, no shotguns. There will be no need for windows to have iron bars in them. We could live on papayas and cashew nuts and when we got tired of them we could eat fish and bananas and maybe a roasted rabbit once in a while."

"No," Rosita said. "But we can pretend for a while."

"We can believe. And if we believe, then it's true. Carmen said so."

"That isn't what she meant, I told you that. Put on your alpargatas. Pretending won't keep thorns out of your feet."

"Alpargatas, then. Nothing else. Savages don't need anything else. We'll leave Sam with the canoe and his aspirin, and we'll build tree houses and green igloos and make fishhooks with hard wood and find bananas. We'll never leave the river jungle."

"No." Her eyes became moist. "The jungle would get us with the teeth of its carribe or the jaws of its caimán negro or the machetes of civilized mestizos like Juanita's father or the shotgun of a missionary. We could live happy for a while, but we would meet the anaconda or the tigre and you would die or I would die and life would not be worth living with one of us gone. The best we can do is pretend for a while, then go wake Sam up and have him help us go home."

"But that's a terrible choice."

"What else can we do?" She rubbed her eyes with her knuckles and said, "There. Over there is a dip in the land maybe down to a place low enough for water where we can find the plants that hold minnows and Jesus frogs that walk on water. I would like to see a Jesus frog again while we're naked savages and the jungle is a good and green place." She picked up her dress and my pants. "You hold the machete to be alert in case something tries to get us."

23
Diamonds and Aspirin

When we got back to the tent, carrying two hands of ripe bananas and dressed for civilization, Sam still slept. Rosita awakened him. "Breakfast is ready," she said. "And it's about to rain."

Sam came from the tent scratching his stomach and grinning. His eye patch had crept up over his brow, and the loose eyelid reminded me of Carmen. "Breakfast?" He reset the patch to become a boy pirate. "The jungle might screech all night, but it's generous with its fruit."

"Not always. We might go days before finding bananas again."

"We need to make fast work of breakfast and get back on the river before those savages come after us in their canoes."

"It's about to rain, and I want to bathe in it. The men won't come for us because we're too far down river, and they know it's a lot of work to paddle back against the current, especially now that the river is higher and running faster."

"I brought banana leaves," I said, "for catching us a drink when the rain hits."

"Good thinking. Rain is cleaner than drinking out of the river."

"Safer," Rosita said.

Sam laughed. "We're in no danger here, unless those guys decide to come for us."

"They won't. But you can drink from the river and risk what it can do to you. Don and I will drink the rain. We'll also bathe."

When the rain began, it came with fierce suddenness, and the three of us got into the tent fast. "You get out there and have a drink first," Rosita told Sam. "Strip and take a bath, if you want. I'll turn this way and not look."

"Why should I go first?"

"Because when you finish, Don and I will go out without clothes, get our drink, and wash off, and you will not watch me."

"But Don will?"

Rosita shrugged. "If he wants. But you will not."

"You're the boss." Sam chuckled. "You kids are the funniest folk

269

I have ever known."

After the rain, after Rosita and I drank and bathed and flipped water from our skin with quick sweeps of our fingers and dried in the sun and dressed—all beyond the tent so Rosita wouldn't worry about being watched—we folded the tent and its canvas floor, loaded the canoe, and pushed off. Rosita kept us in the shade all morning because she feared I would sunburn again. When noon banished shadows from the river, we went ashore to forage for food in the shade of the jungle and to nap beneath a giant rosewood tree, or at least that's what Sam called it. In the early afternoon we again went downriver with Rosita steering us through the shade.

After several hours we found a village large enough to have a cantina, several tiendas where shopkeepers sold cassava, molasses cookies, chinchorros, and other items made in the village.

As we approached the village, Sam pulled a straw hat from his canvas bag, pounded it into better shape, and told me to wear it. Then he handed me light brown chalk and told me to cover my face, hands and feet. "But first, get out of those funny black pants and put on your jeans. Also, put on this shirt." He tossed me the long-sleeved shirt that I had worn while we set up the stage on his pickup.

"You're going to put on another show," Rosita said.

"I am. And you will be the queen of the Nile again. That worked well last time. I'll wedge my green eye in better this time, and we'll be more careful not to insult anyone like we did that wild man with the eyebrow."

"We? We?" Rosita feigned surprise. "I don't remember telling a pack of lies to anyone."

"All right. I won't insult anyone. I'll not clown around with geography. I'll return a Bolivar if some nut demands it back. I won't even pretend to conjure you two from other parts of the world. I'll tell no lies at all. But I'll still put on a great show, and we ought to make more money than before since this is a bigger village."

With me chalked up and my purple hair covered with Sam's hat, we canoed to a pier built high enough to stay above water when the river rose to its maximum. It was necessary for us to climb a ladder to get to it, which meant the river was just beginning to rise. By the time we were on the pier, about half of the villagers had come to greet us. Sam, wearing one blue eye and one green eye, strode up to them and called out greetings as if he were an old friend of the entire village, and people smiled.

Rosita told me later that they were amused by his flaming hair and pink skin, but at the time I thought they were returning his enthusiastic greeting with warmth of their own. Mostly it was women and children who greeted us. All were dark like Rosita and had hair the color of a burnt campfire, and all were short. Sam towered over the women, and most were only a bit taller than I. The women gave Sam much attention, especially one older lady who wore a red hibiscus in her hair. She wasn't old like a grandmother, but old. Rosita whispered that the woman was beautiful, though I couldn't see it.

Sam, carrying his canvas bag, took us to a tienda where he produced from his pockets the coins to buy molasses cookies for every kid there. It wasn't much of a store. Thatching covered the roof and three walls, and the entire front was open. The best thing about the place was the huge mango tree that shaded it and much of the dirt street in front of it. The shopkeeper had set a log on sawhorses, trimmed the top with a machete or a hatchet to make it flat or at least flat enough to pass for a counter, and he had put some pieces of tree stumps on the dirt floor to serve as chairs for customers. Behind the counter were several shelves made from stiff, woven mats. One shelf held wheels of cassava, big around as a pickup tire and thinner than his molasses cookies. They looked to me like compressed sawdust. Another shelf held small baskets stacked together, and another supported short stalks of sugarcane that had attracted a horde of flies. A tray of cookies sat on one end of the counter; on the other were ten or more bottles of brown juice.

When we walked in, the villagers followed us, and our entrance chased out a duck and three chickens. The shopkeeper, a gray man bent over like a dried leaf, hurried behind the counter. "Rum," he said and picked up one of the bottles. "The best. Made in El Tigre. Whiskey." He plucked a bottle from the others and set it before Sam. "Lava Gallo. Good to drink. Good to spit into the eyes of cocks. One bottle? Two?"

"Cookies," Sam said.

The man looked disappointed. "One glass of rum?"

Sam looked at me. "Do you drink that stuff?" The crowd laughed.

"No."

"And my wonderful little friend Rosita: do you drink rum?"

"Of course not." She sounded huffy and offended, much to the amusement of the women and children circling the entrance.

"Do either of you eat cookies?"

I eyed the stack of brown cookies with flies walking on them. "Maybe," I said, adding silently that I did if I could get one from the middle of the stack where the flies hadn't been hopping around, polishing their feet and grooming themselves to flip no telling what kinds of filth on the cookies.

"Then I want all of those for my friends and all their little friends." Sam gestured toward the children in the crowd. He put three Bolivars on the counter. The kids edged closer, the little ones first, moving with caution and glancing up at their mothers and sisters.

The shopkeeper sighed, set aside the Lava Gallo and began peeling off the gooey cookies and handing them out. When the stack was whittled down below the fly line, I stepped forward, got two, and gave one to Rosita. The shop ran out of cookies before it ran out of kids, so the shopkeeper dispatched a boy to run up the street to another tienda, and he returned with a wooden tray heaped with cookies. Sam spoke almost the whole time as if he were already on stage. It amazed me that he could think of that many words to say and never run out of them.

"When the shade of this tree," he told the people gathered around the tienda, "reaches this spot," he walked a few paces into the sun and drew a line in the dirt with his shoe, "I'll put on the best magic show ever seen in South America. The show is free, though anyone who wants can donate to my magic box to help pay for our coming to entertain you. Also, because I am a doctor of rare and special learning, I shall provide you with medicines that stop all kinds of pains. These are wonder drugs that—"

"I thought you weren't going to tell, uh, to talk like that," Rosita said.

"—will help with broken hearts as well as the pain from injuries and age. My little assistant here has just reminded me to tell the good news, to tell the truth about my medicine, and I will, for the medicine will be wonderful news to those who suffer with pain of any kind."

Sam kept up his line of bull and kept an eye on Rosita who stood, hands on hips and head tilted. Her stance made him tell the truth, mainly. I waited until the fly layer of the new batch of cookies had been eaten, then retrieved several more for me and Rosita. Sam saw me get the second round of cookies and paused long enough in his line of bull to say, "Those cookies are good soup, right Don?"

"They're not soup. They're—"

"Hush, Don," Rosita said.

The shopkeeper handed out cookies, paying no attention to the hands that reached for them because he was so intent on counting. When the cookies were gone, he announced that Sam had put almost enough money on the counter and scooped up the three Bolivars. "But I shall donate the remaining cost." He said it in such a way that I knew he was lying. Rosita raised a brow at him, but Sam simply nodded, and I knew from the nod that he didn't realize how he had been cheated.

Sam finally quit talking so much, and people drifted away, most of them. A few children, a couple of sad-looking dogs with ribs showing, and the woman with the hibiscus in her hair remained with us in the tienda. "Rum?" the shopkeeper offered.

"No. Rum is bad soup." Sam made a show of looking at the shelves behind the counter. "What do you have to eat around here besides cookies?"

"Cassava. The best."

"There is no such thing as good cassava." Sam scowled.

"I will make pan de mano," the woman with the hibiscus said. "You can be my guests for dinner. My name is Conchita."

"Thanks. But we have business to conduct. Maybe next time we're in town we'll come to dinner."

"My name is Conchita," the woman repeated.

"I'm Sam." He nodded toward us. "These are Rosita and Don."

"Not El Don—" I began.

"Hush," Rosita whispered, but her statement wasn't necessary. It was obvious that Conchita wasn't listening to me. She hung on Sam's arm and muttered something to him.

Sam slid away from Conchita without giving offense and negotiated with the shopkeeper for renting his place to do the medicine show. At the conclusion of their dealing, Sam said, "You're charging me too much and you know it. For that price, I'll expect you to set up some kind of barrier to keep the people out of the area where we perform." He stepped off the limits of his stage, and the two did much gesturing and arguing. Then Sam asked if there were a car or truck in the village.

"It's parked behind the cantina," the shopkeeper said. "The driver delivered corn, whiskey, and flour, and tomorrow he returns to El Tigre."

"We're nearly home," I whispered to Rosita, feeling no joy.

"We'll be there tomorrow. Will you still be my friend?"

"That will never change." I felt my throat get tight.

"I wish," Rosita sighed. "I wish that we had found a Jesus frog this morning. It would have been so wonderful to see one hop across the water just one more time."

We walked to the cantina with Conchita tagging along, and we found the driver of the pickup swigging from a bottle of rum. Conchita wrinkled her nose in disgust. "That's the man you want? Boracho." She spat the word: drunk. I didn't know if she meant the driver was a drunk or if he had simply become drunk. "I'll wait outside." She left with a flip of her skirt, her chin held high.

"Well la-tee-dah," Sam said. Rosita laughed.

The cantina looked somewhat like the place where Mamacita Moreno fed us beans and the pig ran under my chair: packed dirt floors, tiny windows, thatched roof. Two small tables stood in the center of the room, neither of which had a pig under it. There was, though, a yellow dog sleeping beside one of the chairs, its leg twitching and flies crawling on its ears. The driver of the pickup sat beside the dog, swishing his rum bottle around and looking dizzy. He turned to look at Rosita. "You one of the girls?"

"She is my brother's daughter," Sam said.

"Just as well. I'm too far into the rum to do more than look."

"I'll wait outside, too," Rosita said. "And don't you say la tee dah about me."

"I'll be with Rosita," I said.

"Good." Sam nodded to us. As we left, I heard him say, "Will you drive to El Tigrito tomorrow?"

"Thanks for coming out with me." Rosita gestured toward Conchita who stood across the dirt road talking with a man who had a hoe on his shoulder. "Look at her. I'll bet she flirts with every man in the village as much as she did with Sam."

"She flirted with Sam?" That came as news to me.

"I think I don't like her."

"Why?"

Before she could answer, Sam came out of the cantina. "It's set up. I traded our canoe for a ride in the pickup. Carlos will drive us to El Tigrito tomorrow. Does that make you happy?"

"I guess," I said.

"Thanks," Rosita said.

"What's going on with you two?"

" Nothing. What about my face?" Rosita asked.

"What about it?"

"Aren't you going to make me into the Queen of the Nile?"

"Yes." Sam headed back toward the tienda he had rented, and we followed. "Later. During the show." Conchita tried to get his attention, but he ignored her.

As the shade reached the dirt line, village men who worked in the fields on the edge of the savannah drifted in with their farming tools on their shoulders. Others had arrived in canoes that they docked at the pier. The women and children returned. The shopkeeper drove cane poles into the ground around the perimeter of his shop, then stretched string between the poles to define the area for the show. As people gathered, he told them to stay behind the string. Conchita ignored him and ducked under it to sit on one of the tree stumps set there as chairs.

Sam put his bag on the counter of the tienda and took out the chalk. "Sit there," he told Rosita, pointing at one of the tree stumps. People continued to gather at the string line as he started the job of converting Rosita's face to that of the Nile queen. "This is my chief female assistant," Sam announced. "She looks mestizo, but watch me change her into the royal princess of Egypt." He marked away with the chalk. "I have another assistant, a boy of Mexican royal blood who has suffered more than a boy should ever suffer—but I'll tell about him later. This is Katherine, who will be Queen of Aragon when grown. Do you believe it? No? Then watch as the face of the true queen emerges. She is beautiful without the paint of royalty. With it, she will be stunning."

The crowd grew, and women especially jostled each other for a better view of the Queen of Aragon. Conchita, her arms folded across her chest, seemed not at all interested at first. But when the colors and lines Sam added began to make Rosita look like a grown woman, Conchita stood and moved closer.

"And now I give you Katherine, the Queen of Aragon and the princess of the Nile," Sam said. "Stand up. Here, on the chair." He helped her up. People gasped and pointed. A tiny, nervous smile appeared and disappeared along the corners of Rosita's mouth.

"She's beautiful." Conchita sounded angry. "Paint my face next." She took Rosita's hand and pulled her from the tree-stump chair. Sam caught her and set her on the ground.

"I'll make this woman, this lovely Conchita, into Joan Crawford, the most beautiful of American actresses. But first, you need to know about why Katherine of Aragon almost killed herself."

As he launched into his story about the aspen that nearly bit Rosita's neck, I took the bottle of red pills from the canvas bag, along with a bunch of paper packets. He had used that word before, aspen, and it sounded wrong. It seemed to me that an aspen was a tree and not a snake, and I decided to ask Sam about it later.

Sam was so full of baloney that I almost laughed a few times, but the villagers loved him, and when he set Rosita to selling packets of red aspirin, people lined up to buy medicine powerful enough to ease the pain of a broken heart.

"Now." Conchita said. "Paint my face now."

"First I have to tell about my other assistant, the boy who—"

"No. My face first, the boy after."

A ripple of laughter spread through the crowd and Sam said, "I'll do your face." He leaned close and said so only she and I heard, "then you will leave me alone. Understood?"

"Yes." Conchita arched her eyes and added in a whisper, "My husband died two years ago, can you believe it?"

"I can." Sam went to work on her face. "I can."

"One of your eyes is green, the other blue. Why is that?"

Sam ignored the question. While he marked her up, he told

about the headaches that turned my hair purple and my skin white. He laid it on thick and heavy about my royalty and my extreme suffering and about how his pills cured me. I thought about how I had almost ruined Sam's sales pitch in the last show by forgetting which pills were supposed to cure headaches. The white ones, I thought, and rehearsed how I would say the line properly. White for headaches. White. I wouldn't get it wrong this time.

"There." Sam stepped back to look at Conchita. She looked terrible in a beautiful sort of way. Something about her mouth scared me, and her eyes seemed hard and mean. "She is now the famous Joan Crawford."

"Am I beautiful?" Conchita demanded. "Am I?"

"Find a mirror," Sam suggested.

"Does anyone have a mirror?" No one did, and Conchita grew increasingly agitated. "A mirror. Someone go get me a mirror."

"Go home and use your own," a female voice in the crowd said.

Conchita didn't seem to catch on that people were urging her to go away. She was too bent on finding a mirror. "I guess I will have to go home." She ducked under the string and pushed her way through the crowd.

"Don't send her back here again," Sam said in English, aiming his request at the sky. "And here he is, El Don, the last royalty of Mexico City." Sam stabbed a thumb toward the stump chair, and I sat down. He took a cloth from his bag, dampened it with Lava Gallo and washed my face, talking the whole time. The cloth stank something terrible and I wondered how anyone could drink whiskey. "Some of you can see how disgustingly white the pain turned his face. But wait until you see the real damage." He switched to English: "Turn your back and unbutton your shirt. When I give the signal, turn around and take the shirt off fast. I'll handle the hat."

I faced the collection of bottles on the bar. The shopkeeper was trying to get Sam's attention to tell him he owed for the Lava Gallo, but Sam ignored him. "Behold the ravages of a thousand headaches." Sam reached for my hat and said, "Do it."

He pulled the hat off as I turned around, baring my chest. The crowd shrank back and many people gasped. I shook my purple hair and tried to look mean, but it was hard to keep from grinning. "Those are the ones that did it." I pointed. "The white ones."

"You said that too soon," Rosita said.

"And which pill cured the terrible headaches?" Sam winked his blue eye at me. "He has already told you. The white pills. These will knock out any headache in the world, I guarantee it."

I was a little disappointed that the shock of my purple hair wore off so fast and that I didn't seem to be scaring anyone. When I tried to look fierce, some people laughed. So what was the point of wearing a stupid hat over my ears all afternoon if not much came of it when I took it off? "I've had it with this purple hair," I said to no one in particular.

"Are you mad at the old boy now? It's about time. Not that getting mad will change much." Sam put me to selling pills while he did the rope-cutting trick. Rosita's heartbreak pills sold better, but I had plenty of customers. They were still lined up when Sam brought out the magic box. "Don't do it," Rosita warned.

"This is a different use of the box." Sam held it up and demonstrated the magic of it. "Anything you drop into the box will vanish. Later I'll make it appear and use the money to pay for the expenses of my show. Consider what you drop into the box as payment for being entertained by my magic, and as you drop in the money, you get to see the box hide the coins."

As he snapped the cuffs on my wrist, a boy got to the front of the headache line. "I have no money, but I need headache pills for my grandmother. Will you trade pills for these rocks my father brought from upriver?" The boy held up a rusted coffee can.

"Ask Sam." I moved along the string, holding the box for people to drop their coins into. When I glanced back, Sam was stuffing packets with white pills for the boy with the coffee can. The next time I looked back, I saw Sam putting pebbles into his pockets. That's when Conchita returned.

"I'm beautiful," she announced. "Beautiful." Then she saw Sam holding the coffee can and the boy holding the packets of pills, and she shrieked, "Miguel, what are you doing?"

"Medicine, mama, I'm buying medicine for grandmother's headaches."

"With your father's diamonds?" Conchita's rage parted the crowd. "Give them back. You cannot steal the only wealth my husband left me. Give back the diamonds."

278

"Diamonds?" Sam looked shocked. "I gave the boy medicine because he said his granny needed it. All he gave me was quartz rocks."

"Diamonds." Conchita sounded strange, wild. "Give them back. Now." She ducked under the string.

"I made a trade."

Rosita stepped between Conchita and Sam. "Give them to her, Sam. If they're diamonds, you should give them back. If they're quartz, you don't need them."

The crowd was dead quiet, watching. Sam glanced around at the grim faces, then smiled. "Of course." He dug in his pockets, produced tiny white pebbles, and put them into Conchita's hands.

"More, I had more. Give me them all."

Sam felt around in his pockets, produced one more pebble, and said, "That's it. You have them all."

"I had more than that. I know I had more than that."

"How many did you have?" Rosita asked.

"I don't know. Many. More than he gave back."

"Give them back," someone shouted.

Sam glanced at the sky. "I asked you not to do this to me, you liver-splotched sea slug." Then he spoke Spanish: "The show's over, folks. My assistants will sell more pills to those who need them. Right now I need to convince Joan Crawford that I don't have any of her rocks."

"I'll search you and find them." Conchita put a hand on Sam's shirt pocket and felt around for diamonds.

People laughed and began wandering away. "Search me if you want." Sam held his hands out.

"Not here. In a private place where I can look everywhere for the stones. Come to my house."

"I'll go and search him," I offered. "My brother and I used to take turns searching each other for hidden coins, and I'm good at it."

"Come on." Conchita took Sam's arm.

I started to follow but Rosita grabbed my shirt. "She didn't mean you."

"But I can help solve this problem."

"Conchita doesn't want your help. Get the keys out of the bag

279

and take that box off of your wrist."

"Sorry about the show, kids." Sam turned toward us. "I didn't want things to get out of hand like they did yesterday. You take care of the money and pills. I'll be back as soon as this woman is happy that I'm not a thief."

The shopkeeper took down the strings and pulled up the cane stakes. Rosita gathered pills and Bolivars and put them into Sam's canvas bag while I played with the handcuffs and the magic box and watched Conchita haul Sam into a house made of poles, mud, and thatching. "I could have found the diamonds if he had any hidden on him."

"Stop it. Just stop it." Rosita sounded cross with me, but I couldn't figure out why.

"You must pay for the Lava Gallo that the magician used for washing your face," The shopkeeper told me.

"Pay for getting that nasty stuff on my face? No."

"Take the matter up with Sam," Rosita said. "But don't plan on getting any more money. You already charged him too much for your services. Besides, I counted those cookies. There weren't three Bolivars worth there, and you know it. Don, help me with this bag."

I shouldered the basket that contained the bones of Indios and my blue eyeball that Sam had discarded, and the two of us carried the canvas bag up the street to a shady place under some trees and waited for Sam to come out of Conchita's house.

When he emerged, he was tucking in his shirt. Conchita's chalk makeup looked smeared, her hair was rumpled, and the hibiscus was gone from her hair. Both were smiling.

"Did she find any diamonds?" I asked.

"Hush, Don," Rosita said.

"Don't tell me to hush. Did she?"

"I'm satisfied, completely satisfied that he has none of my diamonds."

"Conchita has invited us to dinner, and I accepted. She says we can sleep here tonight, and she has extra chinchorros."

I looked at Rosita. "What do you think?"

She shrugged. "It'll beat sleeping in the canoe or in a tree." We picked up the bag and started across the street. "I still don't like her," Rosita said.

24
Bones from the Same Finger

"I hate sleeping in a chinchorro," I whispered to Rosita. "A banana leaf mat is better. Even a mat of palm fronds is better. Why don't we just sleep on the floor?"

Rosita was a lump in the dark, an indistinct figure slung in a chinchorro beside the one I struggled with. A tiny bit of moonlight drifted in the window, as did guitar music and drunken singing from the cantina down the street. I could barely make out the cocoon-like form of Rosita in her webbed hammock. Just beyond her Miguel snored in a third chinchorro, the maximum the small room would hold. How he fell asleep so fast was beyond me. A hand span below us lay the cool of the dirt floor and not so far above us hung the tangle of thatching that passed for a roof in Conchita's house. I thought of the beetles and ants, of the mouse with its twitchy whiskers, of the rattling of tiny creatures in the thatching of Sylvia's house and wondered if Conchita's roof was also a city of small crawlies.

"My grandmother told me," Rosita said, "that we sleep in chinchorros to lift us off the floor. She said that if we slept on the floor, scorpions would crawl into our ears."

"Do you believe that?"

"Yes. But I would prefer to be on a banana leaf mat with you. Perhaps above a cave filled with ancient bones."

"And a wild river below."

"And a rock overhang to keep off the rain."

"And a patch of grass to attract a rabbit."

"Yes," she said. "Yes."

Conchita and Sam slept in the next room. Sometime in the night, Conchita made strange noises like someone was choking her, and it seemed clear to me that Sam was too sound asleep to hear her. Certainly he hadn't heard when Rosita and I sneaked out of the tent in the early morning. I struggled out of the chinchorro, awakening Rosita in the process. "Don, whatever are you doing?"

"Someone came into the house and is hurting Conchita." I started feeling my way toward the door. "I have to wake up Sam."

281

"He's awake. You lie down."

"No. He doesn't hear—"

"Don't you dare go in there." Her fierce whisper stopped me. "Lie down. And pay no attention to the sounds they make. You're apt to hear them again before the night is over."

I stood still for a moment listening to Conchita. If she were in real danger, I asked myself, wouldn't she be screaming? Maybe Rosita was right and I shouldn't worry. I got back in the chinchorro and tried to settle with myself that nothing was wrong.

As morning twilight came, Conchita again made her strange sounds. "See?" Rosita said. "They're at it again."

"Sam is making her sound like that?"

"She likes it, but we don't have to stay here and pretend we don't hear. We can get out the front door without disturbing them. It would be nice to go down to the river. Sit on the pier, maybe. In a few hours we'll be home, so this is our last chance to see the wild river."

Sam was still choking Conchita when we left the house. Fog thick as smoke filled the street. A dog barked at us though it didn't sound too enthused about doing so, and it fell silent when Rosita told it to shut up. Roosters crowed all over the village, but other than that, the town was silent under the damp blanket of fog. Even our footsteps seemed muted, softened by the dense water vapor in the air. We walked deeper into the fog as we approached the river so that by the time we reached the pier we could see only a few meters.

"You want to sit in our canoe?" I asked.

"No. Too close to the river to suit me. It's not our canoe anymore, anyway. It belongs to the drunk who'll take us home."

"A candy man brought us to the wild part, and a drunk takes us home. Adults are strange people."

Rosita took my hand and led us to sit on the end of the pier. "Don't you dare become one of them."

"Don't become an adult?"

"Don't become one of those strange adults who wouldn't understand the magic of our adventure along this river."

"I thought you didn't like our adventure."

"Of course I liked it. Some things were terrible, of course."

Far beneath our feet the river gurgled its way toward the sea. Dad once showed me a map that had wavy blue lines like branches of trees coming together and running into the blue mass that he said was the Caribbean. "A big river will send its mud far out into the clear waters," he told me, "making a gigantic cloud of silt in the sea like smoke clouds in the air." I imagined the river, invisible because of morning fog, looking like one of those blue lines on the map. But of course it wasn't blue. It was muddy from the rains.

"I would go back with you," I said. "We could look for the Jesus frog that we couldn't find yesterday."

"We must go home, for now. Perhaps we can travel on the river again, you and I."

"Sneak another ride with the candy man?"

"Not that way, and not soon, not while we're still so young. We should meet when we're grown and go down the river. To the same places. We could get a safer boat, one that held us high enough above the surface to make it impossible for the caimán to leap up and snatch one of us."

"Or the anaconda," I said.

"We could look for the bat cave of dead Indios, and we could avoid going over the waterfall. Would you do that with me?"

"I would do that, yes."

"Promise me?" Rosita's question sounded more like a command.

"I promise."

She nodded, then watched the coming of the sun melting the fog, pockets of it drifting into the trees across the river. Some geese waddled out of the village toward us, and a spotted dog came from one of the houses, stopping to stare our direction. A baby cried then fell quiet. "The village is beginning to awaken," Rosita said. "We'll be leaving soon."

We sat on the pier until people appeared in the streets, then we went back to Conchita's where we found Sam standing outside, barefooted and shirtless, his eye patch hanging below his nose. Conchita came to the doorway, flung his shirt at him, and vanished again. I thought maybe she finally got mad at him for choking her.

"What happened to Conchita?" Rosita picked up the shirt and shook the dust from it.

"I hope she stays mad enough to throw my shoes at me." Sam straightened his eye patch and grinned. "If not, you'll have to go in there and get them, Don."

"I'm not going in there."

Conchita came to the door again. "Take your stinking gringo goat shit shoes with you." She threw the shoes at him. "And your filthy goat shit socks."

Sam picked up the socks and shook them. "I doubt she can throw the bag out the door. You'll have to go in there to get it."

"It's not my bag."

"What about your basket?"

"The bones." I headed for the door. When I got to the entryway, Conchita hit me with the basket and I stumbled back several steps before falling. "Take your goat shit brats and never come back," Conchita said. Rosita helped me up as Conchita set Sam's canvas bag on end and kicked it into the street. "Take your goat shit bag and never show your goat head in this town again." She vanished into the house.

Sam put on his shirt. He seemed amused and broke into a little song in English: "Goat this, goat that, goat everything, goat, goat, this old goat came rolling home."

"What is he singing about?" Rosita asked.

"Goats," I said. "It isn't a bad word in English."

"Is that true, Sam? You sang about goats?"

"This morning I told Conchita I was leaving today. Told her the same thing last night, too, but she didn't believe it, I guess. Why do you suppose goat is such a bad word in Spanish?"

"We should go find the man who'll take us to El Tigrito," Rosita said.

"The night wasn't so bad," Sam said to the sky. "Thanks for that. But why is it only wacky women want to hop in the sack with me? And doing it in that hammock, wowie. That was some trick."

"Tell me what he said," Rosita demanded.

"Don't you do it. This is man talk, Don, if you know what I mean."

"Something about a chinchorro," I said.

"Dealing with a woman like Conchita is like getting in a pissing contest with a skunk. You can't win." Sam hopped around, putting on his socks.

"Talk Spanish."

"Spanish it is. I wasn't talking about you, Rosita." Sam struggled into his shoes. "It's too early to try finding our driver."

"Maybe he's asleep in the cantina, or in his truck," Rosita suggested. "We could wake him up."

"I should have waited until after breakfast to remind Conchita that I was leaving."

A quick check of the basket reassured me that it still held the bones and the eyeball. I slung the basket on my shoulder, Sam picked up his canvas bag, and we headed toward the cantina.

"We'll check the pickup first," Sam said.

Someone had bolted a corrugated zinc canopy, crude and ugly, on the pickup, and the driver made a bed under it using rags and palm fiber. Rosita and I, standing on the back bumper, found him asleep with a yellow dog sleeping beside him, the same one we had seen the previous day in the cantina. A duck balanced itself on one leg beside the dog, its beak tucked into its wing; and a large parrot walked around the rim of the spare tire, which had been flung into the back of the truck beside the driver's bed. The parrot turned its head to look at us first with one eye then the other. "Shut up." The parrot startled me with the English words. "Shut up." The duck's head emerged from its wing feathers enough to regard us with a comical eye ringed in yellow, then slid back into the feathers, and the dog lifted its head to look at us for a few seconds before dropping back into sleep. The driver, shirtless and wearing patched trousers with a rope belt tied below his navel, sprawled on his back with his mouth open and snored in a rasping gurgle.

"That's a disgusting tattoo," Rosita said.

On the man's belly, tattooed in blues, reds, and yellows, was the face of a mustachioed man smoking a cigar, a comic-strip drawing with one eye bulging and bloodshot. The other eye was a gouged-out bloody looking place that made use of the navel to appear like a fresh wound where the eye should have been.

"A bull from San Angelo poked a horn into the tattoo's eye," Sam said. "And you're right, Rosita. That's the most terrible-looking belly button I've ever seen."

"Wake up," Rosita said.

285

"Shut up," the parrot said.

"His name is Alfonso," Sam said.

"A parrot named Alfonso?" I asked.

"Not the parrot." Rosita glanced at me. "Wake up, Alfonso. It's time to go to El Tigrito."

Alfonso snorted and closed his mouth but otherwise didn't move. "Who's there?"

"You remember yesterday afternoon when you agreed to take a canoe in trade for driving us to El Tigre?" Sam asked.

"El Tigrito," I corrected.

"Canoe?" Alfonso sat up and clutched his head. "Ay-yi-yi. What a grievous pain behind my eyes. Get me a bottle of rum."

"No rum. But I'll cure your headache." Sam heaved his canvas bag over the tailgate, opened it, and took out two white pills.

Alfonso raised one brow and eyed the aspirin. "Rum is better." He reached into the rag bedding, pulled out a bottle, and popped a cork from it.

"Swallow these with the rum." Sam handed him the pills.

"Thanks." Alfonso licked the aspirin from his hand and washed them down with the single swallow of rum remaining in the bottle, then looked at me. "I heard about you getting purple hair from having bad headaches. But it's not true. If hair turned purple and skin turned white from bad headaches, I'd be an albino with a head the color of an eggplant. Half the men in Venezuela would be purple-headed bleached freaks from cheap rum, uglier than you." He laid back on the rags, one hand over his eyes. "Canoe, you said? I'll take it. But you drive. I need to rest. The keys are in the truck, and it's gassed up. Go easy over bumps on account of Rocinante. That's my dog. Also on account of the Lady Pato, my duck, and Siatáp, the best parrot in Venezuela. He hates it when you hit hard bumps."

"How do I get to El Tigre?"

"El Tigrito," I said. "We live in El Tigrito."

"Take the only road. When it forks, go left. I'll get up in plenty of time to drive you to the shop."

Fearful that the dog might chew it up, I put the basket in the cab with us. Sam had to pull out a knob on the dash while stepping on the starter in order to get the truck started. The engine popped and sputtered, then quieted down as Sam adjusted the knob. "Looks like I have to choke the engine some to keep it running."

"You seem good at choking things," I said. Sam gave me a puzzled look, then drove into the street and headed for the savannah.

The pickup stirred up plenty of dust until it rained. "Don't you do it," Sam muttered. "Don't you send down enough rain to get the tires stuck, not now, not this close to El Tigre."

"El Tigrito," I corrected.

"I have you talking to the old boy, now," Sam said.

"I was talking to you. Why do you keep saying 'El Tigre' when we're not going there?"

"But we are. El Tigre first. Then El Tigrito. Alfonso told me yesterday that there's a man there who might be interested in buying some things I need to sell so I can get to the coast and hop a boat out of this country."

"Then we go to El Tigrito, right?"

"Right. A deal is a deal. You two did get my truck out of that creek. Besides, I owe you for performing in my magic show."

It rained enough to cool us off and settle the dust but not enough to pose any danger of bogging down the pickup. Alfonso banged on the cab about mid-morning to get Sam to stop and let him drive. Rosita and I rode the rest of the way in the back with Rocinante, Lady Pato, and Siatáp. The dog ignored us, being busy with sleep. Lady Pato spent the whole time beaking oil out of its skin onto its feathers, and Siatáp fluttered around on the spare tire saying "Shut up" from time to time.

The houses of El Tigre were more modern than any we saw along the wild river. Most were made from mud stucco painted white and had corrugated zinc roofs, though there were a few with palm-frond thatching. Alfonso drove us to the business district along the single black-top road that ran through the city. He stopped in front of a store made from cinder blocks and wood. It had a shiny metal roof and large windows that displayed paintings, pottery, traditional Indio clothing, and jewelry.

Inside, the shop was big enough to have several display racks, a jewelry counter, and many shelves stacked with pottery, carved stones, fancy machetes with designs etched on the blades, arrowheads, and other items. I expected Sam to take his bag into the store so he could sell what was left of his collection of aspirin, but he didn't.

Alfonso stayed outside with his pets. Rosita and I followed Sam into the shop. He pulled a tiny draw-string bag from a pocket and approached the old woman who seemed to be in charge of the store. She looked Indio to me with her braided hair and prominent cheekbones. She was short enough to have ancestors whose bones rested in a bat cave, and she wore a bright red-and-yellow dress that I associated with native people of Venezuela.

"Good day." Sam put the tiny bag on the counter in front of her. She nodded but remained silent, her eyes taking in me and Rosita in a way that seemed to measure us. "I heard you might be interested in buying some raw diamonds."

"I might." Her face didn't change.

Sam shook four pebbles onto the wooden counter: two with a yellow tint, one white, and one light blue. The woman picked up the white one. "I like the looks of this one best. Before you say how much you want, tell me why your son has purple hair."

"It was an accident that turned his hair that color," Sam said.

"An accident? That makes no sense—but never mind. I think this diamond isn't clear enough to be worth much."

Rosita drew me aside. "He kept some of Conchita's diamonds. I think perhaps that is wrong."

"But she said she was satisfied that he had none of her stones," I pointed out. "Maybe he found the stones himself.

Rosita shrugged. "Perhaps she gave some to him for staying the night with her." She wandered toward the shelves on one side of the shop, and I followed, leaving the shopkeeper and Sam bargaining over the price of the white diamond. Rosita stopped so suddenly that I bumped into her. "The head." She pointed. "The head."

Hanging beside the shelves, a string through its lips, was a hardball-sized human head, a black one with kinky hair and perfectly-formed but tiny facial features. Stitches held its eyes closed. Rosita and I walked around it, staring. "Why would anyone want such a terrible thing?" I asked.

"I don't. You don't. People are the strangest animals in the jungle. But we do have some finger and toe bones, don't we? Maybe you and I are also strange."

"Old bones are like rocks or sea shells. That was someone's head, someone who might have lived next door or just down the street. Keeping a head is different from keeping fingers and toes."

"Is that the shrunken head my father saw, the one we sneaked into the candy man's truck to go see? If so, it took us a long time to get here. And now that we're here, we don't like it. If we had known that, we might have stayed in our village."

"I doubt there's more than one shrunken head in El Tigre," I said. "And we might have liked the head before our trip into the wild part of the country."

"Before seeing Sylvia get killed. Yes."

"That, too. Also before I was El Don and sent men to hack up one another with machetes and to shoot each other. Before I made Mr. Marlin put the shotgun into his mouth. I hate that shrunken head. It shouldn't be a toy or a decoration to hang in a home."

"My father said there were also bones of ancient Indios in the shop." Rosita looked at the shelves. "There. I think I see them, but not the two skulls he saw. Perhaps someone bought them." She stepped over to a shelf and picked a up bone. "This looks like the ones we took out of the cave."

"Ours are better. Better because we found them, though now I'm not so sure I want them."

"I want only one, a small one. When we found them, the Indios were through with them, unlike that head. I doubt the man who owned the head was finished with it when the headhunters chopped it off."

Sam concluded his deal, and we left. Outside, Rosita said, "You stole those diamonds from Conchita."

"I did not. If I had wanted to steal her stones, I would have gotten better ones and more of them. The diamond I just sold is one I came by honestly enough."

"How much did you get for it?" I asked.

"Enough to pay Alfonso to drive me to Puerto la Cruz. Enough to get me back to Texas on a decent ship. Enough to pay you for your performances in my show."

"You owe us nothing," Rosita said.

"Maybe. Maybe not. In any case, you each get fifty Bolivars." He handed us some bills.

For the short trip to El Tigrito, Alfonso rode in the back with his animals. I thought about what it would be like getting home, about how Rosita and I once pretended to hunt lions in the savannah. Never would we pretend to hunt lions again. I also thought about how my family would make over me. June laughing about my purple hair. Todd loving my new glass eyeball. Mom and Dad punishing me for sneaking a ride in the candy man's pickup. After all the fuss, they would maybe want to go to the movies in the oil company camp, but I wouldn't go, not to a place where kids laughed at natives like Rosita. I'd stay home, even if I got punished for it. The guards at the gate of the camp, I thought, wouldn't let Rosita in if Sam happened to try driving there at night in Alfonso's pickup. I could get in, and so could Sam. Maybe even Rocinante, Lady Pato, and Siatáp could get in. But not Rosita or Alfonso. They would have to get out of the pickup and wait at the gate while Sam and I went to the movie. It made me mad just thinking about it.

As we got into the edge of our village, tears began to roll down Rosita's cheeks. Sam patted her arm. "Tears of joy?" he asked.

"I don't know. I know only that I'm sad and angry. But not at you and not at Don. At the jungle, maybe. The river. At the missionary who killed Sylvia. At that terrible head hanging in the shop."

"Head?" Sam looked amazed. "You kids continue to surprise me. Head? But never mind. Maybe I'm better off not knowing."

He would have driven us all the way to our houses, but Rosita said no; she said she wanted to walk part of the way with me. "Let us out there," she pointed to the corner of the highway and the street beside Mr. Hazri's store. She kissed Sam's cheek, and his red face turned redder.

"Bye, Sam," I said as we got out. I shouldered the basket.

"I'll miss you nutty kids."

"Get you a new eye," Rosita said. "One that fits."

"Good advice," he said. "I'll trade one of my yellow diamonds for it."

We walked down the sandy street past a bungalow on the right with castorbean bushes in the front yard. I stopped beside a stand of banana trees. "Are you in a hurry to get home?"

"No. Maybe. Not much."

"Let's sit in the shade of those banana trees." When we got settled in the shade, I sat the basket beside us and looked around. In the coolness of the shade the faint scent of apples came to us from the underside of the manzanita banana leaves. "Rosita, perhaps we should go back into the jungle."

"We cannot."

"I know."

We sat in silence for what seemed a long time, then Rosita opened the basket, took out the bones, and said, "Select one. Hide it from your family, and I'll do the same."

"What will we do with the rest of them?"

"Here. These look like two bones from the same finger. You take one and I'll take one. And here." She handed me the blue eye that once gave Sam headaches. "Put it in your pocket. I'll keep the basket. The rest of the bones we cover up right here. Later we'll come for them. Together. We'll take them down to the river and bury them properly."

We pulled sand over the bones at the base of a banana tree and began the final part of our journey by stepping from the apple-scented shade into the harsh tropic sun.

Jerry Craven has lived for extended periods in South America, Southeast Asia, the Middle East, and Europe. He now resides in East Texas where he serves as director for Lamar University Press and Ink Brush Press and is editor-in-chief of the on-line literary magazine *Amarillo Bay*. A member of the Texas Institute of Letters, he has published 25 books including fiction, poetry, creative nonfiction, and children's literature. Among his writing awards are *descant's* Frank O'Connor Award for Fiction and first place for novel from both Frontiers in Writing and the Deep South Festival of Writers.

Book Club Discussion Questions for *The Wild Part*

1. How does the story suggest the jungle is in some ways like the Garden of Eden?
2. How do Rosita and Don "fall" from innocence?
3. What are some of the ideas various characters have about the nature of God?
4. What events and circumstances cause Rosita and Don to decide the jungle became an evil place?
5. In what ways does the novel deal with the idea that belief creates reality?
6. Which characters talk about belief creating reality, and how does each think belief can create reality?
7. Which of the main characters do you prefer (and why): Don or Rosita?
8. Examine the minor characters; these include:

El Loco	Mr. Moustache	Mr. Martin	Alfonso
Carmen	Simón	Sam Dean	
Mamacita Moreno	Sylvia	Juanita	
Pepito	Julio	Conchita	

Pick one of these characters you would most like to meet and explain why. If you are less inclined to meet certain characters, explain your reasons.
9. What evidence in the book can you find to support or refute this statement:

  While this is a novel about children, it is not a children's book.
10. What evidence can you find in the novel to support or refute this statement:

  While this is not a children's book, it is appropriate for young readers.

  For the discussion to result in enlightening analysis, please do not give brief or one word answers. Always point to details in the story to explain your response.

*** *

If you enjoyed *The Wild Part*, you will also like the sequel, *Women of Thunder*, published by TCU Press in the spring of 2014. It is the story of Don and Rosita as adults returning to travel down the same river in the interior of Venezuela, a trip they find more dangerous and more wonderful than the one they took so many years before.

293

www.ingramcontent.com/pod-product-compliance
Lightning Source LLC
Chambersburg PA
CBHW021217260626
47172CB00002B/479